W9-BOM-650

FAREWELL TO JACK

David A. Weiss

This book is a work of fiction. The events and characters are a product of the author's imagination and any resemblance to actual incidents or persons, living or dead, is purely coincidental.

"Farewell to Jack" by David A. Weiss, ISBN 978-1-62137-162-5 (softcover), 978-1-62137-169-4 (ebook).

Library of Congress: 2012921012

Published 2012 by Virtualbookworm.com Publishing Inc., P.O. Box 9949, College Station, TX, 77842. Copyright 2012 David A. Weiss. All rights reserved. No part of this publication may be reproduced, stored in a retrieval system, or transmitted in any form or by any means, electronic, mechanical, recording or otherwise, without the prior permission of David A. Weiss.

Manufactured in the United States of America.

To my children, Lori Weiss and Dr. Howard (Adrienne) Weiss, and my grandchildren, Sidney Weiss and Toby Weiss, all of whom are a source of great joy and pride.

I gratefully acknowledge those who have helped me in this endeavor: the members of the Schenectady Fiction Writers' Club who for fourteen years have provided valuable constructive criticism, always in a manner that positively reinforces and assists my efforts; my daughter Lori Weiss (B.A., Brandeis University; Ed., M., Harvard University), who helps design my book covers and critiques my writing; and my dear wife Joyce, who not only critiques my writing, but more important supports and encourages me in the pursuit of this very joyous and rewarding passion.

Preface

Farewell to Jack is a work of fiction set in the historic and charming Village of Cooperstown, New York. As with any novel whose backdrop is a real place, readers may be inclined to draw parallels to actual people who lived or live in the community. Where the community, like Cooperstown, is rural, this inclination can magnify.

Some of the characters depicted in *Farewell to Jack*, including several in highly visible public positions, engage in immoral and/or illegal conduct. It is, therefore, particularly important to stress that all of these characters are entirely fictional and in no way, loosely or otherwise, based upon any real people, living or deceased. Likewise the events depicted are all fictional.

Located on beautiful Otsego Lake in scenic leatherstocking country, Cooperstown was chosen as the site of this book because of its rich and storied texture dating back to and beyond the days of James Fenimore Cooper. Add to this its renowned baseball heritage owing to claims that Abner Doubleday invented the game there, along with the presence of the *Baseball Hall of Fame*, and the halcyon village offers an ideal setting for the story. For those familiar with Cooperstown, there is little need to sing its praises. The village melodizes them far better than words. However, for those who have never visited this uncommon place, let not a novel's fictional characters and events cast even the slightest aspersions on the village. On the contrary, know Cooperstown for the extraordinary place that it is, and seize the opportunity to experience its singular charm.

Chapter I

Twelve years. A full dozen had passed since Skip Maynard had represented a defendant charged with homicide. Back then Eisenhower was President. The cold war was center stage. Fresh from the heyday of Joseph McCarthy, America's incomparable monger of hate, capitalism was pitted in an all-out struggle against communism. Life was simple. *Father 'Knew' Best* and one could tell the good guys from the bad simply by the hats they wore. But that was then. The world had subsequently grown more complicated. Vietnam, a distant unknown Southeast Asian land, had become the centerpiece of America's nightly news. Nearly a half-decade had passed since John F. Kennedy had been assassinated, and little more than a week before, on April 4, 1968, Martin Luther King had met the identical fate. Social upheaval pervaded the cities of America. Pessimists and cynics roamed its streets. Even in sleepy Cooperstown, New York, Skip's home, the thunderous reverberations of distant events could not be escaped. So-called nabobs of negativism could be found, and Skip was among them.

Only an hour earlier Harley Morehead, charged with murder, had telephoned from the county jail requesting that Skip represent him. There was a time when the unexpected opportunity would have triggered excitement. As a youngster Skip had often walked several miles from his childhood home to the County Court House in Cooperstown to watch a murder or kidnapping trial. The high-stakes battle and real-life drama captivated Skip, though admittedly not nearly so much as baseball. However, at a very young age when even the munificence of boyhood pipe dreams could not deny that aspirations to become a major league baseball player were fatuous, he became single-mindedly aimed at a career in law. All the while high school and even college seemed like nothing more than lengthy intrusions on an interminable road to becoming a criminal defense lawyer. At long last when he finally arrived in law school, he heeded his professors, devoured his casebooks and relished moot court. He graduated near the top of his class and breezed through the bar exam. Through his late twenties he quickly gained a reputation as one of the finest criminal defense attorneys in the leatherstocking country of upstate New York. But all that changed when a hit-and-run driver killed the love of his life, his wife Megan, as she jogged alongside the highway. Rage, unchanneled, spiraled Skip downward. The bright, young star of the courtroom dissolved into a black hole. Where once many a late night had been spent imbibing the constitutional principles of Due Process, for a decade he had been burning the midnight oil in libraries of a different ilk. He had been commiserating with a new companion, *Jack Daniel's*.

As Skip drove the short distance from his office on Main Street to the Otsego County Jail in Cooperstown, he was blasé, questioning whether he even wanted to handle the murder case. Sure, the fee would be sizable, but he could do without it. No, he wasn't rich, but his needs were modest and he had only himself to support. Unlike his usual fare, petit larceny, harassment or other charges that could easily be disposed of, a murder case was all-consuming. In the wee hours thoughts about its many nuances were certain to interrupt sleep. Did he want that? Would he give the case the attention it demanded? Skip had doubts. Why too, he wondered, would Harley Morehead, County Chairmen of the Populist Party, hire him, of all lawyers?

Skip pulled his seven-year old *BMW*, purchased used, four years earlier, into the parking lot adjacent to the County Jail. Unlike his cluttered home and office he kept the pricey wheels in mint condition. Like his pal *Jack Daniel's*, the sleek, silver machine provided an escape from a chaotic world. But Skip kept them separate. Out on the road in his *BMW*, *Jack* was *persona non grata*. On the other hand, once Skip arrived home, with his *BMW* locked safely in the garage, *Jack* garnered

Skip's full attention. The same was true at the *Eagle*, Skip's favorite watering hole. The tavern, whose history, both real and fabled, dated two centuries, was but a short walk from Skip's office, as well as the Courthouse. Foot power, rather than German engineering, transported Skip to and from those venues. All too often, however, the indecorous effect of midday hours spent with *Jack* at the *Eagle* manifested itself during the afternoon.

Just before exiting his *BMW*, Skip, six feet tall, with light brown wavy hair and a sinewy frame, restored some semblance of the professional image he had abandoned immediately following an earlier closing. He re-buttoned the collar of his shirt and slipped on his sport jacket. A green tie with blue stripes, the clip-on variety, completed his costume, a far cry from the well-tailored suits he had worn a decade before. He climbed out of his car and headed into the jail. Hundreds of visits had put him on a first-name basis with all the guards. In some respects he felt more at home there than with the black-robed judges and sartorially impeccable lawyers who roamed the halls of the County Court House. Beneath Skip's white dress shirt beat a blue-collar heart.

"What's it today?" said Pete, a stocky guard who got along with everyone, prisoners included. "A petit larceny or a disorderly conduct?"

Skip shook his head. "I'm here to see Harley Morehead."

For an instant Pete's eyes widened, but then he chuckled. "Sure. And I'm the Chief Judge of the Court of Appeals."

"Congratulations. That's quite the promotion." Skip nonchalantly punctuated the retort with a slight smirk.

"You…really here to see Morehead?"

Skip nodded.

Pete flipped a set of keys into the air catching them one-handed. "A murder charge. Sounds like someone got the call from the minors back to the bigs." Pete unlocked the first of two heavy iron doors that led to the cellblock. He unlocked the second and ushered Skip through, securing both doors behind them. "Jake, bring Harley Morehead down. His lawyer's here." Pete ushered Skip into the conference room.

Skip seated himself in the Spartan chamber. About eight-foot square with a single door and a heavy glass window no bigger than a TV dinner—Skip was a connoisseur of the frozen delights—it was basically a cell without bars.

A minute later Morehead, a burly guy, about fifty, with large jowls and a full crop of black wavy hair, arrived in his orange jump suit. "I appreciate your coming," he said.

"No problem." Skip motioned at the chair on the opposite side of a small wooden table. "How you doing?"

Morehead shrugged. "I've been better. And the food, if you can call it that, sucks."

"How they treating you?"

"Who—the guards or my fellow guests?"

"Both."

"No complaints about the guards. As for my compatriots, apart from a few hecklers who get sadistic pleasure seeing someone like me join their shoddy ranks, they leave me alone." Morehead plopped his elbows onto the table. "What are the chances of me getting out of here soon?"

"We'll talk about that in a minute, but first...tell me why you called me."

A quizzical look appeared on Morehead's face.

Skip suspected the reaction might be contrived. "Someone in your position has to know lots of lawyers. And I would assume you have one, given your business."

"Matter of fact, I do—Morgan Witherbee. And he's fine for some things, like when I bought the building for my print shop or for a contract, but he's hardly the guy to defend me for murder."

"Well, as Chairman of the Populist Party, you must know others who are better suited."

Morehead laughed. "You gotta be kidding. They're a bunch of politicians. They trade on who they know, not what. Wheel and deal—that's their game. But try a murder case? Give me a break."

Morehead had a point. But still it begged the question. "Why me?"

4

"I saw you in action when...uh...I don't recall the guy's name. He was charged with armed robbery...at the old Grand Union."

"You don't mean the Porter case? That was nearly a dozen years ago."

"Yeah, that's the one. The guy was convicted before the trial began. God, they had two or three eyewitnesses and evidence up the wazoo. Houdini couldn't have escaped from the fix he was in, at least that's the way it seemed. But by the time you were done, you had convinced the jury and everyone else, me included, the guy was innocent."

Skip thought back to the case. It was arguably his finest moment. Certainly there had been nothing comparable in the past decade. But the Porter acquittal was ancient history, and the lawyer who had displayed those masterful skills was like a distant ancestor Skip had never met.

"Right then and there, I told myself if I ever get in a jam, you'd be the lawyer for me."

Like so many attorneys there was a time when Skip would have jumped at a case that was sure to play big in the media, but that was then. Regardless, he didn't want a client with unrealistic expectations. "Over the past decade I haven't handled many serious felonies, let alone a murder case. You might want to think twice before hiring me."

Morehead shook his head. "Damn, I can't believe you're trying to chase me away. Most lawyers I know, especially out here away from the big cities, take on anything, regardless whether they're up to the task."

Skip shrugged. "Apparently I'm not most lawyers."

"Apparently," said Morehead with a puzzled look. "Anyway, I've been *A to Z* through the lawyers in the yellow pages. The only defense lawyer worth two bits is Charlie Tockler. But he's the last person I'd want defending me, what with him having forced a primary against Biddleford for the Republican line a few years back. Talk about your ass-brained move." Morehead emitted a guttural groan. "Tockler never had a chance. The consequences were inevitable. He pissed off the most grudge-holding Judge from here to Buffalo. And now, day-after-day, week-after-week, he has to go back into court and argue cases in front of Biddleford. To put it bluntly, Tockler screwed himself, and given my mess, the last thing I need is to jump into bed with him, not when His Honor—and I use the term loosely—Harold Biddleford is wielding the gavel."

The logic was hard for Skip to contest. Judge Biddleford, or His Holiness, as Skip often referred to him, was the antithesis of what a judge should be. Most everyone who entered the ultra-conservative Republican's courtroom faced the same disdain. Lawyers, clients, witnesses, court attendants, stenographers—it made no difference. But when it came to decisions, he adjusted the playing field. Political cronies garnered favorable treatment. Others got short shrift. Enemies got worse yet. Biddleford did it masterfully. Favorable evidentiary rulings, the foundation of an appeal-proof record, were the precursor to a screw-job decision. Though Skip was high on Biddleford's crap list, on one occasion several years earlier, he had actually benefited from the Judge's bias. The case, a matrimonial, had Skip representing the wife. His adversary, who represented the husband, just happened to be Charlie Tockler. Throughout the hearing Biddleford treated Skip and Tockler as equals; both were scum. On the other hand, his evidentiary rulings consistently favored Tockler. But that was a setup. When time came for the decision, the alimony award to Skip's client tested the upper limits of judicial discretion. Unfortunately for Tockler, a printed record of the proceeding suggested that Biddleford had given Tockler's client the benefit of every doubt. Tockler had absolutely no avenue of appeal.

Morehead looked Skip in the eye. "I've thought it over carefully. I want *you* to represent me."

It's your funeral. If *Jack* had been along for the visit, a less inhibited Skip might have voiced the thought. Instead he said, "Well, if I'm the one you want, I'm the one you've got." He reached into the inside pocket of his jacket for a small spiral pad and pen. Years earlier when he had shifted to a diet of traffic tickets, disorderly conduct and the like, he had stopped carrying his attaché case. For special court dates he made an exception. He said, "When is your arraignment?"

"Tomorrow morning."

"What makes the police think you killed Squeaky Grimes?"

"My confession."

Skip swallowed hard. Defending Morehead was going to be an uphill climb, one more closely resembling the sheer escarpment of *Yosemite's El Capitan* than the timeworn parabolas of the nearby Adirondacks.

"Hold the phone. I didn't say I killed the Squeaker."

Not to me, but apparently, the police. Once again Skip suppressed the thought. He said, "Why'd you give them a confession?"

"Because I didn't want to wind up like the Squeaker. The detective...what's his face, the tall fellow who looks like Elvis—"

"Ramsey?"

"Yeah, that's it. Anyway, he invoked the power of persuasion." Morehead contorted his face in a manner that made his fat jowls even more pronounced. "You'd be amazed how convincing an officer with a finger on the trigger of a cocked revolver can be."

A part of Skip was skeptical, but another was more receptive. Back in law school he had taken a seminar that traced the historical development of criminal law. He knew the history of southern justice where sheriffs, politicians and judges traded their day clothes for white robes, masks and pointed hats by night. He also knew the way the system had worked years earlier in the North. The police had loads of unsolved crimes. Often they had a suspect. If not, there were plenty of bad actors or flunkies they didn't like. One was as good as the next. A good beating, perhaps some brass knuckles, produced a confession. It was the old kill two birds with one stone. A crime was off the books, and a bum got what he deserved. Whether the crime and the bum were connected didn't matter. Gradually the pattern led the Supreme Court during the nineteen fifties and sixties to expand the protections afforded to defendants. *Gideon*'s right to counsel, *Miranda's* warnings to those arrested and *Mapp's* limitations on searches and seizures were but a few. Horror story after horror story, pervasive abuse, persuaded even conservative justices like Earl

Warren to champion what appeared to be a chain of liberal decisions. Gradually the pendulum swung. Unfortunately victims got lost in the shuffle. Such was the price of a system that had forced citizens to admit crimes they had not committed. Skip understood both sides. But that begged the questions at hand. Was Morehead's confession voluntary? Might he be one of many who used the abuse of others to hide his own guilt? Skip said, "What did you do when he threatened you?"

"I told him I wanted a lawyer."

"How did he respond?"

"He said, *You want a mouthpiece. I'll oblige you.* Then he laughed and sucker punched me in the kisser. An instant later he whipped out his gun and said if I didn't give a confession, he'd blow my brains out and claim self-defense. He said he had a lead pipe in his cruiser, that he was gonna put my fingerprints on it after he shot me and claim that I had come at him with it."

Skip watched Morehead closely, looking for any telltale signs. If Morehead was making up the story, he was good. A bruise on the right side of his jaw lent credence to his claim, not that Skip was convinced how the injury had occurred. He said, "What happened after he pulled out his gun?"

A dumbfounded look came over Morehead. "Whad'ya mean? I wrote out a confession, just the way he told me to. The way I figured, a trip to jail was better than the morgue." Morehead gestured at himself. "But let me assure you, without his threat there would have been no confession. I know better than to spill my guts to a cop. Years ago when I was just starting out in politics, Freddie Smith–you might remember him..."

"Yes, he was still practicing when I got out of law school. But he died before I really got to know him."

"Anyway, Freddie used to handle legal matters for the party...challenges to nominating petitions, voter fraud and the like. He told me if I was ever arrested, I should tell the police I want a lawyer and otherwise keep my mouth shut. He said the cops have two styles, rough and nice. Rough—they beat the information out of you. Nice—they get it by trick. But either way, anything you say will only come back to haunt you."

If it had been a half-century earlier, Skip would have bought the story without a second thought, but so much had changed. Sure, there were still plenty of bad cops, but forced confessions, once the norm, had become far less common. And it was still as easy as ever for a defendant to scream foul, especially when confronted with life behind bars. On the other hand, Morehead was hardly your typical, uneducated hoodlum who ran the streets. Of course, when it came to the criminal justice system and the need to keep one's mouth shut, dropouts were often more knowledgeable than college graduates.

Morehead appeared to study Skip. "You don't believe me. I see it in your face."

"It's not that. I...I was weighing how it's likely to play in court. Judge Biddleford comes from the old school."

"Don't I know. The son of a bitch has had it in for me for years, ever since I accused him of bias when the Republicans stuffed the ballot box in order to get Horthmyer elected to the State Assembly."

The possibility that Biddleford might relish the chance to screw an old political enemy had already crossed Skip's mind. He scribbled the word *recusal* on his pad. "We could move to have Biddleford disqualify himself."

Morehead laughed.

The reaction might have surprised Skip if he were dealing with someone less experienced.

"We did that back in the Horthmyer case. All it did was cost a ton of money. After Biddleford shot us down, we took it up on appeal. The guys upstairs merely parroted Biddleford's assertion that he would be open-minded and fair."

"Nevertheless, passing up any available—"

"I understand. Facing life in prison, I need to try everything, even expensive avenues with little chance of success."

Ordinarily Skip didn't appreciate clients instructing him on the legal aspects of a matter, but Morehead had hit the nail on the head and had said it succinctly. "Let's get back to the facts of your case."

"What about them?"

"What happened after Ramsey took you down to the police station?"

"They booked me, and then Ramsey, along with a couple of other officers, asked me to give a comprehensive statement detailing Squeaky's murder. With other officers around I figured I was safe—at least I hoped I was—and so, I refused and asked to contact an attorney. They locked me up, and here you are."

The events at the station, not atypical when viewed in the context of what had preceded, created an intriguing scenario that arguably lent a modicum of credibility to Morehead's claim that his confession had been coerced. Skip said, "Did you know Ralph Grimes?"

"Yeah, I knew Squeaky. He used to do odd jobs for me—deliver printing orders, fix a jammed door, whatever. The guy knew more folks than the *Cooper Inn* has served draughts. Hell, Squeaky had a finger everywhere. And talk about a weasel."

"Exactly what does that mean?" Skip jotted the words, *Squeaky* and *weasel*.

"Just the way it sounds. He stuck his nose here, there and everywhere. More often than not, places it didn't belong. But give the rodent his due. He had a knack for getting stuff done. Of course, along the way he made loads of enemies."

"Such as?"

"You got all day?" Morehead rocked his chair back on its hind legs allowing his rotund stomach to show itself.

"Suppose we concentrate on those most likely to have killed him."

As he seemingly contemplated the matter, Morehead interlocked his hands behind his head and puffed out his cheeks, a bit like a squirrel with a couple of nuts in its mouth. "I've been trying to figure that out myself. A couple of guys who really stand out are Bernie Feinstein and Jimmie Raines."

"Feinstein...the County Comptroller?"

"Yup."

"And who's the other fellow?"

"Jimmie Raines."

Skip jotted the Greek letter *delta* (ordinarily he used it to signify defendants), along with the two names. "Tell me about this Raines fellow—why you think he might be involved?"

Morehead rocked his chair back and forth a couple more times. "Raines is a piece of work, and his wife Tammy Lee is something else. They live on a hill north of the city in a big house, not that they can afford it. They live way beyond their means. Most of the time you'll see them driving their *Cadillac*. Course on a warm summer day he gallivants around in his bright yellow *Corvette* convertible."

"What's he do for a living?" Skip added Tammy Lee's name to his notes.

"If you ask me, he plays golf. He belongs to the *Leatherstocking Club*." The velvety links adjoined the fashionable *Otesaga Hotel* on Otsego Lake, a resort long popular with the rich and famous who visited Cooperstown, especially those who came for the annual induction ceremonies at the *Baseball Hall of Fame*.

"I assume he does something more than play golf."

"He recently started some kind of art business. From what I know, it's nothing more than a pyramid scheme. His wife—she's a bottled blond with a boob job—inherited some commercial real estate. A small professional building and a couple of apartments, I think. Basically, they collect rents, play golf and live high off the hog."

"What makes you think Raines might be connected to Squeaky's murder?"

Morehead shrugged. "Squeaky was involved in Raines's business. Exactly how, I'm not certain. But one thing sure, Raines couldn't stand Squeaky."

Skip was already forming the foundations of a defense. Regardless of Morehead's guilt, other suspects were a means to create reasonable doubt. "Any idea if Raines ever threatened to harm Squeaky?"

"Not specifically. But one time when I was at the OTB, Raines, in a voice that everyone could hear, told Squeaky he should commit suicide. He said it was the one contribution Squeaky could make to the world."

"Any clue why Raines felt that way?"

"Rumor had it that the Squeaker had crossed him. If and how, you got me."

"Squeaky...the Squeaker—Why the monikers?"

Morehead let his chair rock forward onto all fours. "Damn...if you ever heard the little rodent talk, you'd know why. Fingernails on a chalkboard are harp notes next to his nasally, grating whine. Wouldn't surprise me if someone killed him just to shut him up." Morehead nodded slowly. "If so, it oughta be—what do they call it?"

"Justifiable homicide?"

"Yeah." He heaved a sigh. "I know. You can't kill a guy 'cause he sounds like a freakin' penguin with a walrus tusk jammed up his ass." Morehead shook his head and muttered under his breath. "Bird brains like the Squeaker don't belong on the protected species list."

The offbeat perception drew a rise from Skip, but he was equally conscious of his client's temperament. If and when the case went to trial and Morehead took the stand, a short fuse could spell disaster. Horseshedding him to insure that his acerbic side remained camouflaged would not be easy. Smart birds, like parrots, could be trained in the verbal arts. Nevertheless, some were temperamental, and foul phrases were known to cross their beaks at the most inopportune times. Though Morehead was nobody's fool, he was also the quintessential big mouth, the kind who could warble himself into trouble the moment his feathers got ruffled. And a stiff cross-examination was the perfect device to ruffle the feathers of a warbler. Skip said, "Earlier you mentioned Bernie Feinstein. What makes you think our County Comptroller might be involved with Squeaky's death?"

"Well—Feinstein is a politician. Politicians don't get paid a whole lot. But lots of them, Feinstein included, make out financially. They take care of their friends, and their friends take care of them. Not all of it is above board."

As a political insider Morehead was presumably speaking from personal experience. Skip kept the thought to himself. He said, "So, how does Feinstein tie in to Squeaky?"

"A little patience, and I'll get there." Morehead displayed a put-off look, the kind that reinforced Skip's concerns as to how his client would fare in front of a jury. "It's like this. Feinstein owned a two-family house on the far side of town. A rental. The Squeaker occupied one of the flats. Downstairs...I think. Anyway, the Squeaker was a hanger-on. What you might call a parasite. He did all kinds of odd jobs. Folks knew he could walk in places where the smell was bad. You might say he handled their manure. Along the way he learned their dirty little secrets. Just like J. Edgar Hoover, he gathered information with a purpose. He held it over people's heads."

"I take it he had something on Feinstein?"

Morehead hesitated. "Nothing specific that I know, but I'd lay odds. What I do know is that the Squeaker was behind in his rent to Feinstein. Hardly likely that the County Comptroller, an accountant watching pennies as if they were diamonds, would have let that happen unless the Squeaker had something on him."

Skip scribbled another note: *Squeaky behind in rent to Feinstein. Extortion.* Morehead had painted an excellent picture of Squeaky, one that had Skip wondering whether Squeaky had something on Morehead, and, too, whether Morehead had killed Squeaky. Morehead had pointed fingers in other directions, and he had claimed his confession was coerced, but, as yet, he had not definitively protested his innocence. Down the road when thoughts about his taking the stand would presumably arise, the question would have to be asked. For the time being ignorance had certain benefits. Skip ascribed to the constitutional principle that every defendant was presumed innocent until the prosecution proved guilt beyond a reasonable doubt. The principle was great, at least in theory. Reality, however, cast the concept in a different light. Discovering at the very outset that his client was guilty would dampen Skip's already limited enthusiasm. No reason to risk such an inauspicious beginning. Their first encounter had gone far enough. Skip motioned for Pete to let him out. A minute later, as the doors to the inner sanctum clanged shut behind him, an earlier thought again rang in Skip's head. Why had Harley

Morehead hired him? Admittedly Morehead had provided an explanation. Whether it was true was another matter.

Skip strolled past the *Baseball Hall of Fame* turning at Fair Street into the park that adjoined the national-pastime shrine. Following a brief pause to eye the iconic statues of the pitcher, the catcher and the slugger, he continued on his way to the old cemetery that adjoined the Christ Episcopal Church. Past the gravestone of James Fenimore Cooper and others dating back two centuries, he wended his way to the rear of the graveyard to the youngest of the headstones, perhaps the last that would grace the all-but-full, sacred earth.

Eyes closed, as if reading Braille, Skip ran his fingers over the granite marker feeling the carved inscription: *Megan Maynard, beloved wife, July 13, 1931-September 8, 1958.* Whenever he visited the cemetery, and Skip often did, he touched the epitaph. He longed to caress Megan. This was as close as he could come. The gravestone was simple, about thirty inches high, two feet wide and three inches deep, with a rounded top. Skip would have preferred one like the eight-foot tower with a massive ball at the apex that stood in the next row just to the right, but Megan would have hated such vainglory. Since she, not he, had to rest there into eternity, he had yielded to her tastes.

"I've got a new murder case," he said. "Of all people I'm representing Harley Morehead...No, I'm not doing a whole lot better." During his visits Skip always talked to Megan. She was an excellent listener, and he could hear her responses. He reached into the inside pocket of his sport jacket and pulled out a small leather-encased flask. "I know. You want me to cut down." He took a swig. "I promise to, as soon as you come back." He eyed the flask. *Jack Daniel's* couldn't hold a candle to Megan, but given the darkness without her, it was the best Skip could do. Another swig, and he tucked it back into his pocket. "I love you too," he said, as once more he slowly ran his fingers over the carved letters of her name. He inhaled. The air was fresh, but not with *Chanel No. 5,* her favorite. Skip turned and ambled his way out of the cemetery. The bright, golden glow of the setting sun shone directly into his face. His sunglasses remained buried in his pocket.

———————

Seated in the rear of Judge Biddleford's courtroom, Skip checked the docket. Morehead's case was fourth on the list. If matters moved at the typical rate, he would be at the bench in about fifteen minutes. But one never knew, especially with Biddleford. Time was not to be wasted, except by him. His attitude about humor was much the same. It had no place in the courtroom, unless he was the purveyor, not that his so-called jokes merited a guffaw. Regardless, most of the lawyers, sycophants that they were, laughed heartily, only to brazenly jeer His Holiness once they escaped to the security of the hallway or the lawyers' room. Four-lettered epithets streamed from their mouths as they bitched and moaned, but face-to-face they cowed to the black-robed tyrant.

Skip, however, was the exception. He refused to kowtow to the high priest of the courtroom. It was not in his nature. Skip's disregard—what some termed foolhardy sedition—had a long history. Over the years numerous run-ins with the Judge had fostered mutual animosity. That animosity grew following Megan's death. Though always tough on crime, Biddleford had little compassion for anyone, even victims, Skip included. Irked by the Judge's insensitivity, Skip entered Biddleford's courtroom with a chip on his shoulder. Unfortunately Biddleford held the gavel. And he also rendered the decisions.

The loss of Megan, compounded by Skip's inability to vindicate that loss, had mired him in an ever-deepening depression. His practice had suffered. His once great potential as a trial lawyer had seemingly faded into oblivion, but still Skip persisted until gradually the futility of misdirected rage became inescapable. The better part of a decade had produced no clues regarding Megan's death. Even if fortune suddenly disclosed the perpetrator, little good it would do. The statute of limitations for a criminally negligent homicide prosecution had already expired. Such was the state of Skip's career when Morehead hired him.

As was often the case in Judge Biddleford's courtroom, Skip was lost in his own thoughts. As usual those thoughts included ruminations replete with old resentments. The sound of the bailiff calling the case of the *People against Harley Morehead* roused Skip from his world of dark reflections. He walked forward to the bench. Morehead, who had been seated in the prisoners' bullpen, met Skip there.

Judge Biddleford peered down over the top of wire-rimmed glasses. "Mr. Morehead..." A hint of a smirk appeared on the Judge's face.

That the Judge relished the predicament of the Populist Party Chairman came as no surprise to Skip. That he would be so blatant was less predictable.

Judge Biddleford reached for the murder charge, scanned it for a moment, and then read it aloud. "Mr. Maynard, how does your client plead?"

"Not guilty...Your Honor." The anger from past confrontations made it hard for Skip to add the deferential title when entering the plea, but his client's interests demanded he swallow some pride. "On behalf of Mr. Morehead I request bail. And before Your Honor weighs in on the issue, let me suggest that my client is an appropriate candidate for release on his own recognizance." Skip had no illusions that the request would be granted, but he hoped it might encourage a lower bail. "Mr. Morehead has been a resident of Otsego County his entire life. For more than twenty years he has operated a printing business in Oneonta." An unmistakable, though inscrutable reaction on the Judge's face caught Skip's eye. The curiosity sought analysis, but time precluded the luxury. "As Your Honor well knows, Mr. Morehead is the Chairman of the Otsego County Populist Party. As a pillar of this community, he certainly is not a flight risk. Accordingly, I urge that he be released without bail."

"Mr. Carter, do the People wish to be heard?"

The tall, thin, forty-something District Attorney, who had been standing in front of the prosecution table, took several steps forward. "With all due respect, Your Honor, I take exception to Mr. Maynard's request. We're not here on a misdemeanor. We have a homicide, murder in the first degree. It is all well and good that Mr. Morehead is a long-time local businessman, but the severity of the charge, one that carries a possible term of life in prison, demands financial assurances that he will appear in court. And regarding the charge, let the record note that the People's case is far from circumstantial. We have the defendant's confession, as well as ample forensic evidence. Under the circumstances the People urge bail in the amount of one hundred thousand dollars."

The recommendation was no surprise to Skip. He also knew where the Judge was likely to come out—half the recommendation. The District Attorney surely knew it too, and, chances were, he had asked for twice what he wanted.

Judge Biddleford, his eyes directed to the heavens, rocked back and forth in his big leather chair. For a moment he halted but then folded his arms and rocked some more.

You bogus son of a bitch, thought Skip, willing to bet the display was all show. Then again, there was always the possibility the Judge needed a calculator to divide one hundred thousand in half.

Finally Judge Biddleford lowered his gaze and, looking directly at Skip, said, "Bail is fixed at one hundred thousand dollars. That's cash. Bond is two hundred thousand."

For an instant the number caught Skip off guard. A quick re-assessment suggested he should have anticipated the result. Feelings between the jurist and himself were mutual. Add to that the Republican Judge's sentiments toward the Populist Party County Chairman, and the result was less of a shock. Skip chided himself promising that next time he would know what to expect.

Morehead whispered in Skip's ear. "I don't like it, but I'll manage to post it."

"Is that all today?" said Judge Biddleford.

"I request a date for motions," said Skip.

Judge Biddleford leaned right and examined his calendar. "Three weeks from this coming Thursday. May 14th at ten A.M. Next case."

The bailiff came forward to usher Morehead back to the bullpen.

"I'll be in touch." Skip walked back past the bar and was about to leave the courtroom when he turned and looked back, first, at his client and then, His Holiness. Both were fat, though his Holiness, about five-seven, several inches shorter than Morehead, qualified as a roly-poly. Both were politicians. Morehead had a grating personality, but compared to His Holiness, Morehead was a sweetheart. Before leaving, Skip stared up at the man behind the bench for a few more seconds. They had an extensive history, and despite Skip's longstanding rule that cases not become personal, this case was personal.

Chapter II

Skip arrived back at his Main Street office just a few minutes before noon. He parked in the lot out back and circled around to the front of the two-story Victorian building. The flat front Italianate with bracketed cornices and windows adorned with pediments, typical of the structures along the sleepy village's main thoroughfare, was adjoined on one side by a bakery and a baseball memorabilia shop on the other. Skip's law office, a second floor walk-up, about two-thirds of the way from the *Baseball Hall of Fame* to the Courthouse, was situated over the *Pantheon Pizza Parlor*. Not the greatest location, but the price was right. Roughly two years after Megan's death he had moved there from a classier site around the corner from the storied *Otesaga Hotel*.

Skip inhaled the spiced aroma of fresh-baked pizza as he climbed the twenty-two wooden stairs that led to his office. He turned the brass handle and pushed open the frosted-glass door that bore his name in gold lettering. "How'd the morning go, Lucy?" he said, as he stepped inside. Lucy Walker, his only employee, was his receptionist, secretary and office manager, all rolled into one.

"Quiet. I managed to type the Woodward brief and catch up on my filing."

Skip gestured at a small pile of pink telephone messages. "Anything important? If not, I'll grab some lunch."

"The lawyer for Mohegan Savings and Loan called about the Madison closing. And Mrs. Wells wants to know when her divorce will be final. I told her the decree was on the Judge's desk and as soon as he signs it, we'll let her know. For now, no need to call her back."

Janet Wells had a new boyfriend, about a dozen years her junior, and even before the summons had been served in her divorce action, she was hot to trot. Her rants and raves about her soon-to-be ex-husband's miserly ways, a discourse that Skip had endured on a score of occasions, were insufferable. Not having to return the call was a godsend. Thanks to Lucy and the many responsibilities she voluntarily assumed, such godsends were wide-ranging and frequent.

"When you prepare your check for my signature next Friday," said Skip, "add another twenty cents an hour." The raises he gave her weren't large, but their frequency more than made up for their size.

"If you promise not to quote me, I'll let you in on a little secret. I've got one helluva boss."

Skip feigned a look of disbelief. "All this time I thought you were a good judge of character."

Lucy smiled. "How'd you make out this morning with Morehead?"

"Could have been better. Biddleford set bail at one hundred thousand. And now that you ask, that reminds me–calendar the case for motions on May 14th at ten A.M."

Lucy made a quick entry.

"I'm on my way over to the *Eagle*. Can I get you anything?"

"Not today, thanks." She gestured toward the rear of the suite. "I brought a salad. It's in the fridge." She leaned back and put her hand to her stomach. "For a change I'm determined to stick to my diet."

Skip felt his brow knit. Of all people Lucy hardly needed to watch her waist. Just short of her fortieth birthday, the brunette with high cheekbones still had the figure she enjoyed as a high school cheerleader. Skip, on the other hand, bore hints of an emerging paunch around his midsection. While he still sported the athletic physique that had enabled him to letter in both baseball and basketball at Lehigh, appearances suggested those days were ancient history. He headed back down the stairs and out of his office. The walk to the *Eagle* was easy. He could have opted for the impressive *Cooper Inn*, a favorite gathering place of the village's most urbane citizens, particularly members of the Bar, but the smaller and less fashionable *Eagle*, up a little side street midway between the *Baseball Hall of Fame* and Doubleday Field, befitted him better. It wasn't blue collar, but certainly not starched white either. Legend had it that Babe Ruth and James Fenimore Cooper, among numerous other celebrities, had frequented the place. That the cornerstone bore the year 1907, the best part of a century after the author's death, failed to quell the legend, at least among true believers too wise to allow technicalities to deprecate the charm of their venerated hangout.

Skip had barely seated himself in his usual seat at the left end of the long, finely carved oak bar when Loomis set a highball glass of *Jack Daniel's* on the rocks in front of him.

"What's up?"

"Same old...same old. How's by you?"

Loomis shrugged.

Skip glanced in the direction of the blackboard on the far wall listing the specials of the day, not that he could read them. The look was too brief and the writing too small to discern in the dim light. It didn't matter since his fare, an *Eagleburger*, heavy on the onions, with an extra crisp order of fries, was already determined."

Loomis gave the unspoken order to the cook, got a draft for a fellow near the other end of the bar and then returned to Skip. "I hear you represent Harley Morehead."

"Word travels fast." Not that Skip was surprised.

"C'mon, how often is one of our leading citizens, the Chairman of the Populist Party, charged with murder?"

Skip knew better than to discuss a case. Even when *Jack* was around, Skip maintained his wits. Fish for information, he might, but his tongue never wagged. Well...rarely. A couple of times *Jack* may have gotten the upper hand. Skip wasn't altogether sure exactly what had passed his lips on those occasions.

"Having Biddleford on the bench won't be easy," said Loomis. "Odds are he dislikes Morehead even more than you."

Since Megan's death, apart from Lucy, Loomis was arguably Skip's closest friend. That's not to suggest that the two fraternized outside the *Eagle*, but Skip, once a gregarious lawyer, had basically become a loner. Loomis was a rare confidant with whom Skip often had shared details of his notorious battles with Biddleford. Unlike the facts of a case, skirmishes with His Holiness were not a matter demanding the cloak of attorney-client privilege, and Loomis was a great sounding board. Rarely one to give advice, he listened patiently, and what passed his ears from one patron was not repeated to the next. Skip viewed Loomis as his shrink. True, his office bore beer signs rather than diplomas, but no appointments were required, rates were far cheaper and sessions didn't abruptly halt the moment the minute hand struck twelve. Skip often wondered how Loomis ended up behind a bar. Whatever the subject—literature, art, music, philosophy, history, sports or even science—Loomis was well versed. But bookish he wasn't. Only when others chose an esoteric path did his expansive knowledge reveal itself. Even then there were no airs. Skip knew that Loomis had never earned his college degree. The reasons why or how close he had come remained undisclosed. Loomis was more of a listener than a talker, especially when it came to himself.

"Biddleford is bound to be a problem," said Skip. "On the bright side, he'll treat the District Attorney like dirt, the same as me."

Loomis nodded. "I suppose. But some of that dirt is top soil, while the rest is mainly manure."

As the Chairman of the Populist Party, Morehead definitely fell into the latter category. Chances were Skip did too. Although politically independent, given the years of animosity between himself and Biddleford, four choice letters would have been sufficient for the pompous jurist to characterize Skip. The feelings were mutual.

Loomis put Skip's *Eagleburger* and fries in front of him.

Glass in hand, Skip held it out for a refill.

Loomis reached for *Jack*. He was about to pour but halted. "You gonna resort to your crazy antics when you try the case?"

A breaking smile undermined Skip's effort to feign shock.

"Like the time you lay down on the floor in front of the jury at the start of your summation."

The vivid scene, one that people often threw up at Skip, had Biddleford screaming, demanding to know what Skip thought he was doing. The prosecutor had called thirteen witnesses on an eight-dollar shoplifting case. Only one of them had actually witnessed the theft. Skip told the jury he was sorry, but the prosecutor had put him to sleep. The truth be known, summation came following lunch on the second day of the trial, and Skip had spent the entire noon hour with *Jack*. Any inhibitions, not to mention good sense, had failed to accompany him back to the courtroom.

Loomis filled Skip's glass.

"This time I plan to strangle Biddleford, perhaps when he overrules one of my objections. But rest assured, I'll wear gloves…not to avoid fingerprints, but to avoid catching some loathsome disease."

The stoic Loomis looked Skip in the eye but showed nothing.

At times like that Skip disliked Loomis's psychiatric ways. The lack of reaction, explicit or implicit, forced Skip to confront himself. He could not deny that the man in the mirror was outrageous. His absurd behavior was out of control. His claim that he could hold his liquor didn't hold water. Skip said, "C'mon, you must have a sense of humor."

Loomis shook his head. "I'm just a bartender. What can you expect?"

The question, rhetorical or not, tempted Skip to turn the tables. With all his knowledge Loomis had hardly achieved his potential. And unlike Skip, who had earned both a B.A. and J.D., Loomis had never graduated. But a couple of sheepskins didn't count for much once the score was totaled. Loomis enjoyed his work. In the meantime the fellows whom he served, like Skip, struggled to escape reality.

Skip decided to pursue a more purposeful subject. "By any chance did you know Squeaky Grimes?"

"He came in a few times. But he wasn't a regular."

"What do you know about him?"

"That he's dead."

Skip raised his glass. "Thanks a heap." He looked Loomis in the eye. "Any thoughts about who did him in?"

"Only what I read in the newspapers."

Whether he was serious or borrowing sarcasm from Will Rogers—Loomis often drew upon famous phrases from the past—was hard to discern. "Did he ever talk about himself?"

Loomis laughed.

"What's so funny?"

"Have I ever had a patron who didn't talk about himself?"

Even one as contentious as Skip had to concede the point. Psychiatrists' patients all talked about themselves. An arsenal of mesmerizing techniques and drugs such as hypnotism, Darvon, and sodium pentothal facilitated the process. But Loomis had an even larger arsenal. A bar thirty-feet long lined with soporific liquids, among them *Jack*, pierced inhibitions, stripped away masks, delved the subconscious and unearthed ensepulchered skeletons. But unlike his professionally licensed counterparts Loomis charged by the ounce, not the hour. He wore no muzzle from laws mandating confidentiality. He was free to repeat his clientele's deepest secrets. But that was not his style. The disclosures that crossed his ears rarely passed his lips.

"You must know a few tidbits about Squeaky," said Skip.

Loomis hesitated. "Not really. You might better go up the street a few doors and talk to Buddy Kileen. I understand Squeaky did some odd jobs for him from time to time."

Buddy Kileen, a local insurance agent, had long been active in the local Populist Party. Skip knew him by sight, though not personally. According to the scuttlebutt Kileen had tried more than once to get the nod to run for the State Assembly, but Morehead, as local Populist Party Chairman, had blocked him. Morehead had mentioned that Squeaky had his hands in lots of things, but a link to Kileen had particularly intriguing possibilities. Perhaps it was a coincidence, but maybe not. As for what else Loomis might know about Squeaky, Skip would try some other time to pry such information. In the meantime he decided to pay Kileen a visit. He weighed the possibility of making an appointment but preferred to catch the insurance agent off guard. Skip finished his lunch and then left the *Eagle* heading a block or so north to the storefront insurance operation. As he entered, he was conscious of the first-floor location. It had obvious advantages, among them access and image, but Skip's spot over the *Pantheon* was a helluva lot cheaper.

A frumpy lady, about fifty, seated behind a desk just a few steps from the entrance greeted him. "Hi. Can I help you?"

"I'm Skip Maynard, and—"

"Yes, I know."

He waited a second to see if she might explain. She didn't. "I was hoping to see Buddy Kileen."

"Just a moment." She got up from her seat and went through a door at the rear. Moments later she returned. "Mr. Kileen will see you." She gestured Skip to come through.

With a ruddy complexion and slicked-back hair the wiry insurance agent came around from behind his desk and shook Skip's hand. "What can I do for you? Home, life, auto, malpractice? You name it. We sell it." He motioned Skip to a chair and took the one behind his desk.

"Actually I'm not here to buy insurance. I represent Harley Morehead in regard to the murder of Squeaky Grimes."

"I heard about that, not that you represent Morehead, but that he had been arrested. Then again, everyone around here knows that. Not often that someone of Morehead's stature gets charged with murder, at least around these parts."

"I understand that Grimes worked for you."

"Grimes." Kileen softly repeated the name under his breath. "Not often anyone ever called him that. To the world he was just Squeaky. And to answer your question, he did odd jobs for me now and then. Checked out facts on an accident claim. Took pictures of a banged-up car. Even cleared my sidewalk of snow one winter when my regular guy was laid up with a bum back."

"What kind of guy was Squeaky?"

"Whad'ya mean?"

Skip wasn't sure what he meant. He was simply fishing. "Was he a loner or the type with lots of friends?"

Kileen seemed to ponder. "He definitely wasn't a loner, but friends...that's another matter. You might just say he knew lots of people. He did odd jobs here and there. Whatever. Not that he had any special skills."

"A jack of all trades, but a master of none?"

Kileen shook his head. "The part about master is right, but he wasn't a jack of much. Folks just knew that if you had an odd job, one that didn't take a whole lot of training, Squeaky could probably do it. He didn't have a lot going for him. Definitely not smarts. But one thing, for a little runt, Squeaky had balls. Big brass ones."

The relationship between Kileen and Morehead was on Skip's mind, but discretion, the risk that Kileen might terminate the conversation, demanded the subject be left to the end. "Did Squeaky have any enemies?"

"Enemies...you mean the kind who might do him in? Uh...kinda hard to say. Course that voice of his..." Kileen groaned. "But folks don't usually get killed for that. On the other hand, some, like Squeaky, are so annoying—" Kileen looked away and muttered under his breath, "Badmouthing the clod isn't cricket now that he's sleeping with the earthworms." He turned back to Skip. "Let me put it this way. Squeaky was an odd character. No doubt he rubbed lotsa folks the wrong way, if only because he was like a bad penny. Hard to get rid of, if you get my drift."

"I think so," said Skip, but with skepticism whether Kileen may have dodged the question about enemies. "Anybody at all who might have had a reason?"

This time Kileen broke eye contact.

Skip waited for him to look back. "There's something you're not telling me."

Kileen heaved a sigh.

Again Skip waited.

"I hate spreading rumors...especially about your client."

"I appreciate your concern, but bad news is less painful here than in a courtroom."

Kileen nodded halfheartedly. "Anyway, there's a good chance you know already. Squeaky was a runner for Morehead."

"You must be mistaken." Skip used the line whenever someone surprised him with bad news about a client, not that it was great, just better than spontaneous ignorance.

Kileen chuckled. "Think what you want. But I'm dishing you the facts."

"What makes you so certain?"

"I was among Morehead's suckers. Squeaky took my bets. And when I won—even patsies like me pick a winner once in a while—he brought me my payoff."

"Maybe Squeaky was making book himself. Or working for somebody else."

"Sure. And maybe I'll hit the gigundo lottery three times in succession." Kileen gestured at Skip. "Believe what you like. But sure as I'm sitting here, Morehead's printing business is a front for a bookmaking operation." He glanced at his watch. "Don't mean to rush you, but in four minutes I've got an appointment, the kind that pays the bills. Unlike some others, the fellow is looking to buy some insurance."

With time a sudden luxury, the slow, calculated approach was, like Skip, all but out the door. "I understand you've had designs on the State Assembly."

"I considered it."

"Rumor has it Morehead blocked you."

"Funny you should put it that way. To my face he was always friendly. Said he couldn't muster enough support. Of course backstabbers play that kind of game." Kileen got up from his seat. "I'd be happy to meet with you again some other time. I've got some wonderful policies at great prices."

"Sounds interesting. I'll have to keep you in mind." Skip headed out the door. Another meeting with Kileen was a distinct possibility, but, if so, he'd be looking for information, not insurance.

Skip had started back to his office when just across the street *Wurther's Pharmacy* caught his eye. Up on the top floor of the timeworn, three-story, burgundy-trimmed Victorian structure was the office of private detective Mickey Shore. Skip had used Mickey several times over the years. He wasn't the most professional investigator, but his unorthodox techniques worked, and his price was right. Skip detoured to the other side of the street and climbed the building's side-hall stairs. Past the second floor, up to the third and down the hall beyond a couple of studio apartments was Mickey's office. By comparison Skip had a palace. Skip rapped on the badly marred door, just below the bronze plaque that read, *Mickey Shore, Private Investigator.* The classy sign was the only thing about the office that wasn't seedy. Skip waited several seconds and rapped again.

"C'mon in. It's unlocked."

As Skip opened the door, he inhaled the deeply imbedded smoky odor that permeated the air. Seated in an easy chair over in the corner, not far from a big, old walnut desk, Mickey was rubbing his eyes, beady ones at that. "Don't mind me," said the squirrelly guy with a few days growth on his chin. "Just catchin' a few winks." He rubbed his eyes one more time. "Been a while since I've seen you. How've you been?"

"Can't complain. And you?"

Mickey shrugged as he gestured Skip to a chair adjacent to his own. "What can I do for you?"

"I represent Harley Morehead, and—"

"So I hear." Mickey reached over to his desk and grabbed a pack of *Camels.* "Want one?"

Skip shook his head. "I'd like you to do some investigating. I've got some guys that need checking out."

Mickey pulled out a cigarette and, following a few quick taps on the arm of the chair, lit up. "So, who is it ya need checked out?"

"Buddy Kileen, the insurance man." Skip gestured toward the other side of the street where Kileen's office was located. "Along with Jimmie Raines and Bernie Feinstein."

"The County Comptroller. This sounds interesting." Mickey sat up straighter. "Whose the other fella?"

"Jimmie Raines. He and his wife Tammy Lee live in a big house a couple miles outside of town. It's on Willow Street. From what I've heard, they live pretty high."

Mickey grabbed a pen and pad from his desk and jotted a few notes. "What am I looking for?"

"Links to Squeaky Grimes."

Mickey chuckled.

28

"What's so funny?"

"You've hit the jackpot. Can't tell ya how often Squeaky's name turns up. And always with an odor...the kind ya find in an outhouse."

"Anything that might tie to Harley Morehead?"

Mickey laughed again.

This time Skip simply waited.

"I'm sure ya know that Morehead was a bookie."

Rather than firing off his usual hackneyed line, Skip reacted with a dismissive glance. It was one of several looks he had mastered. Like a light switch he could turn any one of them on and off at will, giving no hint as to his real reaction.

"C'mon. Don't tell me ya really believe your client put food on his table with printing."

"Did you ever place a bet with him?"

"No...but I don't buy lottery tickets either. That don't mean they don't exist."

Debating the issue served no purpose. What mattered was that the Populist Party Chairman might not be a pillar of the community. "Tell me more about Squeaky," said Skip.

"What's there to tell. The runt was a brown nose. Kissed asses quicker than a fox snatches chickens in an unguarded coop." Mickey's eyes, seemingly directed nowhere, narrowed in seeming contemplation. "Ya know, Squeaky may not have been as quick as a fox, but he was a damn side more cunning."

"Why do you say that?"

Mickey gave Skip a look. "Would you want a leech, one with half-a-brain and no conscience, up your ass?" His eyes locked onto Skip's. "You get the picture?"

Unfortunately it was more vivid than Skip would have liked. He said, "I understand that Bernie Feinstein was Squeaky's landlord."

"Now that ya mention it, that rings a bell." Mickey's gaze turned blank. He muttered to himself, "Where did I hear that? The Booker case, maybe." He pulled out another cigarette and lit it with the elfin remains of the one he had been smoking. He dragged the fresh one before snuffing the first in a large, butt-filled ashtray. "Ya know that Feinstein is a slum lord?"

"So I understand." Skip recalled the additional tidbit that Morehead had given him. "I hear that Squeaky was way behind in his rent."

"You think Feinstein oiled Squeaky?"

"Oiled…That a new term for murder?"

"Only in Sqeaky's case." Mickey glanced at the paper where he had earlier jotted a note. "Feinstein, Raines and Kileen. Anyone else ya want me to check out?"

Skip thought for a second. "Not right now." He was about to leave when one last question came to mind. "Apart from what you mentioned about being a bookie, what do you know about Harley Morehead?"

Mickey drew his cigarette to his lips and inhaled slowly. Seconds later smoke poured from his nose. "Only what I've heard third hand."

Anything was better than nothing. "Such as?"

"That as Populist Party Chairman he's a hard ass, the kind with a fuse the length of a firecracker but the explosiveness of TNT. He has two ways of doing things: his way or his way."

"What about his reliability?"

Mickey rolled his eyes.

He had answered the question, and the response had legal significance. If and when Morehead opted to take the stand at trial, his credibility would be in issue. Evidence regarding his reputation for veracity would become admissible. Skip made a mental note as he got up from his seat. "That's it for now," he said. "But…keep an eye open for anything that might link to Squeaky's death."

———

After leaving Mickey, Skip started back to his office. Along the way he thwarted temptation's lure to make another stop at the *Eagle*, not that he could take credit for the good judgment. Past experience had taught him that a second visit would have Loomis on his case. Besides bartender and psychiatrist, Loomis was known to play the role of scrutinizing mother. From time-to-time he donned other hats as well. A

30

voice calling his name had Skip looking back over his shoulder.

"Got a minute?" said Kelly Lane.

As she caught up, he gave his *Timex* a demonstrative look.

"Have you ever known Skip Maynard to be in a hurry?"

She thought for a moment. "Well...there's a first time for everything."

He might have reminded her that he was a creature of habit, but as well as she knew him, the remark was superfluous. Several years after Megan had been killed, Kelly and Skip had dated for roughly a year. Apart from a smattering of isolated dates, she was the only woman he had gone out with since Megan's death. "How've you been?"

"Good. I understand you represent Harley Morehead."

He nodded, noting she looked smart in her stylish turquoise suit. Then again, the shapely brunette with big hazel eyes and fabulous smile always looked great.

"I'm handling the estate of Ralph Grimes."

"No fooling?"

"Yes. He was a client of mine...before someone did him in."

Skip studied her face for clues as to her thoughts. It was opaque. "Any guesses as to the guilty party?"

"Well...nothing personal, but based upon the police investigation, your client is leading the race."

"The cops have been wrong before."

"Admittedly. But more times than not, they seem to be right."

"Spoken like a true estate and corporate attorney."

She flashed one of her tantalizing smiles, the kind that was all but illegal. "I suppose a lawyer who leans toward criminal defense work is more objective."

Debating the point was useless. Conviction rates well over ninety percent in every county demonstrated that the vast majority of those arrested were guilty. Sure, the police were prone to charge crimes more numerous and serious than the offenses committed, but that in no way implied the accused were innocent. And when it came to those overcharged crimes, defense lawyers were the last to complain. Not only did it provide fodder for plea bargains, but it also made it easier to justify fees. Mitigated outcomes impressed defendants in jeopardy of harsh sentences. Skip said, "Did Squeaky leave much of an estate?"

"Not really. He never owned his own home. He rented a flat in one of Bernie Feinstein's tenements...over on Rock Street. Need I say more?"

Though Skip was unfamiliar with the particular property, he knew the area, as well as the dumps the County Comptroller leased. People often claimed his apartments deserved to be condemned. Skip wondered if political influence enabled Feinstein to avoid violation notices. But for the moment another curiosity drew his focus. "How did you come to represent Squeaky? Guys like me usually represent yo-yos like him."

"I handled his grandfather's estate. Squeaky was among the beneficiaries. His grandfather left him a gorgeous diamond ring. More than three carats. As yet it hasn't turned up."

"Very interesting," said Skip, spotting the emergence of another possible defense for his client. "Maybe someone killed Squeaky for the ring."

"Could be...and maybe that someone was your client."

"C'mon, someone with Morehead's kind of money wouldn't kill for...a ten, maybe twelve thousand dollar ring."

Kelly reacted with a look akin to Skip's dismissive special.

"You disagree?"

"No—but that doesn't mean Morehead didn't kill Squeaky and steal the ring."

If Skip were dealing with someone else, he might have treated the remark as gibberish. But coming from Kelly, there was a distinct possibility he had missed something. "You mind explaining?"

"Well, the way I see it, Squeaky knew too much about Morehead's business, the kind of stuff—and I don't mean printing—that could land Morehead behind bars. Morehead may have needed to shut Squeaky up. So he killed him. Once he did, he snatched the ring. Maybe as an afterthought or perhaps because Squeaky owed him money."

"Talk about farfetched." Skip slowly droned the words, flashing a dismissive look reminiscent of the one Kelly had given him moments before. His thoughts, however, bore no similarity to the outward reaction. Her conjecture was plausible. He said, "Did Squeaky leave any other significant assets?"

"A very valuable one." Kelly smiled, the type that hinted there was a kicker.

Skip waited a moment. "You plan to tell me?"

"Sure. A cause of action for pain and suffering and wrongful death against his murderer."

Wheels spun in Skip's head. Lawyers preferred actions grounded in negligence. Insurance policies covered careless conduct. Intentional wrongs, like assault and murder, produced big verdicts, but without insurance, more often than not, those verdicts were uncollectable. He said, "Most damage judgments based upon homicide are Pyrrhic victories. Big numbers, but no dough."

"True. But fortunately I've got a defendant with deep pockets. I'm sure you're aware that your client, who no doubt will be paying you big bucks, is mighty well off. And no doubt you're also aware that he confessed to murdering Squeaky." Kelly reached out halfway as if intending to deliver a poke and then gestured across the street. "I have to make a stop at the bank. Otherwise I'd walk with you. Good seeing you." She flashed one more of her patented smiles.

Skip watched her cross the roadway. No sense letting the unproductive encounter be a total loss. He ogled the tight backside that swiveled seductively beneath her narrow waist. His mind drifted back to the days when they had dated. Their relationship might have led to the altar had memories of Megan not made Skip unwilling to commit, at least that was how Skip had always tried to characterize their breakup. Of course, Kelly probably saw it differently. She had dumped Skip. His inability to commit may have played a role, but bottom line, she couldn't tolerate a guy with a mistress, even a mistress named *Jack*.

Skip parked his car along the curb in front of Morehead's business, *Prime Printing*, located about fifteen miles south of Cooperstown in the heart of Oneonta, Otsego County's largest city. Morehead had managed to post bail a day earlier. Before entering the building, Skip paused taking note of its brick box, *Georgian* style. His late father had been an architect, and the influence had rubbed off. At a very young age Skip had developed a broad knowledge of architectural forms. Where many of his schoolmates were adept at identifying the make and model of most any car, he could recognize the architectural style of most any structure. He also knew the historical development, not that his knowledge impressed his friends. On the contrary, Skip learned to keep it to himself, lest he be shunned as a geek. Were it not for his affinity for the law, Skip might have considered a career in architecture, though limited aptitude for drawing and spatial relations probably would have forced him to rethink such an option.

As he entered *Prime Printing*, Skip took note of the finely crafted, decorative mahogany door. Paralleled by fluted trim and beveled sidelights, it was crowned with an elliptical transom bearing beveled glass and faceted jewels. According to his father doorways revealed a lot about people, particularly their appreciation of culture and history. Straight ahead a man was operating a printing press. Off to his left Skip heard the familiar deep voice of Harley Morehead.

"To what do I owe this unexpected visit?"

"I was in the neighborhood—a closing over at *First Trust*—so I decided to stop in. You have a few minutes?"

Morehead came around from behind a counter. "Sure. We can go into the office." He motioned to one of two doors at the rear.

"Nice building," said Skip, as he followed Morehead. "You don't see many *Georgians* around these parts. Far more common along the New England coast."

Morehead shrugged. "You can't tell by me. All I know is that it was in good condition and the price was right back when I bought it about twenty years ago."

"When was it built?"

"Eighteen-forty...or fifty. Something like that, I guess. Why do you ask?"

"It's different from the rest of the neighborhood. More along the lines of what the gentry were building more than a century earlier. The owner must have had it specially designed."

Morehead shrugged. "All I know is that it's got four walls and a roof."

The response, like cheap paint over beautifully grained wood, might have impugned his father's theory were Skip not willing to resort to the expedient adage that the exception proves the rule.

"You want some coffee?"

"No thanks."

Morehead grimaced. "Don't mind me. Too many hot sausages for breakfast." He pulled a roll of *Tums* out of his pocket and popped a couple into his mouth. "The way I use these things, I probably keep the company in business." He slipped the roll back into his pocket as he ushered Skip into a small office. With a file cabinet, a desk and a couple of chairs, it was nothing fancy. Morehead motioned Skip to take a seat and then, spinning the desk chair around, sat down alongside the file cabinet. "So, what brings you here?"

"A couple things about your case I want to discuss." Skip would have used the telephone, but he preferred to meet with Morehead face to face. That way he could better assess his client's answers. "Let me give it to you straight. I've been hearing rumors that you run a bookmaking operation."

"And?"

"And I need to know if there's any truth to them."

Morehead gestured all around. "Does this look like a bookmaking operation?"

Skip restrained the urge to disparage the unsatisfactory response. He looked Morehead in the eye. "If you want me to give you the best possible defense, I need the unvarnished facts. Going into the courtroom blind is a recipe for disaster. Having said that, tell me flat out, are you in any way involved with gambling?"

"I buy a couple of lottery tickets each week. And I've been known to place a bet on a football or basketball game from time to time." Morehead appeared to study Skip. "Who told you I'm a bookie?"

"It doesn't matter. I just need to know whether it's true."

"Fine," said Morehead. "Now you know. It isn't. I run a printing business. Okay?"

"Good. That's what I needed to hear." Skip was much less sanguine than his words. In the course of practicing criminal law, his clients had lied to him far too often. From the most serious felony down to a two-bit petit larceny or even a minor traffic infraction, he had heard it all. When he had first entered practice, he had accepted what clients said as gospel. Repeated corruption of the truth, a combination of omissions, bending the facts and categorical fabrications, quickly cured that propensity. It did not, however, relieve his clients of the consequences. They fell victims of their own deceptions. While Skip was occasionally singed in the courtroom, fork-tongued clients were ultimately burned. They, not he, did the time.

———————

Mickey Shore circled to the rear of the Otsego County Office Building. There in the space marked County Comptroller was Bernie Feinstein's amber Buick Electra. Cars were a great indicator of people's whereabouts, and Mickey made it his business to know as many as possible. He checked his watch—4:14. Feinstein was likely to appear very soon. A telephone call to the building's chief janitor, long a confidant of Mickey's, had provided heads up on Feinstein's habits. He generally arrived at work between nine-thirty and ten. About once a week, though more during golf season, he took the afternoon off. Other days he made certain to slip out five or ten minutes ahead of the four-thirty rush. The unionized rank and file were strictly governed by the clock. Feinstein was elected. He answered to the voters, not a collective-bargaining agreement.

Four twenty-one. Sure enough, Feinstein sauntered out the back entrance and headed for his car. As Mickey prepared to cut him off, he drew upon his knack for sizing people up. The middle-aged politician with the prominent nose, balding top and paunchy midsection was a typical Jew, smart and shrewd. Ethnic typecasting was a basic facet of Mickey's stock and trade. Political correctness be damned. The old templates were too reliable to ignore. But Mickey prided himself on his ability to identify nuances that made each individual something more than an ethnic cliché. For the moment Bernie Feinstein was a stereotypical chestnut, but soon enough Mickey would refine that superficial profile. "Excuse me. You got a minute?"

"I'm in a bit of a hurry." Feinstein appeared to study Mickey. "Don't I know you from somewhere?"

"Maybe. I'm Mickey Shore, private detective."

"Shore...I remember you. The Morgan kid...the one who was kidnapped. You helped find him. Right?"

Mickey nodded, a bit surprised that Feinstein knew who he was. He was flattered as well. Otsego County spread over a sizeable area, and though Feinstein's job as County Comptroller gave him ties to Cooperstown, his home base was Richfield Springs.

"What can I do for you?"

"I'd like to talk to you...about the murder of Squeaky Grimes. I understand he rented one of your apartments." Mickey pointed to the *Dunkin Donuts* a few doors down the street. "Can I buy you a doughnut, along with a cup of coffee."

"No thanks. But..." Feinstein glanced at his watch. "I'll give you four minutes. Just enough for me to beat the crowd."

Rush hour in Cooperstown was hardly a big deal, but four minutes was better than nothing. "What can you tell me about Squeaky?"

"That his moniker fit."

"What type of tenant was he?"

Feinstein shook his head. "Don't mean to badmouth a guy after he's six feet under, but collecting rent from him was tougher than growing geraniums in January. He was always several months behind."

"Why didn't you kick him out?"

Feinstein shrugged. "Because I'm a nice guy...maybe?"

Whether Feinstein's response, complete with interrogative inflection, was intended as humor or a subterfuge to avoid the question, Mickey wasn't sure. "Did Squeaky have any enemies?"

Feinstein furrowed his brow. "C'mon, Mr. Detective. I wasn't born yesterday. You know as well as I that Squeaky was always on the edge. Everything about him was sketchy. No doubt he rubbed lots of folks the wrong way, not just with his voice. And given what happened, he apparently rubbed someone really hard."

"Any guesses?"

Feinstein smiled wryly.

"Why the reaction?"

"C'mon, this isn't April Fools' Day. We both know that a certain upstanding citizen of our community has confessed to Squeaky's murder. But fair-minded politician that I am, far be it from me to stick pins in the gentleman. I'll let the police, the District Attorney, newspapers and virtually every person who walks the streets of our lovely town do that." Feinstein gave his watch another look, this one far more demonstrative than its predecessor.

With the clock expiring, Mickey shifted to the tidbit Skip had given him over the telephone earlier that day. "I understand Squeaky had an antique diamond ring, a rock the size of a hazelnut, passed down from his grandfather."

"That so?"

"You must have seen it."

"Uh...maybe."

Mickey shot the County Comptroller a wide-eyed look. "You couldn't forget a rock like that."

Feinstein broke eye contact. A moment later he gestured at his car. "Gotta go...before the crowd..."

As Feinstein hurried to his car and drove off, Mickey made some mental notes. When it came to smarts, the Jewish politician failed to measure up to the cliché. As for his ethnic nose, it had all the earmarks of Pinocchio. Feinstein knew a whole lot more about Squeaky's ring than he was admitting. Maybe he knew more about Squeaky's murder as well.

Skip flipped the *Oneonta Daily Star* onto the kitchen table. The local paper was part of his morning ritual, but he never gave it a look until his big mug of coffee was in hand. As the beverage brewed, he stared out the kitchen window. His three-bedroom Cape Cod sat on a half-acre lot with one hundred feet of frontage on the west side of Otsego Lake. Surrounded by huge ponderosa pines on all sides except the lakefront, the secluded house was located a couple miles north of the sleepy village. A slope of nearly thirty degrees down from the house to the water's edge provided a great view, especially of the sunrises off to the east. Skip had seen many, but mostly before Megan was killed. On warm summer mornings they would rise early and sip their coffee on the rear deck. Together in their primeval habitat, the world in which he made his living seemed as distant as the heavenly body that brought light and life to the planet. Only the morning chirp of birds hidden in the trees invaded the otherwise silent sanctuary. Slowly the fiery ball would make its way over the far side of the lake, sometimes as a single yellow disc, while others, through clouds with shades of red and pink and blue. And then there were the mornings when, with a gray mist hanging over the lake, the genesis of the new day arrived in a silky veil. Skip had savored the many variations. But in the years since Megan had died, they were mainly distant memories. Without her, the once entrancing scenes were woefully empty. No longer was he an early riser.

Out beyond his kitchen window the bright sun, already high in the eastern spring sky, shimmered on the placid Otsego Lake waters. Skip filled his mug with high-test java and seated himself at the table in the corner. He unfolded the *Star*. He scanned the front-page headlines: *Middle East Tensions Threaten Wider Conflict*; *Fire Chief Labels Richfield Springs' Blaze as Arson*; *Enforcer to Testify Against Morehead in Exchange for Plea Deal*. The sight of his client's name grabbed Skip's attention. He read on:

*According to attorney Warren Mack, his client Eddie
"the Enforcer" Willis has agreed to plead guilty to
Assault in the Third Degree in exchange for a short
stint in the County Jail and his testimony against
Populist Party Chairman Harley Morehead regarding
the murder of Squeaky Grimes. A representative of the
District Attorney's office, who asked to remain
unnamed, confirmed the deal. Said Mack, "My client
will testify that Morehead's printing business was a
front for his bookmaking operation. He will admit that
he served as Morehead's enforcer and that he beat up
Squeaky Grimes several months ago at Morehead's
behest." Mack also indicated that Willis would testify
that Morehead told him something "more permanent"
might have to be done about Squeaky because the
"runt" had threatened to go to the authorities.*

Skip sipped his coffee. He swallowed hard. The case
against Morehead, already bad, had grown worse. Bad enough
he needed to argue that his client's confession was coerced.
Now, even if the confession were suppressed, there would be
testimony that Morehead was a bookmaker; that he had an
enforcer; and that he had threatened the life of the victim. It
was possible that Willis was lying in order to get a deal. Sure, it
was possible, but Skip didn't buy it. Morehead had insisted he
wasn't a bookmaker. But Buddy Kileen and Mickey Shore had
both said otherwise. Of all people, Mickey would know. Skip
reached for his mug but didn't imbibe. He had lost his appetite,
even for his morning coffee. The odds that Morehead's
confession contained an accurate representation of the facts had
gradually risen from even money to almost a sure thing.

Chapter III

Saturday afternoon. Alone in his office Skip sat with law books spread across his desk. He couldn't recall the last time he had worked on a weekend. In the early days of his career, except for the summer months, he had worked at least a half-day almost every Saturday and occasionally for a few hours on Sunday as well. But that was long ago, long before Megan's death. Long before torpor had replaced passion.

A day earlier the District Attorney had provided him with a *Xeroxed* copy of Morehead's confession. Skip didn't even have to make a motion. An informal request had sufficed. The document, handwritten on a four-by-six inch sheet from a tear-off pad, bore Morehead's signature and the date, April 11, 1968, at the bottom. The unusual confession simply recited that Morehead had stabbed Squeaky approximately six times on April 9, 1968 at Squeaky's apartment when Squeaky had tried to blackmail Morehead.

Skip re-read the confession several times. Extorting money from one's bookie when in debt was a perilous practice. Few would dare. But Squeaky was anything but typical. As Kileen had said, Squeaky had brass balls. He was the kind to pull such a stunt. As for Morehead, his credibility stunk. He claimed he wasn't a bookie. Everyone said he was. Skip banged the arm of his chair. Odds were, he had a guilty client.

He got up from his desk and walked aimlessly around the room. He had defended many a guilty client. The Constitution guaranteed them a defense. They were presumed innocent until competent evidence proved the contrary beyond a reasonable doubt. The prosecution bore the burden of proof. The principles raced through Skip's brain. In the abstract they were great. But buoy him, they didn't. Defending a client he believed innocent had far more appeal than one he believed guilty. Unfortunately, the likelihood that he enjoyed that luxury had become a long shot.

Skip headed back to his desk. Plan B: a defense grounded on technicalities was the way he would have to go. Top priority would be excluding Morehead's confession from evidence. If the jury heard it, Morehead would be dead meat. Without it the case was arguably a tossup. Of course that assumed the mound of incriminating evidence didn't continue to grow.

Skip rocked his chair back and gazed up at the ceiling. He closed his eyes as his mind drifted back to the day when he had first considered the possibility of becoming a lawyer. He was in fifth grade. It was Election Day, 1941, and he had it off from school. He had accompanied his father to the office where he worked as an architect. They had left the house at seven-thirty allowing time to stop for breakfast. They could have eaten at home, but his father, who worked long hours, tried to make the time they spent together special. They had stopped at *Brownie's Diner*, a tiny eatery with a half-dozen booths and an equal number of stools at the art-deco counter. They were seated at the latter. His father might have preferred a booth but yielded to Skip's affinity for the carousel-like, rotating seats. They were enjoying a full breakfast of eggs, sausage, hash browns and toast when two uniformed police officers sat down immediately to Skip's right. They ordered coffee and Danish, which they promptly wolfed down. The officer next to Skip flipped a pair of nickels onto the counter, and the duo walked out. Skip did a double take. He grabbed a menu and checked the prices: coffee, $.10; and Danish pastry, $.15. After quickly totaling the officers' charges, Skip nudged his father. "The policemen who just left didn't pay their bill."

His father put his finger to his lips. "Shush."

Skip pointed at the nickels that lay on the counter. "But they only left—"

His father placed a muzzling hand close to Skip's mouth and whispered, "We'll talk about it later."

Once they had finished their breakfasts and were outside, Skip said, "The policemen left a ten-cent tip but never paid their bill."

His father looked around making certain no one was near. "They eat for free. That's the way the system works."

"Why?"

"Because Brownie doesn't want trouble."

"Trouble?...I don't get it."

His father put an arm over Skip's shoulder. "If Brownie didn't take care of the police, they'd take care of him."

"Like beat him up?"

"No. More likely they'd ticket the trucks that deliver his food or sick the health department on him for some phony technicality. One way or another they'd make his life miserable."

Skip gazed up at his father. "Do they give *you* a hard time too?"

His father failed to answer.

A sinking feeling overcame Skip. "What do they do?"

His father sighed. "Nothing. But only because I give the cop on the beat an envelope every month. A couple bucks for him and some for the higher ups."

"Can't you do something about it?"

"It's...it's not that easy." Skip's father bore a pained look. It was the kind that accompanies that inevitable moment when a son discovers that his father can't lick every other dad. He heaved another sigh. "Here—let me give you a *for instance*. Maybe that will help explain. You know the *Ice House Grill* over on Clark Street?"

Skip nodded.

"Charlie Roper owns the place. Anyway, back in the thirties his beer taps didn't include *Keegan*. It just so happened the brother of our former local Assemblyman brewed it. Charlie was told in no uncertain terms that the time had come for him to sell *Keegan*. Knowing its high cost would sharply trim his profit margin, Charlie refused. A few days later his place was trashed. Word on the street was that the Assemblyman and the police were behind it. Charlie decided to sue. When nobody local would take the case, he hired a big gun from Albany. The lawyer served a summons and complaint. A few days later Charlie got an anonymous telephone call telling him that bad things would happen to his family if the lawsuit didn't disappear. Charlie wasn't afraid of a fight, but jeopardizing his wife and children was more than he could handle. Charlie caved. He put *Keegan* on tap." Skip heard his father's message. Like it, he didn't. He silently stowed the dissatisfaction in the recesses of his brain, hoping someday to confront the injustice. Years later when he was in his first year of law school, unlike many of his classmates, he needed no explanation legitimizing the rash of liberal Supreme Court decisions expanding defendants' rights. He understood how those in power used their positions to suppress challenge and preserve unwarranted spoils. He recognized how the constitutional privilege against self-incrimination was often nullified by a justice system in which the ends, convictions, justified the means. Force readily produced confessions, even from the innocent. Skip's ears were deaf to cries that a criminal-coddling Supreme Court had gone mad. Widespread abuses demanded Draconian measures. Such were Skip's perceptions as a young law student. But impressions change, as do patterns of conduct. By the time he had begun practicing, police were better educated, higher paid and more professional. Abuses had diminished. And the defendants he represented weren't innocent, hardworking architects or tavern owners. They were rapists, robbers and murderers. Still there were two sides to every coin. And Skip's job was to make sure the defendant's side was fully and fairly presented. There were no exceptions, Harley Morehead included.

Skip abandoned the reverie of childhood reflections. He got up and pulled out the volume that held the seminal case of *Brown v. Mississippi*, 297 U.S. 278 (1935), in which the United States Supreme Court reversed guilty verdicts of defendants who were convicted solely on the basis of confessions resulting from torture inflicted with the participation of deputy sheriffs. Years earlier, as a law student, the coerced confessions in *Brown* had outraged Skip. They still did. But the principle begged the question: Was Morehead's confession coerced? That was Morehead's claim. But was that claim worthy of belief? Evidence to the contrary was increasing. Much as Skip wanted to believe Morehead, in his heart of hearts he found it difficult. He told himself that just because Morehead had lied about some things didn't make everything he said false. On the other hand, Morehead's words merited far more skepticism than a client of established integrity.

Skip returned to his desk, rocked back and closed his eyes as he assessed the facts. One, in particular, stood out. Morehead, as Populist Party Chairman, had frequent contact with attorneys. He knew better than to give a confession. At the very least he knew it would erode his chances of making a deal. Whatever Morehead's shortcomings, he wasn't stupid. Even if guilty, he would not have admitted it to the police. The logic gave credence to the claim that his confession was involuntary. That, coupled with righteous indignation from younger days, was all Skip needed. He was ready and willing to fight the good fight. Whether he was able—a decade earlier it would not have been an issue—was far less clear.

———

Skip stepped through the doorway of the *Eagle*. The place was hopping. Several fellows, cues in hand, were crowded around the pool table. Nearly every booth was filled. The same was true of the barstools. Fortunately his favorite seat at the left end of the bar was available, probably because it was farthest from the television up in the corner at the other end. Skip checked the clock on the *Schlitz* sign that hung on the back wall—2:17. He had spent more than three hours in the office doing legal research and planning strategy for Morehead's case. That was not how he preferred to spend a Saturday, but the rest of the day he would make up for time lost.

He eased over to his stool and put a sawbuck on the bar. Loomis was busy down at the other end. A man probably close to eighty seated next to Skip turned his way and said, "Did you see that curve Stottlemyer just delivered? The damn thing looked like it dropped off a table."

Skip shrugged.

Most folks in Cooperstown were baseball fans. As a youngster Skip was as avid as any, fanatically rooting for his beloved Boston Red Sox. With each spring new hope burgeoned. But as the season waned, it became apparent that his heroes would not play in the fall classic. Between his fifth and twelfth birthdays, 1936 through 1943, the Yankees, the despised enemy, copped the American League pennant seven times, and adding insult to injury, they went on to win the World Series six of those seven. Finally in 1946 Skip's Red Sox won the pennant, only to fall victim to the St. Louis Cardinals in the battle for ultimate supremacy. From that day on his interest in the national pastime began to slowly wane. Though he still listened to games on the radio, no longer did he live and die with the exploits of his childhood heroes. No longer was his identity linked to their successes and failures. By the time his college years had begun, baseball, the Red Sox, had indeed taken a back seat to fraternity parties, football games and women—one in particular, Megan.

Megan and he were married the summer after their college graduations. During law school, studying and working part-time left few hours to follow baseball, not that Skip would have if the time had been available. The game had seemingly grown too slow. Batters repeatedly stepped out of the box, pitchers constantly threw over to first base and managers repeatedly visited the mound.

Once Skip had passed the bar and begun practicing law in Cooperstown, he could have found time in the evening or on weekends to renew his interest in baseball, but he lacked the desire. Hall of Fame week, when the new class was inducted into the national shrine and major leaguers took the field at *Doubleday*, was the lone exception. For those few days, but only then, was Skip a fan again.

"Stottlemyre's got a one-hitter going," said the elderly man on the adjacent stool.

"He's with the Dodgers. Right?" said Skip, though he knew otherwise.

"Stottlemyre's a Yankee!"

Skip shrugged. "Well, as Napoleon said—or was it Vince Lombardi?—each man has to bear his cross."

A scowl appeared on the elderly man's face. "Let me guess. You like those bums from Brooklyn."

Skip shook his head.

"Baltimore?"

Skip shook his head again.

The man studied Skip for a few moments. "So, what team is it?"

"None of the above. I'm not a baseball fan. Though it does my heart good when the Yankees lose. Not that I care who wins."

The man muttered under his breath, grabbed his beer and rotated his stool toward the television.

A moment later Loomis delivered a tumbler filled with *Jack.*

"An *Eagleburger* and fries when you get a chance."

A busy Loomis, already on his way, motioned over his shoulder. "Will do."

Skip eyed his glass. *Jack* was his kind of guy. Roughly a hundred years old, his pure spring water still came from the same cave in tiny Lynchburg, Tennessee, from which Jasper Newton (Jack) Daniels had mixed it with corn, rye and barley into a perfect mash. Skip had made it a point to know his pal well. On a trip south he had even visited the ironically dry town of Lynchburg and its meager 361 inhabitants. Just as he had done in law school, he had taken notes as he watched the cooked mash, fermented with yeast, as it was placed into hundred-feet-deep copper stills. If the drop-by-drop filtering hadn't required twelve days, Skip might have stayed for that, as well as the roasting with charcoal from sugar-maple trees. Skip sipped his impeccable *whiskey*. He had tried *Scotch whisky* numerous times. The folks from Scotland were welcome to claim exclusivity when it came to the term *Scotch,* as well as their spelling of *whisky.* Image, avoidance of confusion and price were their concerns. As far as Skip was concerned, *Jack's* older Scottish relatives were nice, but they couldn't hold a candle to the youngster from Lynchburg. Skip took another sip. It was just what he needed. Almost. He looked over at the elderly man who was busy arguing with the umpire that the last pitch was miles from the strike zone.

Get a life. Skip eyed his tumbler. He found it hard to deny that the elderly man wasn't the only one in need of the advice. Skip mused about an earlier time when he would have been more receptive to the man's overture if only out of respect for the codger's age. But that was before the hit-and-run driver had ripped out his heart. Skip didn't like the person he had become, but night after night, forced to return to an empty house, he was who he was. Sure, there were tough days at the office back when Megan was alive, and he often arrived home enervated, but soon enough she would lift his spirits. Without her he spiraled down, deeper and deeper. After a few years friends encouraged him to date, but it was an exercise in futility. No woman could compare to Megan. As wonderful as she was in life, in death she attained perfection. And so, Skip looked elsewhere for companionship. In *Jack* he found a buddy, not one who could replace Megan, but one who could help him escape the reality of her loss. It also helped him escape his failure to fulfill the promise he had made at her grave not long after her death. He had vowed he would find the hit-and-run driver who had struck her as she jogged alongside the road. He had vowed that he would bring the bastard to justice. He never did. That failure, its haunting echoes, magnified his dependence on *Jack*.

"How things going?" said Loomis, as he put Skip's burger and fries in front of him.

"Same old...same old."

Loomis lowered his voice. "Will you have to try Morehead's case in front of Biddleford?"

"Not if I can help it." Skip pointed at the tiny rectangular window on the face of his *Timex*. "In case you weren't aware, it's Saturday. Not a day I come here to talk business."

"Sorry." Loomis gestured to the other end of the bar where a burly fellow in need of another draft was waiving an empty mug. "Gotta go."

Seconds later, frustrated cries, mostly from the far end of the bar, pervaded the *Eagle*.

The elderly man on the adjacent stool turned to Skip. "You see that!"

"What?"

"Parker just hit a three-run shot inches inside the right field foul pole. Talk about a cheapy." The man glared. "You happy now?"

48

What do you want from me? Skip let his eyes voice the reaction.

The man continued to glare.

The look pushed Skip over the edge. "I'll bet you didn't complain back when the Yankees first built the stadium with that short right field for the Babe. It's only unfair when visiting teams take advantage of it." Skip paused just long enough to let the jab penetrate. "As to your question about happy, the answer is *yes*, now that the Yankees are losing."

The old man grumbled and returned to drinking his beer.

Skip reached for *Jack*. His pal was no help. As a youngster Skip hated the bully who lived several doors down the street. Skip was not in the habit of beating up old men. He thought about an apology but couldn't bring the words to his lips. He ate his burger in silence. Ordinarily he enjoyed the company of both Loomis and *Jack*. Loomis was busy. Skip found himself watching the ball game, but only mindlessly. At times he didn't even notice which team was up to bat.

A couple of innings went by. The Yankees trailed by several runs, not that Skip knew the score. Suddenly the old man turned to Skip. "Today's players couldn't be bat boys for Murderers Row. Guys like Ruth and Gehrig and Lazzeri—they were men. The clowns today are nothing but overpaid prima donnas."

Skip had made similar comments in the past, but at times he could be a gadfly. Rather than agreeing with the man, he was tempted to point out that athletes in every sport were bigger, stronger and faster than their predecessors. Instead, invoking his courtroom poker face, he kept his mouth shut.

Beer in hand, the man reached out nearly spilling the brew on Skip. "See—you know I'm right. Otherwise you would have balked."

"That's not—" Skip bit his tongue. Hard as it was to let the distortion pass, pummeling the old man would hurt Skip more than his victim.

"Were you in the military?" The question came with a snarl.

What's that got to do with anything?

"Just as I thought. You take everything America gives, but when it comes to defending the flag, you're AWOL." The man pulled a baseball cap off his head and gestured at the emblem: Veterans of Foreign Wars. "Guys like me fought for this country. I crawled through the mud of Europe in World War I. Damn near froze and starved to death. Took shrapnel in my leg. Some of my buddies weren't so lucky. They got their brains blown open." He scowled at Skip once again, this time with even more disdain. He turned back to the ball game.

Skip finished his burger. He sipped the remains of what was in his glass. Mostly melted ice. Even *Jack* had grown cold and unreliable. Skip looked around. The *Eagle* was busier than when he had arrived. Loomis would have little time, if any, to commiserate. Skip headed for the door. As he stepped out into an overcast day, he kicked the base of the lamppost that stood along the edge of the sidewalk. "That's for nothing," he muttered.

———

"I've got those criminal background checks you wanted," said Lucy. She handed them to Skip. "They contain some—" The ring of her telephone sent her scurrying to her desk.

Eager to see who had been convicted of what, Skip began perusing the information. Jimmie Raines, the loud mouth with the garish gold neck chain, had a reckless driving, an unclassified misdemeanor; County Comptroller Bernie Feinstein was clean; insurance agent Buddy Kileen was also clean; Ralph Squeaky Grimes had served nine months in the county jail for extortion; and Harley Morehead had received three years probation for bookmaking nineteen years earlier.

Skip smacked the papers down onto his desk. "That son of a bitch." He reached for the telephone and dialed.

"*Prime Printing*. Morehead speaking."

"Harley, it's Skip."

"What's up?"

"Couple of things about the case I want to run by you." Experience having demonstrated the folly of going off half-cocked, Skip forced himself to adopt a more measured

David A. Weiss

approach. "First off—what exactly did Squeaky do when he worked for you?"

"This and that. Deliveries, clean-up...stuff like that."

"Did he handle money?"

"Occasionally, when he made a delivery. But most of those were checks. Rarely cash."

"Did you know he served time for extortion?"

"Uh...yeah that he got locked up, but not what for. You think the stints he did in jail are linked to his murder?"

"Possible, but I wouldn't bet on it." Skip's choice of words was not accidental. "On the other hand, the convictions tell us that Squeaky was a shady character. And while we're on the subject...convictions...if my recollection serves me, you don't have any. Right?"

"I got a couple of speeding tickets...and, oh yeah, a wrong way on a one-way street."

"But just traffic stuff?"

"Yup."

Playing along was easy for Skip. Lying criminal defendants had given him lots of practice. When caught, remorse was rare. Outlandish excuses were the norm. Skip's favorite came from the drug dealer who used past lies to excuse his inaccuracies. He claimed his countless fabrications had become so intertwined with the truth that he could no longer separate fact from fiction. Skip viewed the explanation as nothing more than another lie added to the client's lengthy list, and the client's nervous laugh when confronted lent credence to the assessment.

Skip eyed the information that Lucy had given him minutes earlier. He said, "When your case comes up for trial, chances are you'll need to take the stand. Good thing you don't have a criminal record. The District Attorney could use it to impeach your credibility." Skip waited a moment on the chance that Morehead might finally be forthcoming. When it didn't happen, Skip, more jaded than ever, continued. "A few years back I was watching a trial in Binghamton. The defendant testified he had no criminal record. The District Attorney produced a certified copy of a burglary conviction. No surprise—the jury convicted the defendant. One of the jurors, when interviewed afterwards, said the defendant convicted himself." Skip waited again. His normally loquacious client was taciturn. "Funny thing. Public records indicate you pleaded guilty to bookmaking nineteen years ago."

"Oh...that. What about it?"

"What about it? You've got a criminal record."

"Not really."

Skip thought he had heard it all, but perhaps Morehead was about to prove otherwise. "Fine. Then tell me why?"

"I didn't do any time."

"You got three years' probation."

"A slap on the wrist."

Skip pulled the receiver away from his ear and glared at the mouthpiece. He put the receiver back to his ear. "Whom do you think you're kidding? You know as well as I do. You pleaded guilty, and you have a criminal record."

"It was only a misdemeanor."

If Morehead were there with him, Skip might have rung his neck. "Damn it. Is double talk all you know?"

"You aren't—"

"Save your bull for your backroom political pals!" Skip took a deep breath. "You're not fooling anyone. You've got a criminal record, and *you* know it. And let me tell you, if you think your smooth-talking innocence will work on the stand, you, my friend, are a conviction guaranteed to happen." A stranglehold on the receiver underscored Skip's exasperation. "And while we're on the subject of your credibility, why should anyone, including me, believe your confession was coerced?"

"Because I know better than to give a confession."

That Morehead would dare be so cavalier had Skip ready to explode, but damn, the explanation, one Skip had thought about already, made sense. Morehead had been around. He knew the ropes. On the other hand, he was an inveterate liar.

"Just because I've made some mistakes, doesn't mean I'm always wrong."

The point had merit. Indeed Skip had made it in court in the past. There was the time he had represented the fellow who was stopped for a traffic light when he was rear-ended. Despite a rotten driving record with repeated suspensions and accidents, for once the jerk was an innocent victim. But the analogy proved nothing. Even assuming Morehead's confession was involuntary, that did not imply he was innocent. He could still be guilty of murder. Skip said, "As you well know, whatever you say to me is protected by attorney-client privilege. Take advantage of it. From now on, so I can best represent you, be straight with me."

"Fair enough."

The glib response was easy. But Morehead's propensity to lie was equally easy. Skip decided to put Morehead to a test. He said, "All along you've been telling me you don't run a gambling operation. That's not what I hear on the street, and from pretty reliable sources. What do you say?"

There was a long pause. Finally, Morehead responded. "Believe what you want."

The answer, not an admission, was far from a denial. Skip might have reiterated his question had the double talk not provided more significant information. Morehead's propensity to play games had not ceased. The revelation, though not surprising, irked Skip. He said, "You've got an appointment this Friday. We'll talk more then."

———

Seated in front of the television, a take-out order of General Tso's Chicken and fried rice on his lap, and his buddy *Jack* at his side, Skip flipped the footrest lever of his big, family-room recliner. Ever since there had been no Megan with dinner on the table, he had been eating that way. He had mastered the technique to the point where the throw covering the chair needed washing just once a year. On the rare occasion that he had company, he hid the throw beneath the chair.

With his fork in one hand, he channel surfed with the other. Bites of General Tso were interspersed with segments of the local news, a rerun of the Ali-Liston fight and an old episode of *The Honeymooners.* As the weatherman finished the forecast, Skip was about to return to the boxing match when the anchorman's promo stopped him.

"Coming up after the break, we have some just released information regarding the murder of Ralph Squeaky Grimes."

Skip pressed the volume button on the remote upping the level two notches. He gobbled down several mouthfuls of fried rice. He waited through advertisements for *H&B Plumbing*, *Mr. Clean* and the re-election of City Manager Traci LaDieux until finally the anchorman re-appeared on the screen. "This just in," he said. "The Otsego County Sheriff has disclosed that a recently executed search at the home of Populist Party Chairman, Harley Morehead, who is charged with the murder of Ralph Squeaky Grimes, yielded a knife suspected to be the murder weapon. The Sheriff declined further comment, except to indicate forensic tests were being conducted."

Skip let the remote drop between his leg and the arm of the chair. He reached to the adjacent table for *Jack*. "Damn," he muttered. He took a swig. The anchorman moved on to a story regarding water contamination in Cherry Valley. Skip gave *Jack* another go and then laid him down on the table. He grabbed the remote and flipped back to the fight. Bad enough Morehead gave him aggravation in the office. Did he need to spoil dinner as well?

Chapter IV

The packed courtroom arose as the bailiff announced the entrance of Otsego County Court Judge Harold Biddleford.

"Be seated," said the black-robed jurist, taking his place at the bench. He glanced at the District Attorney, and then he turned toward Skip. Their eyes met momentarily.

The feelings are mutual. Whether Skip was misreading the Judge's thoughts, he didn't know. Regardless, he wished someone else were sitting on the case. He had debated whether to make a motion for Judge Biddleford to recuse himself. If he did, the motion, with almost no chance of success, was certain to antagonize the rotund jurist. Still Skip probably needed to take the risk. Having Biddleford preside was arguably worse than the District Attorney's mother.

"Scheduled on today's docket," said Judge Biddleford, "is a motion by defendant Harley Morehead to suppress his alleged confession, along with items obtained as a result of a search of his home on the 13th of April. Mr. Carter, are the People ready to proceed?"

"Yes."

"And the defense, Mr. Maynard?"

"Ready, Your Honor."

"Mr. Carter, call your first witness."

"The People call Detective Theodore Ramsey to the stand."

A strapping man, over six feet, in a brown, Harris-Tweed sport coat, strode forward and took the oath.

"Please state your full name for the record."

"Theodore Charles Ramsey."

"Where do you reside?"

"31 Fairlawn Avenue, here in Cooperstown."

"How are you employed?"

"I'm a detective for the Otsego County Sheriff's Department."

"How long have you been so employed?"

"Eighteen years with the Department, the last eight as a detective."

Skip observed the witness with an analytical eye. Ramsey was poised and his answers, crisp. Shaking his testimony was certain to be a challenge.

"Tell us briefly of your record on the force—whether you've ever been disciplined and/or received positive recognition?"

"I've never been disciplined."

"What about honors?"

"Well..." Seemingly abashed, Ramsey's voice grew softer. "I received a commendation for bravery twelve years ago when I was shot while foiling a robbery at a convenience store. And three years ago I was named the Department's employee of the year."

Testimony was only beginning, but already Ramsey had painted himself with the brush of a model officer. His credibility would be critical. When ruling on Skip's motion to suppress, Judge Biddleford, a former State Trooper, who had earned his law degree at night, would be weighing the issue.

"Officer Ramsey," said the District Attorney, "if I direct your attention back to the afternoon of April 11th of this year, can you tell me what you did on that day?"

"As part of my investigation of the murder of Ralph Squeaky Grimes, I went to the home of Eddie the Enforcer...excuse me...I mean Eddie Willis on Sugarhill Road."

Skip suspected the seeming slip of the tongue might have been intentional.

"Based upon my investigation I had reason to believe that Willis had beaten up Grimes just two weeks before his death. When I confronted Willis, he admitted beating up Grimes but denied any part in the murder. He told me—"

"Objection," said Skip. "Whatever Willis told the witness is hearsay."

"If Your Honor please, I could call Mr. Willis to the stand, but I'm merely trying to establish the circumstances that led Detective Ramsey to interview the defendant. I'm attempting to move this hearing along."

Judge Biddleford nodded. "This is not a trial, and we don't have a jury. I'm going to allow the witness to respond for the limited purpose of explaining what ultimately led him to the defendant's home, not to establish the veracity of anything Mr. Willis may have said."

Skip gritted his teeth. Allegations of a coerced confession in a murder case, and His Holiness, hardly a legal scholar, particularly when it came to the finer nuances of the rules of evidence, appeared more concerned with efficiency than justice.

"Detective Ramsey," said the District Attorney, "what did Eddie Willis tell you?"

"That he worked for Harley Morehead as an enforcer. That Morehead ran a bookmaking operation out of the back room of his printing business. He said that Squeaky, Morehead's runner, wanted a bigger piece of the pie and had threatened to go to the police if he didn't get it. That's why Morehead had Willis beat up Squeaky. According to Willis, Morehead told Squeaky if he didn't back off, he'd wind up in a pine box."

The District Attorney eyed his notes.

The pause, likely a device to allow Morehead's alleged threat to resonate a bit longer, might have annoyed Skip had he not used the technique many times himself. Regardless, his thermometer elevated. The supposed limited purpose for which the testimony had been allowed had become a joke.

"What did you do after you spoke with Mr. Willis?" said the District Attorney.

"I went to see the defendant Harley Morehead at his printing business where I showed him my credentials and explained that I was investigating the murder of Squeaky Grimes. I told him what Willis had said."

"How did the defendant react?"

"He denied having Squeaky beaten up. He claimed he knew nothing about the murder."

The testimony, a pleasant surprise, buoyed Skip, but only briefly.

"What did you do when the defendant denied involvement?"

"I returned to the station to follow up what Willis had told me. Shortly after four o'clock in the afternoon, I got a telephone call from the defendant. He indicated that he had some information about the murder. I asked him what it was, but he refused to say. He told me to come to his home. He insisted I come alone."

"What did you do?"

"Well...the request seemed a bit strange, but I didn't want to pass up a possible lead, so I went to his house on Wideout Road outside Oneonta."

"What time did you arrive there?"

"Four-forty, give or take a few minutes."

"What happened when you arrived?"

"The defendant let me in. We were barely into his living room when he blurted out that he had killed Squeaky Grimes."

A disruptive murmur from the spectators in the rear of the courtroom drew the rap of Judge Biddleford's gavel. "Silence, or I'll clear the courtroom." He motioned the District Attorney to proceed.

"What did you do?"

"I gave him his *Miranda* rights. Even though I hadn't arrested him, we're under strict instructions from the Chief to—"

"Objection," said Skip. "The witness is going beyond the transaction with the defendant and giving self-serving testimony about directions from a third party."

"Sustained."

"Detective Ramsey, just tell us what you did."

"I told the defendant he had a right to remain silent; that anything he said could be used against him; that he had a right to consult with counsel; and if he couldn't afford an attorney, one would be assigned. He said he knew all that but wanted to get things off his chest. Next thing I knew, he began spitting details. He told me how he went to Squeaky's apartment where Squeaky demanded ten thousand dollars or else he'd tell the police about his bookmaking. According to Morehead a shouting match ensued, and he ran to the kitchen where he grabbed a large carving knife from a set on the kitchen counter. He said he stabbed Squeaky in the chest and that when he yanked the knife out, Squeaky tried to run away. He chased Squeaky around the apartment and then near the spot where the living room and dining room met he stabbed him again. Squeaky fell forward onto the floor. Morehead said he stabbed Squeaky several more times making sure he was dead."

"What did you do after the defendant told you how he had stabbed Squeaky?"

"I asked him to accompany me down to the station."

"Did you place him under arrest?"

Ramsey thought for a second. "Not at that moment."

"Did he go with you down to the station?"

"Not immediately. When I told him I wanted to take a written statement, he said he would only give it to me there in his house." Ramsey paused. "Once again, it seemed strange, but I wanted the statement. Where I got it was secondary. The next thing I knew, Morehead got a small pad and pen from a nearby desk and wrote out a confession. Then he tore off the page and handed it to me."

"What happened next?"

"I read his statement. Then I drew a line at the bottom and asked him to sign it. He did. Oh—I almost forgot...I put the date at the bottom as well."

The District Attorney went over to the court reporter and had him mark a paper for identification. He took it to the witness. "I show you People's Exhibit One, marked for identification, and ask if you can identify it?"

Ramsey eyed the document briefly. "It's the confession that the defendant wrote and signed at his home on April 11th."

"The People offer Exhibit One as evidence to be admitted at the time of trial." The District Attorney turned to Skip. "Your witness, Counselor."

Skip got up from his seat and walked forward. "Detective Ramsey, may I see the document?"

Ramsey handed Skip the paper.

"If I may take a few moments, Your Honor," said Skip.

The Judge glanced at his watch. "Suppose we take a ten-minute recess. We'll reconvene at ten forty-five." He got up from the bench.

Skip compared the document to a copy the District Attorney had previously furnished him. The documents, which matched, read:

> Around 8:15 P.M. on April 9, 1968, I, Harley Morehead, stabbed Squeaky Grimes in the chest and back approximately six times with a carving knife at his apartment at 14 Rock Street because he tried to blackmail me.
> s/Harley Morehead
> Dated: April 11, 1968.

The brief confession, written in Morehead's own hand, hardly artful, was arguably more damning and problematic than the detailed work of a law enforcement professional. It was exactly what Skip would expect from someone like Morehead. As County Chairman of the Populist Party, he had seen enough documents to have a vague sense of what they would contain. On the other hand, he lacked the hands-on experience needed to produce a more comprehensive rendition. Skip showed the document to Morehead.

Morehead eyed it for a moment. "As I told you, I wrote out the damn thing and signed it, but only because Ramsey stuck a gun in my face. The way I figured, a trip to jail was better than one to the morgue."

Skip didn't know what he believed. Morehead had claimed he knew better than to give a confession. The point made sense. But most criminal defendants, streetwise as they generally were, knew better than to talk. Prior brushes with the law had educated them. Nevertheless, many, when confronted by the police, spilled their guts. Statistics from a recent article stuck in Skip's head. Seventy-five percent of interrogated suspects waived their *Miranda* rights, and sixty percent confessed. Criminals were sharp, but the police were generally sharper. Tried and true techniques induced confessions. Long and intense questioning, along with food and sleep deprivation were among the devices. The *good cop - bad cop* routine was another favorite. Once the hard ass had softened up the suspect, the good cop feigned sympathy for the plight that led to the crime. That was often followed with hints that a confession might earn the defendant more favorable treatment. A combination of methods over a prolonged period drew admissions from many who otherwise would have remained mute. But Morehead's confession failed to fit historical patterns of coercion. That didn't imply it was voluntary, but it didn't get him off the hook either. Once the reality of a lifetime behind bars had set in, Morehead may have fabricated a story in an effort to recant what was, in fact, a voluntary admission. Skip wanted to believe Morehead. Unfortunately his client had already lied more than once.

"All rise."

The voice of the bailiff announcing the return of Judge Biddleford to the bench interrupted Skip's musing. He had missed his opportunity for a bathroom break. Judge Biddleford would go ballistic if he asked for another recess, even a brief one. Skip glanced at his watch. He wasn't desperate. He could survive the hour or so until noon, at least he thought he could.

"Be seated," said Judge Biddleford. "Mr. Maynard, please proceed with your cross-examination."

Skip got up from his seat, circled the defense table and walked forward about ten feet from the witness stand. "Detective Ramsey, you contend the defendant wrote out a confession in his own home. Rather unusual, wouldn't you say?"

"A little."

"Prior to April 11th, how many times in your eighteen-year career had that occurred?"

"I guess it's a first."

"So, a second ago, when you termed it a little unusual, that was understatement?"

"Argumentative," barked the District Attorney.

"Sustained."

"But Your Honor, this is cross-examination."

Judge Biddleford glared. "Mr. Maynard, I said, *sustained*. If you dislike my rulings, take it up with the Appellate Division. Don't argue with me."

Skip's jaw locked as he fought the urge to snap back at the black-robed son of a bitch. He took a deep breath in an effort to calm himself. "Detective Ramsey, at the time you took the confession, you had your service revolver with you. Right?"

"Yes."

"As a matter of fact, you took it out prior to the writing of the confession, didn't you?"

"No. It was strapped inside, underneath my suit jacket the entire time. As a detective, I wasn't in uniform."

Skip took a step toward the witness. "Over the years how many confessions have you taken as a detective for the Otsego County Sheriff's Department?"

Ramsey shrugged.

Skip gestured in the direction of the court reporter. "We need an audible answer."

Ramsey thought for a moment. "I couldn't say exactly. Two hundred, maybe."

"Of those, how many were taken without another police officer present?"

Ramsey thought again. "About a dozen."

Skip eased back and smiled. Ramsey was following him down the primrose path. "So, about one in fifteen or twenty?"

"Something like that."

"One of the main reasons you have another police officer present is because it helps verify that a *Miranda* warning was given and the confession was voluntary. Right?"

"Well...uh...I don't have to have another officer present."

"Move to strike as non-responsive."

"Denied."

Skip did a slow burn. An application to have Judge Biddleford recuse himself was becoming increasingly necessary, but for the moment it would have to stay on the back burner. "Your Honor, with all due respect, I asked the witness whether it helps to have another officer present, not whether it's required. He didn't answer my question."

Judge Biddleford hesitated. "Uh...fine. I'll permit him to answer."

Sure. You screwed up, and now you're trying to cover your ass.

"May I hear the question again?" said Ramsey.

The court reporter read it back.

"Yes. Having another officer there helps."

"The dozen or so past cases where you took statements without another officer present were all minor offenses, misdemeanors and the like. Isn't that true?"

Ramsey's eyes widened. "Uh...offhand I couldn't say."

"Couldn't or wouldn't?"

The District Attorney leaped from his seat. "Objection. Argumentative and counsel is badgering the witness."

"Sustained. Mr. Maynard, refrain from sarcastic innuendoes."

Skip bit his lip as he struggled to muzzle himself. He remained focused on the witness, refusing to make eye contact with the Judge. "Mr. Ramsey, would it be fair to say that this was the first time you, by yourself, took a confession in a murder case?"

"Well—I've been with the force for a lot of years. It's hard to remember every case all at once."

"But to the best of your recollection there were no other murders where you took a confession without another officer present. Right?"

"I guess so."

"So, what you did with Mr. Morehead was unique?"

"You might say that."

"I might?" Skip folded his arms, but, with the District Attorney moving to his feet, immediately added, "I'll withdraw the comment." He moved a step closer to the witness stand. "Detective Ramsey, on direct examination you told us that you took the defendant down to the station after he gave you his handwritten statement at his home. Correct?"

"Yes."

"Isn't it true that once there, with other officers present, the defendant refused to furnish a more comprehensive statement?"

"It is."

"And not only that, he demanded to see an attorney. True?"

"Yes."

Skip stared at Ramsey before walking back to the defense table where he pulled out his chair as if ready to conclude his cross-examination. "Oh, one more thing," he said. "Isn't it a fact that two years ago in a burglary case involving a defendant by the name of Walter Styles the Appellate Division threw out a confession that you had obtained?"

"Objection," said the District Attorney.

"If Your Honor please, not only am I entitled to have the witness answer the question, but, in addition, I respectfully submit that for purposes of the record being made here, this Court is required to take judicial notice of the findings enunciated in the opinion of the Appellate Division."

"The Court will examine the opinion. Objection overruled." Judge Biddleford turned to the witness. "Answer the question."

"Yeah. The confession was thrown out."

"Because you had failed to advise the defendant of his rights. Correct?"

"Yeah."

"No further questions." Skip took his seat.

"No re-direct," said the District Attorney.

Judge Biddleford surveyed the courtroom. "Mr. Carter, call your next witness."

"The People call Mark Thomas."

A handsome man, tall and athletic, dressed in a blue blazer, came forward and took the oath.

The District Attorney took him through the preliminaries, establishing that he lived in nearby Burlington, was thirty-six and that following his graduation from Cobleskill Community College had been employed for fifteen years with the Otsego County Sheriff's Department. "Detective Thomas," said the District Attorney, "if I direct your attention back to the 10th day of April of this year, do you recall what you did that morning?"

"Yes, I investigated a report from the landlord of Ralph Squeaky Grimes that Mr. Grimes had been seen going into his apartment but had not responded to either knocks at his door or telephone calls."

"And what did you do?"

"Along with Officer Wharton, I went to Mr. Grimes's home, a first-floor flat at 14 Rock Street here in Cooperstown. We arrived around eleven in the morning and knocked on the door repeatedly. Rather than breaking the door down, we contacted the landlord, Bernie Feinstein, who came over and unlocked the apartment."

"What did you find?"

"A body—it turned out to be Mr. Grimes—lying on the floor where the living and dining room met...that is, the edge of the dining area farthest from the kitchen. There was lots of blood. Initial examination of the body indicated he had been stabbed repeatedly. We notified headquarters, and additional backup came. In the meantime Officer Wharton and I checked the flat. There was a knife set on the kitchen counter. It had spaces for six knives, but one slot, the largest, was empty. We searched the apartment for the knife, as well as anything else that might be significant, but found nothing at that time."

"What did you do next?"

"Not a whole lot. I stayed in the background while a detective and a fellow from forensics did their thing."

The District Attorney checked his notes. "When, if at all, did you again have involvement with the case?"

"Three days later."

"How did that come about?"

"Things...not just Grimes's murder, but a bunch of things, were pretty crazy at the Department. Anyway, Harley Morehead had just confessed and—"

"Objection."

"Your Honor, I'll withdraw my last question and approach it another way." The District Attorney again focused on his yellow pad. "Detective Thomas, did there come a time that you learned of the defendant's arrest?"

"Actually it was from the local radio news, several days after the body was found."

"And when, if at all, were you next involved with the case?"

"Well, like I said, things were busy, and incident to the arrest the Chief asked Officer Wharton and I to do a search of the defendant's home and property on Wideout Road in Oneonta, along with his printing business. A search warrant had already been obtained from Judge Versmith."

"And did you conduct those searches?"

"Yes."

"What, if anything, did you find?"

"Nothing at the printing business."

"How about the defendant's home?"

"A large carving knife."

The District Attorney took a clear plastic bag to the court reporter and had him mark it for identification. The District Attorney then went over to the witness. "I show you People's Exhibit Two. Can you identify it?"

Detective Thomas examined the bag and contents. "Yes. That's the knife that I found at the defendant's home on the 14th. My tag is attached."

"Where exactly did you find the knife?"

"It was in the wooden shed out behind the defendant's house...underneath a couple of bags of fertilizer in the right rear corner."

"For the record can you describe the knife?"

"It has a black handle. It's sixteen inches long altogether, a little over nine of which is the blade. I measured it. At its widest the blade is a little more than an inch. It comes to a point."

"What did you do with the knife once you found it?"

"Well—it looked like it matched the set I had seen at the victim's apartment. So, after it was dusted for fingerprints and so forth, I took it to the victim's flat and tested it in the empty slot. It fit perfectly."

"After that what did you do with the knife?"

"With it logged and my tag attached, along with rest of the set, I locked it up in the evidence locker at headquarters for safekeeping."

The District Attorney briefly perused his notes. "No further questions." He returned to his seat.

Judge Biddleford eyed the big clock on the rear wall. "The noon hour fast approaches. Let's break for lunch now. We'll resume at two o'clock with Mr. Maynard's cross-examination of the witness." He rapped his gavel. "Court is adjourned."

Skip might have taken a few minutes to discuss Detective Thomas's testimony with Morehead, but the men's room couldn't wait. He said, "I'll meet you back here at one forty-five. That will give us a few minutes to talk before court resumes."

———

It was roughly one-fifty when Skip, a couple of *Certs* in his mouth, returned to the courtroom. Morehead was already at the defense table. A few spectators were seated in the back, and more were filing in. Skip whispered, "Let's discuss the knife."

"What about it?"

"Ever...uh...see the thing before?"

"Nope."

"Any...uh...idea how it...uh...got in your shed?"

"Nope." Morehead looked Skip in the eye. "You been drinking?"

Skip shrugged. "A little."

"A little?" Morehead shot Skip a jaundiced look. "Based on your breath, not to mention the slurred speech, I'd say a lot."

Skip gestured at his mouth. "I...uh...got a mouthful of breath mints." He made a mental note to watch his speech. The courtroom was not the *Eagle*, and as great a lunchtime companion as *Jack* had been, it was time for the smooth guy from Tennessee to lay low. "What about that fellow...the officer who was testifyin' before lunch. What's his face?"

"Thomas?"

"Yeah. You...uh...think he mighta...planted the knife?"

Morehead shrugged. "Wouldn't put it past him."

"Do you know if—"

"All rise," announced the bailiff.

Skip pushed back his chair, nearly losing his balance as he stood up.

Judge Biddleford surveyed the courtroom. "Be seated," he said, as he sank into his commodious leather high back. "Where were we?" he mumbled with a glance to his notes. "Defendant's cross-examination of Detective Thomas." He motioned to the first row behind the bar. "Detective Thomas, please come forward." He pointed at the witness stand. "You're still under oath." Judge Biddleford looked at Skip. "Mr. Maynard, proceed."

Skip got up from his seat and carefully walked to the vacant jury box. He leaned his hip against the rail for support. "Officer, when you searched the...uh...my client's shed, did you...uh...have a warrant?"

"Yes. It had been granted by Judge Versmith."

"Move to strike everything...uh...except the word, *Yes.*"

"Motion denied."

"Sure," said Skip, with a surly shake of his head. "Let the witness volunteer uncalled for matter."

"Mr. Maynard." Judge Biddleford's tone was sharp. "You have my ruling. Move on."

"Jeze," muttered Skip.

"What was that?" Judge Biddleford's booming voice echoed off the marble floor. "I'll not have you treat this Court with disrespect. Understand?"

A part of Skip's brain told him that he needed to control his behavior. But *Jack* had other ideas.

Judge Biddleford leaned forward and peered at Skip. "Mr. Maynard, I want to see you here at the bench."

Still favoring the jury box rail, Skip hesitated.

"Now!"

Skip stepped across the courtroom in what he hoped was a straight line. In the meantime Judge Biddleford motioned the District Attorney to join them. The two attorneys met in front of the bench. Judge Biddleford eyed Skip for several seconds. "Mr. Maynard, have you been drinking?"

"Only during lunch."

Judge Biddleford continued to study Skip. "It better not affect your conduct." Though Judge Biddleford's voice was soft, it was unmistakably stern. "I have a hearing to run. I will not allow you to turn it into a mockery. Understand?" He waited a moment. "I said: Understand?"

"Absolutely, your Holiness."

"How dare you sass me!" Judge Biddleford's voice was loud enough to be heard throughout the courtroom.

"Sorry. I misspoke." Skip realized he needed to control his tongue; given his condition, doing so was another matter.

"We're going to move ahead now. And let me warn you in advance—I'll be watching your every move. Step out of line, and you'll face contempt."

"I...uh...understand, Your Honor."

"Okay. Let's get on with it."

Skip turned from the bench. All eyes were directed his way, and the stares were anything but sympathetic.

Skip headed back to the defense table. The best plan would be to use his notes, which along with the back of his chair, would offer needed support. Halfway back he caught a glimpse of Morehead. A clenched jaw and eyes aflame suggested his client's rage might exceed that of the Judge. Skip took a deep breath as he tried not to stagger on the way to his seat. The moment he arrived, he placed both hands on the back of his chair.

Morehead glared but said nothing.

He didn't need to. Skip got the message. He took a deep breath. He tried to organize his thoughts. It was useless. His head was spinning. Plain and simple, he was loaded. Under such circumstances he would never have driven. What asininity made him think he could do an effective cross-examination? He said, "Your Honor, I...I know it's a bit unusual, but I..." Skip squeezed the top bar of his chair. "I'd like to request an adjournment until—"

"An adjournment!"

"Uh...yes. Until tomorrow."

Judge Biddleford shook his head and then muttered inaudibly. He reached for his water glass and took a drink. He took his docket book from the far corner of the bench and examined it. "I have a motion for discovery tomorrow morning, along with a conference on another case. And pray tell, just why should I grant you an adjournment? You're the one who requested this hearing. Witnesses have given of their time to be here. And this morning when we commenced, you indicated you were ready."

"I...I know, but..." His brain only half-functioning, Skip struggled to find a good way to explain that he was too drunk to go ahead. It was an invitation for the committee on lawyers' fitness to proceed against his license.

"Mr. Maynard," said Judge Biddleford, "against my better judgment I'm going to grant you an adjournment...not that you deserve it. Not after wasting this court's time." Judge Biddleford pointed at Skip. "Let me assure you that under no circumstances would I be so generous were you my only concern. But you represent a defendant. Our Constitution guarantees him Due Process. That includes representation by counsel. Competent counsel. At this moment you hardly fit that standard." Judge Biddleford reached for his water glass and took a slow drink.

Silence, the kind that bludgeons, pervaded the courtroom. Skip felt it. Morehead, Detective Thomas, the court reporter, the District Attorney, the bailiff and the Judge's confidential clerk—all of their eyes were trained on Skip. And too, he sensed the dagger-like stares of a hundred spectators skewering his back. Even inebriation's anesthetizing benevolence failed to shield him from the arrant contempt. Judge Biddleford perused his docket and jotted some notes. The delay, likely intentional, exacerbated Skip's shame.

Finally Judge Biddleford cleared his throat. "We will continue this proceeding tomorrow afternoon at two o'clock sharp." He turned to the witness stand. "Detective Thomas, that will unfortunately necessitate your returning at that time." The Judge's gaze moved to Skip. "Mr. Maynard, lest you think the matter of your conduct today is a *done* issue, let me dispel any such misapprehension. This Court will take up that matter at the appropriate time." Judge Biddleford reached for his gavel and pounded it three times. "This Court stands adjourned." Even before the assembly could rise, he hurried out the door behind the bench.

Skip stared blankly at the table in front of him as the courtroom began to empty.

Morehead leaned his way. "Thanks a heap."

"I'm sorry," said Skip. The words rang hollow. He waited for Morehead's next volley. It didn't come. Skip looked at his client. "I'll...uh...try to do better tomorrow."

Disgust on his face, Morehead stood up. "You'd better." He started to leave.

"Perhaps we...should discuss strategy...before tomorrow afternoon."

"You're too drunk for that."

Skip had always prided himself on his ability to hold his liquor. Admitting such pride was replete with false bravado was difficult, but denying it in the face of the afternoon's events was impossible. "Uh...suppose we meet in my office tomorrow morning." Visions of a morning hangover suggested that nine might be too early. "At ten. Okay?"

"Fine. I'll be there." Morehead's face tightened. For an instant it appeared he was about to speak. Instead, he turned and marched out of the courtroom.

Skip sat motionless for several seconds before pushing his papers together and stuffing them into his file. He got up from his seat and headed up the center aisle toward the rear of the nearly empty courtroom. Over in the far right corner he caught a glimpse of Kelly Lane talking to another member of the bar. As the attorney for Squeaky's estate, Lane was probably there garnering information for her wrongful-death lawsuit against Morehead. Or maybe she had simply come for the sideshow. She glanced in Skip's direction. The moment she did, he turned away, but not soon enough to escape her look. As much as Judge Biddleford and Morehead's words had hurt, her reaction arguably pained him more. Kelly was the only woman since Megan's death who had seriously interested him. He had loved Kelly, but not enough to marry her, not that she would have accepted a proposal from him. *Ménage à trois* was not her style. Kelly wanted no part of a relationship that included *Jack*.

Head down, Skip left the Courthouse. He was in no condition to go back to the office and work. He was in even less of a mood to do so. Loneliness accompanied his every step. He needed an escape. And he needed a friend. That friend, his only escape from loneliness, was *Jack*. He headed for the *Eagle*.

Minutes later he plopped himself on his favorite stool. He slipped a twenty-dollar bill onto the bar. The tavern was even more subdued than a typical weekday mid-afternoon. Loomis, who had just given a draft to a patron near the opposite end of the bar, glanced in Skip's direction and nodded. Moments later he delivered a tumbler with ice and a clear liquid. Whatever it was, it wasn't *Jack*. Skip pointed at the glass. "What's this?"

Loomis ignored the question. "I heard what happened in Court."

Apparently word had traveled even faster than Skip had imagined. "You heard?"

Loomis nodded. He gestured toward a booth in the corner. "On his way here Pete Broomfield passed the Courthouse. Folks there said you put on quite a show."

Skip shrugged. The reaction was a poor veil for humiliation. Loomis had once told Skip that if he ever needed a lawyer, Skip was his man. The chances that Loomis still felt the same had doubtless diminished. Skip couldn't blame him. He said, "What's in the glass?"

"H₂O."

Rum, vodka, tequila—a variety of clear liquids had all been possibilities. But water had been almost a sure thing.

"You had more than enough at noon today. I should have cut you off then."

"It's not your fault."

"I know."

A moment before Skip had welcomed the chance to be the good guy. Unfortunately he had misconstrued Loomis's message. He looked at the cold beverage sitting before him. He wanted *Jack*. "Give me a break. It's been a really tough day. I'll get my act together tonight."

"You'd better." Loomis pushed the ice water closer to Skip.

Skip pushed it back. "C'mon…be a pal."

"That's just what I'm trying to do."

"You don't understand." The cold expression that greeted Skip's words caused them to echo in his brain. For years

David A. Weiss

Loomis had been his shrink. Day after day, year after year, he had listened with a non-judgmental ear, encouraging Skip to wrestle with unresolved issues. From time to time when Skip drank too much, Loomis would send him on his way. Of course, they both knew that once Skip arrived home, *Jack* was waiting. Skip kept his liquor cabinet well stocked. He said, "Can't you give me a short one?"

"No." Loomis snapped his towel. "And don't ask me again."

The unfamiliar snarl, the look of disappointment, was hard for Skip to swallow. He reached for the tumbler and took a drink.

"I heard your hearing was adjourned until tomorrow afternoon. Is that true?"

Skip nodded.

"What do you plan to do?"

The moment he had left the courtroom, Skip had put the case on the back burner. First and foremost he needed to drown his pain.

"So?"

"So what?"

For a moment Loomis appeared to bite his tongue. But then he shook his head. "No, I can't let you off the hook that easily. Not this time."

"What does that mean?"

"That you're a lawyer, a professional, and provided you put your mind to it, top notch. It's high time you stop wallowing in your misfortune and move ahead."

The glass of water, even the display of disappointment, was understandable. But of all people how dare Loomis play preacher? "Look who's talking," said Skip. "The guy who dropped outta college and became a bartender, rather than an engineer." The pained expression that met Skip's eyes had him regretting the dig. He wanted to blame the remark on his condition, but objectivity kept the rationalization from his lips.

Loomis bowed his head. "You're right. I'm a bartender. Nothing more than a bartender." He looked up. "I've kicked myself a thousand times because I screwed off in college and got my ass kicked out. Worse yet, I kept promising myself I'd

73

go back and finish. But I never did. I lacked the guts. I stayed right here at the *Eagle*. At long last, when I turned thirty, I stopped pretending. I finally admitted I'd never be anything more than a bartender." He turned and pointed at the mirror with the finely carved hickory frame that stretched across the wall behind the bar. "But if you think for one moment that when I reflect back on what might have been, I'm proud of myself, you're dead wrong."

Skip longed to say something encouraging, but sage thoughts were difficult, especially in his state. Telling Loomis he was an excellent bartender was the last thing he needed to hear.

"I am what I am," said Loomis. "But I've never let my failure hurt others. You, on the other hand, are a different story. You represent clients. They put their trust in you. In this case Harley Morehead has his freedom, his whole life, in your hands. And what do you do? Walk into court drunk."

The amateur psychiatrist with the ever-patient ear had blind-sided Skip. An unvarnished dose of reality was more than he could bear. Ice water was the last thing he wanted. More than ever he needed *Jack*.

"Aren't you going to say something?"

What? Like I know you're right. Shoulders slumped, Skip remained mute.

"Tomorrow is another day. You still have a chance to redeem yourself." Loomis crouched slightly as he gently lifted Skip's chin in an effort to make eye contact. "You've got the ability, if only you'll use it."

Skip heaved a sigh. "What's the use?"

"Baloney. Just give yourself a swift kick in the ass, pick yourself up and let the excellent lawyer who has been hibernating beneath a wounded shell emerge."

If only it were that simple. But depression and dependency on alcohol were not so easily overcome. Skip knew he had a problem. No one had to tell him. He had known it for a long time. He recognized that *Jack* was hardly the wisest way to deal with his grief. But he was desperate to numb the pain, and law books didn't do the trick.

74

Loomis reached across the bar and put a hand on Skip's shoulder. "I don't mean to beat you up. You've been pounded enough already. But unless you confront yourself, it's gonna get worse. They'll take your license to practice law, and you could hardly blame them." Loomis headed down the length of the bar and into the kitchen. A minute later he returned with a cup of coffee.

"Try this."

It wasn't *Jack*. On the other hand, it was a whole lot better than ice water. "Is it high test?"

"Absolutely."

Skip took a sip. "Not bad."

A customer near the middle of the bar held up an empty glass. Loomis nodded and hurried off.

Skip slowly downed the entire cup. When Loomis returned, Skip ordered another, along with an *Eagleburger* and fries, extra crisp. The juicy beef on a toasted bun lacked *Jack's* magic, but it helped Skip sober up. A mixed blessing.

Chapter V

Skip arrived at his office shortly after nine A.M. He had slept from seven in the evening until seven-thirty the following morning. A couple of aspirin had helped alleviate a hangover. He opened the bottom drawer of his desk where *Jack*, an unopened fifth, awaited. There was no temptation. Skip had never been a morning drinker. Lunch, dinner and late in the evening were another story. He brought the bottle to Lucy. "Lock this in your desk. And don't give it to me under any circumstances, even if I beg."

"You won't fire me for insubordination?" she said, slipping the bottle into her desk.

"Sorry. Can't promise." He was no more serious than she. Her value was immeasurable. Without her watching deadlines, mollifying upset clients, readying figures for closings—the list was endless—his practice would have gone down the tubes long before. He said, "By the way, Harley Morehead will be coming in at ten." Skip started for his office but turned back in the doorway. "Did you hear about my performance in court yesterday afternoon?"

She motioned toward a newspaper that lay on a table in the far corner of the reception area. "The *Oneonta Star* published all the lovely details. Right on the front page."

Skip shrugged. "I'd read the story, except I haven't got the stomach." He headed to his office and began charting strategy for the afternoon hearing. Minutes later Lucy buzzed him on the intercom.

"Harley Morehead just arrived for his ten o'clock appointment. He knows he's early."

Under other circumstances Skip might have had him wait. "Send him right in." Skip got up from his desk and waited in the doorway. "I'm sorry about yesterday," he said, as Morehead came his way.

Morehead bore a noncommittal expression.

Skip gestured to the chairs on the opposite side of his desk. As they seated themselves, he said, "You have every right to be upset."

"No kidding." Morehead folded his arms. "Last night I debated whether to fire you. Against my better judgment, I'm withholding my decision until this afternoon. But rest assured, unless today's performance is a damn side better than its predecessor, you're history."

"I understand."

"I hope you do." The sarcasm in Morehead's voice was even stronger than his words. "How do you expect to get my confession suppressed?"

Having his client dictate the agenda was not how Skip conducted strategy sessions, but he was in no position to argue. "Frankly, we're in a bind. Having you testify would be risky at best. The DA will get a shot at you. He'll ask you about the crime, as well as the events surrounding your confession and your past. If and when you testify at trial, he'll use it as a weapon."

"But if I don't testify, where the hell will I be?"

"I know what you're thinking, and you're right. If Biddleford hears nothing but the police, he's bound to rule that your confession is admissible at trial."

"If the jury hears the confession, I'm dead."

Skip wanted to paint a brighter picture, but Morehead's assessment was on the mark.

"For Christ sake. Why even have this damn suppression hearing?"

"Well..." Skip heaved a sigh. "We can pin down the prosecution's key witnesses under oath. Knowing what they'll say at trial will help us plan our defense. If by chance they change their stories, we can impeach them with the earlier transcript." The point, although valid, offered little solace in the face of the damning confession.

Morehead ground his teeth. "I want to testify today at the suppression hearing."

The perilous tactic had Skip squirming. "Before you make that decision, you'd better weigh the risks." Across the desk, a frown—no, make that a scowl—communicated that explaining would be difficult. "Here's the situation. First the good news. If you testify today, you're constitutional privilege against self-incrimination will prevent the prosecution from introducing your testimony at trial."

"Great. So, I'm home free."

"Not so fast. There's a problematic side to this coin." Skip paused to make sure he had Morehead's full attention. "The United States Supreme Court has ruled that should you take the stand at trial, your testimony from the suppression hearing can be used to impeach you; that is, the prosecution can show you said something different before."

Morehead shrugged. "No sweat. Why would I say something different?"

Skip struggled to hide frustration. Morehead had heard the message but had failed to digest the significance. Hamstrung by events from the prior afternoon, Skip searched for another route, an indirect one, to explain the risks. He said, "Let's discuss how you came to sign the confession."

"As I told you, Detective Ramsey showed up at my house and started asking questions. Next thing I knew he whipped out his gun. He told me if I didn't write out a confession, he'd blow my brains out. He said he had a lead pipe in his cruiser, and that once he shot me, he'd put my fingerprints on the damn thing. He said he'd claim I tried to kill him with the pipe. It would be his word against...nobody."

Skip tried to allow Morehead the benefit of every doubt, but a gnawing reality, the identity of the man responsible to adjudicate the facts, demurred. Selling the dubious allegations to Judge Biddleford would be tougher than convincing him that *Alice in Wonderland* was the gospel truth. Over and over Skip took Morehead through the details. His story grew less and less credible. Skip said, "Any idea why Ramsey forced you to confess?"

"How the hell should I know?"

"That won't fly in court."

"Christ. What do you want from me? I'm not a mind reader."

"Fine..." Skip took a deep breath as he tried to contain exasperation. "Sarcasm and arrogance will kill you on the stand."

"Great. So what should I say?"

"Look—I can't tell you what to say. But you have to be smart. You can't let the DA get your goat."

Morehead muttered incomprehensibly.

Skip shook his head. "What's the matter now?"

Reaching Morehead was becoming ever harder. "If you take the stand today—"

"What's this *if*? I told you. I'm testifying."

Skip started to throw up his hands. "Fine—*when* you testify...the DA will hit you with a tough cross-examination. You need to think. And most of all, you need to keep your cool."

"Yeah, look whose talking. You were really cool yesterday."

The jab, one Skip couldn't deny, cut deeply. For the next hour he tried to prepare Morehead. Progress was non-existent. Morehead, as arrogant as ever, left the office with arrangements for them to meet at the Courthouse just before the hearing reconvened. Skip longed for *Jack*. He settled for a cup of coffee and a tuna-fish sandwich at the diner. The hearing was certain to be a nightmare. Skip had lost the respect of his client. Worse yet, he had lost respect for himself. If that weren't enough, in his heart of hearts, Skip disbelieved Morehead. The cannons of ethics prohibited him from knowingly allowing Morehead to testify falsely, but those principles raised nothing more than a hypothetical. Skip had no proof that Morehead was lying about the confession.

As Detective Thomas seated himself on the witness stand, a murmur permeated the packed courtroom. Murder cases, rare in Cooperstown, always drew a crowd, but Skip's fiasco the previous afternoon had consigned numerous would-be spectators to view the proceedings from without the four walls of the Courthouse.

Judge Biddleford shuffled some papers and then rapped his gavel twice. "May I see both counsel at the bench."

Skip got up and met the District Attorney in front of the jurist. Judge Biddleford, as he often did, peered over his narrow, wire-rimmed glasses that hung low on his nose. "Mr. Maynard," he said, his voice loud enough that even those in the rear could hear, "I trust the inebriation which disrupted proceedings yesterday is distant history."

"I apologize for my behavior, Your Honor. It was inexcusable."

"To say the least." A glower twisted the dagger. "But for the moment my concern is not with recriminations, only assurances a repeat performance does not await us." Judge Biddleford eyed Skip for several seconds. "Unlike the police who patrol our roads, my time should not be wasted with sobriety tests. That said, have you consumed any alcohol today?"

"None whatsoever, Your Honor." Skip's vantage point in front of the bench required him to gaze upward at the jurist. At that moment, his ego dwarfed, Skip, the Lilliputian, felt as though he had been called before the royal personage of Brobdingnag.

"Then let us continue with your cross-examination of the witness."

The District Attorney headed back to his seat at the prosecution table.

"Detective Thomas, I remind you that you're still under oath," said Judge Biddleford. "Mr. Maynard, proceed."

Skip walked to the table next to the court reporter and picked up the knife that had been marked for identification the day before. He gazed at it for several seconds as he endeavored to re-adjust his perspective to proper proportions. Knife in hand, he moved to the rail of the empty jury box. The preceding afternoon he had used the wooden bar for physical support. This time, moral. It also served to distance him from Judge Biddleford. A hush came over the courtroom. Skip felt the laser-like stares that were doubtless coming at him from all directions. He needed to take the offensive. He held up the knife. "Detective Thomas, yesterday you indicated that you found this knife in the shed behind the defendant's home. Is that correct?"

"Yes."

"As a matter of fact, the shed was unlocked, wasn't it?"

"Yes."

"So anyone could have gone into the shed?"

"I guess so."

Skip eyed the long blade and then refocused on the witness. "You don't know how the knife got into the defendant's shed, do you?"

"Well, no, but I have my—"

"Of your own knowledge, you don't know."

"That's true."

"Anyone could have put it there."

"I suppose."

Skip took a step forward. "That includes someone who wanted to frame the defendant."

"Objection, counsel is asking the witness to speculate."

"Your Honor," said Skip, his gaze met with a cold stare from the bench, "I'm asking Detective Thomas something he would no doubt need to consider as a police investigator."

"Mr. Maynard, this is a *Sandavol* hearing to suppress evidence, not a jury trial. The witness acknowledged that the knife could have been put there by anyone. I'm astute enough to discern that includes someone who wished to frame the defendant."

An acerbic tone, an intense stare, opaque to the record, verified Judge Biddleford would extend Skip no slack. He refocused on the witness. "You found no fingerprints on the knife. True?"

"Yes. It had been wiped clean."

"Detective Thomas, you can't be sure that this knife was in fact the murder weapon, can you?"

"Not one hundred percent, but..."

Skip had hoped for an unqualified *no*. Detective Thomas had proved himself far too experienced. He had phrased his acknowledgment in a manner that suggested he was all but certain. Pressing the matter was likely to make it worse. Skip laid the knife on the jury box rail. "The defendant's alleged confession was what led you to search his shed. Correct?"

"Yes."

"So, if the confession was illegally obtained, then the knife would be an inadmissible fruit of that illegal confession?"

"Objection!" The District Attorney was on his feet. "The question calls for a legal conclusion."

"I'll withdraw it," said Skip, his sole purpose to remind Judge Biddleford of the point. Skip refocused on the witness. "Detective Thomas, even assuming the knife matched the set in the victim's apartment, you don't know that it actually came from that set, do you?"

"No."

"That's all I have," said Skip, conscious it was better to end on a positive note than continue to belabor weak points. He returned the knife to its proper place and headed back to the defense table.

"Mr. Carter, please call the People's next witness."

"The People rest."

"Mr. Maynard, defense witnesses?"

"Yes. We call the defendant, Harley Morehead." Skip caught a slight reaction from the bench. And why not? Putting the defendant on the stand was a dubious tactic. True, his testimony was necessary if the motion to suppress was to have any chance, but even with it, lottery tickets were a better bet. On the other hand, exposing Morehead to the prosecutor's cross-examination increased the likelihood of a conviction. But Skip had already explained the dangers to Morehead, and he was insistent on testifying.

Jacket unbuttoned, stomach extending over his belt line, Morehead, dressed in a gray suit and a red and black power tie, walked forward and placed his hand on the Bible.

"Do you swear to tell the truth, the whole truth and nothing but the truth?" said Judge Biddleford.

"I do."

Judge Biddleford gestured at the witness stand, and Morehead took his seat.

"Would you state your full name for the record please?" said Skip.

"Harley Malcolm Morehead." His deep voice resonated in the acoustically designed chamber.

"Where do you reside?"

"457 Wideout Road, outside Oneonta."

"How old are you?"

"Forty-seven."

"What is the nature of your employment?"

"I'm self-employed. I run a printing business."

Morehead was sitting tall. His answers were clear and brief. He was doing better than he had done in the morning preparation. But this was only direct examination, and the questions were still innocuous. "How, if at all, are you involved with the community's political affairs?"

"I'm the Chairman of the Populist Party for Otsego County."

"You were here yesterday when Detective Theodore Ramsey testified about certain events that took place between the two of you at your home on April 11th of this year. Right?"

"Yes."

"Did he, in fact, come to your home on that date?"

"Yes."

"At about what time did he arrive?"

"Shortly after four-thirty in the afternoon."

Skip took a deep breath. "Tell the court what transpired."

"I answered the door, and Detective Ramsey, after displaying his credentials, said he wanted to speak to me about the murder of Squeaky Grimes. I invited the Detective into my living room where we sat down. He asked me if I had any thoughts about the crime, and I said I didn't."

"What happened next?"

"He accused me of killing Squeaky. Next thing I knew he...he stood up and pulled out a revolver from the inside of his jacket."

Skip stole a glance at the bench. Judge Biddleford was actually concentrating on the witness. That was a good sign. But the chance that the conservative Republican jurist, a former state trooper with a streak of jaded bigotry, would take

Morehead's word over Ramsey's was nil. In the courtroom His Holiness gave lip service to the presumption of innocence, but off-the-record comments in more private venues revealed that the hard-ass, no-nonsense Judge believed police officers arrest only guilty persons. Skip said, "What happened once Detective Ramsey took out his revolver?"

"He took a step toward the chair where I was sitting and aimed it down into my face."

"How far away from you was he? Just approximately."

"About four...maybe five feet. But the gun was right in front of my forehead...about a foot or so away."

"And what did you do or say?"

"Not a whole lot, except to kinda press back in my seat...and put up my hands like this."

"Let the record show that the witness raised his hands with palms open on either side of his head," said Judge Biddleford.

"What did Detective Ramsey say or do?"

"He told me if I didn't confess he'd blow my brains out, then put my fingerprints on a lead pipe he had in his cruiser and claim that I had tried to attack him with it."

"What happened next?"

"He took a pen and small pad out of his pocket and laid it on the coffee table next to my chair. He ordered me to write exactly what he dictated."

"What did you do?"

"With a gun pointed my way, I did as he said. I wrote out a confession just the way he told me."

"Then what happened?"

"Ramsey...I mean Detective Ramsey demanded I sign it. When I hesitated, he cocked his gun. I didn't want to die. So, I added my signature."

The story, one Skip had heard from Morehead before, sounded crazy. But it was just crazy enough to be believable. Or at least it might have been if there were a logical explanation why Ramsey would want to pin the murder on Morehead. Skip stared into space as he contemplated his next question. A murmur from the spectators behind the bar hinted that Morehead had them thinking. But whether anyone believed his story was another matter. "What happened after you signed the confession?"

"Detective Ramsey handcuffed me and took me off to jail."

"Your Honor," said Skip, "if I may take a moment?"

"A brief one."

Skip went over to the defense table and got his yellow pad. He ran his finger down his notes making sure he had covered all that he wanted to. Once done, he retrieved the knife from the jury box rail and then went over to the evidence table next to the court reporter where he picked up the confession. He handed the confession to Morehead. "I show you People's Exhibit One, marked for identification, and ask if this is the confession you signed at your home on April 11th?"

Morehead examined the document. "Yes, it is."

Skip took a couple of steps back, momentarily surveyed the courtroom and then refocused on Morehead. "Would you have signed that confession if Detective Ramsey had not threatened you with his gun?"

"Definitely not."

"Mr. Morehead, who, if anyone, besides you and Detective Ramsey, was present at your home during the events of April 11th that you just described?"

"No one."

Skip took the confession from Morehead and handed him the knife. I show you People's Exhibit Two, marked for identification. "When was the first time you saw this knife?"

"Yesterday in court."

"Did you hear Detective Thomas say that he found it in the shed behind your house?"

"Yes, but I have no idea how it got there."

Skip hesitated a moment. All along Morehead had claimed his confession was coerced. He had implied he was innocent of the murder. Never, however, had he specifically said so. Skip had assiduously avoided the question for fear of the answer. If and when he would make the inquiry remained unclear, but one thing sure, this was not the time. A denial while helpful, was far from necessary for purposes of the suppression hearing. The only issues currently before the court were the admissibility at trial of certain evidence. Skip had been careful to confine his examination of Morehead to the events of April 11th. If the prosecutor attempted to explore occurrences on April 9th, the date of Squeaky's murder, Skip would argue they were beyond the scope of direct examination, as well as the purposes of the hearing. Whether the tactic would work was another matter. Skip said, "No further questions." He looked over at the District Attorney. "Your witness."

Carter got up from his seat and slowly stepped around the prosecution table. His face appeared irresolute, but Skip saw through the mask. Ordinarily forced to show his entire hand without knowing what the defendant might claim, Carter was getting a shot at Morehead long before trial. No doubt the District Attorney was licking his chops, especially with a hothead like Morehead on the stand.

"Mr. Morehead, you indicated to your attorney that you run a printing business. Right?"

"Yes." Morehead uncrossed his legs and sat up taller.

"Isn't it also true that you run a bookmaking operation from the back room of that business?"

"Objection."

"Overruled." Judge Biddleford turned to the witness stand. "Answer the question, please."

"I'm not a bookmaker." Morehead was emphatic. "And might I add that rumors to the contrary—I've heard them—are false."

Skip's stomach sank. Morehead had just begun his cross-examination, and already he showed signs of that worst of courtroom diseases, diarrhea of the mouth. And that might be only the lesser disaster. Unless several people, including Mickey Shore, were mistaken, Morehead had just perjured himself.

His tone sharp, the District Attorney said, "Mr. Morehead, isn't it true that nineteen years ago you pleaded guilty to Promoting Gambling in the Second Degree in violation of Section 225.05 of the Penal Law?"

"Objection." Skip had no basis, but he needed to do something.

"Overruled. By opting to take the stand, the defendant has put his credibility in issue, and prior convictions are relevant to that credibility. The witness has also testified as to the nature of his business." Judge Biddleford directed his attention to the witness stand. "Did you plead guilty to said charge?"

Morehead hesitated.

Skip held his breath. Denying that which was a public record would instantly prove Morehead a liar.

"Yes...but that was nineteen years ago. Of course, what happened then probably explains the ongoing rumors."

"The question called for a *yes* or *no*," said the District Attorney. "Move to strike the rest of the witness's comments on the grounds they're not responsive."

"Stricken."

The District Attorney eased his way back to the prosecution table and leaned his butt against it. His face bore a seemingly friendly smile. Smugness, however, showed through. Skip couldn't blame him. Down the street at storied *Doubleday Field* how often did a seasoned hurler get a chance to pitch to a schnook who had a bat in his hands for the first time? And this was no exhibition game. Morehead, charged with murder, was in the big leagues.

"Mr. Morehead," said the District Attorney, the cadence of his speech very deliberate, "isn't it true that you killed Ralph Squeaky Grimes?"

"Objection," shouted Skip, leaping from his seat. The prosecutor's question, not unexpected, underscored the peril of Morehead's decision to take the stand. Allowing the District Attorney to explore the matter could spell disaster. Concern was not that Morehead would actually admit the crime, but that he might arm the prosecution with testimony bolstering its case or, worse yet, hamstring the defense with untenable positions. Unfortunately Skip's objection suggested the defense had something to hide. Maybe it did. "Your Honor," said Skip, my direct examination was strictly confined to the April 11th transaction in which Detective Ramsey obtained the defendant's alleged confession. The crime itself was never discussed, and as this Court quite properly indicated, this is a suppression hearing, not a trial. The issues here today are limited to the admissibility of the defendant's confession and a certain knife."

Judge Biddleford's face grew pensive. His gaze moved upward as he rocked back and forth in his big chair.

Skip held his breath. They had ventured into rocky waters, and the man at the helm was anything but a scholar when it came to the principles of navigation. But with Skip treading tenuously, a helmsman whose days as a jurist were spawned amidst the cigar smoke of politically connected back rooms, rather than the stacks of quiescent libraries, was arguably advantageous.

Seconds slowly ticked until finally Judge Biddleford said, "I'm going to sustain the objection. As defense counsel noted, this is a suppression hearing and direct examination did not open the door."

Skip's heart moved back from his throat to his chest.

"Mr. Morehead," said the District Attorney, "let's talk about the 11th. Earlier you told us what transpired between you and Detective Ramsey on that day. You said that when you answered your door the Detective indicated he wanted to speak to you about the murder of Squeaky Grimes. Correct?"

"Yeah."

Like a rubber ball, Skip's heart was back in his throat.

"And you told us Detective Ramsey accused you of the murder. True?"

"Yeah."

"What did you say in response?"

"Objection." Skip was on his feet again. The question, not even leading, was a trap. "Your Honor, the District Attorney is trying to do by indirection that which you have already ruled he cannot do directly—explore the murder itself."

"If Your Honor, please," said the District Attorney, "on direct examination counsel questioned the witness about the conversation that took place between the defendant and Detective Ramsey. Having opened that door, I'm entitled to fully explore the conversation."

Judge Biddleford nodded. "Objection overruled."

Once again Skip held his breath. Obviously Morehead could not confess to the murder. But a denial was perhaps more perjury. On the bright side, perjury was nothing compared to murder. And too, as a lawyer it would make Skip's job easier. He would be representing a client who had stated under oath that he was innocent.

"Mr. Morehead," said the District Attorney, "what did you say when Detective Ramsey accused you of the murder?"

Morehead folded his arms and spoke decisively. "I told him he was nuts."

The response had Skip's legal mind racing. Even if Morehead had killed Squeaky, assuming the words accurately reflected what Morehead had said, they were not perjurious.

The District Attorney stepped closer to the witness stand. "And it's your testimony that Detective Ramsey immediately pulled out a gun and threatened you if you didn't sign a confession?"

"Yup. That's what happened."

The District Attorney went over to the table next to the court reporter and got the confession. He took it to the witness. "I show you People's Exhibit One and ask if that's your signature?"

"Yeah, that's my signature."

"No further questions."

Skip had many more questions he could have asked on re-direct, but getting Morehead off the witness stand was priority number one. "No re-direct and no further witnesses."

"Then I believe that concludes this—"

"Excuse me, Your Honor," said the District Attorney. "The People have a rebuttal witness."

A frown on his face, Judge Biddleford glanced at his watch.

"I assure the Court this will be extremely brief."

"Very well. Proceed."

"The People call Sean Kileen."

A man about fifty, gray around the temples, came forward from the back row of the spectators and took the oath.

"Mr. Kileen, please state your full name for the record."

"Sean Alan Kileen, but folks call me Buddy."

"Where do you live?"

"Above my insurance agency on Main Street here in Cooperstown."

"What brought you to court today?"

"A subpoena from your office."

"Within the past year have you placed any bets on any sporting events, and I mean with a bookmaker, not a wager with your friends?"

"Yes."

Skip could see where the testimony was headed. "Your Honor, this is far afield from a suppression hearing."

"Subject to prompt connection—and I do mean prompt—I'll allow it."

"What have you bet?"

"A bunch of Yankee games and the Super Bowl and stuff like that."

"With whom did you place your bets?"

Kileen pointed at the defense table. "Harley Morehead."

"How did you place those bets?"

"Well, Squeaky...Squeaky Grimes would give me a sheet with odds, and I'd mark my bets and give him the money. Then he'd deliver the bets to Harley Morehead."

"Objection as to what Squeaky did or didn't do out of the presence of the witness."

"Sustained."

"Did you ever win any of those bets?"

The witness chuckled. "Fewer than I'd like, but yeah...sometimes."

"If Your Honor, please," said Skip, fearing the potential damage, "there was supposed to be prompt connection. Mr. Carter is traveling farther from the relevant path."

"On the contrary," said Judge Biddleford. "Your client has indicated he is not engaged in illegal gambling. His credibility is a critical facet in sorting out what happened between him and Detective Ramsey on April 11th. And that is what this suppression hearing is all about." The Judge looked to the District Attorney. "Proceed."

"What happened when you won a bet?"

"Squeaky delivered my winnings."

"So—Squeaky was what's called a runner on the street. Right?"

"Objection...leading."

"It's merely terminology. I'll allow it." The Judge turned to the witness. "Please answer the question."

"Yes, he was a runner."

"For whom?"

"Objection. Calls for a conclusion."

Judge Biddleford turned to the witness again. "Do you know of your own knowledge for whom Squeaky worked?"

"Yes. Harley Morehead."

"No further questions," said the District Attorney.

Kileen started to get up.

"Excuse me," said Skip. "I have some questions."

Kileen glanced toward the bench and then re-seated himself.

"Mr. Kileen, you never placed any bets face-to-face with Harley Morehead, did you?"

"No."

"The betting sheets you referred to didn't have his name on them, did they?"

"No, but betting sheets—"

Skip held up his hand. "That's fine. You've answered my question." Skip took a moment as he carefully planned his next inquiry. "Mr. Kileen, as you sit here today, you have to admit it is possible that Squeaky Grimes actually worked as a runner for someone other than Harley Morehead. True?"

Kileen shrugged. "Well...I guess so."

"Or he could have even been in business for himself?"

"Uh...I suppose."

Skip slowly turned to the District Attorney. "Your witness."

"No re-direct and no further rebuttal witnesses," said the District Attorney.

"Your Honor," said Skip, "I would like to make a brief oral argument."

"Well—" A facial contortion accompanied a momentary pause. "All right. Proceed."

Skip wished the court reporter could have captured the Judge's tone and demeanor. Proof that deaf ears awaited the argument was lost. In the event of an appeal, the record would manifest an attentive jurist. Aware he needed to be brief, Skip said, "If Your Honor, please, we all know how devastating a confession can be at trial. As a result the outcome of this suppression hearing is critical. We have a detective who ignored usual protocol and, with no other officer present, claims to have gotten a voluntary confession from the defendant. Why in an extremely serious case, one involving murder, would an experienced detective do that? That fact alone casts a foul odor on the confession. Detective Ramsey's past history makes the smell of the confession here even more rancid. In *People v. Styles* the Appellate Division threw out one of his so-called confessions. Suppression here hinges on credibility. Detective Ramsey lost his several years ago."

Skip cleared his throat. "Furthermore, I ask this Court to examine the logic behind the alleged confession. Harley Morehead, as Chairman of the Populist Party, deals with lawyers all the time. Assume hypothetically that he *was* guilty. What would he have done? He would have remained silent and asked to see a lawyer. Indeed he did exactly that once he was at the police station in the presence of other officers. If the defendant is to have a fair trial, the confession must be suppressed."

Judge Biddleford shuffled some papers.

Skip got the message. His time had nearly expired. He said, "As for the knife, the cases are well settled that fruits of the poison tree must be suppressed. The alleged confession occasioned the search that led to the knife. Thus, the knife is poison fruit." Skip picked up the confession from the small table adjoining the court stenographer and waived it in the air. "In summary, Your Honor's decision whether to suppress this so-called confession will be crucial come the trial. Give the defendant Due Process. Let the case go before the jury on the evidence, but don't allow their judgment to be poisoned by the likes of this." With a thrust of disdain Skip smacked the confession back down. He circled back to the defense table.

Morehead whispered, "Good job."

"Mr. Carter," said Judge Biddleford, "any closing argument?"

The District Attorney nodded. "Ever so briefly." As he stood up, he gestured toward the defense table. "Mr. Maynard asks Your Honor to suppress his client's confession. He calls that Due Process. May I suggest that a free pass for murder would be more accurate. Due Process dictates that the jurors see the defendant's confession. Allow them to listen to the witnesses. Let them determine what happened at the defendant's home on April 11th. They can decide whom they believe, the defendant, a convicted bookmaker, or a disinterested police detective. That, Your Honor, is Due Process." The District Attorney returned to his seat.

Judge Biddleford made some notes. A murmur could be heard from the rear of the courtroom. The onlookers were perhaps speculating what the Judge would do. Skip's eyes drifted to the large mural on the far wall depicting the scales of justice. Many times before he had read the inscription beneath the painting: *Let Justice Be Done.* Indeed, the handwriting was on the wall. Judge Biddleford, still a law enforcement officer at heart, would deny the motion to suppress. Objectivity forced Skip to concede he would do it too if he were on the bench.

"Gentleman," said Judge Biddleford, "having heard the testimony, together with the argument of counsel, I am taking the matter under advisement and will render my written decision in due course. If there is nothing further this afternoon, this court will stand adjourned." He waited several seconds and then rapped his gavel.

As the courtroom emptied, Skip began stuffing his papers back into his file. Morehead put an arm over Skip's shoulder.

"Way to go."

"Thanks," said Skip, the positive feedback a shot in the arm.

"I picked the right guy, the same one I saw in the courtroom years ago."

Morehead gave Skip another pat. "We're gonna win this thing. Biddleford's gonna toss the confession."

Hello. Skip allowed his widening eyes to hint at the thought. "I wouldn't get your hopes too high. We've got a rough road ahead. When it comes to motions to suppress, Biddleford is like a kid in the terrible two's. The only word he knows is *no*."

Morehead took his hand from Skip's shoulder and held it out as if prepared to shake hands. "Tell you what. I'll bet you a fin Biddleford suppresses my confession."

"I'll pass," said Skip, pushing Morehead's hand back to his side. "And given the circumstances, you're the last person who should be doing any betting."

Morehead shrugged. "Fine. But we'll see who's right when Biddleford makes his ruling."

Chapter VI

Skip reached out to shake the hand of his new client.

"Lenny Gardner," he said, his limp fingers a squirmy fish in Skip's normally firm grip.

"How can I help you?" Skip gestured him to a chair across the desk.

"My wife and I are divorced." The slight fellow with the high-pitched voice and purple ascot seated himself with one leg crossed over the other. "She's looking for an increase in her child support payments."

"How many children do you have?"

"Just one. A daughter. She's eight years old."

"How much do you currently pay?"

"Forty dollars a week. I've been paying that amount for over three years, ever since the divorce settlement. I've never missed a payment." He handed Skip some legal papers, an Order to Show Cause and supporting affidavit.

Skip perused them quickly, noting the application was returnable in front of Judge Biddleford, rather than in Supreme Court or, more likely yet, in Family Court. A copy of the Divorce Decree, attached to the affidavit, provided the reason. County Court Judge Biddleford had been sitting as an Acting Supreme Court Judge at the time of the divorce and, as he was known to often do, had retained jurisdiction of future issues. "I see your former wife wants to raise your payments to one hundred twenty-five dollars per week."

"Can she do that?"

"If she can show a sufficient change of circumstances."

"Gee…I don't get it. We agreed upon all the terms of our divorce, including child support. And the court blessed the agreement."

"I understand." Skip hesitated knowing the explanation would not be pleasing. "The agreement or contract between you and your wife affected the rights of your daughter. Not only was she not a party, but, in addition, she was a minor. The court has the power to protect her interests. Even though the original award may have been fair at the time, the court can modify it based upon a change of circumstances."

Gardner nodded.

The willingness with which he seemingly accepted the unappealing explanation was atypical. "Did anyone explain this to you when you got your divorce?"

"No. My ex and I agreed on terms, and I signed the papers so she could get it uncontested. I didn't have a lawyer. But maybe that was a mistake." He heaved a sigh. "You think I'll end up paying a whole lot more?"

"Depends on the circumstances...whether there has been a change. What do you do for a living?"

"I operate a hair salon in Oneonta."

Signs that he might be gay had been visible the moment he had entered the office. The probability had just increased. His sexual persuasion made no difference to Skip. Unfortunately the same couldn't be said for Judge Biddleford. The conservative jurist was homophobic. For the moment Skip avoided the issue and remained focused on facts that might legitimately justify a modification of support. "Were you in the same business at the time of your divorce?"

"Yes."

"Then and now, how does it compare?"

"Well, back then it was fairly new. I had just one chair. Now I have two other hairdressers working for me."

"What about your income? Has that changed?"

Gardner nodded. "This past year I earned nearly eighteen thousand, almost double what I was netting when we were divorced in 1965."

"What about your ex-wife? Any change in her work status?"

"Not really. She's been a secretary ever since high school. Her raises have pretty much mirrored the inflation rate."

Skip made a few notes. "Any other changes that might be relevant, such as financial circumstances; special medical, educational or other needs of your daughter; or any other differences that would affect your daughter's needs or the ability of you or your ex to provide for her?"

Gardner thought for a minute. "Not that I can think of." His shoulders sagged. "I'm gonna take a hit, aren't I?"

"Well..."

"Before you give me the bad news, there's one more bit of information you should know. I live with a guy. Judge Biddleford knows that. It was in our original divorce papers." Gardner looked Skip in the eye. "I understand if you'd rather not represent me."

"Relax. As far as I'm concerned, your sexual preference is your business. As for Judge Biddleford, that's another matter."

"I suspected that. According to my wife, when she went to court for the divorce, the Judge said I was lucky there was an agreement and she hadn't sued for an annulment based on fraud." Gardner shook his head. "I thought this might be a rough ride. That's why I'm getting an attorney this time around."

A motion to have His Holiness recuse himself was a possibility, but the idea, one that crossed Skip's mind in virtually every case before Judge Biddleford, held little allure. The volcanic jurist, belching smoke and fire, would almost surely deny the application. The avenue of appeal was always available, but that was an expensive proposition with little chance of success. A settlement, one that avoided a decision by the biased Judge, offered a more practical approach. "Would you be willing to pay something more than forty dollars per week for child support?"

"Given the situation, if I could get away with seventy-five, I'd consider myself very lucky."

Gardner was the kind of guy Skip was happy to have for a client. That he was straight or gay was immaterial. What mattered—he was realistic and flexible. All too often Skip had represented mules. At great expense they stubbornly spurned any compromise as they opted for costly courtroom battles, only to suffer the consequences of their own intransigence.

"Perhaps we can minimize your pain with a negotiated settlement. I'll certainly try."

"I appreciate that."

"Regardless, don't let your wife know you're willing to settle. We've got a better chance if her lawyer thinks I'm twisting your arm."

"I understand."

Skip proceeded to outline some other details of his representation, including his hourly rate. Just before concluding the meeting, he said, "If you don't mind, I'd like to inquire why you came to me, as opposed to someone else. The reason I'm asking is that I've started to do some advertising, a larger display in the yellow pages and the like. I'm trying to get a sense of what's worthwhile."

"Well...the only ad that brought me in was your performance in the courtroom last week. I watched you in that murder case, the one involving Squeaky Grimes. Squeaky lived in the house next to mine. That's what drew me to court."

"You knew Squeaky?"

"Uh...just to say *hello*. He was..."

Skip waited a moment. "You were about to say something about Squeaky?"

"Not really. Just that it was too bad what happened to him."

The possibility of a conflict of interest, though it seemed remote, crossed Skip's mind. "Does the fact that I represent Harley Morehead concern you?"

A puzzled look appeared on Gardner's face. "I'm not sure what you mean. The guy's entitled to a defense."

Skip nodded. "Just making sure that your interests and those of Morehead won't clash. You said you knew Squeaky."

"I knew him. But...not in the biblical sense." Gardner chuckled.

Whether the humor or something subtler prompted the laugh, Skip couldn't tell. He wondered if Squeaky might have been gay. He was debating whether to ask when Gardner said, "As I told you earlier, I saw you in the courtroom when I went to that hearing, the one about the confession."

"The suppression hearing?"

"Yeah, that's it. Anyway I needed lawyer. I've never had one, except for the fellow from First National who did my real estate closing, and he represented the bank, not me. But to make a long story short, I thought you did a great job and decided to give you a call."

Skip's ego welcomed the flattery, though he suspected Gardner must have only been there the second day. Had he seen Skip slur and stagger a day earlier, presumably he would have gone elsewhere.

"The way I see it," said Gardner, "Judge Biddleford has it in for me. I need someone who isn't afraid to take him on. A friend from up north, a court stenographer, told me that in rural areas like Cooperstown most of the lawyers are pretty tight with the judges. According to my friend few would jeopardize their relationship on a small-potatoes case like mine."

Though the assessment contained more jailhouse fallacy than truth, that wasn't the point. Skip also realized his earlier self-satisfaction might have been misplaced.

Gardner glanced at his watch. "I've taken more than enough of your time." He got up from his seat.

Skip ushered him out of the office.

A minute later Lucy buzzed him on the intercom. "Mickey Shore is here for his two o'clock."

"Send him in."

A moment later, dressed in khaki slacks, a multi-colored sport shirt and a cigarette behind the ear, the detective entered. "Hope you had more success than I did."

"Pardon me."

"With your investigation." He gestured toward the waiting room as he took a seat. "Was Gardner any help? He refused to talk to me."

"About what?"

Mickey studied Skip for a moment. "You sober?"

"Completely. What's this about?"

"Gardner—I assume you know where he lives."

"Yes, on Rock Street. Next door to Squeaky's place. But what about it?"

"What about it? You gotta be kidding." Mickey's eyes widened. "You don't by any chance represent him?"

"He's a new client. Just met him today."

Mickey shook his head. "Did he talk to you about the Morehead case?"

"That had nothing to do with his visit."

"You sure about that?"

Suddenly Skip wasn't. "What do you think?"

"That it's mighty strange for Squeaky's next door neighbor to walk into your office out of the blue. A sawbuck says it's no coincidence."

Skip might have taken the bet had he disagreed with the assessment. "Earlier you said you tried to talk to him."

"Yup. But he refused. He seemed mighty defensive. If you ask me, he knows a whole lot more than he lets on. As to why he hired you, I haven't a clue. But gold to garbage says he's got something up his sleeve."

"Damn," muttered Skip. He had always ranked his ability to judge people among his greatest strengths. Gardner had struck him as a square shooter. If the guy was a con man, he was good. "See what you can find out about Gardner."

Mickey took the cigarette from behind his ear. "Don't worry. I'm not gonna light up." He looked Skip in the eye. "And don't be judgmental."

Much as Skip detested the cancer sticks, especially their smoky wake, his ties to *Jack* were far too similar to sermonize. Still he had no intention of making an exception to his office policy prohibiting smoking. The same as clients, Mickey could wait until he was out on the street to feed his habit.

Mickey inhaled on the unlit *Camel*. "I've been nosing around, and it seems that Squeaky, jack of all trades, was even more parasitic than I had realized. He had loads of interesting connections, especially the kind that make him a threat to folks in high places."

"Such as?"

"The City Manager for one. And Gino Morelli, the contractor."

"I've heard the name, but...don't know much about him." On the other hand, City Manager Traci LaDieux was far more familiar to Skip. She had been in his high school class. Back then he had been tempted to ask her out, but older guys were more her style. Even in high school she had shown a propensity for politics. Senior year she was elected class vice-president, but that was strictly a popularity contest. If someone had suggested she would become City Manager, Skip would have laughed. As a student, she was nothing special. Hot? No doubt about it. And brassy too. But City Manager? Skip would not have imagined that. He said, "Tell me about Morelli."

"He built those chicken-coop apartments south of town. He also refurbished the city office building."

"Wasn't that the deal a year or so ago where one of the bidders squawked because the bid specifications allegedly showed favoritism?"

"Yup, and Morelli was the one favored. To make matters worse, he wasn't the low bidder. The firm that came in first was rejected for technical reasons. Supposedly they lacked the experience needed for the project. If you ask me, Morelli had the contract locked up even before the bidding started."

"Where does Squeaky tie in?"

"From time to time he worked for Morelli."

The information was interesting but hardly enough to suggest a link to Squeaky's murder. "Even assuming the bidding was rigged, how would Squeaky know?"

"He probably wouldn't. But he'd know if he helped install a finished basement in LaDieux's home." Mickey displayed a big smile.

"You suggesting the City Manager got a kickback from Morelli?"

"Well...let me put it this way. Her basement has been redone in style. Morelli did the work. And a friend of mine at the Leatherstocking Bank and Trust—that's where the City Manager maintains her account—confirms she didn't pay Morelli by check. She may have paid him in cash, though that alone would raise some interesting questions. There's also the possibility she paid Morelli with a credit card, but that seems unlikely."

"Interesting," said Skip, as he leaned back in thoughtful contemplation. Regardless whether the disclosure had actual ties to Squeaky's murder, it had potential. Anything that might suggest someone other than Morehead had a motive to kill

Squeaky was fodder to create reasonable doubt in the minds of a jury. In a murder case where the evidence against the defendant was strong, that was generally the goal. Sure, it was nice to convince the jury the defendant was innocent, but creating reasonable doubt was a more realistic possibility. In Morehead's case, if his confession were ruled admissible, even reasonable doubt would be an ambitious goal. "Do you think Morelli or the City Manager might be involved in Squeaky's murder?"

Mickey shrugged. "It's a long shot, but..." His voice trailed off briefly. "I'll have to see what else I can dig up on them. In the meantime I've got another angle. You had asked me to investigate Buddy Kileen. I found a rather odd pattern. In the past three years a bunch of his insureds have settled cases without a lawyer. Most of them were fender benders with neck or back injuries."

"What's so strange about that? After all, Kileen is an insurance agent."

"I know. But in two of them Theodore Ramsey signed the police report. Ordinarily detectives don't spend their time investigating car accidents. And add this to the pot. In one of those accidents—it happened a little over a year ago—the passenger was none other than Ralph Squeaky Grimes."

"Intriguing," said Skip. "Tell me more."

Mickey slipped his *Camel* between his lips. A moment later he pulled it out, giving the unlit cigarette a hostile look. He said, "Yesterday I did a background check on Squeaky."

"Perhaps he had a history of insurance fraud?"

Mickey shook his head. "No, but eight years ago he pleaded guilty to extortion. He served nine months in the county jail, along with three years' probation."

The familiar tidbit, when coupled with Mickey's other facts about Ramsey and Kileen, was arguably better than the information about the City Manager and Morelli. The prosecution's chief witness, Ramsey, might not be a Boy Scout. Better yet, he might have had a motive to kill Squeaky and frame someone else. "You did a helluva job, Mickey. Twenty minutes ago Morehead was a conviction waiting to happen. Now I might have something to talk about. And

depending how the facts shake out, it could be a whole lot."
Skip eyed the cigarette that was back behind Mickey's ear. He
reached for the *No-Smoking* sign that sat on the front of his
desk and turned it face down. "Go ahead and light up," he said.
"You've earned it."
Mickey hesitated and then flipped the sign upright again.
"Thanks, but I'll survive until I'm out in the fresh air."
"Fine, but in that case I won't keep you. Just a couple
quick things before you go. See what else you can learn about
Morelli and the City Manager and Ramsey and Kileen,
especially the latter duo."
"That's already on my to-do list."
"Just one last question: Any idea whether Squeaky was
gay?"
A puzzled look appeared on Mickey's face.
Skip wanted to explain, but the confidence owed to Lenny
Gardner forced him to be circumspect. Once again, the possible
conflict of interest loomed in the back of his mind. He said,
"See what you can find out about Squeaky's lifestyle."
"Will do," said Mickey, and he went on his way.

———

Skip pushed the containers of orange juice and one-
percent milk aside on the chance there might be a can of
Budweiser behind them. He knew there wasn't. He had made
sure a week before when he had emptied his house of alcohol.
Giving two unopened bottles of *Jack Daniel's* to the fellow
who did his lawn wasn't easy. The cost was immaterial, but
bidding farewell to the one friend who was always there for
him on lonely nights was another matter. Eight days had passed
since he had taken a drink. How many more might go by until
he succumbed was hard to say.
A bowl of *Cheerios* in hand, he sank down into his
favorite easy chair in the den. He reached for the television
remote and began pushing buttons. Sunday morning offered an
insipid potpourri. A round table interview of City Manager
Traci LaDieux and County Comptroller Bernie Feinstein won

out easily over an infomercial for *Ronco's Vegematic*, Oral Roberts and *Oil Painting with Preston*.

The interviewer said, "I understand that both of you are considering a run for the vacant seat in the State Assembly."

"If I do," said Feinstein, "I'll make my announcement in about a month."

The interviewer turned to LaDieux. "What about you?"

"I leave such speculations for members of the press, like yourself. I'm too busy with my current job to spend time contemplating others."

"Are you saying you won't run?"

"I didn't say that." She gestured at the interviewer. "Tell you what. If and when I decide to run, you'll be among the first to know."

"Along with the rest of the world," said the interviewer.

LaDieux turned to Feinstein. "Our journalist friend is a quick learner."

Skip's eyes remained focused on the screen, but his thoughts drifted away from the bland audio portion. The City Manager still enjoyed the well-endowed body that had made her a hot commodity in high school, and she still liked to show it off. Her tight black sweater, cut low to reveal ample cleavage, made far better viewing than a tête-à-tête about any possible run for the State Assembly. Too bad he didn't get the chance to date her in high school. Rumor had it she was easy.

The camera switched back and forth between the interviewer and his subjects. Skip confined himself to only one, and her words passed mindlessly through his ears. His ruminations continued until the interviewer said, "What, if any, role will Harley Morehead's problems play in your decision whether to run?"

The mention of Morehead's name grabbed Skip's attention.

LaDieux furrowed her brow. "As a Republican, my decision won't be affected by anything that happens to the Populist Party Chairman."

"I understand." The interviewer turned to Feinstein. "Mr. Comptroller, how about you?"

"Hold the phone. The last thing I need is a connection to Harley Morehead. His difficulties have nothing to do with me."

"Well...there have been indications that his intervention precluded you from getting the Populist nod more than once in the past."

Feinstein folded his arms. "Maybe those indications are mistaken. At no time did I ever toss my hat into the ring."

"That may be...but it seems he's been a thorn in your side for years. I doubt you'd mind having him out of the way."

With a seemingly warm smile painting his face, Feinstein shrugged.

To Skip the masked anger was evident. Feinstein lacked the polish of a seasoned veteran, the kind needed to move upward and onward in the duplicitous world of politics.

"Perhaps your audience would be better served," said Feinstein, "if you direct any inquiries related to Mr. Morehead's problems to her Honor, the City Manager."

"Excuse me," she said with bristling indignation.

Feinstein looked her way. "Not to cast any aspersions, but the auditors in my department tell me the name Squeaky Grimes comes up far too often when auditing contracts involving your office."

"Are you insinuating something?"

"No. As I said, I'm not casting aspersions. I'm merely making note of a matter which might be of interest to the viewing audience."

Feinstein may have been amateurish, but Skip realized the Comptroller was not afraid to play hardball, even to the point of pitching a grenade. Whether he had anything of substance that might link to Squeaky's murder was another matter. Skip made a mental note to include Feinstein on the list of people he might subpoena for Morehead's trial. But first Mickey would have to follow up on Feinstein. Calling him as a witness without knowing what he would say would be a risky business, but getting him to open up voluntarily before the trial might be impossible.

The interviewer glanced at his watch. "Interesting as this discussion may be, it appears the fast moving hands of time dictate that we conclude. Who knows? Perhaps our guests will meet again at the ballot box in the next race for the State Assembly."

Maybe they'll meet elsewhere, thought Skip, conjuring an image of them in Judge Biddleford's courtroom.

After what had been a relatively productive day, Skip left the office early for a visit to the *Baseball Hall of Fame*, his first in many months. Though he had long since ceased to follow the annual pennant races, the shrine's embodiment of a bygone era, its link to his childhood, still lured him through its doors. The moment he passed through the entrance, reality and the world around him were left behind. With its many busts and copious memorabilia, the great hall beckoned him to journey back to bygone eras. Skip, a part of him still residing in the past, welcomed the chance to mingle with boyhood heroes whose legendary exploits time had embellished. His heart still beat for former loves, among them, though hardly foremost, was his also-ran Boston Red Sox. Growing up in Cooperstown, the stars of the game were his heroes. In junior high school Ted Williams, the Splendid Splinter, was Skip's idol. Day after day, season after season, he and his two buddies, Jerry and Slicker, debated who was the best outfielder. Jerry, a New York Giant fan, argued for Mel Ott, while Slicker, a Yankee lover, touted Joe DiMaggio. With endless statistics—home runs, batting averages, slugging percentage, runs batted in, fielding average, or anything else available—they endeavored to substantiate their claims. Far more than bragging rights were at stake. The boys' identities, inexorably linked to their heroes, were on the line.

Season after season the boys ate, drank and slept baseball. They lived and died with the success of their favorite team. But hardly a year went by that Slicker failed to get the last word. With few exceptions his beloved Yankees emerged as World Champions. Skip could do no better than borrow the mantra of the *Bums* from Brooklyn: *Wait until next year.* But gradually as he moved through his teens and on to college, he was able to shed that mantra. No, the Red Sox didn't win, but that was their problem, not his. Still his love for Cooperstown, his boyhood hometown, never waned. Neither did his love for its ultimate personification, the *Baseball Hall of Fame*. Indeed Skip was a member, not because of deeds on the ball field, but because he always paid his annual admission fee.

Entering the lobby of the shrine, the sights that met his eyes failed to reach his brain. His mind was conjuring images decades old. He could see himself, Red Sox cap on his head, seated on the first base line at *Doubleday Field*. As a youngster he never missed the Hall-of-Fame game at Cooperstown's iconic ballpark. Back then the opportunity to see bigger-than-life major leaguers in person was the closest thing to paradise. He still had the ball that Ted Williams had autographed for him years before. Countless times while in Little League he had played at *Doubleday*. Out there in center field he was the Splendid Splinter. Though Skip never hit for power, when he stepped to the plate, he was his hero.

Skip seated himself on a bench in the lobby of the *Hall of Fame*. Numerous times in the past he had occupied that identical seat, and recollections from those occasions remained vivid. As a child more than once he had sat there and imagined himself being enshrined in the venerable edifice. At the age of thirteen he had stopped there after striking out three times and making two errors in a Little League game. It was there on the familiar bench that his mediocre talent became a harsh reality. Even his rich imagination could no longer sustain the fantasy of a career as a professional baseball player. The ensuing week was terribly painful, but with youthful resilience Skip adjusted to the verdict. He resolved that his future rested with gray matter, not physical attributes. His life lay in an arena up the street from the *Hall of Fame* and *Doubleday*. The nearby Courthouse, the magnet that drew him when, in the depths of winter, baseball bats had been stowed away, was where his bread would be buttered. Though the courtroom stars never matched the superhuman icons of the ball field, still they wowed Skip. Being one of them, unlike a master of the diamond, was an ambition to which he could realistically aspire. A career as a trial lawyer became his goal.

Well over two decades later the *Hall of Fame* remained a place where Skip could think, a place where time travel was easy. In an instant he could move from his youth to the present or back to the era of Cy Young and others whose exploits long predated his birth. As always, Skip made sure to stop in the room that housed the busts and plaques of all the enshrined greats. Unlike childhood days when his focus was directed almost exclusively to his Red Sox heroes, men like Ted Williams, Jimmie Foxx and Joe Cronin, Skip's attention was broader and his observations different. No longer were the stars of baseball bigger than life. Like Skip, they were mortal. They had suffered the vicissitudes of that mortality. Jackie Robinson, the man who had broken the color barrier, had died at the age of fifty-three, several years after losing a son to suicide. Grover Cleveland Alexander, the great fireballer, had succumbed to a poverty-stricken death after years of battling alcoholism and, worse yet, epilepsy in an era when the disease was deemed the devil's revenge. And Roy Campanella, the three-time most valuable player, had seen his career cut short by a motor vehicle accident that had left him wheelchair bound for the rest of his life. So many icons of the diamond had become dust amidst darker days. Their worst pain was familiar territory for Skip. It was more than vicarious. The loss of Megan had sabotaged Skip's life. And unlike the inglorious day on the diamond when his dream of a baseball career had been quashed, the impact was not short-lived. Megan was not just a childhood fantasy. She was real. She was his soul mate. And she was gone.

After Megan's death the *Hall of Fame* took on a dual role for Skip. In the company of his boyhood idols, so many of whom had faced hard times on the ball field of life, Skip sought refuge and solace. The old adage *misery loves company* played a part. And too, the *Hall*, like *Camelot*, allowed him to visit a simpler time when, with a bat on his shoulder, he nobly defended his strike zone. He had a cause. It was important. And potential glory was a constant companion. Such was the world of his youth. While others boarded airplanes and ships to escape to idyllic locations, Skip walked through the doors of the legendary shrine. Having parted ways with his dear friend

Jack, that means of escape, albeit brief, had grown even more important. Less than thirty minutes after entering the impressive structure, he was back on Main Street. As he passed the Courthouse, Kelly Lane came down the sidewalk leading from the entrance. A taut mouth hinted she was not in her usual upbeat mood.

Even before Skip could exchange pleasantries, she said, "That man, and I use the term advisedly, is impossible!" She gestured back toward the building.

"By any chance are you referring to His Holiness?"

She nodded, turning her gaze back to the Courthouse. "Such a prime example of church-like, Victorian Gothic deserves better than an ogre like Biddleford on the bench."

"Impressive," said Skip. That he knew the architecture of the hundred-year-old structure was no big deal. His father, the architect, had exposed him to the many designs that graced the buildings of Cooperstown. However, Kelly's awareness was more surprising.

"What's impressive?"

"Your architectural acumen."

She gestured at Skip. "The credit is yours. And don't look so puzzled. Back when we were dating, you spruced up our walks with details regarding the features of Cooperstown's finest buildings. You were a regular encyclopedia of architecture."

"Was I really that boring?"

"Well..." A breaking smile hinted her response was amiable ribbing rather than a real jab.

"So, knowledgeable as you are, no doubt you can provide the term that most accurately describes the features of the stained-glass windows, towers and façade."

"Sorry, my teacher was very mediocre. You'll have to tell me."

"Queen Anne Revival."

Her scrunched face revealed little excitement for the tidbit. "As far as I'm concerned, particularly after a morning the likes of which I just endured, they're windows, towers and whatever."

Skip got the message. Back in his youth it had taken him longer to realize that enthusiastic displays of his expertise painted him with the unenviable image of a bookish nerd. The picture became clearer many years later when a fellow member of the bar, a self-proclaimed wine connoisseur, superciliously droned on for ninety minutes about the bouquet, vintage and other forgettable aspects of the wine he had ordered for lunch. As far as Skip was concerned, wine was wine. *Jack*, on the other hand, had class.

"You did a nice job at Morehead's suppression hearing. I was in the Courthouse and caught the tail end."

"Unless I'm mistaken, you also witnessed the fiasco the day before."

Kelly displayed a sheepish smile. "Well...at least you managed to rebound."

"You still thinking about suing Morehead on behalf of Squeaky's estate?"

For an instant she appeared noncommittal. "As I told you, I plan to sue his killer. For now my money is on your client. Got anything to change my mind?"

Revealing strategy was not a wise idea. "Come to the trial and decide for yourself." As he encouraged her to make her own observations, he was making some of his own. Her shapely body had drawn his attention. Recollections of intimacies shared several years earlier when they had dated reminded him how fine it was. "That blue suit is very becoming." His mind, aided by both imagination and memory, penetrated well beyond his eyes.

"Thanks. And I like your sport coat."

A compliment, yes, but hardly the flirtatious response he had solicited. He was contemplating an invite for dinner at the *Otesaga* on Saturday night when she glanced at her watch. "Gotta go. I've got a client coming into the office at four." She patted him on the arm. "It was good seeing you."

"You too." He barely got the words out, and she was on her way. He watched her slowly disappear down the street, his mind again conjuring thoughts of the charms that lay beneath her trim outfit.

Chapter VII

"So, what have you got, Mick?" Telephone receiver to his ear, feet up on his desk, Skip rocked back.

"I checked out Morelli. Very interesting. He definitely worked on the City Manager's basement. And guess whose name also came up during my investigation?"

Skip thought of Morehead. His client had too many bad ties already. If there was to be another, let Mickey say it.

"Take your time. My cigarette needs replacing, unless I want to smoke my fingers."

Skip switched the receiver to the ear closest to the telephone. "You tell me."

"Squeaky Grimes. It seems he did framing and paneling for Morelli when he was short on help. Nothing more than a few weeks a year. A source of mine who once worked for Morelli was willing to bet that Squeaky got paid under the table."

Mickey had previously said that Squeaky was a jack of everything. Sure enough, his name was popping up everywhere. On the other hand, that begged the underlying question whether his work for Morelli had anything to do with his murder.

"I went to City Hall in Oneonta and checked out Morelli's building permits for the past year. I followed up with a couple of the homeowners he worked for. One was satisfied. The other was pissed. Halfway through the job Morelli demanded more money. His written estimate contained fine print on the back of the form allowing for the charges. I asked the homeowner how he came to hire Morelli. Turns out the homeowner got three bids, and Morelli came in lowest. A glowing recommendation got him the job. Guess who provided the recommendation."

111

This time Skip was willing to speculate. "Squeaky?"

"If you were on Groucho's show, the duck would be delivering one hundred smackaroos. Anyway, the homeowner said that Squeaky told him Morelli gave his kitchen a masterful makeover. Mighty interesting, given that Squeaky, who rented one of Feinstein's flats, didn't own a kitchen."

Skip began jotting notes. "Any idea whether Morelli was paying Squeaky for the endorsements?"

"Nothing concrete. But if I were in the business of a certain bookmaker—his name to remain unmentioned—I'd call it a sure thing."

"Any chance Squeaky may have begun blackmailing Morelli?"

A breathy sound came over the telephone. Whether it was a sigh or Mickey exhaling cigarette smoke was unclear.

"Squeaky Grimes was the kind of guy who would blackmail his mother, even on her deathbed. The son of a bitch was a charmer. But he was a son of a bitch."

The extraordinary rancor in Mickey's voice had Skip contemplating the possibility of personal animosity. "If I recall, you knew about Squeaky before I hired you."

"Uh, yeah...by reputation."

Skip scribbled the response on his yellow pad. He had used Mickey before and had the utmost confidence in him. Nevertheless, he drew a question mark next to the entry.

"One more tidbit, and then I'll let you go. Morelli has a criminal record. About fifteen years ago he was charged with fraud. He plea-bargained it down to a misdemeanor and got away with a fine. According to the file he admitted gouging customers of his contracting business. The details were sparse, but from what I could tell it was very similar to what he does now—starts a job and then halfway through demands more money."

"He sounds like a real sweetheart."

"Hey...it's to be expected."

The logic escaped Skip. "Why?"

"Anyone with links to Squeaky is bound to be an eight ball."

The point had merit, and, unfortunately, the list of those connected to Squeaky included Morehead.

"I got Xeroxed copies of the records relating to Morelli's plea. I'll send them to you."

"Thanks. I appreciate that." Skip exchanged good-byes with Mickey and hung up the telephone. His cache of ammunition to raise doubts about Morehead's guilt was growing. But the case still appeared to hinge on the confession. The chances that Biddleford would suppress it were slim. That meant Morehead still faced long odds.

———

Skip parked his *BMW* along the margin of 57 Columbo Way in Oneonta. He headed up the tapestry brick walkway, past two life-size stone lions that led to the expansive home. On either side of the approach were impressive gardens. The one to the left had a circular fountain which sent a spray nearly fifteen feet into the air, while the display to the right included what appeared to be a replica of Michelangelo's *David*. The lot, certainly more than an acre, was meticulously maintained. Skip could hear his father's voice describing the exterior of the structure: *modern neoclassical and Tuscan, amalgamated into sheer and utter gauche.*

Skip climbed the stairs of the portico. At the top of the threshold, the name *MORELLI* was engraved in the marble surface several feet in advance of the heavy double doors with stained-glass side lights leading into the structure. Skip rang the doorbell.

A minute later a muscular, dark-complexioned man, a couple inches under six feet, with forearms like a blacksmith opened the door.

"Mr. Morelli?"

After a probing look, the man said, "Yes."

"I'm Skip Maynard. I represent Harley Morehead. I wonder if I might speak to you."

Morelli eyed his watch.

Skip had intentionally come unannounced at seven-thirty in the evening in the hope of catching Morelli off guard.

"Well...okay, I guess. But this better be brief. At eight I'm watching the *Mets*, and I don't intend to miss a pitch." He ushered Skip into a large foyer, which faced two curved staircases that met at a landing about fifteen feet above the rear of the foyer.

"Impressive home you have."

"I find it comfortable." He guided the way into a large den with a pool table and long bar at one end and loads of leather furniture at the other. He gestured Skip into a club chair and seated himself in another that was kitty corner to the first. "So, whad'ya wanna know?"

Before coming Skip had mapped out his strategy. Save the questions that were more likely to ignite sparks for the end. "I thought you might be able to tell me a little about Squeaky Grimes."

"Ask your client. I'm sure he can tell you far more."

Morelli would not be easy. "I appreciate that, but a second view always helps. I understand Squeaky worked for you."

"An odd job here or there. Nothing much."

"What kind of guy was he?"

"Hey, with a name like Squeaky, you figure it out." Morelli hesitated. "Bad mouthing the dead ain't my style. I say let the clod rest in peace."

"I gather he wasn't too bright."

"He wasn't no Einstein, if that's what ya mean. But he was a helluva lot foxier than the chump he seemed. He knew how to hang on here and hang on there, just enough to work an angle."

Skip wondered what angles Squeaky may have worked with Morelli. The question, however, was premature. "Good worker?"

"Not bad. He could handle a hammer and nails, but a craftsman...no way."

Skip gestured left and right. "It's obvious you take pride in workmanship."

Fingers taut, Morelli displayed his huge hands. "When you've got a fine piece of mahogany or marble, it's a sin to waste it. Most folks don't understand that. Spit and sand, wrapped in vinyl and aluminum—as long as it's cheap—that's what they want. I quit school when I was sixteen." There was a look of disdain as his eyes met Skip's. "Today every Tom, Dick and Harry goes to college. They come out spouting philosophy and social whatever, but they can barely wipe their asses. They don't know shit from *Shinola.*" He smiled, the self-satisfied kind.

"I hear you," said Skip, pretending to be too callow to recognize the jab was meant for him. "You built the apartments near the warehouse south of town, didn't you?"

"Hey...business is business. If that's what people want, that's what they get."

"Did Squeaky work on that project?"

"He might have."

"How about the refurbishing of the County Office Building?"

Morelli hesitated. "Can't say I recall."

Skip was edging carefully into a more controversial realm. "If I remember correctly, you weren't the low bidder on that project."

"So?" Morelli's expression hardened.

"I forget why the county rejected the low bidder."

"Inexperience, lack of skill...bad performance record. Ask the county, not me, if ya wanna know." Morelli's tone had taken a turn similar to his face.

"You also did major improvements on City Manager LaDieux's home, didn't you?"

Morelli leaned forward. "You're mighty nosy, aren't ya?"

Skip feigned a look of surprise.

"Do ya tell the world what ya do for your clients?"

"Only if I have their permission. The practice of law by its very nature involves confidentiality. But with a public figure, like City Manager LaDieux, folks expect transparency. They're entitled to know how and where she gets her services."

"Ya insinuatin' something?"

"Me?" Skip shook his head.

Morelli folded his arms across his huge chest. "Shootin' one's mouth off is a dangerous pastime. Bad things can occur."

"You mean like Squeaky's fate?"

Morelli shrugged. "You said it. Not me."

"But that's what you're thinking."

Morelli failed to respond.

Skip got up from his seat. "So—should I take your remark as a threat?"

"A threat?" Morelli shook his head. "I never make threats." His saccharine tone shifted amidst an icy stare. "But rest assured, I don't take no shit neither." He gestured toward the front entrance. "You, my friend, have overstayed your welcome." He motioned at the door and started in that direction.

Skip followed.

Morelli opened it. As Skip was about to pass through, Morelli said, "Now I know why the members of your profession are known by that nasty name."

Whether Skip's face showed confusion, he couldn't say, but if so, it was real.

"Ya know," he said. "Liars." He spelled the word. "Isn't that the common term for attorneys?"

Skip pressed his hand to his chin. "Could be....Kinda like the way folks in your line of work got their name."

This time Morelli was the one with the puzzled look.

"CON...tractors." Skip stepped out onto the porch. He turned back toward Morelli. "No doubt it comes from the term, *CON man*." Skip smiled broadly.

Morelli glared, just before slamming the door.

———

With his client Lenny Gardner at his side, Skip sat at the respondent's table. Off to the left at the petitioner's table sat Gardner's ex-wife, Samantha, along with her attorney Karl Fuller. A court attendant, the court reporter and Judge Biddleford's confidential clerk rounded out the assemblage. Issues arising out of matrimonial actions were closed to the public.

Skip gazed around the courtroom. The large chamber with lofty ceilings, timber trusses and stained-glass windows evidenced the ecclesiastical influences of its 1880, Victorian-era construction. Skip wasn't particularly religious. He had grown up in a Protestant home where hard work and self-discipline were emphasized. Temperance, on the other hand, was not a byword. Church was not a part of the family's activities. His father, who worked long hours, contended that free time should be spent enjoying lively conversation with real men. He found it at the local pub. He refused to endure the pompous sermonizing offered in the stodgy confines of a church.

A part of Skip was happy to escape the humdrum routine of Sunday morning services. His school friends often complained about them. Nevertheless, Skip had mixed emotions. At times he was even jealous of his chums, worrying that he was missing something. Worse yet, he feared the eternal inferno about which they warned. After school, especially in the winter months, he would occasionally stop in the church about three blocks from his home. At that hour the sanctuary was all but vacant. He would seat himself near the back, though never in the last pew. Sometimes he would read a paragraph or two from a prayer book, but mostly he just sat there. He would always say *Amen* before he left. Why, he wasn't sure, except it seemed the right thing to do.

Seated in the Otsego County Courthouse, childhood recollections raced through Skip's mind. The appearance of Judge Biddleford coming through the door behind the bench interrupted the musings. Along with the others, Skip was on his feet. A motion, one he had made in numerous other cases, was on the docket. Like the past he was virtually certain to lose.

Judge Biddleford seated himself and motioned the others to do the same. He surveyed the parties at their respective tables. "Let the record show that the plaintiff, Samantha Gardner, who was granted a divorce in the action entitled, *Samantha Gardner, Plaintiff, against Leonard Gardner, Defendant,* has petitioned this court to increase support for the minor child from forty dollars to one hundred twenty-five dollars per week. The matter is scheduled for a hearing three weeks from yesterday. In advance of that proceeding Mr. Gardner, through his attorney, has moved that I recuse myself." Judge Biddleford interlocked his fingers, resting his hands on the bench. "Mr. Maynard, on what basis do you make such application?"

Skip got up from his seat. Telling Judge Biddleford that fairness dictated he bow out of a case was always a tricky issue, but the present situation involving a client's sexual persuasion, was particularly so. Calling the Judge a narrow-minded bigot, even with more delicate phrasing, was a disaster waiting to happen. But smoke screens that danced around the issue had little chance. Nevertheless, Skip had decided to try the latter method first. "Your Honor," he said, "my client, Mr. Gardner, lives in the building next door to an apartment where Ralph Squeaky Grimes was murdered. It is possible the two cases may involve a common thread or witness. I'm sure Your Honor would not want information from one case to infect the other." Skip found it hard to believe he was resorting to such a ludicrous argument. "In order to obviate this potential problem, I thought it wise that Your Honor recuse yourself from this matter."

"Mr. Maynard, do you have any specific facts which create a link between this child support issue and the murder of Ralph Grimes?"

"No, but I hoped to avoid any circumstance that might place Your Honor in such an awkward position."

"Your thoughtfulness is certainly appreciated, but I assure you this Court can deal with such an eventuality." Like viscous oil, the sarcasm oozed from Judge Biddleford's tongue. "Mr. Maynard, if by chance the two cases bear a problematic connection—though I doubt they do—I believe *you* are that connection. Perhaps you should ask yourself whether you have a conflict of interest representing both Mr. Gardner and Mr. Morehead."

Judge Biddleford had managed to shift the shoe to the other foot, and in so doing had struck a nerve more tender than he could have imagined. Skip recalled Mickey's concern about Gardner's unwillingness to discuss Squeaky and the murder. Was Gardner's hiring of Skip more than a coincidence? Skip glanced down at his client. Might there be a conflict of interest or, worse yet, something more sinister. Possibilities, but Skip had nothing concrete to indicate Gardner had ulterior motives.

"Your Honor, at this time no facts have come to my attention as would preclude me from representing both clients." "And this Court knows of no reason it cannot handle both cases. That said, unless you have more substantive grounds, I will deny your motion." The real issue, Judge Biddleford's prejudice against gays, begged to be addressed. Doing it was another matter. "Your Honor, may I suggest that this case might better be referred to Family Court where the vast majority of support issues are litigated." Judge Biddleford turned to Skip's adversary. "Mr. Fuller, do you wish to be heard?"

The very fact the Judge had not dismissed the recommendation out of hand was positive, not that Skip had high hopes.

"Yes, Your Honor," said the middle-aged lawyer as he got up from his seat. "We have a date for a hearing of this matter in less than three weeks. If it were sent to Family Court, it would be a couple weeks before we could even appear there. And given the backlog on that calendar, we might have to wait another two months for a testimonial hearing. Such an unnecessary delay would be prejudicial to my client. In addition, Your Honor granted the divorce of these parties. Family Court, unlike you, is totally unfamiliar with the background. Duplication of effort makes no sense when the judiciary already suffers from overcrowded dockets."

Judge Biddleford nodded. "Points well taken." He turned to Skip. "You disagree?"

"With all due respect I believe Family Court would be more appropriate."

"Fine," said Judge Biddleford. "I don't. And that being so, I'm denying your motion."

"Excuse me, your...uh Honor." Skip caught himself just before he referred to Judge Biddleford as your Holiness. "There's another reason we believe recusal is in order."

A disgusted look, a seeming hint of clairvoyance, came over the Judge. "Tell me why."

Skip swallowed hard. The fun was about to begin. "My client, though unrepresented at the time, came to court when his former wife put in her proof for their divorce. I understand that at that time the record included information that my client was gay. I also understand that Your Honor expressed sympathy for Mrs. Gardner while criticizing Mr. Gardner." A glare from the bench confirmed the trouble Skip had anticipated. "Under the circumstances one can only presume that Your Honor has a predilection in favor of Mrs. Gardner and against Mr. Gardner. At the very least there is the appearance of bias. Accordingly, I believe sound judgment, as well as fairness, dictates that you recuse yourself from this matter."

"Mr. Maynard!" Judge Biddleford's voice boomed. "Of all people, how dare you calumniate this Court!" The Judge pointed a menacing finger at Skip. "You, who recently begged this Court's indulgence for an adjournment when you were too intoxicated to proceed. You have the nerve to cast aspersions on this Court." Judge Biddleford took hold of his gavel. The stranglehold with which he twisted it from either end evidenced his rage. "Let me cleanse the record of your distortions. First off, understand that as provided in the decree of divorce, this Court expressly retained jurisdiction, including issues involving support of the minor child. Facts previously adduced are part of the record giving rise to this proceeding. Those facts suggest that your client married his former wife under false pretenses. He undertook a lifelong commitment of marriage when in fact he had a sexual preference favoring men." Judge Biddleford looked over at Mrs. Gardner and said in a softer voice, "Do you think this woman would have married Mr. Gardner and had his child had she known he intended to cohabit with a man?" Judge Biddleford turned back to Skip. "The record in this case is not about the merit or evil of the gay lifestyle. It is about misrepresentation and deceit. My job is to look out for the interests of the minor child. Your client, as a consequence of his dishonesty, has deprived that child of a home that includes both a father and a mother. That, Mr. Maynard, is the record in this case."

You pompous slug. If Skip were at the *Eagle*, he would have voiced the sentiment. But not in the courtroom, especially this one. Judge Biddleford had managed to camouflage his prejudices against homosexuality with a veil of fraud. No doubt when the time for decision came, he would invoke his prejudices and screw Leonard Gardner.

"Mr. Fuller," said Judge Biddleford, "do you wish to weigh in as to my fitness to handle this case vis-à-vis the matters we have just been discussing?"

"On behalf of my client, we see no reason whatsoever for Your Honor to disqualify yourself. On the contrary, as noted earlier, we believe that the interests of justice and the need to avoid undue delay demand that you proceed."

Judge Biddleford nodded. He looked over at Skip. "Motion to recuse denied. Hearing for a modification of support will be held, as scheduled, three weeks from yesterday. We'll conference it a week before." He hammered the bench with his gavel. "This Court is adjourned."

Skip turned to Gardner and whispered. "That was hardly a success."

Gardner shrugged. "What we expected."

The courtroom emptied leaving Skip and Gardner alone.

"Biddleford hates me," said Gardner. "He's sure to shaft me. What do you suggest?"

"As I've said, we should try to settle."

"I understand. But how without any bargaining power?"

"Well..." Skip thought for a moment. "There's always an appeal."

Gardner sighed. "Isn't that drawn out and expensive?"

"Yes, but the threat isn't."

Gardner showed a puzzled look.

"If your ex thinks we plan to appeal, she may be willing to settle."

A smile came over Gardner's face.

"Speaking of settlement," said Skip, "what would you consider acceptable?"

"Given the circumstances, the increase to seventy-five I mentioned in your office would be a Godsend."

Skip started to get up.

"Before we go," said Gardner, "all that stuff about conflicts—you don't have a problem representing me, do you?"

"Not based upon what I know. Of course, if there were a link between you and Squeaky or that case, that could be another matter." Skip looked Gardner in the eye. "You don't know of any connection. Right?"

Gardner glanced off into space as he seemingly contemplated the question. "No."

Skip found himself playing lie detector. Gardner's break of eye contact appeared to be part and parcel of a thoughtful response. Nothing more. But it was also possible that anxiety, an effort to conceal something, was at work. Objectivity told Skip he was overreacting. Cynicism persisted. He said, "Squeaky lived in the house next door to you. What did you know about him?"

"Not much."

The line between cavalier and candid was hard to discern, especially when the imagination was running rampant. "What kind of guy was he?"

"I don't know. Like most any other...I guess."

Skirting the issues was taking him nowhere. Skip decided to be more direct. "Do you happen to know if he was straight or gay?"

Gardner gave Skip a rankled look. "I didn't know him that well." A pique slipped into his voice.

"I didn't mean to put you on the spot."

Gardner shrugged. "I understand. You're doing your job."

Or being paranoid. Skip had no idea which. He said, "Is there anything at all, however minor—a stranger in the neighborhood, unusual noises or anything—that you're aware of regarding Squeaky's murder?"

Gardner hesitated but then shook his head.

Skip wanted to press him further, but Gardner was a client, not an adverse witness on cross-examination. They got up from their seats and headed out of the courtroom. A thin fellow with dyed-blond hair, wearing skin-tight, black pants and a pink shirt, approached them in the hall.

Gardner gave the fellow a hug and then gestured at Skip. "This is my lawyer, Skip Maynard." He motioned the other way. "And this is my friend Darrell."

"Nice to meet you," said Skip, suspecting the fellow might be Gardner's boyfriend.

"Likewise." Daryl turned to Gardner. "In case you didn't hear, the *Yankees* came from behind last night to win in the thirteenth."

"Well..." said Gardner, "it's a long season, and if they don't win the World Series, you'll have to take a high, hard one for the team." He turned to Skip. "Just a little personal bet that Darrell and I made."

A curious mind might have sought more information about the wager between the two flamers. Skip preferred ignorance. He exchanged quick good-byes and went on his way. The duo headed in the opposite direction. Skip glanced back. Lenny Gardner seemed like a nice guy. As a client he was cooperative. Nevertheless, questions gnawed. Had Squeaky's neighbor actually wandered into the office by innocent happenstance? If not, what did he know? And what were his motives?

———

Seated at the breakfast table with a large mug of coffee, Skip unfolded the Sunday edition of the *Oneonta Star*. Coffee and the newspaper had long been a Sunday morning ritual. Across the top of the front page the headline read: *Justice Department Investigates Local Government Corruption.* The banner spurred Skip to forsake his customary practice of first perusing the entire front page. He charged directly into the story:

> *A confidential source indicates the United States Justice Department is looking into the possibility of government corruption in Otsego County. According to the source, area contractor Gino Morelli lies at the center of an investigation that focuses on alleged no-bid contracts and favoritism in exchange for kickbacks, including work done on the private properties of certain unidentified public officials. A former member of Morelli's crew, Woody Wilson, indicates he helped*

with major renovations at the home of City Manager
*Traci LaDieux. Wilson had no knowledge whether
Morelli billed LaDieux for the work. Wilson noted that
ordinarily work done for Morelli's customers was laid
out in a written contract. In LaDieux's case it was
performed pursuant to verbal instructions from the job
foreman. When asked, the Justice Department refused
to confirm whether a probe is underway and, if so,
whether City Manager LaDieux is a target. The
Oneonta Star has filed a Freedom of Information
request with the office of the City Manager regarding
any contracts, whether bid or not, that were awarded
to Morelli over the past five years. A similar request
was also filed with the office of the Comptroller
regarding details of any and all audits of those
contracts. Thus far, both offices have declined to
furnish any information.*

Skip sipped his coffee as he contemplated the significance
of the story. At the very least it provided fodder for additional
smoke screens to create reasonable doubt whether Morehead
was responsible for Squeaky's death. Mickey had described
Squeaky as the kind of guy who would blackmail his mother,
and Morelli had used Squeaky as a phony reference. Perhaps
Squeaky was blackmailing Morelli or, maybe, the City
Manager. Either or both may have silenced Squeaky. Skip
doubted the scenarios, but if properly presented, they might be
enough to make a jury think twice.

The City Manager and Comptroller had both rejected the
newspaper's Freedom of Information request. Were they hiding
something? If so, subpoenas might be the way to go. If called
to the stand, it would be dangerous for the City Manager to
deny Morelli did the work for her, given what Woody Wilson
had said. The key was whether the City Manager could prove
payment from her own pocket. If not, she might be forced to
take the Fifth Amendment. That would be a perfect scenario.
Regardless whether she and/or Morelli were involved with
Squeaky's murder, her refusal at Morehead's trial to answer

questions on the grounds they may be incriminating would make it hard for any jury to convict Morehead.

The old adage about smoke and fire crossed Skip's mind. In this case the Justice Department apparently smelled smoke. Flames would be nice, but they were not a prerequisite. The Constitution demanded that the prosecution prove Morehead's guilt beyond a reasonable doubt. Skip's job, smoke screens and all, was to hold them to that burden. Skip's odds of an acquittal seemed to be increasing. He reached for his coffee and took a drink. The brew, like his enthusiasm, was cool. Try as he did, he could not convince himself that Morehead's confession was coerced. Deep down Skip still believed his client was guilty.

Skip's mind drifted back to earlier days before he was admitted to the Bar. Youthful images that someday he would defend and vindicate the wrongfully accused were magnificent. It was *Don Quixote*, except the quests were real. Like doctors who cured suffering patients, teachers who turned would-be jailbirds into scholars, architects who decorated sterile ground with magnificent edifices, and scientists who unlocked the world's mysteries, Skip envisioned himself doing great things as a trial lawyer. But enabling a murderer to escape justice fell far short of the mark. True, the Constitutional protections were imperative. Someone had to preserve them. Defense, even of the guilty, was important. The logic was impeccable. Why then did it leave him empty? Skip knew the answer. Whatever his foibles, he had a conscience. If his assessment of Harley Morehead's guilt was accurate, defending him was hardly a glorious quest.

Chapter VIII

About ten miles north of Cooperstown Mickey turned west on Route 20 on his way to Richfield Springs. The road, a miniscule section of the highway that was once a main artery from east coast to west coast, had languished. The four-lane, divided byway through scenic valleys and rich farmland was fine, but all along its margins economic stagnation prevailed. Cabins dating from the first half of the twentieth century, most boarded up with peeling paint, hinted at a bygone era when commerce had thrived. Just as the railroads had snuffed out the inns and general stores that had flourished along the banks of the Erie Canal, and the automobile, in turn, had made Route 20 a prime route leaving railroad tracks to show their age, so too, the construction of the New York State Thruway in the middle of the twentieth century had turned Route 20 into a faded vestige.

Mickey wended his way past the aging *Petrified Creatures Museum of Natural History*. With its life-size dinosaur restorations and fossil digs, the museum exemplified how economics, coupled with travel patterns, had dictated the history of the landscape. Like the surroundings Mickey felt his years. As a youngster fascinated by dinosaurs, he had often entreated his parents to stop at the museum. Always on their way to somewhere, the visit was left for another day. That day never came. As an adult Mickey had passed it time and again. He had the time and might have stopped, except digging for fossils, along with the possibility of a souvenir, lacked the appeal of an earlier day. He told himself he had to take his little nephew there. He could still enjoy the experience vicariously. Unfortunately, once again time had slipped by. Little Scotty had grown. He was playing linebacker for a community college football team in the Adirondacks. Just before Mickey reached the turnoff for the road where Woody Wilson lived, he glanced in his rearview mirror. He could barely see the museum's sign. All too quickly, life, like travelers on the east-west corridors of the Leatherstocking Region, was passing him by.

He flipped his right turn signal and headed north about a half-mile on Osprey Road. Apart from a couple of farms, the winding road was all but deserted. He slowed his pace until he spotted a mailbox with the number nine. He turned into a gravel driveway and followed it about sixty yards through a grove of pines to the one-car garage of a small, wood-framed ranch. As he climbed out of his Mustang, he took note of a half-dozen old cars, some without wheels, that decorated the property. It looked like a junkyard. But given its out-of-the-way location and the many trees that obscured it from the rural road, it likely prompted little concern from folks in the community. Mickey ascended the two steps that led onto the small wooden stoop. The floorboards, in need of paint, creaked as he reached the front door and rang the bell.

A minute later a short, skinny fellow, about thirty-five with thinning hair on top and a few days growth on his chin, answered the door. "Can I help you?"

"I'm Mickey Shore. I'm looking for Woody Wilson."

"You lookin' to get your car fixed?"

"Not really. I'm a private detective."

The man, who a moment earlier had appeared ready to open the screen door, hesitated.

"I take it you fix cars."

"Yeah, when they're banged up. Ain't a better body man around these parts. I also do engine repairs, but that's strictly for fun." He looked Mickey in the eye. "But you ain't here to get a car fixed. So, why you lookin' for Woody Wilson?"

"Would you be him?"

"Answer my question first, or we're done talkin'."

Mickey preferred to do things the other way, but the man was already moving his hand to close the wooden door. "My client represents Harley Morehead. He's charged with the murder of—"

"I know—Squeaky Grimes."

Mickey, still unsure to whom he was speaking, welcomed the interruption. Over the years he had discovered that the more he allowed others to speak, the less defensive they became. And the less defensive they became, the more apt they were to open up. "I take it you know him."

"Who? Grimes or Morehead?"

At the moment it didn't matter. Anything to keep the door open. "Either or both."

"Never met Morehead. Don't know him at all. Only know his name from the news. Course, around these parts, even the woodchucks do. Don't get no bigger than a politician charged with murder."

"How 'bout Squeaky? Did you know him?"

The fellow nodded.

"Would you be Woody Wilson?"

He hesitated. "Yeah...but I'm not sure I wanna talk to you."

Not exactly what Mickey wanted to hear, but it was a step in the right direction. "I understand. If I were you, I'd feel the same way. Tell you what. Just hear me out. You'll be free to stop me whenever you want."

Wilson shrugged. "Fair enough." He pushed open the screen door and, with a pronounced limp, led Mickey into a small living room with a threadbare couch on one side and an adjacent easy chair in the corner. Across the way was a television, along with another easy chair and a lamp with no shade. He gestured Mickey to the couch and took the chair near the television.

As Mickey seated himself, he made some mental notes. The slight man with rounded shoulders hardly fit the physical image that Mickey had imagined before Wilson had answered the door. On the other hand, Wilson's manner and speech were four square with the yokel that Mickey had predicted.

"So, what do you wanna know?"

Wilson's connection to Morelli topped the menu, but an uninvited guest with designs on a full-course meal couldn't ask for filet mignon right off the bat. "Whatever you can tell me about Squeaky."

"He wasn't my kind of guy."

Skip had asked Mickey to find out if Squeaky was gay. Whether Wilson was alluding to that or something else, Mickey didn't know. "Whad'ya mean?"

"I didn't trust him none. Always droppin' names of people he claimed to know. Truth was, he was just an ordinary Joe like me. But he loved to play the big shot. That and he was always fishin' for information. I was never sure why. Sometimes it was like he was spyin' on folks."

"Why would he do that?"

"Got me. But a couple times when I was workin' a job and he was brought in as a fill-in, he kept askin' questions about the boss."

"Did he say why?"

Wilson chuckled. "Nope. And when I asked him, he spit some double talk, claimin' he was just makin' conversation. And speakin' of guys who ask questions...odds are, just like Squeaky, you got an angle."

Years of experience had taught Mickey that disagreeing was the bane of detective work. When confronted, an admission could be disarming. "You're right."

Wilson's eyes widened.

"As you know, Harley Morehead is charged with murder. His life is on the line. I'm trying to gather as much information as I can about the murder victim."

"Yeah...so you can pin the murder on some other slob."

"Exactly," said Mickey, once again willing to agree.

"How do I know that someone, the guy you're lookin' to point a finger at, ain't me?"

Mickey swallowed hard. Acquiescence was great, but it had its limits. "From what I know, you didn't have any reason to kill Squeaky. I can't say the same for some others. They're the ones who need to be concerned about pointed fingers."

"You really think someone other than Morehead knocked off Squeaky?"

Mickey shrugged. "Don't really know. But that's what I hope to find out."

"Well...if Morelli or one of his rich pals did it, it wouldn't bother me none if they got caught. Though I never cared much for Squeaky—damn, that voice of his was like a Model T with a twisted piston—he didn't deserve to be sliced into hamburger meat. Permanently lockin' him in a sound-proof booth woulda been enough." For a moment Wilson appeared pensive. "As for Morelli, there's no love lost between him and me."

"You still work for him, don't you?"

Wilson shook his head. "Not since the son of a bitch screwed me."

Mickey waited, hoping Wilson might explain.

"You like a beer? 'Cause I could use one."

Mickey had no desire for a beer. He was dying for a cigarette. The absence of ashtrays or the smell of smoke suggested that Wilson was not a smoker. Verbalizing his craving for a nicotine fix might earn Mickey an invitation to leave. On the other hand, sharing a brew with a guy who wanted one might foster increased chatter. "Kind of you to offer. I'd love one."

Wilson got up and limped to the kitchen. A minute later he returned with two cans of Budweiser. He handed one to Mickey.

"Thanks." He popped the top and took a swig. The cold brew tasted better than Mickey had anticipated. "Hits the spot." He eyed the can briefly. "Let's see. You were telling me about Morelli."

"Yeah." Wilson heaved a sigh as his gaze drifted briefly into space. "Sleep with a pig, and you wake up in crud."

Questions surged in Mickey's head, but he held his tongue.

"Morelli paid me under the table. His idea. Not mine. Of course, stupid here thought it was great. No taxes, Social Security or stuff like that taken out. Who knew I was gonna fall off a ladder. Only about twelve feet, but enough to bust up my knee and hip. Can't do much of what I did before, especially the luggin'. Worse yet, I can't hardly do my auto-body work neither. Fifteen minutes and the pain is awful." He gestured at the yard full of wrecks. "Ain't got no way to earn a decent living. I filed a Workmen's Compensation claim. Wouldn't you know? They bounced me out the door 'cause I couldn't prove I was Morelli's employee. Told me they'd reconsider if I came back with my pay stubs and tax returns." Wilson displayed a disgusted puss. "Fifty dollar bills don't come with pay stubs. As for my tax returns, they ain't gonna prove I worked for Morelli neither." He guzzled a few ounces. "A buddy of mine suggested I go to the police. Thinks they might help me in exchange for gettin' Morelli. I'm thinkin' about takin' the advice, but I ain't sure. If I start screamin', I could have the IRS on my ass. For all I know, I might end up in jail. Maybe they'd give me a slap on the wrist in exchange for Morelli, but who needs that? A criminal record won't pay for no groceries. Hard to know what to do."

"I hear what you're saying." Mickey nodded slowly as he expressed the sentiment as thoughtfully as possible; his motive, however, was to keep Wilson talking.

"You're probably curious why I'm tellin' you all this."

"I'm sure you have your reasons."

"Well...it's 'cause I'm desperate. And seein' as how you're a private detective, I thought you might be able to help. Folks gettin' paid under the table must be nothin' unusual to you. Right?"

Mickey always preferred to ask the questions, but in order to get answers, sometimes he had to trade positions. "Let's just say I've seen it from time to time."

A look, the kind that communicated, *you can do better than that*, showed on Wilson's face. "Did any of those guys throw in their employer to get some benefits?"

Mickey thought for a moment. In his line of work he often came in contact with the underground economy. More than one client had paid him in cash. But he was aware of no instances where anyone had turned around and used such employment as a basis to get public benefits. "Can't say I know of anyone who came forward and made a claim."

Wilson looked him in the eye. "Let me guess. If you were in my shoes, you wouldn't risk it."

As always, Mickey weighed his words, but in this case concern for Wilson was part of the equation. The fellow was down on his luck, and Mickey wasn't about to exacerbate his problems. "I'd be reluctant," said Mickey

Wilson nodded.

"On the other hand, if you have information incriminating a bigger fish—say a public official or, better yet, Squeaky's murderer—you might have a stronger bargaining position." "Yeah, I suppose I would." Wilson hesitated. "Course, if someone linked to Squeaky's murder thought I was gonna finger him, he'd want me out of the way. Given what he done to Squeaky, I doubt he'd hesitate." Wilson raised his can and gulped the remaining contents. He squeezed it crushing it into an hourglass frame. "Workmen's Compensation benefits would be real nice, but stayin' alive ain't chopped liver."

The comment had Mickey wondering if Wilson knew more about Squeaky's murder than he had thus far let on. "You've got a point. Of course, the sad part is a fellow, no matter what he knew, would be in danger if the killer thought he was wise to something and apt to talk."

"Yeah, I suppose so," said Wilson, peering stolidly into space.

Mickey waited patiently hoping Wilson might yield more.

Wilson mumbled, "A little knowledge could get a guy whacked. But it also could get him a pile of dough." He looked at Mickey inquisitively.

"Depending on the knowledge, that's a pretty fair assessment."

Suddenly Wilson got up from his seat. "It's been nice talkin' to you."

Mickey did a double take. Patience had gotten him little, and time had become an evanescing luxury. He said, "What do you know about Squeaky's lifestyle?"

Wilson failed to react.

"Did he have a girlfriend...or maybe he preferred guys?"

"Don't know. Don't care." Wilson headed for the door.

Mickey followed. "If you don't mind, I have some other questions."

Wilson looked back and, revealing a wry smile, nodded. "I suspect you do." He leaned against the door frame. "Well—at the moment, I can't say I care to hear them."

"Maybe just a—"

Lips taut, Wilson held up a silencing hand. "Got a fender that needs fixin'." He gestured toward the front yard. "Gonna

hurt my knee to work on it, but if I wanna eat, I better get to it."
He swung the door open.

"Could you—" This time Mickey cut himself off.

A stone-faced Wilson was refusing eye contact.

Mickey stepped out onto the porch. "I appreciate your talking to me. Perhaps we can do it again. I'll give you a call. And next time I'll bring a six pack."

Wilson hesitated. "Better yet. You got a card?"

Mickey took a business card out of his wallet and handed it to Wilson.

"You never can tell. I might call you."

The possibility was welcome, but waiting with no guarantee still came up short. "If I don't hear anything, can I contact you in a couple of days?"

"What the hell. It's your nickel. Course don't expect nothin'." Wilson closed the door.

Mickey stood motionless for a few seconds before reaching into his pocket for his pack of *Camels*. He lit up even before his first foot struck the unpaved ground adjoining the porch. Unlike the dromedary that could roam the sands for days without a drink, Mickey couldn't store up his nicotine. An hour without a cigarette was like a trek across the desert without water. But the analogy ended there. Where a dehydrated hike demanded a copious intake to alleviate the distress, one drag, fully inhaled, coupled with the security of more between the index and middle finger, instantly eased the physiological affliction of a smokeless hour. Mickey ambled to his Mustang and climbed in. Just before pulling away, he looked back at the house. Intuition convinced him that Wilson had information concerning Squeaky's murder. Some might have termed it a hunch. Not Mickey. Expensive lessons sixty miles to the northeast at the betting windows at *Saratoga* had taught him that hunches were unreliable. Intuition was different.

———

Estate citations filed in Surrogate's Court, Skip headed out through the Courthouse lobby. Just as he reached the main entrance, a familiar voice called from behind.

"Skip, if you wait a second, I'll walk you out."

He stopped and held the door open as Kelly Lang hurried to catch up. "How've you been?"

"Good, other than a crazy morning."

As he followed her into the sunshine, he gestured down the street. "I'm on my way to the *Eagle*. Can I buy you lunch?"

She gazed skyward and muttered to herself, "Files in the office won't walk away just because I eat." She looked back at Skip. "Don't mind me. I always talk to myself. But it doesn't do any good. I keep running the rat race. And yes, I'd enjoy having lunch. Not that you'd be dining alone if I passed up your offer."

"If you're referring to Loomis, this hour of the day, he's awfully busy what with noon-hour traffic and all."

She shook her head. "I wasn't referring to Loomis. I meant your other pal, the one from the back hills of Tennessee."

Skip got the message. It stung. But he couldn't blame her. Back when they had dated, he had often referred to *Jack* as his friend. More than once he had told Kelly how *Jack* had been there in the long, dark days after Megan's death. Worse yet, Kelly had seen first hand how *Jack* ruled Skip's life. The smooth guy in the bottle had drowned their romance.

"Sorry," said Kelly, her voice sheepish. "That was a low blow, especially given your invite."

"Apologies unnecessary. You were only parroting things I've said myself." His eyes met hers. She appeared as uncomfortable as he felt. The possibility that friends and colleagues viewed him as an alcoholic was painful. Even Loomis had recently chastised him. He wondered what others in the community said behind his back, especially following the recent inebriated episode in court. His thoughts remained introspective as he and Kelly walked to the *Eagle*. Her arm brushed against the sleeve of his suit jacket. He felt an urge to take her hand, not that he seriously considered doing it. Perhaps if *Jack* had been along for the stroll and calling the shots, Skip might have. As they arrived at the *Eagle*, he reached for the large brass handle of the tavern door. The fragrance of her perfume enhanced his senses. He guided her to

David A. Weiss

a booth on the far side about equidistant from the entranceway and his usual barstool. The familiar spinning seat may have been perfect for *Jack*. Kelly, on the other hand, deserved a table.

A minute later Mary, a long time waitress at the *Eagle*, came their way. Greetings exchanged, she focused on Kelly.

"What can I get you to drink?"

"A glass of Chablis."

"One Chablis and a *Jack Daniel's* on the rocks coming up."

"I think I'll have an iced tea," said Skip.

Mary did a double take. "You feeling okay?"

"Yes...fine."

"Then iced tea it is." Mary hurried on her way.

"It's because of what I said earlier, isn't it?" Kelly's reticent tone matched her abashed expression.

"Not at all. I would have ordered iced tea regardless." However, had Skip planned to order *Jack*, her earlier remark would have given him second thoughts. Two was a couple. If *Jack* joined them, the old adage would have rung true. Lunch at their table would have become very crowded.

"If I knew you were ordering iced tea, I probably would have opted for a *Diet Coke.*"

"Then I'm glad you didn't know. You should have what you want."

"Well...to tell the truth, after the morning I had, I can use a little wine. Don't get me wrong. I enjoy practicing law, but some days—exhibit number one, today—I could do without."

"I know what you mean." His response, however, rather than mirroring her attitude, reflected nothing more than distant recollections. The days when only occasional frustrations interrupted a profession he loved were distant. Dulled emotions, stifled motivation and lethargy had supplanted enthusiasm. Much of the time he merely went through the motions. He said, "Assuming it's not confidential, you want to talk about your morning?"

"I'm happy to talk. The question is whether you can stomach my griping."

Their drinks arrived. She took a sip.

135

"So, tell me what happened."

"Well...I was back in front of Biddleford again."

"Say no more." Skip looked around to be sure no one was within earshot. He lowered his voice. "His Holiness can spoil anyone's day. What did he do this time?"

"The bastard—excuse my French—screwed up my vacation."

"How'd he do that?"

"I represent a lady charged with shoplifting. The DA wanted a misdemeanor plea and a fine. My client says she's innocent. So, I set the matter down for trial. Naturally I asked for a jury. Biddleford got pissed. He told me he has more important things to do than try a misdemeanor involving three dollars worth of cosmetics."

"Let me guess—his comment came outside the courtroom."

She nodded. "In chambers. And he didn't say it in so many words. He told me if my client wanted a trial, that was her right. But the look on his face, not to mention the sarcasm in his voice, made it clear he wasn't happy. The next thing I knew he docketed it for three weeks from today. I had already told him I'd be out of town that week. I was planning to visit my sister in New Mexico. I purchased my airline tickets four months ago."

"Couldn't you prevail upon him to pick another date?"

"I tried, but Biddleford wouldn't—" Kelly cut herself off as Mary came and took their food orders. Once she had left, Kelly continued. "When I reminded him about my trip, he began shuffling some papers. He reconfirmed the trial date without even looking at me. Pete Harper, the Assistant DA, tried to jump in on my behalf. He suggested we could try the case a couple of weeks later. Rather than go along, Biddleford pointed at me and said, *The defendant has a Constitutional right to a speedy trial. Far be it from me to trample on the defendant's Constitutional rights.* Of all people, throw-away-the-key Biddleford, pretending to be concerned about Constitutional protections."

Ordinarily Skip was not a great listener when people carped. His nature, as well as his training as a lawyer, prompted him to play devil's advocate. That, plus he didn't care for whining. But when it came to the robed buffoon, the vent was welcome.

Kelly lifted her narrow-stemmed wineglass and gazed analytically at the contents. "Compassion and equity mean nothing to that man. Worse yet he lacks judicial temperament. How did he ever become a judge?"

Though the question was rhetorical, Skip couldn't let it pass. "Politics. That wonderful game where *whom* you know counts more than *what* you know. And just for the record, when it comes to gray matter, His Holiness is hardly a heavyweight. And as long as we're on the subject of the creep..." Judgment, one of Skip's strengths, so long as *Jack* wasn't in control, counseled that he curb his tongue.

"C'mon, don't leave me hanging. I had a rough morning. A little trash talk will do my heart good." Kelly flashed a beguiling smile.

Judgment melted under the rays of her persuasive look. "Between you, me and the time-worn timbers that support the ceiling here, I don't trust the fat windbag any farther than I can throw him."

"You think he's on the take?"

Candor forced Skip to weigh the question rather than simply vent. "I guess not, at least in the usual sense. On the other hand, he takes care of his friends. If he likes you, he bends over backwards to go your way. If he doesn't—guys like me fall into the latter category—he screws you to the wall."

Kelly gestured at herself. "If this morning is any indication, I'm in the latter category too."

"Let me guess. You don't contribute to his campaign fund."

"Why should I?" She plunked her wineglass down. Had she rapped it any harder, the stem would have broken.

"You shouldn't. I don't either. But that's not the point."

Amidst a puzzled look her pique was evident.

"You remember Charlie Landers?" said Skip.

"Only to say hello. He retired about seven or eight years ago. Right?"

"That's the guy. Well...a few years before he retired he gave me some friendly advice. He recommended I send a check to Biddleford's election campaign committee. Though he remained circumspect when I tried to pin him down, I got the message: Those who give do a whole lot better than those who don't. And as Charlie pointed out, in a rural area like Otsego County where judges are few in number, being on the wrong side of even one is an inevitable disaster."

Kelly leaned back, her hands interlocked behind her head.

Skip grabbed for his iced tea before her ample magnetic charms snatched hold of his gaze.

"So, why didn't you take Charlie's advice and contribute?"

Skip had asked himself the same question loads of times. A part of him saw it as a matter of principle. But there was another reason, perhaps more important. He said, "I'm too stubborn to kiss his fat behind. And apparently, you're the same way."

She chuckled. A slight nod accompanied the laugh. A moment later her face grew thoughtful. "I hear what you're saying, but one thing doesn't add up. Biddleford gives everyone a hard time. How do you explain that?"

"He's a bitter, brooding curmudgeon who lives alone in his big, old Victorian house. I doubt he has any real friends. As for a wife, that's an impossibility. A woman foolish enough to marry the likes of him doesn't exist. He's—" Skip clipped his tongue just long enough to focus on Kelly's question. Over the years he had watched his Holiness, and together with Loomis, his amateur psychiatrist, Skip had developed what he considered an accurate analysis of the surly jurist. "He's your quintessential Napoleon, constantly trying to build himself up by putting others down. Up on his little throne, wearing his black robe, he treats everyone with disdain. Lawyers, witnesses, jurors, clerks, stenographers—to him they're all nothing more than jackstraws."

"Agreed. But doesn't that contradict your theory about favoritism?"

Skip had anticipated the question. Thinking ahead, with an eye to fine distinctions, was what had made him an excellent lawyer, at least when he was prepared and sober. He said, "In court, Biddleford belittles everyone. Come decision time, he does right by friends and shafts the rest."

Kelly nodded slowly. "You know...that's a pretty fair assessment." She hesitated. "Have you ever considered bringing him up on charges?"

Skip laughed.

"What's so funny?"

"Hell, if I did, they'd be more apt to sanction me. Recent history bears that out."

"You...referring to the day you had too much to drink?"

"Exactly."

Kelly's silence confirmed he had made his point. Their food arrived. Skip was picking at his fries when he felt a tap on his shoulder. He looked up and saw Harley Morehead.

"You got a moment?" Morehead's tone was acerbic. He gestured to the corner across the way.

Skip got up and followed his client there.

"Real sweet, finding you here fraternizing with Squeaky's attorney."

Technically Kelly was the attorney for Squeaky's estate, but the distinction was hardly consequential.

"Perhaps you're helping her plan strategy for her wrongful death lawsuit."

"C'mon, you know that's not the case."

"Do I?" Morehead looked Skip in the eye. "I'm not blind. The chick is hot. And this isn't the Courthouse."

Skip resented the sarcasm, as well as the innuendo. While lunch at the *Eagle* with Kelly, especially a cozy one with wine, might arguably create some semblance of a possible conflict, Skip would have debated the point had not their attorney-client relationship included his drunken courtroom fiasco. He could ill-afford additional issues, legitimate or not, regarding his fitness. He said, "I hear what you're saying."

"You damn well better!"

Skip eyed the booth where Kelly waited. "I'll pay my check and go."

139

"Do that." Morehead stormed over to a booth on the far side of the tavern, one occupied by a good-looking chick twenty years his junior.

Skip seethed, irked by the idea that Morehead, while complaining, could fraternize with whomever he pleased. It had been a long time since he had kowtowed to a client. A year before when he had represented a demanding blowhard in a divorce action, he had told the jerk to take a hike. Morehead was demanding and, at times, a blowhard. But Skip's earlier indiscretion, one that had occurred in open court, had put him in a tough position. If Morehead, armed with the transcript of proceedings and statements of disinterested spectators, went to the lawyers' fitness committee, Skip's license to practice would be in jeopardy. He reached for his wallet as he shuffled back across the room. His job had just grown tougher. Arrogant clients were always hard to control, and one who held the upper hand would be especially difficult.

———————

Skip stepped through the doorway of City Manager Traci LaDieux's office. The buxom blond shook his hand and ushered him in.

"Nice digs," he said, as they seated themselves on either side of her desk.

She glanced around the large office almost as if she were discovering the place for the first time. "I suppose, but it comes with all the headaches." She looked him in the eye. "Can you believe our twentieth reunion is coming up?"

High school. In some ways it felt like eons earlier. Still it was hard to imagine that two decades had slipped past. "Back then, did you ever imagine you'd be City Manager someday?"

For a moment her face bore a distant look. "Not really. Of course, it was a different time. A woman lived in the kitchen with a string of pearls around her neck. You know, like the *Beaver's* mom. What's her name?"

"June Cleaver."

"Good memory. Then again, you were always good with names and dates and stuff like that. Seems to me they voted you most likely to succeed...or some such thing."

"Actually, it was most likely to be a professional, whatever that meant." Skip avoided the temptation to mention that the City Manager was voted, though only by the guys and not in the yearbook, most likely to have a baby without knowing the father.

"Ah...those were the good old days. Football games, cheerleading, dances and beer. But damn, just when you get used to it, they give you a bunch of responsibilities and force you to get old."

"Beats the alternative." The instinctive cliché turned Skip's stomach. A moment's thought conjured a familiar refrain, one that made him question the old saw. Might it have been better if he, not his beloved Megan, had been the one jogging the day the hit-and-run driver had struck and killed her.

"How's your law practice?"

Doubtless she knew his office was upstairs over the *Pantheon Pizza Parlor*. Location, location, location. "I can't complain." The insipid comeback echoed in his ears. Ordinarily Skip was not one to react without thinking. In part it was his legal training, but mainly it was his nature.

"So, what brings you here?"

"As you no doubt know, I represent Harley Morehead."

"Yes...but what's that got to do with me?"

Telling her he was interested in rumors that she may have gotten a kickback from Morelli in the form of free work was a bad idea. "Well...you and my client, both being politicians probably travel in the same circles."

"Hardly, given that we're in different parties." A smug look appeared on her face.

Playing cute wasn't going to work. Traci LaDiuex was a politician. Most everyone who came through her door had an agenda, and she knew that. He said, "Did you by any chance know the victim, Squeaky Grimes?"

"A little bit. But from what I've heard, he made it his business to know anyone with money or status."

Skip's urge to point out that he didn't know Squeaky was quelled by a reluctance to label himself a nobody. "I hear that Squeaky sometimes worked for a contractor named Morelli. Did he ever do any work for you?"

"Might have."

Though her tone lacked the edge indicative that Skip should mind his own business, there was still the possibility she was sending that message. "What can you tell me about Squeaky?"

"Not a lot. Except one thing sure...Squeaky Grimes was a leech."

Skip recalled that Mickey had referred to Squeaky as a parasite. Apparently he was not alone in his evaluation. "You think it was just a case of wanting to rub shoulders with important people?"

She shook her head. "Nah. He always had ulterior motives. Most were designed to make a fast buck. As a matter of fact, it was work for your client that got Squeaky into the pyramid scheme business."

"Work for my client? Pyramid scheme?" Though Morehead had mentioned that Squeaky was involved with a pyramid scheme, Skip preferred to play dumb. "What are you talking about?"

LaDieux rolled her big brown eyes. "C'mon, don't tell me you didn't know your client was a bookie and Squeaky, his runner."

"That ridiculous rumor." Skip did his best to dismiss the accusation, not that he thought it false.

"Hey, believe what you want."

Playing the credulous fool for the sake of his client rankled Skip. He said, "So, what's this pyramid scheme stuff?"

"As I said, Squeaky was a runner. He hung out at the OTB. Not only did he like the ponies, but what better place to drum up suckers. Easier than finding bubbles in a brew. With the offer of better odds, folks were happy to move their action to Morehead. Anyway, OTB is where Squeaky hooked up with Jimmie Raines and his wife Tammy Lee. Pretty soon the three of them went into the flimflam business selling distributorships

David A. Weiss

called *Artway.*" LaDieux hesitated, appearing to study Skip. "You've got something on your mind."

Her reaction was no surprise. His feigned show of perplexity had invited it. "Now that you mention it, I do. You know an awful lot about Squeaky."

LaDieux laughed.

Skip scratched his head, strictly for effect. "Did I say something funny?"

"Frankly, yes. But then again, back in high school, especially in old lady Whipple's class, you had quite the sense of humor."

His mind diverged with recollections of the countless times his unsolicited quips had brought levity to the study of biology. Of course, Whipple had a different view, and several times she had communicated it with an award of detention.

"Where was I?" said LaDieux. "*Artway* and—"

"Not exactly." Skip was not about to let the artful politician duck the issue. "We were discussing how familiar you were with Squeaky."

"You're right. We were," she said. "I hardly knew the bird until he began soliciting me to become a distributor. The guy had chutzpah. And talk about persistent. To him the word *no* meant *maybe*. Or perhaps even *yes*." She heaved a sigh. "But if that wasn't enough, he sicked Jimmie Raines on me too. Like me, Raines belongs to the Leatherstocking Club. This past spring he corralled me in the grill room there and asked me to play with him in the mixed member-member best-ball tournament. Stupid me said okay." Her face bore a look of disgust. "Damn, if the creep didn't start with *Artway* on the first tee. Eighteen freakin' holes, five hours, he hocked me to sign up. Let me tell you, Raines and Squeaky—I know them both." She chuckled. "Let me correct that. I *know* Raines. I *knew* Squeaky."

The comprehensive answer compelled Skip to reassess his earlier surmise that she had dodged his question about Squeaky. He said, "So, what is *Artway*?"

"You interested? Cause I can arrange—" She flashed her long, sexy eyelashes his way. "Only teasing." She leaned back. "*Artway*, just as I said, is a pyramid scheme. Their product is paintings, the kind churned out by starving artists and sold at places like the *Holiday Inn.* "

Skip had seen pyramid schemes before. He had even been approached. But the weird, new angle was hard to figure. "Don't tell me they turn five-dollar canvases into million-dollar masterpieces."

"Not quite, but...I'll explain. Raines and his wife rounded up about forty initial recruits, some of them local. The rest were from places like Albany, Utica, Little Falls and other cities in upstate New York. They even have a few on each coast of Florida and a couple in Massachusetts. Each of these initial recruits paid five thousand dollars for ten paintings, along with a franchise as a certified *Artway* dealer."

Five thousand dollars for ten worthless paintings made no sense to Skip. "What's in an *Artway* franchise that someone would pay that kind of money?"

"You really wanna know?"

The cockamamie scheme was weird enough to intrigue Skip. "Yeah."

LaDieux rotated her chair toward an adjacent file cabinet. She took out a sheet of paper. "Give me a moment to refresh myself. It's been a while since Raines hit me up." After a brief hiatus she continued. "It works like this. Each of the initial franchisors has the right to buy future paintings for one hundred dollars apiece. No franchisor may sell a painting for less than five hundred dollars."

"Who in their right mind would pay five hundred dollars for—" The image of the humongous white canvas with one black dot that Skip had seen years earlier on the wall of the *Guggenheim* forced him to bite his tongue.

"I wouldn't give you two cents, but the painting isn't what's really being sold."

The explanation left Skip more puzzled than before. "Run that by me again."

"Franchisors are buying tax deductions. They become *Artway* dealers. Their homes become art galleries. They hang the paintings in their homes, especially spare rooms and basements. They deduct about half of their living expenses—heat, electricity, telephone, lawn maintenance, you name it. The same with their car, restaurant expenses and even vacations."

The logic, if one could call it that, bordered upon the absurd. "Just how do they deduct vacations?"

"Wherever they go, they carry photographs of their paintings, along with their business cards. A siesta poolside becomes a business meeting, an attempt to make a sale to a would-be customer. The amazing thing, if you can believe Raines, the paintings sell. Regardless, the franchisors enjoy huge tax deductions year after year."

Questions about how the Internal Revenue Service would react were bubbling forth in Skip's head. Before he could explore them, LaDieux continued.

"But here's where the franchisors really make out. Using the lure of tax deductions, they sell their paintings. Every painting bears an *Artway* seal on the back. Once an individual has purchased five thousand dollars of *Artway* paintings, he automatically becomes a franchisor entitled to buy certified *Artway* paintings from Raines for a hundred dollars apiece. Remember—the paintings can't be resold for less than five hundred dollars."

Skip's legal mind was spawning issues such as illegal restraints on alienation and anti-trust price-fixing, but pyramid schemes were always on the edge. The contrivance was wild, but it was also ingenious.

"If a newcomer to the game can find just two new recruits, he's ahead of the game. And after that it's almost all gravy. All the while he's writing off the high life on his tax returns." She winked at Skip. "Tempting, isn't it?"

Artway, like LaDieux, was. Both were sexy. Both also had all the earmarks of fatal appeal. Look, but don't touch. Skip said, "The trouble with every pyramid scheme is there's always a sucker at the bottom who gets left holding the bag. In this case…paintings."

"True…there's always that risk when one buys an expensive painting. But even then, Raines has a silver lining. The sucker can donate the piece of junk to charity and take a tax deduction for what he paid. You know what they say, *Beauty is in the eye of the beholder.*"

The adage did nothing for Skip. Her underlying point was harder to dismiss. The person donating the painting could back up the deduction by showing he actually paid that amount for it.

"The amazing thing," said LaDieux, "assuming you can believe Raines, is that a couple of the no-name artists who do his paintings are becoming cult masters. Their works are selling for big bucks. In the meantime, *Artway* people are raking in the dough."

Fascinated though Skip was, he realized the canvas was getting lost beneath impressionistic brush strokes. He said, "Why would someone like Raines take Squeaky on as a partner?"

"I asked Raines the same question. If I'm not mistaken, it was on the fourth fairway." With a nauseated expression LaDieux shook her head. "What a way to spend a day on the links. Anyway, Raines didn't solicit Squeaky."

Skip felt his brow furrow. The reaction, unlike an earlier one with guile, was spontaneous.

"Squeaky came up with the idea. While he may have known lots of people with money, the kind needed to make the scheme work, he lacked the credibility. Folks knew he was a low life. So, he pitched Raines, a flashy dude with a gift for gab and a little larceny in his blood. With Squeaky that last item was always a prerequisite."

"Interesting," said Skip, his mind on a tangent. Although LaDieux didn't buy into *Artway*, her relationship with Squeaky seemed more than casual. Did that imply she possessed the prerequisite? Skip pressed the notion back into his memory bank and refocused on the broader issue. "So, what's your take on how Raines fits in with Squeaky's murder?"

LaDieux jerked back. "Hold the phone. My money is on Morehead. The guy confessed, and that's good enough for me." She thought for a moment. "On the other hand, if I were in your shoes, I'd check out Raines. Squeaky definitely got on his nerves. At least a half dozen holes, especially on the back nine, Raines badmouthed Squeaky. Not that it was surprising. Backstabbing is hardly a shock with two guys both capable of screwing their own mothers."

146

Skip waited a moment to see if she might share more. When she didn't, he said, "Is there anything else you can tell me about Squeaky?"

She took a deep breath as she leaned back and stretched, perhaps to evaluate the question.

If this were still high school biology class, Skip would have had no doubts as to her purpose. Drawing the attention of her male classmates was among her favorite pastimes. Regardless whether she was employing the old technique, her move drew Skip's eyes. Her translucent silk blouse provided a provocative wrapping, and just enough unlatched buttons to reveal ample cleavage.

She said, "Squeaky may have been small of stature, but he always had his eye out for big things."

At that moment Skip did too.

LaDieux smiled.

Had her gaze been at him, rather than empty space, Skip might have interpreted it as a come-on. "Whatcha thinking?"

"Oh...nothing."

He shook his head. "Definitely something. The question is what?"

She shrugged. "Just high school and..."

"And?"

She remained pensive for several seconds. "Oh...what the hell. I was thinking back. I would have liked to go out with you, but you never asked me out."

At the time he hadn't considered it because he assumed she preferred older guys. He said, "Gosh, had I known, I certainly would have." His reaction was more than a polite response. Hell, if she were anywhere near her reputation, a good time certainly would have been had by all.

"Too bad. We may have missed a good thing."

The fact an earlier opportunity had been wasted didn't dictate a repeat performance. They could make up for lost time. Temptation enticed Skip. But it wasn't going to happen. Not then. Not while he was defending Harley Morehead. She had managed to point potential incriminating fingers in various directions. But she had links to Squeaky. She also had ties to Morelli. Embarking on a relationship that had conflict of interest written all over it was a dilemma Skip would have to forgo, at least for the present. He said, "You never can tell what the future might bring."

"You never know." Her wry smile appeared as provocative as his earlier musings.

He smiled back, but his thoughts were less sunny. *Life wasn't fair.* An instant later Skip chuckled to himself. Mr. Ames, their history teacher, may have had the same reaction years earlier. Like the guys in the class, Mr. Ames was known to steal a peek at Traci. But as a teacher, a relationship with a student was *malum prohibitum*. Then again, there were rumors about Mr. Ames. Maybe he got luckier than Skip. The possibility was tantalizing. Skip got up. "I've taken enough of your time. I appreciate your seeing me, Your Honor."

"My pleasure, Skip. But please, it's still Traci." Her luring eyes bore more than a polite RSVP.

As he left, Skip smiled again, more warmly than before.

Chapter IX

The moment Morehead entered the office, Lucy buzzed Skip. His instructions were to interrupt him, even if busy. After the scene at the *Eagle* a couple of days earlier, Skip was determined to present his best side. Rather than have Lucy show Morehead in, Skip went out to the reception area and greeted him personally. He ushered Morehead into his office and directed him toward the pair of easy chairs in the corner.

"So, what's up?" said Morehead, as he plopped his rotund body into a seat.

"I got a call yesterday from Mickey Shore, my private investigator. He's got an interesting lead. He tracked down this fellow, Woody Wilson, a yokel from the sticks not far from Richfield Springs." Skip caught what appeared to be a reaction from Morehead. "Do you know Wilson?"

"Can't say as I do." Morehead delivered the reply with a deadpan. "So, did your investigator make some earth-shattering discoveries?"

"Not really. But he thinks Wilson knows something about Squeaky's murder."

"Does he think Wilson killed him?"

"Not really...though he hasn't ruled that out. He says Wilson worked for Morelli. Wilson also knew Squeaky. How well...isn't clear."

An inscrutable look appeared on Morehead's face.

"What's the matter?"

"I don't get it. What makes Shore think Wilson knows something?"

"An uncanny knack for reading people, coupled with the fact that Wilson dropped a few hints. Unfortunately he clammed up and shuffled Mickey out the door."

149

"Any idea why?"

"Wilson is in tough financial straits. He's got a bum leg and apparently can't work. Mickey figures he wants to trade what he knows for a payoff." Skip waited to see if Morehead might bite at the possibility. He didn't. "Mickey suspects Wilson is exploring his options, perhaps hoping to cash in on the most fertile opportunity."

"What do you plan to do?"

"That's why I had you come in. I was hoping you knew something about Wilson that could improve our bargaining position."

Morehead shook his head. "So, now that Plan A flopped, brighten my day with Plan B."

The tone, even more sarcastic than the comment, underscored that bygones were not quite bygone, not that Skip was surprised. He said, "At my behest Mickey is gathering information about Wilson. With a little luck, he'll unearth something to improve our bargaining power."

Whatever Morehead was thinking, he displayed no enthusiasm.

"If it doesn't work out, I could always subpoena Wilson to testify at trial, but—"

"Jesus. You don't have to tell me. That would be a goddamn crap shoot."

"Exactly."

Morehead's look of disgust punctuated a groan.

Skip needed to spin the situation more favorably. "I know you have concerns, but I think you're focusing on the negatives. We've found someone who seems to have some information relevant to your case. Up to now that was hard to come by. Ferreting out what he knows may be tough, but just locating him is a step in the right direction." The logic was excellent, except there were no guarantees Wilson knew something. Worse yet, there was always the possibility that Wilson might incriminate Morehead.

"Well—I suppose." Morehead frowned. "And this is why you wanted to see me?"

Skip nodded.

Morehead got up, his goodbye hardly a rousing farewell.

"Karl Fuller for you on line two," said Lucy over the intercom. "He's calling on the Gardner matter."

"I'll take it." Skip was happy to hear from Fuller. It offered an opportunity to discuss a settlement without appearing too anxious. "Hello Karl. How you doing?"

"Other than being swamped, okay. But you have your own problems. You don't need to hear mine. The reason I'm calling—I've got a little complication in the Gardner case."

The concern in Fuller's voice was welcome, not that Skip wished Fuller anything bad. In fact, Skip liked Fuller. He was a straight shooter and a genuinely nice guy. But an adversary's difficulties could provide leverage, and leverage was critical when negotiating.

"My brother's daughter is getting married out in Colorado on the morning after we're supposed to have the support hearing. I forgot all about it. My wife booked our flight for the day before, but I never put it on my office calendar. I need an adjournment."

Skip was more than happy to oblige. No doubt Gardner would be ordered to pay increased child support. Delaying that increase could save Gardner money, though the order might be made retroactive to the proceeding's commencement. "Have you run it by Judge Biddleford yet?"

"He hard-timed me but finally said okay, provided I got your consent. He's taking three weeks off the beginning of August and suggested the 28th at one-thirty."

Skip checked his calendar. "Works for me, but I'll have to check with my client and let you know. In the meantime, as long as we're on the phone, you want to discuss the case?"

"Always willing."

Skip waited a moment, hoping Fuller might initiate some discussion. He didn't. Skip said, "So, tell me, what does your client want?"

"A hundred twenty-five dollars per week."

"C'mon, that's what her petition says. But what does she *really* want?" In countless prior cases Skip had been down the same route. Whether it was a support issue, a liability claim or anything else involving dollars, neither side was willing to bid against itself. That is where an effective judge could mediate. By talking to the lawyers one at a time, the judge could press the lawyers with the weaknesses and risks of their cases and learn their bottom lines. With proper massage, he could enable the parties to reach common ground. Unfortunately Biddleford was ineffective, and, worse yet, Skip didn't trust him, especially in non-jury situations like support hearings. Biddleford was renowned for bludgeoning settlements with thinly veiled threats of adverse decisions. Skip said, "My client thinks the forty he's currently paying is more than fair."

Fuller chuckled.

"But if Mrs. Gardner would indicate a willingness to accept a modest increase—say five dollars per week—I'd talk to my client about it."

"She might take a hundred to get it resolved, but don't waste your time offering nickels and dimes."

Progress. Discussions, which on their face had seemingly showed no potential, had begun. "From what I understand, your client would really like to avoid the agony of a contested hearing." Skip had nothing more concrete than the knowledge that most people had little stomach for courtroom battle.

"Whatever she may have said to her former husband, push come to shove, she'll be up to the task. I assure you. And the way I see it, Lenny will be the big loser. If what we hear is true, he can afford the increase. Word has it his hair dressing business is doing very well."

"He's doing okay, despite increased expenses." Skip was thankful that the liberal, pre-hearing financial disclosure requirements adopted in some jurisdictions were yet to come to his part of the State. Regardless, he knew the hearing would demonstrate that Gardner's net income had grown significantly.

"We'll be glad to take our chances in court. I may be wrong, but, my guess, your client's lifestyle may play a part. Not in the written decision perhaps, but the mental process that leads to it."

Fuller had played his trump card. The last time they were in court, the homophobic Biddleford had hinted that he had no sympathy for a gay man who would wed an unsuspecting woman. Gardner had privately expressed his willingness to up the child support to seventy-five dollars per week. That provided considerable leeway, but Biddleford was likely to pick a much larger number. "Talk to your client, and see what she's willing to do. I'll do the same, and I'll get back to you about the August 28th hearing date."

"Sounds good. And before you go, one more thing. The last time we were in front of Judge Biddleford, when you asked him to recuse himself from the case, you mentioned the Grimes murder. Do you think Lenny Gardner—and I don't mean that he's involved—has a link to those who are?"

Fuller's question may have been innocuous, but Skip didn't see it that way. From the outset he had wondered if mere coincidence had led Lenny Gardner, Squeaky's next door neighbor, to hire him. Admittedly Cooperstown was a small village with few lawyers, and Lenny needed one. But too often seeming coincidences were more than serendipity. Skip said, "Knowing you as I do, Karl, your question didn't come from nowhere. You have something specific on your mind, don't you?"

"Uh...not really."

Skip wanted to probe. The impediments were manifold. Without a judge to compel answers, aggressive questioning, the kind used in the courtroom on cross-examination wouldn't work, particularly on an experienced lawyer. Regardless, Skip had no idea what, if anything, he was fishing for. "Did your client know Squeaky?"

"Nope. In fact, I asked her right after we argued your motion to have Judge Biddleford recuse himself."

"Did she indicate whether *my client* knew Squeaky?"

"No offense. But since when does my adversary interrogate me about conversations with my client?"

The point was indisputable. Unfortunately that detail did nothing to alleviate concerns that Lenny Gardner might bear a link to Squeaky Grimes and/or the circumstances surrounding his murder. "I understand what you're saying," said Skip, "but if there's—"

"Stop right there. I don't intend to be interrogated, not when I owe a duty of confidentiality to my client."

"An attorney also has duties if he has information relating to a crime."

"Excuse me!" A snarl had replaced Fuller's normally cordial voice. "Are you insinuating—"

"Sorry," said Skip. "I...I was totally off base." Skip knew lawyers whose integrity he would have questioned without apology. No way did Karl Fuller belong on that list. An aspersion suggesting otherwise, especially one not grounded upon any evidence, merited rebuke.

"Enough said. Consider the issue closed."

Ordinarily Skip preferred to do business face to face. He was glad they were on the telephone. "I'll check with my client about the adjournment. I don't expect a problem. I'll get back to you."

"Great. And we can talk more about the case."

"Good enough. And once again, I apologize for—"

"Don't even mention it. I understand. Defending a murder case is no afternoon at *Doubleday*. You take care."

"You too." Skip hung up the receiver. He reached for his *Rolodex* and looked up the number of Lenny Gardner's hair salon. He confirmed his client's willingness to postpone the court appearance. He dialed Fuller. He was with a client. Skip left a message with his secretary okaying the request for an adjournment. The immediate action helped mitigate remaining embarrassment. He stared at Lenny Gardner's file as he laid it aside. Possible links to Squeaky Grimes's murder were probably nothing more than Kafkaesque handiwork of Skip's imagination. He had no evidence, the coin of his realm, to support a contrary verdict. On the other hand, the legal system was far from perfect. Juries were known to be duped. Lawyers, as well.

Just before entering, Skip eyed the big, gold-lettered sign emblazoned across the front of *Prime Printing*. The gaudy emblem besmirched the striking brick, *Georgian* edifice. How perverse that the structure had fallen into the hands of a philistine like Morehead. The image of Skip's own digs upstairs over the pizza joint flashed into his mind. There were pangs of jealousy, but he had no one to blame other than himself. Choices he had made, among them *Jack,* had him practicing law from a second-floor walk-up rather than posh offices.

Bells jingled as he stepped through the doorway.

Morehead looked up from behind a large press. "To what do I owe this unexpected surprise?"

"I was in the neighborhood." The statement was true, but there was also an ulterior motive.

"Give me a sec." Morehead pushed a couple of buttons, and the big machine he had been operating halted. He motioned to a small office along the rear wall. They went into the Spartan room and seated themselves at the art-deco table and chairs.

"What's up?"

"Back when we first talked, you gave me the names of a few people to check out, individuals who might have had it in for Squeaky. Among them you mentioned Jimmie Raines."

Morehead perked up. "You got something on him?"

"No."

As fast as enthusiasm had bubbled, a dour puss appeared.

"You said he runs some type of pyramid-type business. I understand its called *Artway.*"

Morehead laughed.

"Did I miss something?"

"Nah. Just that the word, *Artway,* stirs memories that makes me reach for my *Tums.* One day at the *Leatherstocking Club,* Raines tried to sell me on *Artway.* The son of a bitch called to play golf. We no sooner reached the first tee than he began his freakin' pitch."

For Skip the scenario echoed a familiar refrain.

"This past season he's gained a reputation. No one wants to play with him, not that they were all that anxious before."

"I take it *Artway* didn't interest you."

"Jeze! Why would I buy into a pyramid scheme when I've got a viable printing business. I told Raines no way on the first hole. Unfortunately his ears were like a vacuum hose, two openings with nothing in the middle. He went on and on. And for the most part he was selling nothing more than tax deductions. What do I need with an art business in order to get tax deductions?" Morehead gestured toward the main room beyond the office. "I've got all the tax deductions I want." He lowered his voice. "And between you and me, I milk them for all they're worth."

Hoping his client might proceed on a stream of consciousness, Skip waited.

"Let me guess. Raines invited you to play at *Leatherstocking?*"

"Nope."

"Consider yourself lucky. The day he hooked up with me, I shot over a hundred. Exactly what I couldn't tell you 'cause I stopped keeping score long before I hit two in the water on the seventeenth. Me—a twelve handicap shooting triple digits on my home course. God, I wanted to jam my wedge up his ass. I coulda killed the jerk." Morehead studied Skip for a second. "What's the matter? You don't play golf?"

"I...I play a little. But that's not why I reacted. Remarks about killing someone is far from recommended when you're charged with murder."

"Jesus! Give me a break. It's only a..."

"A figure of speech?"

"Yeah."

"Well, a figure of speech like that can get you into trouble. Just imagine if someone heard you say that about Squeaky. Wouldn't that make great testimony for a jury?" Skip gave Morehead a hard stare. Making an impression on the cavalier client was never easy. "And speaking of Squeaky, I assume you know he was involved with *Artway.*"

"*Artway.* If I hear that name one more time, I'll puke. In the grill room at the *Club* you hear it more than golf. The few dolts who have bought into it are as bad as Raines. It's all they know. As for the rest of us, we're left to bitch how some *Artway* asshole screwed up our game."

Skip gave Morehead another look.

"What's your problem now?"

"You didn't answer my question." Whether the puzzled look that greeted Skip's eyes was feigned, Skip couldn't tell. "Did you know that Squeaky was involved with *Artway*?"

Morehead thought for a moment. "Yeah, I heard that he and Raines were partners. Of course, Raines didn't make a big deal of it, not with his ego. It's bigger than Otsego Lake. Hell, to hear him talk, you'd think the *Golden Bear* would need strokes if they played a match. Raines, a freakin' fifteen handicapper…and he'd be a few strokes higher but for his sharp pencil."

"Sharp pencil?"

"The bastard cheats!"

Skip was finding it hard to keep the conversation on point. "Didn't Squeaky ever approach you about *Artway*?"

"Why would he when Raines was already on my case?"

In the courtroom Skip would have moved to strike the non-responsive answer and demanded a *yes* or *no*. He said, "How well did you know Squeaky?"

"As I told you before, I knew him. He knew everybody. But he wasn't my buddy."

"You know, some folks claim he worked for you as a runner."

Morehead rolled his eyes.

"What now?"

"You. I shoulda known. You're back on that kick again. Checking me out for bookmaking." Morehead shook his head. "Let's get it straight, once and for all. Squeaky may have been a runner, but it wasn't for me. Folks may have thought he worked for me on account of my prior record. For all I know, Squeaky could have claimed he did."

"Why would he do that?"

"How should I know?"

Skip had anticipated the answer. He had used those exact words more than once back in junior high when old lady Burgess wanted to know why Skip's buddy Clint wasn't in class. Back then the answer was a dodge. The identical possibility existed now that he was on the receiving end. But unlike junior high, where Burgess ultimately confronted Clint,

Skip lacked that same luxury. Squeaky was permanently indisposed.

———————

Mickey pulled his Mustang into the driveway at Woody Wilson's home. Since his previous visit, he had telephoned three times. Each time he had left a message. Wilson hadn't returned any of them. It was possible that Wilson was out of town, but given the way he had clammed up the last time Mickey had gone to see him, Mickey was betting that Wilson was avoiding him.

As he climbed out of his car, Mickey surveyed the scene at the out-of-the-way location. The afternoon sun was dipping lower in the sky, but darkness was still a few hours away. Mickey climbed the stoop. He listened attentively, trying to ascertain if there were sounds inside...music, a television or someone walking around. Apart from the caw of a crow somewhere in the pines, all was still. Mickey pressed the doorbell. He waited. No answer. He leaned his ear to the door as he pressed the bell again. He heard it ring. Again he waited. And again, no answer. He pulled open the screen door and rapped hard on the wooden door. Still no answer. He stepped off the porch and began circling the house clockwise. He peered through the base of the living-room window, but apart from furniture saw nothing. He continued around to the back of the house. The small windows there were too high for him to look in. He proceeded around the corner where, peering through the window on the far side of the garage, he observed a green *Chevrolet*. Inside the vehicle Wilson was seated in the driver's seat. Mickey watched him for several seconds. Wilson sat motionless. Mickey rapped on the window. Wilson neither responded nor moved. Mickey rapped again. He called out. Wilson remained silent and still.

Mickey sniffed the air for fumes. There were none that he could detect. He watched for another minute. He rapped again, harder than before. Wilson looked like a zombie. The possibility of suicide or even foul play crossed Mickey's mind. He went around to the rear door of the garage. It was locked.

Discretion told him not to jimmy the door. He had a habit of ignoring discretion, but intuition, a bad feeling, sent him back to his Mustang and his car phone. The device was one of his few luxuries, though he justified it telling himself that in his line of work it was a necessity. Regardless, the expense was worth it, if only for the reactions it evoked. And Mickey milked it for all he could. When questioned about the uncommon technology, he would say it was an *AT&T IMTS, Improved Mobile Telephone Service, using UHF 454/459 MegaHerz radio frequencies.* Then he would add, *a darn side better than Radio Common Carrier's AMPS.* He had memorized just enough jargon from an article, along with the literature that accompanied his car phone, to come across as well versed. Mickey dialed the technological toy and notified the police what he had found.

Minutes later a patrol car with lights flashing and siren sounding pulled into the driveway. Once the officer climbed out, Mickey showed a business card identifying himself as a private detective. As he directed the officer to the window at the side of the garage, he said, "Fifteen minutes, and Wilson hasn't moved a muscle."

The officer peered in and watched for the better part of a minute. He called out, but there was no response. "I think we need to go in."

Mickey gestured toward the back of the garage. "There's a door at the rear. Although it's locked, it looks like an easy access."

The officer went to his patrol car and got a crowbar from the trunk. Along with Mickey he went around to the back door. A couple of skillful yanks of the crowbar and the door opened. The officer went directly to the car and tapped on the driver's side window. "Sir, are you okay?" There was no response. The officer opened the door and examined Wilson. He turned to Mickey who had waited a few steps away. "No pulse. He's dead." The officer took several deep breaths. "Air seems okay, but carbon monoxide is odorless." He opened the garage door and then climbed into the vehicle from the passenger side. He said, "The key is in the *on* position." He checked the dashboard. "But the fuel gage is on empty." He reached over and turned the key, cranking the engine. The car failed to start. "No gas." He examined Wilson more closely. "From what I can see, at least at first blush, there's no evidence of trauma. Looks like it might be a suicide."

"Apparently so." Mickey's words differed from his thoughts. There had already been one murder, and his conversation with Wilson several days earlier had convinced Mickey that Wilson knew much more than he was willing to share.

"Be right back after I radio for assistance." Minutes later the officer returned. He checked the tailpipe and all around the vehicle. He looked inside the car. He spent a minute or so examining the glove compartment. "No note, at least none that I see. Of course, the house might prove otherwise." He circled the garage, stopping for several seconds at a workbench adjacent to the rear door. He removed the keys from the ignition and unlocked the trunk. "Paintings."

From his position adjacent to the driver's side, Mickey stepped to the back of the vehicle to get a better look as the officer leafed through the several canvases. There were a couple of landscapes, a floral bouquet and a man playing a violin. Each canvas had a cardboard encasement that covered the entire back but only the four corners of the front. On the upper left hand corner of each encasement, printed in bold letters, was the word, *"Artway."*

"Not bad," muttered the officer. He looked at Mickey. "Any idea if the fellow might have been an artist?"

"Got me. Didn't know anything about him." Mickey remained as circumspect as possible. He was trying to imagine why Wilson would have *Artway* paintings. Sure the fellow worked with paints, but the kind used on cars. A pyramid scheme like *Artway* hardly seemed to fit with a guy like Wilson. It was possible that physical problems had made him desperate, but Mickey didn't buy the explanation.

The officer spent a few more seconds checking the trunk. He turned to Mickey. "What brought you here?"

For Mickey, one who viewed his business like chess, a game focused several moves ahead, it had only been a matter of *when*, not *if*, the question would be asked. "I wanted to speak with him."

"You knew him?"

Discussing a case was something Mickey ordinarily avoided, but being present at the scene of a dead body modified the usual ground rules. "No. I spoke to him for the first time just a few days ago. I wanted to talk to him again."

The officer appeared to scrutinize Mickey. "You want to tell me why?"

Not really. The truth was a bad answer, unless Mickey was prepared to take a ride with the officer down to police headquarters. "I'm doing some investigation in regard to the Squeaky Grimes murder. I wondered if Wilson knew anything about it."

"What made you think that?"

Mickey was determined to provide as little as possible. "I understand that Wilson knew Squeaky. I hoped Wilson might be able to provide some information."

"Who you working for?"

Once again, refusing the officer's inquiry was a bad choice. He said, "Skip Maynard."

"Oh...Morehead's attorney."

Mickey could see the wheels spinning inside the officer's head. What he was thinking, however, was impossible to discern.

A moment later another police cruiser, along with an ambulance, pulled into the driveway. The officer greeted the new arrivals and then returned to Mickey. "You can go. We'll take it from here." He pointed at Mickey's Mustang. "Is that your car?"

"Yup."

"Loop it around on the grass, and you'll be able to get out. We'll be in touch."

Mickey went over to his car and climbed in. He preferred to stay and see what the police found. Unfortunately the invitation to leave was an offer Mickey wasn't free to refuse. He drove off, turning onto Route 20 and then south towards Cooperstown. Several minutes later he pulled into the lot of a long-vacant diner. He sat for a minute just to be sure he hadn't been followed. He dialed Skip and let him know what had transpired. He jotted a few notes while matters were fresh in his mind. Though he had talked with Wilson just once, Mickey, who prided himself on his ability to judge people, was convinced that Wilson wasn't the type to take his own life. Add the *Artway* paintings in the trunk, and the picture hardly looked like suicide.

Skip seated himself at a table near the front window of Oneonta's *Off Track Betting* establishment. He had chosen the location because he could observe any cars entering or leaving the parking lot. Mickey had given him a good description of Jimmie Raines and his wife Tammy Lee, but their yellow Corvette convertible would be even easier to spot. According to Mickey's information they were Friday-night regulars.

Though the ponies had never appealed to Skip, he needed to give the appearance that he was there to play. Unlike the track where bettors often chose a horse because they liked the name, most at *OTB* were serious handicappers. They didn't come to simply gaze at beautiful thoroughbreds on a big television screen. They were there for the action. Forty minutes before the first race at *Belmont*, Skip put two dollars on the favorites in the daily double and another two on the favorite to place in the second race. He also bet a long shot, *Megan's Pride*, five dollars across the board in the seventh race. Odds were by the time the seventh rolled around, Skip would be back home. The possibility of winning a few dollars was neither here nor there. If by chance he did, the proceeds would go to the local soup kitchen. Back when she was alive, every Thanksgiving Megan and he helped there serving meals to the homeless. The first year after her death Skip thought about continuing the tradition but found it too painful. He needed to find other ways to preserve Megan's memory. For a time he laid bouquets next to her gravestone. The abundance of flowers that dotted the cemetery made the gesture all too commonplace. Megan was unique and spontaneous. Gradually

David A. Weiss

Skip gravitated to more impulsive tributes. Such was his bet on *Megan's Pride*.

Skip ordered a draft beer, along with a bag of pretzels. The alcoholic beverage, the first in several weeks, was for appearances only, at least that's what he told himself. The very fact he eschewed *Jack* proved the point. A part of him knew he was playing with fire. The logic almost convinced him to dump the brew in favor of a *Pepsi*. But the ability to have a beer, just one beer, was indicative of control. An alcoholic lacked control. Ergo, discipline could prove Skip was not an alcoholic. Admittedly the purported syllogism was grounded in spurious logic, but it sounded good. It was also familiar territory. As a lawyer Skip often handled difficult cases armed with nothing more than arguments that sounded good.

He sat back and focused on the parking lot. Roughly thirty minutes had elapsed when a yellow Corvette pulled in. Any question whether it might be someone other than Jimmie and Tammy Lee was erased the moment the bottled blond with bouffant hair and low-cut top opened the passenger-side door. As the duo entered the establishment, they were greeted by several other patrons. They seated themselves at a table along the wall adjacent to Skip's back. He got up from his seat and strolled over near the betting windows. After a brief look at some television screens, not that he was interested, he meandered back to his table. He seated himself on the opposite side of his booth so he now faced them. His improved view did nothing to prove the old maxim that opposites attract. Jimmie was arguably as garish as Tammy Lee. Several gold chains, one of which bore a large medallion, circled his neck. A purple sport shirt unbuttoned nearly to the level of the table revealed a hairy chest. His long, slicked-back hair was as shiny as his black, patent-leather shoes.

Skip focused on his race program stealing an occasional glance at the couple. He allowed them time to settle in and place a drink order. Tammy Lee got up from her seat and headed down the hallway that led to the ladies room. Skip seized the opportunity and headed over to their table.

"Excuse me," he said. "Aren't you Jimmie Raines?"

The fellow looked up. "You got it."

"I'm Skip Maynard. I understand—"

"Catch you in a couple. It's gettin' close to post time." Jimmie squeezed out of the booth and hurried to the betting windows.

Skip debated whether to return to his own table but decided he had a better chance of conversation if he stayed close to Jimmie's drink.

Several minutes later Jimmie returned. "Didn't mean to give you the fast shuffle, but I got a good one at *Pimlico.* Easy money." As he slipped into his seat, he motioned Skip to the other side of the booth. "So—Skip Maynard, what do you want with me?"

"You know who I am?"

"You told me your name, didn't you? Anyway, I know who you are. I saw you on TV coming out of the Courthouse. You represent Harley Morehead."

Skip nodded.

"Can I buy you a drink?"

"Thanks, but I got one." Skip motioned to his own table.

"So, what's up?"

"I understand you run *Artway*. It sounds like something that might interest me. I'd like to get the lowdown."

"That so." Jimmie glanced to his right. "Tammy, we've got company," he said, as his wife approached. Sliding over to make room for her, he added, "This is my wife Tammy Lee."

Skip stood up, as much as his position in the booth allowed. "Skip Maynard. Nice to meet you," he said, as he shook her outstretched hand.

"Mr. Maynard is interested in Squeaky." He looked Skip in the eye. "Isn't that right?"

"What prompted—"

Jimmie turned to his wife. "Mr. Maynard was—"

"Skip...please call me Skip."

"Like I was about to say, Mr. Maynard here wants to find out what we know about Squeaky's murder."

Tammy Lee's eyes, decorated with long, artificial eyelashes and extensive black makeup, widened.

Skip glanced in Jimmie's direction.

The flashy forty-something bore an insistent stare.

"Well," said Skip, "let's just say I'm interested in both *Artway* and Squeaky."

Jimmie looked at his wife again. "Our friend here represents Harley Morehead. Says he wants to talk to us about *Artway*. As a lawyer with his own office, no doubt he already has more tax deductions than *Churchill Downs* has horse manure." Jimmie refocused on Skip. "So...just what is it you want to know about Squeaky?"

"I understand you were partners with him."

"Dear," said Tammy Lee, "Charlie said we should refer any questions to him."

"Relax. Just because I encouraged him to ask, doesn't mean I intend to answer." Jimmie turned to Skip. "Case you didn't figure already, Charlie...Charlie Hagadorne is our lawyer. He warned us to be on the lookout for vultures like you."

Cocksure and obnoxious, with a gift for gab. It fit the image Skip had formed the instant Jimmie had climbed out of his Corvette. It went with the car, jewelry and bimbo he called his wife. But Jimmie was proving even more insufferable than Skip had imagined.

"So...have we talked enough about Squeaky and *Artway*?"

Disclosure that Jimmie and Tammy Lee were represented by counsel hindered Skip's ability to delve into what they knew about Squeaky's death. He said, "As far as I'm concerned, the subject is closed."

Jimmie leaned over to his wife and whispered, but loud enough for Skip to hear. "If you believe that, he'll find you a long shot that's a sure thing." Raines winked at Skip. "C'mon, make me look good."

Skip reached into his pocket and pulled out his win, place and show tickets on *Megan's Pride*. He said, "Seventh race...M*egan's Pride*. But keep it under your hat. Otherwise, before you know, the odds will drop from forty down to ten-to-one."

A puzzled look appeared on Jimmie's face.

"Something the matter?" said Skip.

"Common sense says any tip from you is a candy-coated cow chip. But you dropped three fins on that mare's nose. You really got some inside information?"

Skip struck a sober pose. "I wouldn't put fifteen dollars on just any lady. I can assure you, Megan is a lady. A very special one." Skip winked. "You can take that with you to the betting windows."

Jimmie shrugged. "You never can tell. I might."

"Any tips for me?" said Skip.

"Well...I suppose one good turn deserves another." Jimmie leaned back. "Tell Morehead he should get his affairs in order. 'Cause dollars to daffodils, he'll be behind bars until the day they dig his grave."

Skip remained impassive as he shifted his focus to Tammy Lee. "Your husband seems awfully sure. Makes a fellow mighty curious as to what he knows."

"That's too bad," she said. "Because one thing sure, he certainly won't tell you."

Skip shook his head. "I beg to differ. As a matter of fact, I suspect you'll both rethink today's reticence." He got up squeezing his way out of the booth. From the corner of his eye he caught a glimpse of the sneers that painted the faces of the tacky twosome. Just as he began to walk away, he looked back and, drawing on an aphorism he had uttered before, said, "Funny thing how a subpoena can turn taciturn turkeys into garrulous gobblers." He pulled a business card out of his pocket and tossed it onto the table. "Have Charlie Hagadorne give me a call once he changes your mind."

————

"Don't worry. I'm not gonna light up." Mickey slipped a *Camel* between his lips.

"You ought to give them up." With one hand Skip pushed his *No Smoking* desk sign directly in front of Mickey, gesturing at the cigarette with his other. "They're bad for your health."

"Look whose talking." Like a ventriloquist, Mickey managed the remark and the cigarette at the same time. "Alcohol isn't a whole lot better."

Skip was tempted to point out that apart from a single beer at the *OTB*, and that was for appearances, he had been on the wagon for a month. The risk that he, like most inebriates, would revert to the bottle kept him from voicing the boast. "Let's talk about everything you've learned so far."

Mickey removed the cigarette from his mouth, but not before he feigned a drag. "For a nobody Squeaky was quite a guy, amazingly adept at attaching himself to people with money and prestige who didn't need to give him the time of day. He had a clever technique. He looked for an angle, something he could do for them. Once he leeched on, he gathered information. Mainly he searched for skeletons, the kind he could use as leverage. Pretty soon the little parasite had power over the big fish. The more I've talked to folks, the more I've caught the hang of his *modus operandi.*"

"You think one of those big fish may have killed Squeaky because he was blackmailing them?"

"That's my guess."

"Anyone win the gold statuette for most likely?"

Mickey hesitated.

"Hard to pick anyone in particular?"

Mickey shook his head.

"So...what's the problem?"

"You won't like the answer."

"Morehead?"

Mickey nodded. "No offense, but he's my odds-on favorite."

Skip might have debated the point, except his money was on Morehead as well. "Let me modify my inquiry. If you were on a jury and knew everything you do, would you convict Morehead?"

"Nope. I've got doubts. Lots of them."

At that moment it was exactly what Skip wanted to hear. Whether Morehead was innocent or guilty, the foundation for an acquittal was being laid. At other times, when he was alone, especially late at night, Skip had pangs about the great abyss that divided justice and reality. Too often he had seen the guilty walk free. And worse yet were the innocent who had been convicted. The criminal justice system, like the people it served, was a paragon of imperfection. Unfortunately no one could offer a better alternative. But sitting there with Mickey, trying to plan a defense, esoteric questions regarding flaws that taint the system were as relevant as qualms about war for a soldier in the midst of a raging battle. As an attorney Skip's job was to ensure that Morehead, even if guilty, enjoyed the full breadth of constitutional protections. The prosecution, using only competent evidence, bore the duty of proving every element of the crime beyond a reasonable doubt. "So, take me through the various candidates."

Mickey reached into the vest pocket of his tartan plaid sport shirt and pulled out a slip of paper. "Here we go—alphabetically…sorta. City Manager Traci LaDieux. A hot broad who could beguile a eunuch with her charms. She likes life in the fast lane. No doubt political favoritism is her stock and trade. Graft is even a good possibility. Murder, on the other hand, seems out of her league. Of course, that's not to say she might not be in bed, both figuratively and literally, with the killer." Mickey glanced at his paper. "Bernie Feinstein. A part of me says rule him out, but a little voice in the back of my brain refuses."

"You think our dear Comptroller is capable of murder?"

"Not really, but…he's much too defensive. And then there's the matter of Squeaky's big diamond. I'm certain Feinstein knows more about it than he lets on. Let's not forget he was Squeaky's landlord." Mickey's gaze drifted into space as he tapped his unlit *Camel* on the arm of his chair. "Buddy Kileen," he murmured in an expressionless voice. He repeated the name and then laughed.

"Why the reaction?"

"I can't figure the son of a bitch out. He seems to do okay with his insurance business, but he's much too tight with our detective friend Ramsey. A buddy of mine spotted the two of them drinking in a little hole-in-the-wall outside Worcester. As I previously mentioned, more than one of Kileen's clients with connections to Squeaky had accidents that were investigated by Ramsey. And always with the same injuries, neck and back."

"Could be a coincidence," said Skip, playing devil's advocate.

"Yeah, and apples falling to the ground, rather than the sky, might be as well." Mickey eyed the ceiling and shook his head. "I'll bet on gravity."

"Why would Kileen kill Squeaky?" Once again Skip was playing provocateur.

"The same reason anyone on the list may have—extortion. Squeaky may have looked and sounded like a mouse, but let me tell you, he was a rat."

Would he risk jail time? This time Skip kept the question to himself. The authorities were quick to give parasites like Squeaky immunity in exchange for testimony that netted bigger catches. He said, "Larceny is one thing. Murder, another. Like LaDieux, Kileen hardly seems the type."

"That may be. But I'm not sure I'd say the same for Ramsey. He's a cop from the old school. What my Uncle Sean—may he rest in peace—used to term a thug with a badge."

Skip recalled the decision of the Appellate Division throwing out a confession Ramsey had obtained in a prior case. Maybe Ramsey was a rogue cop. If he and Kileen were staging phony accidents, who better than Squeaky to find characters willing to fake them. But what if Squeaky wasn't satisfied with his share of the pie. He'd blackmail God for the chance at a buck. Ramsey and Kileen wouldn't head off to prison without a fight. Killing Squeaky and framing Morehead for the crime was not out of the question. Skip said, "See what else you can find out about Kileen and Ramsey."

"Already on my agenda." Mickey went to his list again. "Morelli. Now there's one tough bastard. I know he was paying people under the table to avoid Workmen's Compensation and unemployment taxes. Wilson told me that."

"You think he may have killed Wilson?"

"Don't know, but I'd bet two cartons of *Camels* that Wilson didn't commit suicide. The fact that it looked that way doesn't mean a damn." Mickey held up his crib sheet. "If I had to pick a winner of the *Most Likely to Murder Award* from the clowns on my list, Morelli would win hands down. Rumor has it his late father had Mafia ties. Sonny boy learned from papa. If Wilson or Squeaky even thought about crossing Morelli, they were dead meat." Mickey eyed his list again. "Jimmie

Raines—a gambler who lives way beyond his means. A big talker with a taste for fast cars, glitzy jewelry and big boobs. His slicked-back hair may shine like a thoroughbred after a workout, but underneath beats the heart of a yellow chicken. Around his neck there's lots of gold, but inside there's no brass. Jimmie Raines didn't kill Squeaky."

"Tammy Lee?"

Mickey's eyes widened. "Frankly, I hadn't considered her. But don't get me wrong. At best she's a long shot." He pointed the coffin nail he held in the fingers of one hand at the list he held in the other. "I didn't even put her on the program." He shook his head and muttered to himself, "Getting sloppy in your old age, Mickey." He snatched a pen from Skip's desk set, jotted a note and then looked up. "So, where would you put your money?"

If Skip were a betting man, Morehead would still be the favorite. The sentiment was best left unvoiced. Regardless, there was a more salient point. He said, "We've got a lot of ponies in this horse race, enough that the District Attorney will have a tough time convincing a jury that Morehead is a sure thing."

"Even with his confession?"

"Even with—" Skip heaved a sigh. For a while the telltale document had faded into the back of Skip's mind. The reminder gave him second thoughts. On summation, just before the jury retired, the District Attorney would remind them. Indeed, he would probably read the confession to them one more time. Like all juries, they would be loath to let a killer walk. Morehead still faced a harsh reality.

Chapter X

His real estate closing at the *Oneonta Savings Bank* completed, Skip stepped out of the venerable building. He no sooner started down the street then he stopped to take note of the structure's large cornerstone—1902. Apparently there was a time several generations earlier when folks in upstate New York still appreciated the transcendent architecture of ancient days. Skip moved his gaze upward along the broadly fluted Doric columns that led to the emblature beneath the gabled roof. The edifice reminded him of the *Temple of Poseidon* at Paestum, Italy. The recollection radiated warmly from Skip's brain to the tips of his extremities. Architecture was for his eyes what music was to the ears of a devotee of Motzart's symphonies, what Braille was to fingers of a blind lover of the written word. Styles and techniques intrigued him. Often he made connections, some symbolic, between architecture and other facets of life that most people could never have contemplated. With the *Oneonta Savings Bank* the symbolic link was especially strong. Less than a year before the hit-and-run driver had taken Megan's life, she and Skip had journeyed for four weeks from London to Paris, south through the Swiss Alps, west to the French Riviera and then south again through Florence and Rome and finally, Paestum. They had spent three days basking in the beauty of the Tyrrhenian Sea before returning to Rome for their flight home. Four glorious weeks, never to be recaptured except with isolated memories. None was better than the late afternoon visit to the *Temple of Poseidon.*

Skip closed his eyes. He could feel the caress of the setting sun and, even more so, the caress of his beloved Megan. For an instant she was back in his arms. For an instant he was whole again. He opened his eyes. The *Oneonta Savings Bank* wasn't the *Temple of Poseidon*, but the divide between them was far narrower than the vast Atlantic waters that lay between.

Skip stepped off the curb into the street to gain a better view of the frieze that adorned the wall beneath the gabled roof. As he did, he caught his toe and stumbled. He managed to maintain his balance using his rarely carried attaché case as a support. The jolt brought him back to reality. He gave the building one more look. In a short time he would be back in his office upstairs over the *Pantheon Pizza Parlor*. With its prosaic storefront it was light years farther from the *Temple of Poseidon* than the *Oneonta Savings Bank*. True, the owner had personally decorated the restaurant with murals of impressive Italian structures and scenes, but his artistic talents bore no similarity to his culinary skills as a master pizza maker.

Skip glanced at his watch—12:07. Difficult years had taught him that one must settle for what was available, not that he had reconciled himself to the proposition. Back at the office Lucy wouldn't have taken her lunch break yet, and she loved the *Pantheon's* pizza. Skip did too. He went to his BMW and, using his mobile car phone, dialed the *Pantheon* and ordered a fourteen-inch, mushroom and pepperoni pie with anchovies on just one half. What Lucy saw in the salty fish, he had no idea. Regardless, with all she did to make the office run smoothly, not to mention putting up with him, it was the least he could do.

Once back in Cooperstown, Skip picked up the pizza, along with two sodas, diet for Lucy and regular for himself. If cola had to replace *Jack*, he could at least have high test from time to time. He headed up the long staircase at the front left corner of the building. The moment he entered the office, Lucy looked up from behind her reception desk. Eyes wide, she drew in a deep breath. "I smell pizza."

"Damn," said Skip, "are the odors from downstairs creeping up through the floorboards again?" He motioned her to the small room to his right, a combination storage area, kitchenette and Xeroxing station.

"Don't you want to go over the mail first?"

"Not really."

172

David A. Weiss

"I'll bring it with me," she said.

The seemingly insignificant phrase underscored her dedication and value. The practice of law was a minefield with potential malpractice lurking at every step. Skip had learned the lesson the hard way just one year into his practice. A man came in with an automobile accident case, a minor fender bender. He signed a retainer agreement hiring Skip. Investigation, including a police report and the statements of two disinterested eyewitnesses, revealed that the client, contrary to his initial interview, had run a red light. Skip called the client and told him he had no case. He considered the matter closed. A few years later, just after the statute of limitations to sue had expired, the client called to see how his case was progressing. Skip reminded him of their conversation. The client denied it had taken place. Skip had no record to substantiate his position. The client threatened action with the lawyers' disciplinary committee, along with a malpractice suit. It didn't matter that the client's original accident claim had a minuscule chance of success. From all appearances Skip's failure to sue within the allotted time had deprived the client of a day in court. Having taken the case, no matter how bad its merit, Skip was obligated, unless the client signed off, to see he got his chance to be heard. To avoid a conflict of interest, Skip had the client select another lawyer who determined the high-end value of the case assuming the client prevailed on the issue of liability. Skip paid the client that amount, seventeen hundred dollars, plus the fee of the other lawyer. All that for what was likely a phony backache.

More than once since coming to work for Skip, Lucy had saved him from a similar fate. She had set up a special diary. Every morning she would check it for statutes of limitation, orders requiring service of papers, compliance with the rules of practice, and other matters with time requirements. Lucy was a secretary, but she knew more than most paralegals, and none were more conscientious. A guy like Skip, especially one with a friend like *Jack*, was indeed fortunate to have a secretary like Lucy. Skip knew it and did all he could, much more than pizza, to express his appreciation.

173

He finished chewing a bite. "How'd you do in your bowling league last night?"

She shook her head. "I'd rather discuss the mail than my 327 triple. Didn't even break a hundred the last game."

"Fine. What have you got?"

"The proposed deed for the Hilliard closing came in. There's a curious restriction that runs with the land. You'll want to look at it. Oh...and Karl Fuller called you on the Gardner case."

"Hopefully he wants to talk settlement." Like a jack-in-the-box, the voice of his high school English teacher popped up in Skip's brain. Whenever he misused the word *hopefully*, which he often did, her chiding voice was there to highlight the error.

"He didn't say." Pizza in one hand, Lucy thumbed through the mail with the other. "Most of this is neither here nor there." She held up a letter. "*Prudential* offered seventy-eight hundred on the Koznecki case."

"Get Eddie in. He'll be thrilled. In the meantime, I'll see if I can squeeze out a few extra bucks for him."

"Jasper Redwine's reckless driving charge is scheduled for next Wednesday over in Cobleskill. I put it in the book." She continued shuffling papers. "You'll love this last one, not that it's of any consequence. The *Committee to Re-elect Judge Harold Biddleford* is soliciting campaign contributions."

"That slimy son of a bitch."

With a wry smile Lucy shook her head. She held the paper out so Skip could see it. "The Committee, their names are listed on the left margin, not Judge Biddleford, is making the request. According to the letter the Committee is certain that all members of the Bar will want to contribute in order to perpetuate, in their words, *Judge Biddleford's extraordinary judicial talents.*"

"Extraordinary. They make me sick." Skip pointed at the remaining slices of pizza. "Even those damn anchovies are a helluva lot more appealing." He took the letter and eyeballed it. "His Holiness has some nerve."

"We get similar letters from the committees for all the judges."

"True, but other jurists, unlike Biddleford, stay out of it. A couple years back, just after I had finished conferencing a case in his chambers with Elmer Woodbridge, Biddleford patted Elmer on the back and, loud enough for me to hear, said, *I want you to know how much I appreciate your generosity.* He did everything but say he would go out of his way to repay the favor."

Lucy gave Skip an odd look. "Any chance you might contribute this year?"

Skip, who had never put a dime in the jurist's coffers, was unsure whether the question was rhetorical. He bit hard on a thick crust. A contribution might make life easier. "I don't know," he said. He chewed the thick dough. "Damn it. I don't know."

A few minutes earlier the clock on the mantle of Skip's office had struck seven. It had been an exhausting Monday, one that had begun earlier than usual. He had finally finished the motion papers he had been working on. Though another meal of pizza was hardly what he wanted, had he not insisted that Lucy take the two remaining slices home with her, he probably would have opted for them. The thought of a TV dinner alone at home was unappealing. In recent days he had eaten too many of them. A thick, juicy *Eagle Burger*, with a side order of fries, was far more inviting. Some lively conversation with Loomis would be an added bonus. The danger, however, was that *Jack* might crash the party.

Skip locked the office and, rather than drive, leisurely strolled down Main Street to the *Eagle*. The scant exercise, walking there and later back to his BMW, was a far cry from the resolution he had made the preceding January. But anything was better than nothing. The place was busy for a Tuesday, but his favorite stool at the left end of the bar was vacant.

"A while since I've seen you," said Loomis, as Skip climbed onto his seat. "What'll it be?"

Ordinarily Loomis would have simply brought *Jack*. If he had, Skip might have done the courteous thing and welcomed his guest. The question forced him to make a decision. He said, "*Eagle Burger*, heavy on the onions, an order of fries, extra crisp, and...a coffee."

"Still swearing off the hard stuff?"

Skip shrugged.

"Gotta hustle." Loomis gestured in the direction of some waiting customers and hurried away.

Skip peered down the length of the bar. Most of the stools were occupied, and, apart from a couple of empty glasses, in front of each was an alcoholic beverage, except a tall one at the far end. It could have been a *Pepsi*, but a dark amber draft was equally possible. A few minutes later Loomis delivered a coffee, along with several packets of sugar and a pair of creamers. Skip eyed the steaming beverage. It left him cold and lonely. He slowly swiveled his stool a full three hundred sixty degrees taking in the entire establishment. The place was buzzing. Despite being a long-time regular, Skip felt like an outsider. Good company, his pal *Jack*, was what he wanted. If nothing else, *Jack* could dull despondency.

Two sugars and a creamer later, chin sunk deep into an elbow-propped hand, Skip recalled the warm, sun-drenched images of Paestum that had filled his head earlier in the day. They were far too distant. For too many years his life had lacked meaning and direction. Memories were nice but, superimposed on a vacuous present, insufficient. He carefully sipped his coffee lest he burn his tongue. Though richer and more flavorful than the instant he made at home, it failed to warm his heart.

His burger arrived. It was probably as good as usual, though he couldn't say for sure. He was down to the last bite when he realized he had eaten it mindlessly. One by one he ate his fries with his fingers until the last was gone. He reached again for his coffee. It was cold. Loomis would have given him a fresh cup, but that wasn't what he wanted. He waited patiently until Loomis had a free moment. Skip motioned to him. "A *Jack* on the rocks."

Loomis hesitated before walking over to Skip. "I think I misunderstood you."

"*Jack*...You know, the usual."

Loomis shook his head.

"What's that mean?"

"Dram Shop Law...You're the lawyer. You know exactly what it means."

Skip was familiar with the statute. It had come in handy a decade earlier when a client's car was struck by an uninsured motorist with no assets apart from the rusted junker he was driving. The fellow blew a .31 on the police breathalyzer. Just before the accident he had been drinking for hours at a watering hole only a half-mile down the road. Skip used the Dram Shop Law to sue the establishment. The owner had continued to serve the inebriated patron knowing that he would drive away drunk in his truck as usual. But why was Loomis making reference to the law? Skip pointed at his coffee. "Unless you filled this cup with *Kahlúa*, rather than *Folgers*, I don't think you have much to worry about."

Loomis shook his head again. "I'm not gonna serve you."

"You're what?"

"You heard me."

"I heard you, but I certainly didn't understand."

"Look...I'm doing this as a friend. I—"

"A minute ago it was because of the Dram Shop Law."

The normally relaxed Loomis fidgeted with the rag he used to wipe the bar. "Under the law I'm uh...supposed to watch whom I serve."

"And all of a sudden you can't serve me?"

"Not when you're trying to get off of the stuff. And more important, not when you need to."

The comment was a sledgehammer. Many times Skip had dismissed the idea he might be an alcoholic. He didn't stagger around. He didn't drive after drinking. He didn't miss appointments, at least not very often. He didn't wake up with hangovers. Well—even when he did, he still made it into the office, albeit late. The evidence had always seemed clear, and the verdict, easy. But Loomis, his friend, the man who knew Skip's drinking better than anyone, had just told him he needed to stop. "What do you mean by that?" said Skip.

"Just what I said."

"What—you think I'm an..." Skip couldn't bring himself to use the word. "Just why do I need to stop drinking?"

Loomis hesitated, seemingly struggling with a response. He gestured to a bottle of *Jack Daniel's* on the shelf behind him. "Your buddy has been running your life. Or maybe ruining it would be more accurate."

Skip wanted to object, and he probably would have if Loomis hadn't continued.

"For instance, take a few weeks back when you put on that show in Biddleford's court."

The recollection, blurred though it was, of the horrible afternoon when, in front of a packed courtroom, the suppression hearing had to be adjourned, was painful. Sure, Skip had redeemed himself the following day, but that didn't erase what had preceded. Skip bowed his head between slumping shoulders. An instant later he felt the friendly pat of Loomis's hand.

"Sorry...I didn't mean to hurt you. I...I probably went about it all wrong."

Skip raised his head. "Well, it certainly came out of the blue."

"I suppose it did, though I've been meaning to tell you for a long time."

The disclosure only added to the pain. "Why now?"

"You had finally taken the first step on your own." Loomis heaved a sigh. "Years ago after Megan was killed, back when you started drinking, you needed to dull the pain. Who could blame you? As time passed, I assumed your hurt would ease and your dependence, subside. I kept hoping. I thought about telling you to quit, but experience—if nothing else, I know alcohol and those who drink it—said you had to make the decision." Loomis chuckled for a moment. "It also gave me a great excuse to avoid the issue. Anyway, when you finally bit the bullet, I made myself a promise. No longer would I be your enabler."

Skip looked Loomis in the eye. "Am I..." He drew a breath as he prepared for the first time to ascribe aloud the offensive term to himself. Entertaining the thought, as he had in the past, was one thing. Asking someone else, a man he respected, to make the judgment was very different. "Am I an alcoholic?"

Loomis looked away. He said nothing. He didn't need to. He had answered the question.

The lawyer in Skip instantly conjured a wealth of arguments, the same ones he had so often used to silently dismiss the issue. Unlike drunks who couldn't hold a job and slept in the park, he was a professional with a nice home. He, not alcohol, was in control. The logic was excellent, but only as a rationalization, not reality. Loomis had forced him to finally come to grips with the latter. Skip gestured at his coffee cup and said, "A refill, please."

Loomis nodded and headed to the kitchen. A minute later he returned and filled the cup. He motioned down the bar. "My customers await." He hurried off.

Skip started to reach for a packet of sugar but let it be. He would drink the libation straight up and unadulterated. Creamy and sweet may have been tasty, but playing the martyr was more palatable.

"We've got a trial date of October 6th," said Skip.

Morehead showed no reaction.

If Skip's lifelong freedom faced a date with fate just eight weeks off, no way would he have been so blasé.

"You hear anything from Biddleford about throwing out my confession?"

"Not yet." A favorable decision would give Morehead a fighting chance for an acquittal. Unfortunately the Red Sox would sooner make Skip their shortstop than His Holiness would grant the motion to suppress.

"Well, I'll be surprised if he doesn't go our way."

The response helped explain Morehead's nonchalance. It was also bad news for Skip. A client's wildly unreasonable expectations were an attorney's bane. "As I've told you before, motions to suppress are hard to win, especially with a judge like Biddleford. And speaking of him, I've been thinking. If you'd like, I could probably get the trial date moved back."

"Why would you do that?"

"With the November election, you never know. Gruzman might pull the upset. You'd be a whole—"

"Forget about what I'd be. Gruzman isn't going to beat a Republican incumbent, not around here. Anyway, I'd just as soon take my chances with Biddleford."

Everything Morehead had said made sense except the last point. "Why do you want Biddleford, a throw-away-the-key conservative who detests us both?"

"Well...you never know. That may backfire. A jury may be offended if they think he isn't giving me a fair shake."

From a theoretical standpoint the jailhouse-style strategy had some appeal, but Skip knew better. "Jurors are inherently skeptical of lawyers. They trust the judge to guide them. They focus on his instructions. If I were you, I'd choose Gruzman over Biddleford."

"I'll do that...when I'm in the voting booth. Regardless, come January 1st, we both know who will be wearing the black robe."

The point had merit. Whatever the trial date, Biddleford would be on the bench.

Morehead put his hand to his chest and grimaced. "Damn heartburn."

"You ought to get those pains checked out."

Morehead leaned forward in visible discomfort. He reached into his pocket and pulled out his familiar roll of *Tums*. He popped a couple into his mouth and then held out the roll in Skip's direction. "Have one. They're good for the digestion."

Skip shook his head. "My stomach is fine. As for my liver, that might be another story."

"That about it for today?" Morehead started to get up.

Skip had one other matter on his mind. "You remember a couple weeks back I mentioned a fellow by the name of Woody Wilson?"

Morehead's eyes appeared to widen at the mention of Wilson's name, but it was equally possible Skip was attaching significance to nothing. "Mickey Shore suspected he might know something about Squeaky's murder."

"Yeah...and?"

"Wilson died of carbon monoxide poisoning about a week ago. According to the police, a suicide."

A curious stare replaced Morehead's cavalier manner. "You think Wilson's death might be linked to Squeaky's murder?"

"I don't know. But I understand Wilson worked for Gino Morelli, the same contractor for whom Squeaky provided glowing, but phony references."

"Maybe Wilson killed Squeaky and then committed suicide fearing the police were hot on his trail."

The scenario had crossed Skip's mind, but the logic failed. With Morehead charged, assuming Wilson was guilty, if anything, he had reason to believe he was beating the rap. "I doubt it," said Skip. "On the other hand, it's not beyond the realm of possibility that Wilson's death, which may not be a suicide, is tied to Squeaky's murder."

"What makes you think Wilson's death might involve foul play?"

"Mickey Shore has doubts."

"But if I understood you, the police—I assume they investigated—termed it a suicide."

"Yes...but Wilson's death seems rather coincidental. And Mickey has me wondering. His methods may be unconventional, but his instincts are excellent."

Morehead thought for a moment. "Let me try again. You think...whoever killed Squeaky killed Wilson as well, but made it look like a suicide."

"Well, I'm not saying that's what happened. Just that I wouldn't rule it out."

"Interesting," said Morehead. "Unfortunately, unless I'm missing something, it doesn't take us any closer to Squeaky's killer."

"Not for the moment. But it could give us two chances to find a murderer. That, plus it gives us a reason to look for someone with motive to kill both Squeaky and Wilson."

Morehead nodded. "Now I see where you're going—Morelli. Both Squeaky and Wilson knew his operation. Morelli needed to get rid of them before they spilled their guts to the Justice Department."

Once again the scenario had crossed Skip's mind. It had possibilities, but there were others. He said, "Correct me if I'm wrong, but if recollection serves me, you didn't know Wilson?" "Not personally." Morehead flashed a peeved look. "By any chance you lookin' to pin a second murder on me?" "Easy. I just want to be sure I've got my facts straight. Walking into the courtroom with blinders is a disaster waiting to happen."

"I suppose," said Morehead reluctantly.

"So, what exactly did you mean when you said you didn't know Wilson *personally*?"

Irritation again showed on Morehead's face. "I've heard of the guy—that he was in the car repair business. Years ago somebody told me he was the best auto body man around these parts. Could make a crumpled fender loaded with rust look showroom new."

"But you didn't know him personally?"

"Nope." Morehead chuckled.

"What's so funny?"

"Well, under the circumstances, probably just as well that I didn't." He checked his watch. "We about done, 'cause I got a fellow coming over to the shop at two who says he's got a big print job for me. And with my checks to you well into five figures—in case you haven't noticed, your rates aren't cheap—I need all the business I can get." Morehead displayed a rare, good-natured smile as he got up and left.

Skip stared at the open doorway pondering the all-too-numerous facets of the case. Permutations abounded. In one respect that worked to his advantage. But Morehead's confession was still the key. Presumably Judge Biddleford would allow the jury to see it. If so, they were likely to convict, unless Skip could convince them it was, as Morehead claimed, forced. To do that he would need to discredit Detective Ramsey. Ramsey had investigated automobile accidents with links to both Squeaky and Kileen. Perhaps Ramsey had ties to Wilson as well. But what if Wilson's death was a suicide that had nothing to do with Squeaky's murder? And there was always Morelli. And LaDieux and Feinstein and Raines. Skip heaved a sigh. His head was clear of *Jack's* influence. Why then was his mind more boggled than ever? As a single practitioner he lacked the luxury of a partner's assistance. Perhaps he needed *Jack's* help.

———————

Skip flipped the pages of one of the many deed books in the Otsego County Clerk's Office. He could hardly imagine how tedious the practice of law must have been before the advent of typewriters and *Xerox* machines. Hand-written deeds and mortgages with metes and bounds descriptions that traced angles and distances to towering trees and big rocks were the norm. A hand gently moving across his back interrupted his thoughts. Before looking to see who had come up from behind, he paused briefly, if only to savor the caress.

"Hi Skip."

Even as he turned, he recognized the voice. "Hello Kelly. I didn't see you coming."

"Sorry, I didn't mean to sneak up on you."

Recollections of the times they had spent together when dating flashed into his mind. Indeed he knew her touch far better than a mere pat on the back. "How've you been?"

"Can't complain. On second thought, I could. But why bore you with my problems? You, like any lawyer, no doubt have more than enough of your own."

Ordinarily Skip was not much for vapid small talk, especially when in the midst of accomplishing something. But most every rule had its exceptions, and Kelly was certainly an exception. "Your hair looks great."

"A client of yours does it."

"My client?"

"Lenny Gardner. He's been doing it for nearly a decade. Of course, when he needed a lawyer, he didn't come to me. But that's no surprise."

Skip tried to make sense of the remark. "Why wouldn't he hire you?"

"C'mon," said Kelly, jabbing a finger into Skip's arm. "No doubt you've noticed he prefers men."

The comment offered a perfect segue to an issue that Skip had been trying to explore for several weeks. "I understand your late client, Squeaky Grimes, lived next door to Lenny. I also understand that Squeaky had a voice worse than fingernails on a chalkboard. Maybe Squeaky, like Lenny, favored men. Perhaps the duo were more than neighbors."

Kelly shrugged. "No idea as to Squeaky's sexual preferences. Of course if I did, unless I knew he had come out of the closet, I wouldn't share them. My job is simply to probate his estate. As for his personal life, that should be left to rest, along with him, six feet underground."

The unequivocal message left Skip at a momentary loss for words.

"I understand *Pepsi* has become your recent drink of choice."

"Who told you that?"

"Our mutual friend at the *Eagle*."

"Loomis?"

She nodded.

A part of Skip was glad she had heard, but another feared the pressure of expectations. Boarding the wagon was easy. Staying on as it rumbled down a steep slope laden with rocks and ruts was a different matter. "I thought bartenders were supposed to be discreet."

"Apparently you didn't read your law books very well. Doctors, clergymen and folks like us owe a duty of confidentiality. Not bartenders."

"It may not be codified, but the wise ones know to keep what passes their ears off their lips."

"Well...Loomis is hardly a gossip. Some lawyers and doctors I know could take a lesson from him."

Skip found it hard to argue the point.

Kelly glanced at her watch. "I'd better be going. I have an appointment back at the office, and no doubt you're anxious to return to your work."

This time her point was wrong. Debating it, however, would serve no purpose. He said, "As always, it was great seeing you."

"And you too." She smiled.

David A. Weiss

As she went on her way, the scent of her perfume filled his head. It wasn't *Chanel No. 5*, Megan's favorite. That much Skip could tell. Regardless, the enchanting fragrance commandeered his thoughts. Her big eyes, small turned-up nose and demure smile were innocently provocative. A neat blue suit understated her slim, curvy figure. Kelly had a certain, singular aura, that indefinable something. Her quiet, unobtrusive entrance into a room somehow echoed like an exclamation point. Though it bore no similarity to the thunder accompanying the voluptuous Tammy Lee Raines or City Manager Traci LaDieux, still its decibel level was paradoxically higher. Perhaps Skip's high school pal, Slicker Storch, could explain it best with his celebrated classification of the three varieties of dynamite: Tammy Lee was the quintessential one-nighter, a duct-taped mouth special; the City Manager, a three-monther, with options for extensions; and Kelly, a lifer...marriage material.

Skip sat with Lenny Gardner in the hallway outside Judge Biddleford's chambers waiting to conference the support issue. He curbed the urge to quiz his client about his former next-door neighbor Squeaky Grimes. Skip was there to represent Gardner, not interrogate him. The least Skip could do was hold his questions until after the conference.

Judge Biddleford's secretary stepped out into the hallway and approached Skip. "His Honor is ready to see you in chambers." She had already rounded up Karl Fuller. A moment later the two lawyers entered the jurist's office.

The telephone to his ear, Judge Biddleford motioned them to take seats on the opposite side of his desk. "I tell you that Pete Filmore is nothing but a goddamn sandbagger. Saturday afternoon the son of a bitch shot 91. Took me for twelve bucks...His handicap? It's seventeen...I don't care if 91 is a fair score for a seventeen. The guy is a..."

Skip tuned out the rants. Too many times he had heard the pompous jurist whine about a match. But Skip knew the truth. His Holiness's reputation was notorious. He sported a fifteen

185

handicap, far fewer strokes than he needed. Most of the time he played with partners in a foursome. If he knocked a ball out of bounds, he'd bitch and moan and simply walk the hole, but then he'd write down a score only one shot more than his partner. If his partner hit one stiff for a birdie, His Holiness would pick up his ball and take a par, even if he was already lying six. If he counted all his strokes, his handicap would have been well over twenty. As a result, when he played an opponent head-to-head, he ended up giving strokes, instead of getting them. Losing was inevitable. But as far as His Holiness was concerned, his opponents were all sandbaggers. There was one group of exceptions. He did well against members of the Bar. The explanation was simple. His Holiness was a sore loser. Letting him win a few bucks on the links was preferable to having him get even when on the bench.

"I'd like to talk more golf, but unlike yourself, judges don't get a morning and afternoon break."

Give me a break, thought Skip. You take all the breaks you want, not to mention that most days you show up after nine-thirty, take two-hour lunches and sneak out before four.

Judge Biddleford finally hung up the telephone. "Okay, give me the good news. You fellows have settled this matter and want to put it on the record. Right?"

Skip glanced at Fuller, who returned the look. Skip could read his adversary's mind. Neither wanted to bear the bad tidings.

"That's hardly a resounding yes." Judge Biddleford shook his head. "Don't tell me you've just been twiddling your thumbs instead of negotiating a resolution. Why do you think I kept myself distracted well after you arrived?"

You should have been a used-car salesman. On second thought, even used-car salesmen aren't that slimy. Skip ground his teeth.

The Judge flipped open a folder and muttered just loud enough for Skip to hear. "This is the case where *Little Lenny*, the queenly coiffeur, dumped his wife for tutti-frutti." He looked at Skip. "Your client is paying all of forty dollars per week for the support of his daughter. You call that fair?"

"That was the parties' agreement, Your Honor."

186

"That may be. But the minor child is not bound by that agreement. It's my job to ensure her interests are protected." He turned to Fuller. "Counselor, what do you have to say?"

"At the time of the divorce, Mr. Gardner had limited income. Thus, the tiny award. He now runs a very successful shop with other hairdressers working for him. We understand his income has more than doubled. Very simply, there has been a material change of circumstances."

"Change of circumstances." With the zip of a fast ball pounding the catcher's mitt, the phrase snapped off Judge Biddleford's tongue. "That's grounds for a modification, Mr. Maynard."

Judge Biddleford's cold stare told Skip he was in a bad bargaining position, not that it was a revelation.

"Mr. Fuller," said Judge Biddleford, "if you would briefly excuse yourself, I will explore with your adversary the possibility of settlement."

Fuller got up and left.

With someone else Skip would have welcomed the standard negotiating procedure whereby a judge, as disinterested go-between, ferreted out the parties' bottom lines. But not with a predisposed judge who was prone to bludgeon results.

"Let's see," said Judge Biddleford, eyeing his papers. "The petition seeks one hundred twenty-five dollars per week, and your client is paying forty. Why doesn't your client want to support his daughter?"

The old when did you stop beating your wife routine. Just what Skip had anticipated. "My client has been supporting his daughter. He's even willing to increase his payments."

"Fine. Tell me one twenty-five, and we're outta here."

Skip bit his tongue, though no doubt his facial reaction was less restrained.

"Okay. You tell me. How much is your client willing to pay? And don't hold anything back."

The vise was beginning to tighten. Bidding against oneself was a losing proposition. Skip said, "Assuming it would resolve the matter, he'd go for a twenty-five percent increase. Fifty dollars per week."

Judge Biddleford put a finger next to his ear. "Damn…I must have wax. I thought you said fifty."

"I did."

The jurist laughed as he rocked back and peered over the top of his slim reading glasses. "Mr. Maynard, I asked you for your bottom line, not some two-bit low ball." He leaned forward. "You didn't happen to drink your breakfast this morning, did you?"

Skip resented the aspersion, though recent history forced him to concede its justification. "Assuming it would settle the matter, my client would pay fifty-five dollars. Let's see what the petitioner will take."

"Fine. You want me to press your adversary? I will. But before you go out into the hall, understand your risks. If this matter goes to trial, I intend to protect the minor child. That's my duty. Don't expect my sympathies to lie with a…" The homophobic jurist paused long enough to allow Skip to fill in the blanks. "Not after he abandoned his family for some *Tinkerbell*."

Skip left the Judge's chambers, and after trading places with Fuller, related the discussion to his client.

"As I told you, I'd be happy to get away with seventy-five," said Gardner. "Maybe we should tell the Judge."

"He'd only squeeze us for more. Anyway, for the time being, I want to try for something less. If necessary, we'll up the ante."

"Okay. But I'd hate to have the Judge fix the number after a hearing. Given his feelings, he might go higher than one twenty-five, assuming that's possible."

If needed to protect the minor child, a simple amendment of the petition could increase the upper limit. The point underscored that Skip needed to proceed cautiously.

Minutes later Judge Biddleford's secretary summoned Skip back into chambers where Judge Biddleford and Fuller were waiting.

"Discussions are fruitless. You fellows are too far apart. We'll have to try the thing, though I'd rather devote my time to more important issues." He looked at his docket. "We already have a hearing date: August 28th at one-thirty. We'll see you gentlemen then."

Skip, along with Fuller, started to get up.

"By the way," said Judge Biddleford, "I was talking with my re-election campaign chairman the other day. Amazing how generous folks have been, especially members of the local bar. It really gives me a warm feeling to know the lawyers who practice before me appreciate my efforts." He nodded slowly. "Yes—it sure is nice to be appreciated."

Skip stole a peak at Fuller as they headed for the door. His adversary revealed nothing, but Skip knew what he was thinking. Biddleford had solicited them both for contributions. Nothing he had said had linked it to the pending case. There was certainly no suggestion of a *quid pro quo*. Still the timing of the remarks could not be denied.

As they stepped out into the hallway, Fuller said, "My client is willing to talk, but if it comes down to the Judge's ruling, that's fine with her."

If Skip were in Fuller's shoes, he too would have been happy to try the matter. The need for a settlement was obvious. Communicating that need was the last thing Skip could afford. He said, "I understand your thinking. My client feels the same way. But he also understands that he has a right to appeal. He's prepared himself for any eventuality here. He's more than willing to take it up to the Appellate Division." Skip patted Fuller on the back. "You have a good day, Karl." Skip headed down the hallway. Lenny Gardner no more fancied an appeal than he did women, but as far as Karl Fuller was concerned, if the issue didn't settle, a long, arduous road lay ahead.

Chapter XI

The police file on Woody Wilson was closed. They had investigated the scene, the autopsy was done and the medical examiner had issued his report. Woody Wilson had died of carbon monoxide poisoning, the result of suicide. Living alone and apparently despondent, he had taken his life. Mickey Shore didn't buy it. He was convinced that whoever killed Squeaky Grimes also killed Woody Wilson. If Mickey was right, there was a killer on the loose, and no one, apart from Mickey, was looking for him. The question was who? Unfortunately, Harley Morehead topped the list of possibilities. But there were lots of others, and a number of them would be at the ribbon-cutting ceremonies for the opening of the new local museum.

The building, a small two-story Victorian home bearing a broad porch and gabled roof with a dormer and turret, was vacant and in need of repair when the village had purchased it. A desire to preserve the village's proud history, coupled with the ability of a local Congressman to bring home some pork from Washington, had led to the museum. From the outside it was the typical small town gallery, but within its walls exhibits revealing a storied past belied its modest exterior. Displays depicting the birth of the nation's pastime, artifacts of James Fenimore Cooper, including signed copies of the *Deerslayer* and *The Last of the Mohigans*, and early *Singer* sewing machines, emblematic of the opulent family whose estate lay on Lake Otsego, evidenced Cooperstown's impressive lore. Several photos and early scorecards from the *Otsego Lake Golf Club*, situated at the north end of the lake, about ten miles from the more famous *Leatherstocking Course* at the south end, served as a reminder that golf had come to Cooperstown at a time when just a handful of courses dotted America and only the wealthy partook.

As Mickey entered the vestibule, he noted a placard on an easel indicating that *Artway* had graciously provided some paintings of local landmarks. Mickey quickly spotted a couple in the room to his right. A depiction of the *Farmers' Museum* bore a thirteen-hundred-dollar price tag. A rendering of the legendary *Cardiff Giant* was marked at eight hundred. Jimmie and Tammy Lee Raines's so-called generosity was an opportunity to display their paintings for free. They knew the right people and were pushy enough to arrange the showing. Mickey gave the paintings a second look. The amateurish *Cardiff Giant* looked like something a junior high school student might do. The *Farmers' Museum*, a string of buildings, including an apothecary and blacksmith shop, all buzzing with people in costume, was surprisingly good.

"Well—look who's come to the museum opening."

Mickey turned to see Bernie Feinstein.

"Who you investigating today?"

"Can't a fellow appreciate his community's culture without abuse from a surly cynic?"

"A fellow could." Feinstein smacked Mickey on the back. "But not Mickey Shore."

The conversation was headed in a direction Mickey didn't like. "And what brings you here—the free lemonade?"

"Duty...Public service."

"I'm impressed," said Mickey, unmoved by the politician's spin.

Feinstein pointed at the painting of the *Farmers' Museum*. "What do you think?"

"Nice. But hardly thirteen hundred dollars nice."

"Well..." Feinstein eyed the painting more closely. "Good art carries a hefty price."

Mickey chuckled.

"What's so funny?"

"For a second—at least until you reminded me—I almost forgot that you were a politician. Maybe you're an *Artway* dealer as well."

"Not me...though I was solicited."

"Why didn't you bite?"

"Looking at paintings is enough for me. I don't need to become a peddler."

"Who solicited you? Jimmie Raines…or was it Squeaky?"

Feinstein laughed.

"Now I'm the one who missed the humor."

"You're here on Squeaky's case. I should have figured."

Before Mickey could react, Jimmie Raines approached. "You fellows like the artwork?"

"My friend here was just admiring it." Feinstein gestured at Mickey. "Are you two gentlemen acquainted with one another?"

Mickey held out his hand. "I'm Mickey Shore."

"The private detective?"

"Yes. Is that bad?"

Raines shrugged, but then shook Mickey's hand.

Mickey gestured at the painting. "I like it."

"It can be yours, along with an opportunity to make a lot more money. By any chance, you ever hear of *Artway*?"

Mickey might have played dumb and listened to Raines's spiel, but not when the act would have been obvious to Feinstein. "I've heard about it, not that I know the details."

"It's a great opportunity, a chance to enjoy fine art and make money, all while getting huge tax savings."

"Sounds interesting. Does it require up-front money?"

"Hardly. Five thousand, and you're an *Artway* dealer."

"Five thousand…" Mickey sighed. "That may be chump change to someone like you or our County Comptroller, but—"

"Hold the phone," said Feinstein. "Just because I track large sums in my professional capacity doesn't mean I can toss them around in my personal life."

"Come on. We're only talkin' five grand."

Mickey suspected that the bank balance of the politician in the blue suit was far larger than that of the big talker with the flowered print shirt and gold chain around his neck. Investigation had confirmed that Jimmie Raines and his wife Tammy Lee lived high but were in debt up to their ears. "If I were to invest, what would I get for my five thousand?"

"You'll excuse me," said Feinstein, "but I'll let you gentlemen discuss business by yourselves."

Once Feinstein was out of earshot, Raines said, "Just what you'd expect from *his* type."

"Huh?" said Mickey, feigning a puzzled look and hoping Raines might open up more.

"The guy's an accountant. He watches pennies." Raines looked Mickey in the eye. "If you want to make real money, you have to think big."

"I take it *Artway* will let me do that."

"How does four thousand percent profit sound?"

"A thousand times better than the four percent the bank pays on my little account." Mickey scratched his head for effect. "But let me guess, I have to wait forty years."

"How's twenty days sound?"

"Great, if only you were serious."

"I am." Raines motioned Mickey into the next room. He pointed at a painting with a small *sold* sign next to its nine-hundred-dollar price tag. "I paid fifteen dollars for that two weeks ago. While preparing for the show yesterday, I sold it for six hundred. Cash money."

Mickey pretended to study the canvas. "It's not bad. Forty, maybe fifty bucks. But six hundred? You must have found the world's biggest sucker."

"Not really. In fact I told him I bought it for fifteen dollars."

Mickey eyed the canvas again. The skills the high school drama coach had taught them years earlier when rehearsing for the school play were coming in handy. "I don't get it."

"Let me explain." Raines looked around, as if checking that no one was listening. He proceeded to detail how an investment of five thousand dollars for ten paintings enabled one to become an *Artway* dealer; that dealers got paintings for a hundred dollars apiece; and then resold them for no less than five hundred dollars. Then he came with the kicker, the tax advantages.

Once he finished, Mickey said, "You know, five thousand dollars sounds a whole lot better than fifteen minutes ago. But one question: Isn't this like one of those pyramid deals?"

"Absolutely. And if you know pyramids, those at the top make out big." He put a hand on Mickey's shoulder. "You, my friend, have a chance to get in just a little below the apex."

"Sounds interesting." Based upon his investigative sources Mickey had assumed he had a clear picture of Raines, but the bragging hotshot who had never matured beyond exaggerated exploits from his high school days was even more unbearable than expected. Mickey said, "Funny, not long ago someone told me about *Artway*, but I dismissed it right away when I heard that Squeaky Grimes was involved."

Raines gave Mickey a look.

"So, Squeaky wasn't involved with *Artway*?"

Raines shook his head. "Save the charade. I know who you are. You're investigating Squeaky's death. You obviously know he was my partner."

Mickey had prepared himself for the eventuality. "Investigation was among my purposes. I was hoping you could provide some information. As Squeaky's partner I'm sure you want to see his killer brought to justice."

Raines nodded. "Absolutely. And fine fella that I am, I'm gonna give you the benefit of my expertise."

Mickey waited anxiously. "So?"

Raines took a deep breath. "The way I see it...the police got their man."

"You mean Harley Morehead?"

"Hey...he confessed. That's good enough for me."

"Anyone else who might have had it in for Squeaky?"

"How should I know?"

"He was your partner."

Raines scowled. "In name only. We traveled in *very* different circles. He had a good idea, and I knew all the right people. Unusual circumstances led to odd bedfellows. And let me tell you, Squeaky was odd."

Explanations were superfluous, but keeping Raines talking was not. "In what way?"

"His voice to begin with. My wife, Tammy Lee, says he sounded like a hyena. If I were a hyena, I'd take that as an insult. A few hours with Squeaky could send a sane person to the booby hatch."

"You must have spent quite a few hours with him?"

"No more than necessary. And if you're insinuating I did him in because he got on my nerves, forget it."

Though the reasons differed, that was what Mickey had in mind. Raines might have killed Squeaky because he disliked splitting *Artway's* profits with him. There was always the possibility that Raines was cutting Squeaky out of his share, and Squeaky got wise. "I'll bet he was a shrewd little fella."

"Shrewd...that's one way to describe him. The animal kingdom gives a better picture. Foxy, sly, stubborn as a mule...annoying, like a mosquito. The guy latched onto folks like a bloodsucker. That was Squeaky."

Mickey already had a good picture of Squeaky, and Raines had added a few details. There were lots of people with possible motives to kill Squeaky, but nothing concrete. Perhaps Raines could change that. Mickey said, "I assume you know both the City Manager and Buddy Kileen. I understand they're members at the Leatherstocking Club."

"Yeah, but Kileen's a hacker. The fellows I play with shoot in the eighties. LaDieux plays in the women's league." Raines leaned closer and lowered his voice. "But damn, I wouldn't mind playing with her. And I don't mean golf."

"By any chance do you know Gino Morelli, the contractor?"

"Not personally, but I read about him in the newspapers. Gonna be interesting to see if he and LaDieux get indicted for corruption." Raines hesitated. "If I recall, the paper said that Squeaky worked for Morelli. Maybe that corruption stuff is what led to Squeaky's murder."

"How so?" said Mickey, containing excitement over the possibility that Raines might be on the verge of a significant disclosure.

"Well—the way I figure..." Raines pawed at his chin. "Workin' for Morelli, Squeaky was there at LaDieux's place. Hammerin', nailin', puttin' in screws. Puttin' 'em here." He gestured with one hand. "Puttin' 'em there." He gestured with the other. "You never know, maybe LaDieux screwed Squeaky. Screwed the little runt to death." Raines shook his head. "Dyin' ain't ever easy. But what a way to go."

Mickey realized he had been had.

"You ought to investigate my theory. Check out LaDieux." Raines motioned toward the adjoining room. "Our charming City Manager is in there now."

Mickey nodded. "I'll take your advice."

"Before you go, can I sign you up as an *Artway* dealer?"

"I'll have to think about it."

"Fine. For now you just wanna buy a painting?"

"I'll think about that too." Mickey headed into the adjoining room, directly to City Manager Traci LaDieux. "Excuse me, Your Honor," he said, as she took a plastic cup of Chardonnay from a refreshment table. "I'm Mickey Shore. I voted for you in the last election. You're doing a great job."

"Thank you. And I know who you are. You're a private investigator. I understand you're involved in the Morehead case. I imagine that's why you want to speak to me."

Trying to fool the politician was an exercise in futility. "You come right to the point."

"Sometimes." She looked him the eye. "What about you?"

"Sometimes."

She laughed.

He had seen her on television from time to time. He had even passed her on the street once or twice. But up close and smiling she was even sexier than he had realized. He had all he could do to keep his eyes from dipping lower, not that his peripheral failed to take in the sights. Her smart yellow top was not cut particularly low, but it hugged her body enough to yield ample hints.

"Let me make your job easy. I didn't kill Squeaky, and I don't know who did." She gave him a look as if to say: *Are we done?*

Her experience as a politician had demonstrated itself. Her self-serving denial, which supposedly made his job easier, had done exactly the opposite. "Did you know Squeaky Grimes?"

"A little...Did you?"

Like him she was adept at turning the tables. "Not really."

"He was quite the character. Unforgettable to say the least. But I'm sure you're well aware."

"Did you—"

"I understand you're working for Skip Maynard. Did you know that he and I graduated high school together?"

"You're kidding," said Mickey, though the information was already familiar. "You must have skipped a dozen grades." She patted him on the arm. "Flattery will get you everywhere."

It had gotten him nowhere.

"You'll pardon me. I'd love to talk longer, but duty calls." She disappeared through the hallway and around the corner.

Mickey took a Chardonnay from the nearby table. Though likely the cheap stuff, it wasn't half-bad. Regardless, one of the *Camels* in his pocket would have been better. It had been nearly an hour since he had last lit up. He was about to head outside when he spotted Buddy Kileen coming through the front door. Mickey had anticipated that politicians like Feinstein and LaDieux would be at the museum's opening. Kileen was a bonus. Mickey headed over to the insurance man.

The moment he approached, Kileen said, "Let me guess. You're Mickey Shore."

"How'd you know?"

"I bumped into Jimmie Raines on the sidewalk as I was coming in. He warned me to be on the lookout."

Mickey tried to ignore the unenthusiastic greeting. "You got a couple minutes?"

"For you?...No!" Kileen walked away.

Mickey watched him for a moment. He had accomplished as much as he could. Nothing. He glanced at the stairway that led to the second floor exhibits. He liked museums, but not ones that prohibited smoking. He headed out the front door. The moment he stepped outside, he lit up.

———————

Skip seated himself on the family-room couch in front of the television. Famished as he was, his *Swanson* Salisbury steak dinner with mashed potatoes, carrots and apple crisp looked appetizing. A can of *Pepsi* stood close by on the end table. Foregoing *Jack* might have been tough had Skip not expelled his pal from the liquor cabinet several weeks before.

The local newscast, a typical potpourri of fires and auto accidents, had been blindly passing before his eyes when the anchor caught his attention.

> *Following an application by the Oneonta Star for disclosure of public records, State Supreme Court issued an order today directing Cooperstown City Manager Traci LaDieux to turn over all records relating to any contracts awarded to area contractor Gino Morelli. County Comptroller Bernie Feinstein was also directed to furnish all records relating to the review and approval of such contracts. Corporation Counsel for the City Manager's office when contacted by this station indicated it was immediately filing a notice of appeal to the Appellate Division of Supreme Court. The Corporation Counsel contended the order of disclosure violates executive privilege.*

Legal wheels spun in Skip's head. Executive privilege was an excuse to withhold the information. A smoke screen. Where there was smoke, fire was likely. Unfortunately the notice of appeal would automatically stay the order requiring disclosure. It would likely take a year or more before the appeal was decided. Even then, an appeal to the Court of Appeals could not be ruled out. But there were other ways to get the information. Skip would subpoena LaDieux, Feinstein and Morelli to testify at Morehead's trial. Whether Judge Biddleford would compel answers was another matter. But a refusal might not be so bad. In the event of a conviction, Skip could argue on appeal that Morehead was deprived of a fair trial. Skip's focus returned to the television as the scene shifted to the steps of the State Capitol.

The on-the-scene reporter was soliciting thirteen-term State Assemblyman Horris Goodhouse's reaction to the continued refusal to turn over the records. "The public has a right to know how public contracts are awarded. The case is especially disturbing in light of the pending investigation by the United States Justice Department. Secrecy casts shadows

David A. Weiss

over our entire system of government. I intend to immediately introduce a bill to prevent such outrages in the future."

"Give me a break," barked Skip at the television. Normally he reserved such audible retorts for the referees during broadcasts of the *Knicks'* games, and those reactions came with *Jack's* encouragement. But Goodhouse, three-dollar bill that he was, had earned it. Years earlier during law school, when Skip was a summer intern in the State Legislature, he had come face-to-face with the Assemblyman's methods. In the midst of a tough campaign Goodhouse had sponsored legislation to make pork-barrel spending transparent. The provision prevented legislators from hiding their pork deep in the nethermost reaches of voluminous bills with no indication who was behind the expenditure. Goodhouse went on the airwaves decrying pork and the evils associated with it. Behind the scenes in a closed-door meeting with Skip's boss in the Senate, Skip watched as Assemblyman Goodhouse, puffing a fat cigar, caved in on legislation that would have protected children from sexual predators in exchange for assurances that his bill to control pork would never reach the floor of the Senate. He made sure it was a one-house bill. He no more wanted to limit pork than the tobacco industry wanted to ban cigarettes. His only goal was to get himself re-elected. Do-good liberals and church-going conservatives could waste their time on drivel such as the public interest. Goodhouse would be damned before he'd allow it to interfere with his status.

Skip bit into his Salisbury steak. With all the people who were linked to Squeaky Grimes, too bad Horris Goodhouse wasn't on the list. Subpoenaing Goodhouse would provide a unique pleasure. Skip imagined what it would be like to sink his cross-examining teeth into the two-faced, cigar-smoking egotist.

———

"Quiet reigning here at the fort?" Skip had just returned to the office after a morning session in Family Court.

"Not exactly," said Lucy. She reached to the corner of her desk and held up a blue-backed folio. Harley Morehead

199

dropped this off about an hour ago. He said a process server delivered it to his printing office. He was none too happy."

"What is it?"

"A summons and complaint in a wrongful death action brought on behalf of the Estate of Squeaky Grimes."

"Damn, I was hoping Kelly would await the outcome of the criminal case before suing."

"Apparently not."

Skip took the papers from Lucy. He skimmed the first cause of action. "Looks as if Squeaky didn't have any family dependent upon him for support." Skip moved on to the claim for conscious pain and suffering. Once he finished skimming, he muttered aloud, though mainly to himself: "Five million, plus another ten in punitive damages. Based upon the autopsy report, Squeaky died quickly. There's not a lot to support a huge verdict for conscious pain and suffering. Punitive damages might be another matter." He turned to Lucy. "Apart from being unhappy, did Morehead say anything when he left the papers?"

"Not really, unless you count a nasty growl."

"I'll have to give him a call. But first, I'll talk to Kelly and see exactly where she's coming from."

Lucy pointed at the papers. "Don't they tell you?"

"Yes and no. Possible she served these just to get the ball rolling. Maybe she still plans to await the outcome of the criminal case." Potential complications that the wrongful death action could create with the pending criminal prosecution were already dancing in Skip's head. He headed into his office and dialed Kelly's number. Her secretary answered, and a minute later Kelly came onto the line.

"What a pleasant surprise."

"As if you have no idea why I'm calling."

"Social call...or might it have something to do with the summons and complaint I served on your client?"

"Gosh, you're clairvoyant."

"Don't I wish. But here—let me test my skills." She paused. "Something tells me you're not calling to say that a check for fifteen million is in the mail."

David A. Weiss

Coming from most adversaries, the banter might have irked Skip, but not from Kelly. Had the shoe been on the other foot, she would have accepted the razzing. She fought hard for her clients but didn't treat matters as personal, at least so long as her adversary didn't make it such.

"I assume you plan to hold the action in abeyance pending the outcome of the criminal case." Skip was far less sanguine than his words.

"Sorry, but I plan to move ahead. I'm convinced that Morehead is responsible. If and when the contrary is established, and I don't anticipate that, I'll go after someone else. In the meantime, your client is it."

"So, I need an acquittal before you'll get off his back."

"More than that. You'll have to convince me he's innocent. As you well know, unlike the District Attorney who has to prove guilt beyond reasonable doubt, I need only prove it's better than 50-50 that your client killed Squeaky."

"You can do that once the criminal case is over. Why not wait?"

"The pending criminal charges can work to my advantage."

"You can't mention them to a jury." Skip knew he wasn't fooling Kelly.

"But I can schedule a deposition."

Skip had worried she was headed there. Pointing out that Morehead could take the Fifth Amendment served no purpose. Unlike a criminal case where no unfavorable inference could be drawn from his refusal to testify, Morehead could be called to the stand in the wrongful death action. If he then declined to answer questions based upon the possibility of self-incrimination, the jury could use that against him as grounds to conclude he had killed Squeaky. Skip wanted to tell Kelly she was putting him in a horrible position, but the point was as absurd as it was valid. Kelly represented the Estate of Squeaky Grimes. She was duty bound to do whatever she could to protect and promote the interests of the Estate, including tactics inimical to Morehead.

"It's not personal. I assure you."

Skip knew that, but he refused to concede the point, not when she was making his life difficult.

"C'mon, you and I go way back. Need I remind you of what we shared in the past?"

"Aha...so that's it." As long as she was giving him a hard time, he might as well give her a good-natured jab. He said, "You're getting even for our old breakup."

"That's hardly what I meant. And need I remind you that I was the one who terminated our relationship?"

There was no getting around that. There was also no getting around her obligation to do the best she could for Squeaky's estate. "I know, you're only doing your job. I understand."

"I'm glad you do, because *I never did.*"

Her comment, its reference to the past tense, suddenly cast a cloud over her position, one that theretofore had seemed painfully clear. "What didn't you understand?"

"Exactly why our relationship didn't succeed."

Five years earlier when she had broken it off, he had analyzed what had happened a hundred times. He thought he had figured it out. His analysis had always been predicated upon the assumption that the reasons, at least in her mind, were clear. He said, "You don't know why we split up?"

"Yes and no."

"What does that mean?"

"There were a variety of reasons, some real and others...I don't know. Anyway it's water over the dam."

Maybe it was, but he wanted to pursue the issue.

Before he could, she said, "You have a nice day."

"You too." The telephone clicked in his ear. He held it there for a moment before hanging it up. Her comments about their breakup stirred old thoughts, the kind that had kept him awake night after night. He leaned back and stared at the wall revisiting bygone ruminations, how and why he had let Kelly slip away. Megan—Skip had been unable to get beyond her loss—had played a role. Commitment was impossible. But that was a copout. Kelly had never asked for Megan's place in his heart. She had made that plain. As long as he had room for her as well, that was enough. Unfortunately, a foursome, one that included *Jack*, was too crowded. But at the time he still needed his friend and the anesthetized world he provided. That was then. Perhaps times and needs were finally changing. He had been on the wagon for more than a month. Maybe he was ready to commit. But what about Megan? The excuse, one he had used before, reared its odious head. As fast as it did, he was forced to dismiss it. Megan wasn't the problem. She would have wanted him to move on. She would have wished him the best life possible, just as he would have wished that for her if their roles had been reversed. On the other hand, *Jack* was more complicated. It was hard to give him up. That didn't mean that Skip was an alcoholic. Common sense told him he was making familiar rationalizations. Regardless, it didn't matter. The issues were all academic. Whatever Kelly and he had shared in the past, whatever had caused their breakup, they couldn't go back. They were adversaries in litigation, and the canons of ethics precluded a personal relationship.

"Karl Fuller on line one," said Lucy over the intercom.

"Damn," muttered Skip.

"I can tell him you're in a meeting."

"Oh...no. I want to talk to him. The *damn* was for me. I never returned his last call." Skip pressed the button for line one. "Hi Karl. Sorry I didn't get back to you." Skip paused just long enough to see if recriminations would be forthcoming. They weren't. That wasn't Karl's style. "So, what's up?"

"You might say this is your lucky day. I spoke with Samantha Gardner, and she knows she's in the driver's seat. I told her I thought Biddleford would award a hundred dollars per week or maybe more. She said she isn't looking to take your client to the cleaners. She's willing to accept seventy, provided she can avoid a trip back to court."

The proposal was sweet music. Lenny was more than willing to pay seventy-five. But if Fuller was offering to take seventy, there was a possibility his client would accept less. "Sixty and we have a deal."

"You're pressing your luck, Skip. Take seventy now, or we'll let Biddleford settle it. That's a promise."

Most times Skip negotiated long and hard, but there were exceptions. Fuller had made an excellent offer. Only a fool would let it slip away knowing that given the chance, His Holiness, homophobe that he was, would come down hard on Lenny Gardner. "Seventy a week it is."

"My client will pay her own attorney's fees, provided the order is retroactive to the date the petition was filed."

If they fought it out in court, not only was the order likely to be retroactive but Lenny could also expect to get hit with his ex-wife's attorney fees. He was fortunate she wasn't out for blood. "Okay," said Skip. "You've twisted my arm." He knew better than to gloat over the good deal. No matter how pleasing a settlement might be, when dealing with an adversary, Skip maintained a subdued or even a dejected façade. Lawyers were competitive. Rubbing success in an adversary's face would only make him fight harder the next time they crossed swords. And in a rural area where lawyers were few in number, that next time generally came quickly.

"I'll notify Judge Biddleford that we'll be putting a settlement on the record when we go back to court."

"Sounds good. And before you go…" Skip hesitated as he searched for the best approach to the delicate issue. "Any chance, now that the support matter is resolved, of finding out if your client has information about a possible connection between her ex and Squeaky Grimes?" The question made Skip uncomfortable. He was venturing into the never-never land of a conflict of interest. What might be good for Harley Morehead might be bad for Lenny Gardner.

"Actually, I discussed it with my client already. I spoke with her a few weeks back when you first raised the issue. She authorized me, if and when we resolved the support matter, to discuss it with you."

Anticipation mounted. "And?"

"There's not a lot to tell. When she and Lenny were married, they lived in Oneonta a few blocks from his hair salon. Following the split, she stayed in the house, while he moved to Cooperstown, next door to Grimes."

"Even so, she might have information. According to Lenny, he and Samantha stay in regular contact."

"Yes, from what I understand, they're still friends, and, as a matter of fact, that's why your client is getting off so easy. Samantha says he's reliable, as well as flexible, when it comes to visitation with their daughter. Perhaps more important are the odd jobs he does helping to keep her house in shape. But whether Lenny's connection to Squeaky went beyond the proximity of their respective flats, she has no idea."

"Did she, by any chance, know Squeaky?"

"Not personally. But a couple of times Lenny had referred to him as the quirky neighbor with the ungodly voice. Based on what Lenny told Samantha, Squeaky was a nobody who not only knew everyone on the block, but also everybody who was anybody. Mention a name of someone in the area with political, social or financial clout, and Squeaky claimed to have an in with them."

The characterization, a repetition of everything Skip had heard, was no surprise. If only it were as easy to garner details about others with possible links to Squeaky's murder. "By any chance did your client know whether Squeaky was gay?"

"She didn't, though, when I asked her, she said it crossed her mind. No surprise, given Lenny's leanings."

Skip sensed there was more to the link between Lenny and Squeaky, but getting at it was another matter. In all likelihood the difficulty lay not in his questions, rather his source. Samantha Gardner had probably shared what little she knew.

"Do you think Lenny might be tied to Squeaky's death?"

"No." Skip's emphatic tone exceeded his certainty.

"Sorry, I should have known better. No way would you be representing the person charged and someone else who might be involved."

The potential conflict was all too obvious. Skip knew of nothing concrete precluding him from representing both Harley Morehead and Lenny Gardner. But that begged the question. The mere possibility, as well as Mickey's sixth sense, provided reason enough to steer clear of the pitfall.

205

Rather than immediately calling Lenny Gardner with news of the settlement, Skip procrastinated until after lunch, hoping the noon-hour break would provide a sage strategy to explore potential links between Squeaky and Lenny. A telephone call to Mickey, the best idea Skip could conjure at the time, accomplished nothing. An hour later, with food in his stomach, but a want of ideas in his head, Skip dialed the hair salon.

"*Sublime Coiffeurs*...Gardner speaking."

"Hello Lenny. This is Skip Maynard. Am I catching you at a bad time?"

"No, I just finished putting my customer's hair in curlers." Gardner lowered his voice. "Can you hold a moment while I switch to the phone out back? It's a bit more private."

Moments later Gardner answered again. "Sorry to keep you waiting. What's up?"

"I don't mean to interrupt your work, but I wanted to let you know that I managed to settle your support issue. I would have waited, but I wanted to be sure you heard it from me rather than your ex-wife."

"So, give me the bad news."

"It's not that bad. Seventy dollars per week."

"Seventy—did I hear you right?"

"That's what I said."

There was a momentary silence.

"I can't believe you got me off that cheap. As I told you, I would have been thrilled with seventy-five. You did a helluva job."

The praise made Skip's day. All too often clients were unhappy with results, especially in support cases. It didn't matter which spouse one represented. The one seeking support complained of being shortchanged while the other screamed about being hosed. "I appreciate the kudos, but much of the credit is yours. Your ex was reasonable thanks to the goodwill you've garnered through visitation and helping to keep her house in shape. But about the settlement, there's one more thing: the increase is retroactive seven weeks to the filing of the petition."

"No big deal. Anyway, you warned me that was likely."

Skip was about to shift the conversation to Squeaky.

"I don't mean to sound impatient, but, unless there's something pressing, I should get back to work."

"Well, I would like to talk some more, but...under the circumstances it can wait."

"Whatever you say. And thanks again for a super job."

"My pleasure." Skip hung up the receiver. He had what he arguably valued most about the practice of law, an appreciative client. Regardless, he felt a distressing undercurrent. Was Gardner a piece of the Morehead puzzle and, if so, might he turn out to be problematic?

Chapter XII

Papers in hand, Lucy stepped through the doorway from the reception area into Skip's office. "Judge Biddleford's decision on the motion to suppress Morehead's confession just arrived in the mail."

"You don't have to tell me. His Holiness told us to go to hell." The expected result fit perfectly with the way Skip's morning had gone. An engineer's report had indicated that the house one of Skip's clients was selling was structurally unsound. And the morning's research on a brief in opposition to an adversary's motion for summary judgment revealed case law dead against Skip's position. "Go ahead, give me the bad news."

"I'll let you read it yourself." Lucy handed him the papers.

Skip immediately flipped to the last sheet of the three-page decision. He could get the nuts and bolts behind the ruling afterwards. He focused on the paragraph just above the Judge's signature.

> *Accordingly, the motion to suppress the confession of the defendant Harley Morehead is granted. As for the knife, the alleged murder weapon, which was found in the shed at the rear of the defendant's property, it too must be suppressed as a fruit of a search resulting from said confession.*

Skip did a double take. He carefully read the paragraph a second time. "Holy freaking hell!" he bellowed, as he turned to Lucy. "Wonders never cease. The son of a bitch granted our motion. Can you believe it?"

Lucy stood there grinning

"Of all people, His Holiness, the throw-away-the-key conservative, the guy who presumes every defendant who walks into his courtroom must be guilty, is suppressing Morehead's confession. And not just his confession, but the knife too."

"Hard to believe, isn't it?"

Skip shrugged, still struggling to digest the ineffable. He flipped back to the first page of the decision. Before he got too carried away, he needed to read the whole thing. He perused it quickly. It was fairly well-reasoned, allowing for the fact it had come from Judge Biddleford. Among its underpinnings, it noted that the hand-written confession had been obtained by Detective Ramsey at the defendant's home without the presence of another police officer. That, in and of itself, was rare, and in felony cases, particularly murders, unprecedented for the long-time detective. The opinion indicated that Morehead, as Chairman of the local Populist Party, was a savvy individual, who presumably would have consulted with an attorney. The claim that he had contacted Ramsey and offered the hand-written confession strained credulity, especially given that he refused to provide a statement once he was at the police station in the presence of other officers. Finally, the opinion noted that the Appellate Division had thrown out a confession obtained by Detective Ramsey in a prior case.

Skip looked up at Lucy. "This is amazing!"

"I know," she said. "Morehead may get acquitted."

Skip already had the same thought. Arguably the odds had shifted in Morehead's favor. Without the confession and the knife, the District Attorney would be hard pressed to prove a case beyond a reasonable doubt. "It's a whole new ballgame. If the District Attorney appeals this decision, I doubt he'll be successful. Biddleford had the chance to observe Ramsey on the stand and weigh his credibility. The Appellate Division knows that Biddleford almost never grants these motions. Merely examining a transcript, they'll be reluctant to substitute their judgment." Skip eyed the credenza that occupied the far corner of his office. On past occasions when he got an especially good decision or settled a big case, *Jack*, stowed away in the bottom of the cabinet, led the celebration.

Lucy glanced at the credenza and shook her head. "Not a good idea." She knew Skip as well as he knew himself. She also knew that he hadn't taken a drink in weeks.

"Don't worry," he said. "There's no semblance of alcohol there. In fact, that was the bottle I gave you a few weeks back, along with instructions to keep it from me, even if I asked." He thought for a moment. "That doesn't mean we can't celebrate." He checked his watch—11:34. At twelve o'clock you and I are going downstairs to the *Pantheon* for pizza, soda and a cannoli." He gestured at the decision. "But first I want to call Morehead with the good news."

"In the meantime, I'll type the *Porter* complaint. I promised myself I'd get it done this morning." Lucy headed out to the reception area.

Skip turned his *Rolodex* to the letter *M* and looked up the number for Morehead's printing office. He dialed it.

"*Prime Printing.* Harley Morehead speaking."

"Harley. It's Skip. You sitting down?"

"Don't tell me Biddleford, that lousy bastard, revoked my bail."

"No...no. It's nothing like that. I've got good news."

"Well, I'm sitting. So, fire away."

Once more Skip scanned the key sentence at the conclusion of the decision making sure he hadn't imagined it. "I have Judge Biddleford's decision on our motion to suppress. He suppressed your confession. The District Attorney won't be able to introduce it at your trial. He's also barred from offering the knife into evidence."

"That's good."

Good? Skip had anticipated that Morehead would be ecstatic. Perhaps he failed to comprehend the significance of the decision. But that was all but impossible. He and Skip had discussed the importance of the motion to suppress repeatedly. "You hardly sound excited?"

"I am."

"Could have fooled me."

"Sorry. I guess it's because I was an observer at the hearing. You did such a great job that I knew we'd win."

Skip recalled their conversation after the hearing. Unlike Skip, who anticipated an unfavorable decision, Morehead was confident. Skip tried to put himself in his client's place. If he were facing life imprisonment, anything that enhanced the likelihood of an acquittal would have evoked an ebullient reaction. On the other hand, Skip had seen defendants do nothing more than breathe small sighs of relief when juries returned not guilty verdicts on serious felonies.

"I assure you. I'm one happy guy. I really appreciate what you've done. At the same time I don't want to get too excited, at least not yet. I'm still not out of the woods. As Yogi put it, *It ain't over till it's over.*"

The sobering point had merit. The prosecution had a rocky road ahead, but unless and until a jury returned a verdict of not guilty, the final score remained in doubt. Skip envisioned the all-too-familiar moment when the foreman would rise to deliver the outcome. Skip's stomach would tie in knots, and with good reason. A single, tiny three-letter word on the lips of the foreman was the difference between a free pass out of the Courthouse and a permanent stay in a prison cell.

"Gentlemen, I understand the parties have reached a settlement and are prepared to put it on the record. Is that correct, Mr. Fuller?" said Judge Biddleford.

"Yes, Your Honor."

"Mr. Maynard?"

"That's right, Your Honor."

"Mr. Fuller, would you place the terms into the record?"

Fuller got up from his seat. "It is hereby agreed by and between the parties to this proceeding that Leonard Gardner will pay the sum of seventy dollars per week to his former wife Samantha Gardner for the support of their minor child Judy Lynn Gardner, and that said payments will commence retroactive to May 15th of this year when the petition was filed with this Court."

"Is that your understanding, Mr. Maynard?"

"Yes, Your Honor. And I'd like the record to show that Mr. Gardner has already caught up on the retroactive portion and his payments of seventy dollars are current through the week ending this Saturday."

"That's correct, Your Honor," said Fuller.

"Is there anything else this Court needs to consider today?"

"No, Your Honor," said Fuller.

"Nothing more," said Skip.

"Then apparently, just that quickly, we're done." The Judge rapped his gavel. "This Court is adjourned."

Skip started slipping his papers into his file when the Judge came down from the bench to the respondent's table. He focused on Lenny Gardner. "Fortune has shined upon you today."

Gardner displayed a puzzled look.

"Seventy bucks per week. That's a cheap price for a fellow who traded his wife for his boyfriend." The Judge turned to Skip. "Wouldn't you agree, Counselor?"

Coming from any other jurist, the injudicious remark would have shocked Skip, but not from Biddleford. Regardless, Skip wanted no part of it. He said, "I believe the parties reached an equitable result. It's always good when differences can be resolved amicably."

"It would have been my pleasure to assist them had they not done so on their own. Unlike some, I refuse to endorse the gay lifestyle, not when statistics prove it's anathema." He peered at Gardner. "You look confused. So I'll spell it out. Take a look at our prisons. Homosexuality is rampant there. Why?—Because criminality and homosexuality go hand in hand." He turned and marched out of the courtroom.

Once he was out of earshot, Gardner whispered, "Thank God we settled." He pointed to the mural on the wall depicting the blindfolded woman holding the scales of justice. He shook his head. "I've always assumed that judges were a cut above the politicians in the other two branches of government. How naïve."

Reality, at least Skip's version, lay somewhere between the cynical assessment and something more idealistic. He said, "Most judges aren't like Biddleford."

Gardner shrugged. "Yeah...I suppose. Anyway, I'm glad you were able to work things out. You did a great job." He shook Skip's hand and started to leave.

"Before you go, can we talk a little about Squeaky Grimes?"

Gardner said nothing, but his body language was a picture of discomfort.

"Did you know him?"

"Well...not in any real sense."

The denial, pregnant with admission, or what lawyers refer to as a *negative pregnant*, amplified Skip's curiosity. "What does that mean?"

"I'd rather not talk about it."

Gardner's reluctance suggested the subject might involve something adverse to his interests. The possibility of a conflict was rearing itself again. "Representing both you and Harley Morehead is becoming increasingly difficult."

"It's fine with me. Does Morehead have a problem?"

"No. But that's not the point."

A ripple in Gardner's brow hinted at confusion.

"Your interests appear to conflict."

"In what way?"

Broaching the delicate issue was proving a challenge. "Representing Morehead, I need to explore every avenue that might aid his defense. That includes finding out what, if anything, you know about Squeaky and his murder."

Gardner pulled back. "You don't think I'm involved?"

"No, but..." Skip couldn't rule out the possibility. "Perhaps I can better explain by summarizing what I do know. You lived next door to Squeaky. Shortly after he was killed, you walked into my office and hired me. Coincidence? Maybe. But for reasons known only to you, you're reluctant to discuss the subject."

"So, what are you saying?"

"I don't think I should represent you anymore." The offended look on Gardner's face told Skip his attempt to explain had failed. "Please, it's nothing personal. The canons of ethics dictate it. A lawyer is prohibited from representing clients with inconsistent interests. Morehead's interests demand that I press you about Squeaky. You, on the other hand, want me to beg off. I can't do both."

Gardner nodded. "I think I understand...not that I'm enthusiastic." He looked Skip in the eye. "Does that mean we're parting ways?"

"I guess so," said Skip, though the outcome was hardly ambiguous.

"Well...I can't say as I like it. But if that's how it has to be...what can I say, except thanks for keeping my child support down." Gardner shook Skip's hand and left the courtroom.

Alone, Skip contemplated what had just occurred. He gathered his papers. The dilemma spawned a wealth of familiar questions. At the top of the list—What did Lenny Gardner know about Squeaky's murder?

Skip hesitated outside the door of the *Eagle*. Mickey, who had been doing follow-ups on those with a possible motive to kill Squeaky, had suggested the evening site. Skip might have objected had he not established the precedent several years earlier. When work demanded a ten or twelve hour day, a relaxed atmosphere, plus the company of friends, helped mitigate the burden. No place had a more relaxed atmosphere than the *Eagle,* and back then Skip had no better friend than *Jack.*

Conscious of sweaty palms, particularly his left, Skip pulled open the tavern's heavy wooden door. He was right handed, but he had always held *Jack* in his left. Drinking was one of a very few things he did with his left hand. He had developed the habit years earlier at the family dinner table. His fork was always in his right hand. Between bites he would take a sip of milk. The two-handed approach, utensil in the right and glass in the left, carried over. He wiped his left hand on the side of his trouser leg, just below the bottom of his sport jacket. Off to his right in a booth along the far wall, Mickey, a cigarette between his fingers, was motioning to Skip.

"What would you like to drink?" said Mickey, as Skip arrived at the table.

The tall dark brew that sat in front of Mickey was tempting. *Jack* was even more so. Skip said, "I'll have a...*Diet Pepsi*." If he couldn't have *Jack*, why waste the calories on so many grams of sugar?

"You sure you wouldn't prefer something with a little more kick?"

The answer was a resounding *yes*. Unfortunately what Skip preferred was not the issue. He said, "A *Diet Pepsi* will be fine."

"Suit yourself." Mickey motioned to the barmaid and ordered the soft drink. "Don't know how you can do it. I couldn't." He thought for a moment. "I wouldn't." He held up his *Camel*, briefly appearing to watch the smoke that billowed forth. "Life is too short, not to mention too tough, to give up the few pleasures that are available whenever you want them."

He had a point. It wasn't what Skip wanted to hear. Or maybe it was. Did he really want to put *Jack*, the one friend he could always count on, out of his life? When Skip had Megan, *Jack* was at most an acquaintance. Next to her, the silent friend in the dark bottle paled. Admittedly at a party or after a hard day Skip sometimes relaxed with *Jack*, but a single tumbler, or occasionally a second, was plenty. There was no desire, let alone need, to escape reality. Skip watched Mickey inhale on his cigarette. "Did you ever consider giving up smoking?"

"Don't *you* start with me."

"I won't. I promise. I was simply wondering if you had ever tried to give them up."

Mickey heaved a frustrated sigh. "Yeah, when I was about thirty. I had already been smoking for over fifteen years. The Surgeon General had recently linked cigarettes to cancer. At the time I was doing about two packs a day. My goal was to cut it to one the first month and then chop that in half the next. Within a week I was back to my two packs." He took another puff. The cigarette was little more than half an inch. He used it to light another. "It's my life, and I intend to live it my way. Isn't that what the *Bill of Rights* is about?"

Despite an extraordinarily broad brush, Mickey was not completely in left field. But legal arguments to the contrary were also familiar to Skip. The public, which was bearing the costs of tobacco's health hazards, claimed the authority to regulate smoking. Arguments involving individual freedoms were always that way. Collisions of conflicting interests at opposite ends of a linear spectrum. With neither side able to see the other's viewpoint, invariably the question: Where should lines be drawn? But as with most such issues, economic factors colored the debate. In this case powerful tobacco money, the omni-present lobby, had its say. The lawyer in Skip or, perhaps more precisely, the gadfly was tempted to pursue the debate. But he was in no position to preach, not when he had his own vice. Discretion, the knowledge that Mickey wanted to hear none of it, kept the homily from reaching Skip's lips. He said, "I hear what you're saying. It makes sense. But for the time being I'm sticking to *Diet Pepsi*."

"Fine with me." Mickey held up his cigarette. "Live and let live. Do that, and you'll get no arguments here." He took a puff and inhaled deeply.

The barmaid delivered Skip's soda. He sipped the carbonated beverage. Though knowledge he was doing the right thing helped, he resented the inherent inequity. Day after day the battles would continue. He could win a hundred in a row, but one defeat, and the war might be lost. Addiction was that way, not that Skip was an alcoholic. That's what he told himself in a conscious effort to quell the depressing thought. He said, "So, have you made any more headway with any of our persons of interest?"

Mickey took another puff.

The action was symbolic. Mickey could deliver good news with or without a puff. With bad news a drag was always an indispensable precedent.

"Everyone seems to be clammin' up. Detective Ramsey—he never wanted to talk to me anyway—won't even return my calls now. And Morelli, Feinstein, Kileen, even your lady friend, City Manager LaDieux, are givin' me the fast shuffle. They have more excuses than *Doubleday* has seats. They don't have time. They have nothing to say. They prefer to let the judicial process take its course. It's all the same. Not so friendly hints that I should get lost." Mickey flicked some ashes onto the floor and puffed again. "Speaking of LaDieux, I think she has the hots for you. Before she chased me away, she hinted a visit from you might make her more talkative. Based on her tone and body language, I'd say she wants more than talk. And with that body, there's no doubt she could fill the bill." Cigarette in one hand and brew in the other, Mickey drew a curvaceous outline in the air.

Skip had no need for the artistic assist. His brain had already conjured a vivid image of LaDieux's voluptuous figure. The last time he had seen her she had given him the come on. She was anything but subtle. As long as he had to bear a widower's misfortune, he might as well enjoy the rare perks. The logic was impeccable. The damn canons of legal ethics—they had been showing their ugly face all too often—forbade the pleasure. He would need to subpoena the City Manager for Morehead's trial. A lawyer was prohibited from being in bed, whether literally or figuratively, with a witness, particularly an adverse witness. Skip reached for his goddamn *Diet Pepsi*. The beverage had already proved itself a lousy substitute for *Jack*. The icy glass was an equally poor surrogate for the beguiling charms of Traci LaDieux.

Mickey shook his head.

"What's that supposed to mean?" said Skip, his bark a consequence of frustration that was no fault of Mickey.

"I can read your mind." He shook his head again. "You oughta try livin' life a little more on the edge, like me. An illegally taped telephone conversation here, a trespass there—you do what you gotta in order to get information. And when a looker with a rack like LaDieux comes lookin' for action, you rock and roll."

Skip summoned one last, lustful image of the City Manager. The time would come when Morehead's case would be past history. He would have to be patient, but patience would ultimately be rewarded. He said, "What about Jimmie Raines? Did you talk to him again?"

"Yeah...but I didn't get anywhere. All he did was hock me with his cockamamie pyramid scheme. Art something."

"*Artway*."

"Yeah, that's it. Anyway, when he talked about Squeaky, there were no kind words, not that he fed me anything useful." Mickey took a swig of his brew. "But that doesn't mean I didn't discover some interesting tidbits about Raines. Some fellas told me that back in March in the Grill Room of the *Leatherstocking Club* they heard Squeaky accuse Raines of stealing from their business. The two got animated, and Raines threatened Squeaky." Mickey pulled a slip of paper from his pocket and handed it to Skip. "The three guys listed here—they're all members at *Leatherstocking*—heard Raines make the threat."

"Good work," said Skip, as he eyed the paper. He sipped his *Diet Pepsi.* "What about alibis?"

"From what I've been able to piece together, apart from Kileen, who was in Hawaii, nobody really has one."

The information was not a surprise. The coroner had estimated that Squeaky had been dead for ten to twenty hours before he examined the body around noon on the tenth. That left a ten-hour window between four in the afternoon on the ninth and two in the morning on the tenth when he was killed. It was hard for most people to account for that much time."

The lack of alibis was helpful. Skip planned to subpoena all the persons of interest. Each had a connection to Squeaky, and some, a semblance of motive. Ordinarily the shotgun approach was legally unsound, but in criminal defense work it had its place. Spray ammunition. Create lots of possibilities, enough to leave the jury with doubts who committed the crime. The wide window of opportunity made it easy to include a long list of possible suspects. Unfortunately Harley Morehead was among those with no alibi.

"Anything new regarding Wilson's death?"

Mickey shook his head. "The police closed their investigation. Except for the fact that he worked for Morelli, I haven't been able to link him to any of the others we've been talking about. Basically he was a loner." Mickey used the remaining butt of his *Camel* to light another.

218

"What about his auto-body business?"

"Wilson did it all at his house. He fixed the wrecks, and that was that." Mickey puffed his cigarette. "I talked to some of his customers. They all said his work was excellent and his prices reasonable. Best that I could tell, none were linked to Squeaky."

Skip sunk his teeth into the shrunken remains of an ice cube. "Perhaps the police are right. A loner, disabled by a bad fall, grew depressed. Maybe Wilson did commit suicide."

Mickey launched a smoke ring into the air. "Maybe...but I still don't buy it."

A television remote crew, along with about fifty people, was milling around in front of the Otsego County Courthouse as Skip came out following some research in the law library.

"Gonna be some fireworks," said a man in jeans and a tee shirt with a New York Mets logo.

"What's it about?" said Skip.

The man pointed. "That fella over there in the pink shirt, the one next to the TV guy, is gonna make a big announcement. Ain't sure what."

Skip gazed in the direction where the man had pointed. The fellow in the pink shirt was vaguely familiar, but for the moment Skip couldn't place him. "Who is he, the one about to make the announcement?"

"Don't know. But I'll tell ya this. He's a fruitcup, if you get my drift."

The remark jogged Skip's memory. He was the same individual that had met Lenny Gardner after he and Skip had finished an appearance in court. At the time Lenny had engaged in an odd exchange with the fellow about some kind of World Series bet.

"Are you a lawyer?" said the man.

"Yes," said Skip.

"I kinda guessed that, what with you comin' outta the Courthouse and all sportin' one of them brief cases." The man nudged Skip. "Wanna hear a joke?"

Not really, thought Skip. He was staying around only because he was curious about the fellow's announcement.

"Where can you find a lawyer who doesn't lie?"

Skip had heard far too many lawyer jokes already. "You tell me," he said, making no effort to curtail a sarcastic inflection.

"In the graveyard." The man laughed and slapped Skip on the back.

Skip remained stone-faced.

"In the graveyard…Don't you get it?…The only lawyers who don't lie are dead ones." The man waited a moment. "Ain't you got no sense of humor?"

Skip shook his head. "How could I? I'm a lawyer. Did you forget?"

The man peered at Skip with a flummoxed look.

Skip might have continued the banter had not the television reporter begun speaking into his microphone.

"This is *TV Seven* newsman Riley Ripley coming to you from the Otsego County Courthouse in Cooperstown. Here with me is Darrell Plane with what we understand is a disclosure that's certain to rattle the upcoming November election for County Court Judge. Mr. Plane, what is it that you want the public to know?"

"I had a four-month affair with Judge Harold Biddleford."

A gasp from the crowd briefly interrupted the announcement.

"It ended shortly before Thanksgiving last year."

"Let me understand," said the reporter. "Are you telling us you engaged in a homosexual relationship with Judge Biddleford?"

"That's exactly what I'm saying."

"And where did this relationship take place?"

"Mostly at my flat over on Oak Avenue. Occasionally at his home just off Main Street. He lives alone there." Plane hesitated. "Ordinarily, I'm not one who believes in kissing and telling."

"Then why are you coming forward with this information?"

"Actually I've agonized for some time. But ultimately it came down to a matter of principle. I decided I had to. It's one thing to be homophobic. And don't misunderstand, as one who is gay, I take great offense at those, especially those in positions of power, who attempt to treat me as a second class citizen. But what we have here goes much further. It's the height of hypocrisy for Judge Biddleford to publicly maintain an anti-gay posture. It raises fundamental questions about his integrity. The public has a right to know."

The newsman turned toward the Courthouse. The camera shifted there as well. "Behind these walls there sits a Judge who must face some serious questions about his conduct. This reporter passes no judgment on the veracity of the allegations, but there is no doubt that Judge Harold Biddleford owes answers to some tough questions. The constituency that has repeatedly returned him to the bench is entitled to know if his conduct and rhetoric have been one hundred eighty degrees apart. We look forward to hearing Judge Biddleford's response. Regardless, *News Seven* will follow the story. In the meantime we return you to our studio."

Skip watched as the news crew packed up its gear. The crowd was buzzing. Several of them tried to corral Darrell Plane, but he resisted and disappeared down the street. The bombshell he had dropped was likely to turn the race for Judge Biddleford's seat on the bench upside down. Perhaps it explained why the jurist had never been married. Skip wondered if the disclosure might work to his advantage in the Morehead case. Having anyone other than Biddleford preside would certainly be an improvement. On the other hand, Biddleford had suppressed Morehead's confession. Would another judge have ruled that way? An old adage, *The devil you know is better than the one you don't*, popped into Skip's head. Fortunate rulings and adages be damned. Skip would gladly take potluck in place of Biddleford. But it wasn't going to happen. Regardless how the election turned out, Morehead's trial would not be delayed beyond Biddleford's current term.

The moment Skip arrived home from the office, he switched on the television. He glanced at his watch—4:56. The allegation of the homosexual relationship was likely to garner top slot on the local news. How would His Holiness react? A denial would spark controversy. An admission would unleash a hornet's nest. Whatever approach he adopted, repercussions were inevitable.

With an ear to the television Skip popped his usual fare, a TV dinner, into the oven. Five o'clock, and sure enough the lurid accusation led the broadcast.

"Today," said the anchorman, "a bombshell struck the race for Otsego County Court Judge. Cooperstown resident Darrell Plane announced that he had a four-month homosexual relationship with incumbent County Court Judge Harold Biddleford. For details we take you to the Otsego County Courthouse where this afternoon Mr. Plane leveled his claim." Skip watched the broadcasted replay of what he had observed earlier in the day.

"Immediately following Mr. Plane's disclosure," said the anchorman, "this station endeavored to speak with Judge Biddleford. His law clerk, Weldon Casper, indicated His Honor was busy with judicial duties. Mr. Casper did, however, issue a brief statement labeling Mr. Plane's allegation—and I quote—*a scurrilous and unmitigated lie unworthy of any response beyond a flat-out denial.* Mr. Casper raised the specter that the accusation might be a desperate ploy by Walter Barndecker, Judge Biddleford's Democratic opponent, to compete in an otherwise futile campaign. Late this afternoon I again attempted to contact Judge Biddleford, this time at his home, but was unsuccessful. Here with me in the studio is our legal commentator, attorney Gerald Hanson. Tell me, Mr. Hanson, how do you think this is apt to play out, particularly its effect on the race for County Court Judge?"

"At the outset let me emphasize that nothing I say in any way reflects either positively or negatively on the veracity of Mr. Plane's claim."

Skip laughed out loud. Typical lawyer. A disclaimer to protect against libel. Skip conceded he would have done the same.

"It's my opinion that Judge Biddleford, a staunch conservative, is in an especially difficult position. Having ruled in a previous case that homosexuals, unlike other classes such as racial or religious groups, merit no protected status, he plays to a constituency that regards such behavior as immoral. The very possibility that he has engaged in such conduct will stir a backlash within his conservative base. Voters closer to the center of the spectrum, who tend to be more accepting of homosexuality, are apt to view him as a hypocrite, unworthy of a place on the bench. And those on the left, never his supporters, will use the controversy as ammunition against him."

"How would you rate his re-election chances at this moment?"

"Much will depend on whether the allegations bear out. Of course, as so often is true with *he-said, she-said* controversies—in this case *he-said, he-said*—the dust never settles, and we're left to speculate. Having said that, I believe Judge Biddleford, who heretofore was a shoe in, now faces an extremely tough race."

"Any thoughts about the suggestion of Mr. Casper, Judge Biddleford's law clerk, that the Judge's Democratic opponent, Walter Barndecker, might be responsible for the rumor?"

"I'm glad you asked," said Hanson. "I've known Walt Barndecker for nearly two decades. Debate his qualifications to be County Court Judge all you want, but as far as his integrity, there is no question. Dirty tricks, innuendo and character assassination are not his way. I'm certain he did not precipitate the accusation. Might I add that Mr. Casper's suggestion to the contrary offends me."

Skip eased down into his favorite chair. Were the allegations about His Holiness true? Skip had no idea. Regardless, he had no sympathy for the black-robed bastard. For years he had sat on his elevated throne treating everyone—lawyers, parties, bailiffs, clerks and even jurors—with disdain. At long last the tables were turned.

———————

"What's this?" said Lucy, as Skip adorned her desk with a tiny bonsai tree. She pointed at her calendar. "National Secretaries' Day is months away."

"It's a small way of saying I have the best secretary and office manager this side of the Mississippi."

Lucy feigned an indignant look. "You trying to tell me I'm not as good as the ones from the west side of the river?" Her bright smile confirmed that she appreciated the thoughtful gesture.

To some their interactions appeared strange, but Skip preferred it just as it was. Although he was the lawyer and she, the employee, in his mind they were a team. Mutual respect was at the heart of their relationship. He placed a *Pantheon* pizza box, atop of which he had carried the plant, onto her desk.

"Pizza!...You do appreciate me."

"No, but I figured your favorite lunch would make you more efficient." He waited, anticipating she might continue the banter. She didn't. He said, "Let's go out back and indulge."

As she got up, she grabbed a paper from the corner of her desk. "The District Attorney's witness list for the Morehead case came in the morning mail. I think you'll find it interesting."

They headed to the back room where he removed two diet sodas from the refrigerator. With pizza in hand, no anchovies on his half, he reached for the witness list. It was part of the procedures that over the past two decades had altered the practice of law. Disclosure was the objective underlying the change. Depositions, bills of particulars and other devices enabled each side of a lawsuit to discover what evidence the other intended to introduce in court. Skip found it hard to deny that the rules made sense. Regardless, he had mixed feelings. He had begun practicing law when disclosure was in its infancy. Surprise and gamesmanship were elements of the judicial process. Opponents of the new procedures—Skip was among them—resented the idea that a lazy adversary could dig into the file of a diligent lawyer. Skip liked to play his cards close to his vest. Disclosure made it tougher. But the judicial process was aimed at finding the truth, not identifying the most

David A. Weiss

skillful master of courtroom illusion. While cleverness and the art of surprise were entertaining, in his heart of hearts Skip conceded they often allowed dramatics to supersede justice. Whether Skip liked it or not, trial by ambush, as it was sometimes termed, had become a relic. He read the prosecution's witness list which, among others, included: Detective Theodore Ramsey; Officer Mark Thomas; the county coroner; a hematologist; Warren Holt and Guy Devine, both of whom would reputedly testify that Morehead was a bookie; and Eddie the Enforcer Willis, Morehead's collector of bad debts. Their names were all anticipated. But there at the end of the list was one Skip hoped he would not see: Leonard Gardner. Skip pointed at the name. "What do you think of that?"

"My guess, your former client knew Squeaky a whole lot better than he let on."

"And his hiring me was no coincidence." Skip bit into a slice of pizza, masticating both the mouthful and the revelation. What was Gardner's connection to Squeaky? What did he know about the murder? Might he be the linchpin in the prosecution's case against Harley Morehead? He said, "I can't believe the son of a bitch was using me. Sugar sweet, and all along he was conning me."

"You can't be sure."

"Would you like to bet on it?"

"No thanks. I'll leave the wagering business to Harley Morehead."

Lucy's sardonic comeback underscored one more problematic element of the case. Skip eyed the witness list. Presumably the District Attorney knew that Skip had represented Lenny Gardner. If so, why hadn't the District Attorney contacted Skip? A setup crossed his mind, but that seemed unlikely. The District Attorney wasn't foolish enough to play that game, not when it could earn him a date with the disciplinary committee. More likely, the District Attorney minded his own business while Skip dug himself a hole. But maybe the District Attorney didn't know about Skip's connection to Gardner. Neither matrimonial cases, nor the personal problems of witnesses were of concern to the prosecutor's office. But whatever the District Attorney did or

225

didn't know, Lenny Gardner knew a whole lot more than he had let on.

Once Skip had finished his lunch, he dialed Lenny Gardner's apartment. He got the answering machine. Rather than leave a message, he called Gardner's hair salon.

"*Sublime Coiffeurs*. Gardner speaking."

"Hello Lenny. It's Skip Maynard. You got a minute?"

"Yup. My customer is out front under the drier. I hope there isn't a problem with the support settlement."

"No problem. But just this morning I received the prosecution's witness list for the upcoming Morehead trial. Your name is there." Skip waited for a reaction. There was none. "They obviously have a reason for including you as a witness."

"Well...I suppose they do."

"You mind telling me?"

"It'd be better if you asked them. I'd rather not speak for the District Attorney."

The dodge came as no surprise given Gardner's earlier failure to be forthcoming. "The District Attorney would recommend I talk to you. I'd appreciate your telling me what you know about Squeaky Grimes's murder."

"I don't mean to be difficult, but I'd rather not discuss it."

Skip was on thin ice. Gardner was a former client, and pressing him on a subject that might be adverse to his interests was hardly appropriate. The problem could have been simpler had Skip not opted to represent Gardner in the first place. He said, "I assume you discussed it with the District Attorney's office."

"No."

"Are you telling me you have no idea why they want you as a witness?"

"That's not what I said."

Skip wished he had Gardner on the stand. No judge would let him get away with such double talk. "Why do they want you to testify?"

"I'd rather not discuss it. That's what I told the police as well. They threatened to charge me with interfering with governmental administration or something like that if I didn't cooperate."

"I take it you told the police what you know about the case."

"Yes."

"And you expect to testify?"

"Maybe. I don't know."

The soft-spoken fellow who had seemed so nice in the office had become a pain in the ass. Polite, yes, but extremely obstinate. "What do you mean—you don't know?"

"They told me I could expect a subpoena for the trial, but I haven't received one yet. If and when I get one, I'll have to go to court, I guess. That, or maybe I'll discuss it with a lawyer first. I'd like it to be you, but based on what you told me after the settlement, I assume that isn't possible."

The comment underscored that the conversation had already gone too far, but Skip could not resist the temptation to explore one last nagging matter. He said, "Darrell Plane, the fellow who claims he had a homosexual relationship with Judge Biddleford—isn't he the same guy with whom you made some kind of bet a couple months back?"

"So?"

"Is the allegation true?"

"You'd have to ask Darrell. Just like you straight folks, most of us who are gay keep our sex lives behind closed doors. Often in the closet, if you know what I mean."

Skip longed to press Gardner as to what he knew, not just about Judge Biddleford's alleged affair, but even more so, Squeaky's murder. Curiosity, however, surrendered to judgment. Skip was only looking out for Morehead's interests. Gardner needed someone who would do the same for him. That someone wasn't Skip. Reluctantly he said, "Under the circumstances, I should probably let you go." His words echoed in the earpiece of the receiver. It wasn't *probably*. "You may need to speak with an attorney, one who will evaluate the situation based exclusively on what's best for you. Mind you, I'm not telling you what to do. It's merely a thought."

"I'll keep that in mind. And thanks again for the great job you did on my child support."

The receiver clicked.

Skip hung up the telephone. He stared into space trying to put the situation into perspective. Lenny Gardner had been as sweet as ever. But was it all an act? The first day Gardner had walked into the office, he may have come armed with ulterior motives. All along Mickey had been skeptical that mere coincidence explained how Gardner had come to hire Skip. The possibility existed that Skip had been baited into a trap.

Chapter XIII

Skip glanced at his watch—9:41, eleven minutes after the scheduled commencement of the trial. He had lost his cigarbox gamble, a bet with himself, that with the pending allegations of sexual impropriety His Holiness would go out of his way to make a favorable impression, especially with the huge public interest in the homicide case. Skip made a mental note. Judge Biddleford's arrogance apparently knew no bounds. Underestimating him at the wrong moment could be disastrous.

Skip gazed at the finely carved wooden framework that wrapped around three sides of the Judge's bench. Nearly four feet high the varnished hardwood had character. At regular intervals scrupulously sculpted cutouts resembling the playing-card symbol for *clubs* hinted that elements of gamesmanship had their place within the impressive hall. But unlike the smoky backrooms where many card games were played, the courtroom in the Otsego County Courthouse bore the stately elegance that exemplified its Queen Anne Revival exterior. No doubt it was an arena for high stakes games. And none were higher than a murder trial.

Out of the corner of his eye Skip peered at the man he was representing. Ordinarily attired in natty sport jackets and colorful silk shirts, Harley Morehead, per Skip's insistence, wore a dark suit and a tie with a conservative stripe. Glib and brawny, with proportions suggesting he might have been a football lineman in his high school days, the defendant looked more like an undertaker than a gregarious businessman and politician. Finding a jury had not been easy. Owing to preformed opinions about the widely publicized case, many prospective candidates had to be dismissed. Others with views

229

about Morehead, mainly owing to his involvement in local politics, had met the same fate.

Morehead whispered in Skip's ear, "We're gonna win this thing. I'm certain."

Glad you're sure. Though Skip said nothing, he suspected his face may have hinted at his reaction. Never in the years that he had practiced criminal law had a defendant made such a cocky remark at the commencement of a trial. Even those who seemed confident during pretrial proceedings were apprehensive once facing the reality of a tense courtroom.

Judge Biddleford finally stepped through the door behind the bench. All rose as the self-important master of the realm sank his bulbous torso into his generous leather throne. He briefly surveyed the scene before inviting the throng to take their seats. He shuffled some papers and then turned to the prosecutor. "Mr. Carter, are the People ready to proceed?"

"Yes, Your Honor."

"And the defense?"

"Yes, your...uh...Honor." Skip, who was still digesting the demeanor of his client, caught himself just before referring to Judge Biddleford as your Holiness.

"Mr. Carter, your opening statement."

The handsome, six-foot prosecutor got up from his seat and walked slowly toward the jury box. He carried a yellow pad. That came as no surprise to Skip. Though Carter would maintain eye contact with the jury much of the time, he was one to read his opening statement. That approach was certainly easier, but in Skip's mind, a distinct disadvantage. Still Skip knew better than to sell Carter short. Far from an insecure litigator who hoped to script his proof, the District Attorney was adept at rolling with the punches and improvising as the case moved along.

"Ladies and Gentlemen of the jury. At the outset let me thank you both individually and as a group for giving of your time for this civic duty. The case you are about to hear charges the defendant Harley Morehead (Carter gestured at Morehead) with the murder of Ralph Grimes, more commonly known as Squeaky. The testimony will show that the defendant did willfully and intentionally stab the victim Ralph Grimes to death in his Rock Street apartment. The testimony will also show that the defendant was a convicted bookmaker who—"

"Objection, Your Honor." The trial had barely commenced, and Skip could hardly believe he was on his feet shouting. "The District Attorney has poisoned this jury with information he cannot prove."

"What is it you contend the prosecutor can't prove?" barked Judge Biddleford, his annoyance with the objection undisguised.

"Your Honor, may I approach the bench along with the District Attorney?" Skip sensed that Biddleford had missed the point. "Discussing the matter openly could compound the wrong."

"Well...all right. Come forward, but understand this proceeding will not become a disjointed series of incessant interruptions. I get enough of that every evening when commercial intrusions distract from my favorite television shows."

The analogy drew a chuckle from spectators behind the bar. Even several of the jurors joined in. But those like Skip who were in the courtroom regularly were not laughing. They had heard Judge Biddleford utter the hackneyed gripe before. What the uninitiated also failed to realize was that an important legal point had escaped the Judge.

As the prosecutor and Skip met in front of the bench, Judge Biddleford, his voice soft, but also stern, said, "Exactly why have you interrupted the District Attorney's opening statement, Mr. Maynard?"

"He labeled my client a *convicted bookmaker*."

"Excuse me," snarled the prosecutor. "I said I intend to prove that he is a *convicted bookmaker*."

"That's my recollection too." Judge Biddleford's impatience was unmistakable.

"That's not the point," said Skip. "The prosecution can only introduce evidence that Mr. Morehead was convicted for bookmaking to impeach his credibility, and that will only occur if and when Mr. Morehead waives his rights under the Fifth Amendment and opts to take the stand. The District Attorney has prejudiced my client."

Judge Biddleford's eyes widened.

"Your Honor," said Skip, "I move for a mistrial."

"A mistrial!"

"Absolutely." Skip had no illusions that his motion would be granted, not that he wouldn't have welcomed it. A mistrial would insure that the case would not be tried until after the November election. With Plane's allegations of a homosexual affair, the possibility that a new judge might occupy the bench was real. Even potluck was preferable to Biddleford. Skip said, "To have this case begin with the jury aware that the defendant is a convicted bookmaker, a fact that may not be provable by competent evidence, is grossly unfair."

"Mr. Carter," said Judge Biddleford, "your adversary has a point. Having created this complication, what do you have to say for yourself?"

"Your Honor, Mr. Maynard is making a mountain out of a mole hill."

"A mountain out of a mole hill!" Judge Biddleford's bark, though far from a shout, may well have been picked up by the jury. "Do you deny the potential harm to the defendant owing to your error?"

Skip would have jumped in, but there was no need. For once Judge Biddleford was carrying the ball, though his motive differed. While Skip was protecting the defendant, His Holiness was protecting himself. Even more than most judges, the egotistical jurist hated to be reversed by appellate courts. While a single mistake of lesser magnitude would not bring that about, several—and accumulations were often rapid—could.

"Your Honor," said the District Attorney, "if you instruct the jury to disregard my use of the word *convicted*, I'm sure they will."

"Mr. Carter, you seem to be treating this matter rather cavalierly. Need I remind you that it is your mistake that has occasioned this predicament."

"Your Honor, I...uh...didn't mean to minimize the situation. I was merely suggesting what I believe is the appropriate remedy."

Skip knew the District Attorney was not taking the *faux pas* lightly. With a highly publicized murder in a county where homicides were few, a mistrial resulting from his inability to deliver a proper opening statement would be a political disaster. That it occurred in the first minute of the trial would spark charges of incompetence. The local press would chop him to bits.

"Mr. Maynard, would it satisfy you if I admonish the jury to ignore the remark?"

Skip shook his head. If Judge Biddleford thought the absurd ploy would get him off the hook, he needed to think again. Skip looked the jurist squarely in the eye. "I am requesting a mistrial."

After grumbling briefly under his breath, Judge Biddleford said, "I'm denying your motion." Judge Biddleford turned to the District Attorney. "Your misconduct has placed this Court in a difficult position. A mistrial would come at significant expense to the taxpayers, not to mention a waste of the time of many. I will not allow that. But from here on out you had better demonstrate greater prudence. Do you understand me?"

"Yes, Your Honor."

"Fine, return to your respective tables, and I will unravel this mess, so we can move forward."

Once the prosecutor and Skip were back at their stations, Judge Biddleford turned to the jury. "Ladies and Gentleman, we have all endured a protracted delay. This unfortunate interruption was caused because the prosecutor suggested that the defendant was previously convicted of bookmaking. The District Attorney's statement was entirely improper. I am directing you to ignore it. Give it no credence whatsoever. The defendant enters this courtroom with a clean slate. Whatever you learn about this case, including anything about the defendant's background, must come exclusively from the evidence."

Morehead whispered in Skip's ear. "What did you do up at the bench? Threaten him with more allegations of homosexual liaisons?"

Skip quickly put a finger to his lips.

"Mr. Carter," said Judge Biddleford, "please continue with your opening statement."

Skip watched his adversary closely as he got up from his seat. The prosecutor's gait had slowed. Doubtless the jury didn't know the details of what had transpired, but they knew the District Attorney had done something wrong. They appeared to study him with a new vigilance. Perhaps Skip was reading more into the triers of fact than actually existed. In any event, the District Attorney seemed more defensive. His speech had become more measured. He was less animated. The polish and self-confidence that had made him such an attractive candidate when he had run for office had seemingly tarnished. His message had become less compelling. The scene reminded Skip of the first presidential television debate nearly a decade earlier. Minutes before District Attorney Donald Carter bore the look of the dashing and mellifluous John F. Kennedy. A misstep had turned him into the perspiring, five-o'clock shadowed Richard Nixon. What Carter said mattered less than how he said it. The prosecution was off to a shaky start.

Once the District Attorney completed his opening statement, Skip got up, but only after the prosecutor was back in his seat. Skip never tried to script a trial. That wasn't his style. In a world that always held surprises, he valued flexibility. As he walked past the prosecutor's table toward the jury box, his brain was working overtime. The prosecutor's misstep made it advantageous for Skip to shorten his opening statement.

> *Good morning, Ladies and Gentleman. This is my first opportunity to speak to you. You have heard from Mr. Carter. He has told you what he intends to prove: motive, premeditation and the actual homicide. Not one word he has spoken is evidence. These are the elements he is required to prove. And he must prove each and every one of them beyond a reasonable doubt. Otherwise you are duty bound to return a verdict of not guilty.*
>
> *As you know from the process during which you were selected to serve on this jury, the defendant, Harley Morehead, walks into this courtroom with a presumption of innocence. Each of you assured me you*

234

would approach this case with a full respect for that principle. Skip looked the homemaker in the second row directly in the eye. During *voir dire* he had questioned her on that very matter, and now he was holding her to that promise.

As of this moment not one scintilla of evidence has been adduced. The slate on Harley Morehead is blank. Skip's eyes moved slowly over the panel. The elderly man at the right end of the first row was looking straight ahead. His stare was icy. Perhaps Skip should have used a peremptory challenge to excuse him. Hindsight had advantages. Skip hoped it wasn't twenty-twenty.

At the conclusion of the prosecution's case the defense intends to call a number of witnesses. What you will hear is testimony demonstrating there were other individuals with motive and opportunity to kill Ralph Squeaky Grimes. I submit to you that the testimony will convince you that someone other than the defendant killed Mr. Grimes and that the defendant Harley Morehead is totally innocent. However, it is not the duty of the defense to solve this crime. That is the obligation of the prosecution. Not just to convince you that the defendant may have committed the crime, but to convince you beyond any reasonable doubt.

My client asks only that you listen to the testimony—all of the testimony—and then with the guidance contained in the Judge's instructions deliberate the case. Do that, and I am confident you will return a verdict of not guilty. Thank you.

Skip walked slowly back to the defense table. He had been briefer and less dramatic than he might otherwise have been, but he was satisfied the jury would closely scrutinize the evidence and hold the prosecution to its burden. That was as much as he could ask.

Judge Biddleford checked his watch. Hardly half-an-hour had elapsed since he had taken the bench. He said, "Although we haven't been convened that long, it would be well to allow those in need of the opportunity to visit the rest room. We'll take a fifteen-minute break."

Give *me* a break, thought Skip. Judge Biddleford was the one needing a delay. Too much coffee, and he would likely have another cup. Skip also knew that the ploy fooled none of the court clerks or attendants. More than once he had heard them remark about the Judge's addiction to the caffeinated beverage. What irked them most were his demands that they fetch his brew. His Holiness treated court personnel like serfs. Compounding the indignity, he was the type of lord who degraded. The musing reminded Skip of the occasion when, after a conference in chambers, Judge Biddleford had directed Skip to tell a court attendant to pick up a birthday card for a friend over the noon hour. Instead Skip simply informed the attendant the Judge wanted to see him. His Holiness could do his own dirty work.

Skip headed out into the hall. Kelly Lane was milling around there. "What brings you here?" he said, not that he needed an explanation.

"In case you forgot, my client, or should I say former client, was the victim of the murder you folks are debating in the courtroom. As the attorney for his estate, I have a distinct interest in the outcome."

"You mean that wrongful death action you brought against my client?" Skip waited a moment. "I know, a guilty verdict would suit you just fine."

Kelly shrugged. "I can't say it would break my heart. On the other hand, what I'd really like is a little justice for Squeaky."

Skip contemplated a recommendation that she focus on others instead of Morehead, but soon enough he would be back in the proper forum for that argument.

"By the way," she said, "that was a cool move you made during Carter's opening statement. It reminded me of the Skip Maynard I saw in the courtroom a dozen years ago, my senior year in law school. I had a crush on that guy." She headed off.

His eyes followed the motion of her tight butt as it moved to the swivel of her shapely hips. She looked great in a brown suit. Then again, she looked great whatever the apparel. As she disappeared around the corner, thoughts of the trial overshadowed the vision of her pleasing silhouette. Litigation, with its heightened focus and all-consuming nature, had that effect. Skip valued that blessing. He also detested its curse.

———————

"Mr. Carter, please call your first witness."

"The People call Detective Mark Thomas."

As the witness stepped forward and took the oath, Skip eyed the jury. All five men and seven women were keenly attentive. *Voir dire* had revealed that only one woman had ever sat on a criminal case before. The shoplifting charge in a local justice court had been resolved with a plea and a suspended sentence shortly after the commencement of testimony. From all indications the jury embarked upon their duty appreciating the magnitude of their responsibility. For the system to work properly, that was essential. For the defendant, Harley Morehead, it could, depending on the evidence, be problematic.

The District Attorney, after quickly moving through the details of Detective Thomas's background and experience, said, "If I direct your attention back to the morning of April 10th, do you recall that day?"

"Yes, I was on duty. It was a few minutes before eleven when I received a report that the landlord of Ralph Grimes had expressed concern for his tenant. Mr. Grimes had previously been seen going into his apartment but failed to respond to either telephone calls or knocks at his door."

"Do you know the name of Mr. Grimes's landlord?"

"Yes. It's Bernard Feinstein, the County Comptroller."

"And once you received the report, what did you do?"

"Along with Officer Watson, I went to 14 Rock Street, where Mr. Grimes lived."

Following a glance at his yellow pad, the District Attorney said, "Kindly describe the exterior of the premises."

"An older, two-story frame house with a porch in front. It had two adjoining doors, the right for the flat on the first floor and the left for the one on the second. Mr. Grimes occupied the lower flat."

The District Attorney gestured at the jury box. "Please tell the jury what transpired once you arrived there."

"Officer Watson and I rang the doorbell. There was no answer, so we rapped on the door several times. Still no answer. We tried to look into the windows but couldn't see much. Blinds and shades, as well as some curtains, blocked our view. We had been in contact with Mr. Feinstein, the landlord, and so, rather than break down the door, we waited a few minutes for him to arrive and unlock the front door of the apartment."

In his seat at the defense table Skip remained focused on his notes. A look was unnecessary. The engaging prosecutor had drawn the full attention of the entire jury. Despite his early miscue, the prosecutor was back on his game.

"What happened next?"

"Officer Watson and I went into the apartment. Unsure what we might find, we asked Mr. Feinstein to wait outside. The door led directly into the living room. At the far end, where the room met the dining area, a body—I assumed it was Ralph Grimes—was lying on the floor."

Judgment kept Skip from moving to strike what Detective Thomas assumed. The point, though valid, would be quickly cured, and in its wake the jury would come away with the impression the defense was trying to obfuscate the facts with technicalities.

"Please describe for the jury how the body was situated."

"It was face down, parallel to the line that separated the living and dining room. The head was to my left and the feet, my right, as I entered."

"What did you do once inside the apartment?"

"Officer Watson called for backup and an ambulance, just in case Mr. Grimes wasn't dead. In the meantime I checked his body. He wasn't breathing, and he had no pulse. With all the blood I was certain he was dead. I checked the apartment to make sure no one else, dead or alive, was there. While Officer Watson secured the crime scene, I brought Mr. Feinstein in, just long enough to make an identification. He confirmed it was his tenant, Squeaky Grimes. That's what he called him. Oh...and I also notified the Coroner's office."

"You mentioned blood. Where did you observe it?"

"It was all over Mr. Grimes…his shirt and his pants. It was everywhere. And there was a large pool of blood next to his body about a foot from the dining room. There was also a trail leading from the center of the living room. It made me think Mr. Grimes may have been stabbed there and that he was stabbed again after—"

"Objection as to what the witness thought." Skip completed the words as quickly as he reached his feet.

"Your Honor," said the District Attorney, "experienced as Detective Thomas is, he is entitled to express an expert opinion."

"Excuse me," said Skip, "even assuming he might be an expert—and he's yet to be qualified as such—he was merely speculating, not giving an expert opinion."

"Objection sustained."

The District Attorney took a moment to review his notes before refocusing on the witness. "What did you do next?"

"I examined the living room and dining room."

"And to give us a clearer picture of the flat, can you describe its layout?"

"At the front, the area nearest the front porch, was a large living room. Moving back through the flat was a small dining room with two tiny bedrooms off to the left. At the rear of the apartment, just beyond the dining room, was the kitchen."

"A few moments ago you mentioned that you examined the living room and dining room. What did you observe about them?"

"They were anything but neat. A few newspapers were strewn about the living room. On the table in the dining room there was all sorts of stuff: the guts from a couple of old radios, a dirty jacket and work pants, some magazines, a bunch of rags, four or five rolls of toilet paper, and a few other things."

"What else did you observe when examining the apartment?"

"There were several spots of blood, four to be precise, on the hardwood floor leading through the living room towards the front door."

"Can you describe those spots?"

"They were generally round and ranged in diameter from about an inch down to about a quarter of an inch. Oh, and I also found some blood on the interior handle of the front door. It was located toward the bottom, near what would be five o'clock if you picture the handle as a clock."

"What, if anything else, can you tell us about that trace of blood?"

"Well, it might best be described as a smear. About a half-inch by a quarter of an inch."

"What did you do next?"

"I went into the kitchen. There were dirty dishes on the table and in the sink. On the counter I observed a wooden knife block. It had slots for six knives. Only five knives were there. The largest slot was empty."

Skip's focus, already sharp, heightened. Evidence that linked the missing knife, the murder weapon, to Morehead could be critical, a potential linchpin that could lead to a conviction. Remarkably Judge Biddleford had not only suppressed Morehead's confession but also the knife. The ruling that it was a fruit of the poison tree, a consequence of the confession, had surprised Skip, almost as much as it had pleased him. Consistent with legal principles, the Judge could have easily ruled that the knife was admissible on the grounds that investigation independent of the confession would have led to the search of Morehead's shed and, ultimately, the weapon. Skip needed to exercise the utmost care to ensure he did nothing that would open the door to the knife's receipt in evidence. That the District Attorney would try to accomplish indirectly what he could not do directly was a foregone conclusion. And already the prosecutor had started down that Machiavellian road.

"How wide was that empty slot?"

"An inch and a half."

"The wooden block. Can you describe it for us?"

"It had a rectangular base, about six inches square. The top sloped. It was roughly ten inches tall in the back and about eight inches in the front."

"Was the slot for the missing knife in the front or back?"

"The back."

Out of the corner of his eye Skip caught the District Attorney stealing a glance his way. The testimony about the knife block was a *Pandora's Box*. But as long as the box remained unopened, as long as the knife wasn't linked to Morehead, the box was harmless. On cross-examination Skip could ask many questions about the knife and its holder. He would ask none of them. No way would he touch *Pandora's Box*.

"In the course of your investigation, what did you do next?"

"About that time the ambulance, along with another squad car, arrived. Just before they did, Watson took a picture of the body and several of the crime scene. The emergency medical personnel examined the body and rushed it away."

The District Attorney went over to the court stenographer and had nine photographs marked for identification. He took them to the witness stand and handed them to Detective Thomas. "I show you People's Exhibits Number One through Nine and ask if you can identify these?"

"They are the pictures, the ones I mentioned, that Officer Watson took."

One by one Detective Thomas explained what the pictures depicted: two of the body of Squeaky Grimes on the floor where they found it; the spots of blood; the living room, dining room and kitchen. One by one the District Attorney elicited testimony establishing that each was a fair and accurate representation of what was photographed. Finally he said, "I offer People's Exhibits One through Nine in evidence." The District Attorney handed the photographs to Skip, who methodically examined them.

"Mr. Maynard," said Judge Biddleford, "any objection?"

"I'd like to *voir dire* the witness." Telltale tightening of the Judge's lips was not lost on Skip. "Very briefly, Your Honor."

"Proceed."

Skip stepped forward. "Detective Thomas, you indicated that Officer Watson took these pictures. Is that correct?"

"Yes."

"And where is he?"

"Objection, Your Honor. Detective Thomas is here on the stand and is familiar with the pictures."

"Overruled. The witness testified that Officer Watson took the pictures and, therefore, he is relevant to their admissibility." Judge Biddleford turned to the witness. "Kindly tell us what you know about Officer Watson's whereabouts."

"He's in the State of Oregon, I believe. He left the force and moved there about a month after we did this investigation. But he had announced that he was leaving the force several weeks prior to Mr. Grimes's murder."

"Move to strike the last comment as gratuitous and beyond the scope of the question."

"Denied."

The predictability of Judge Biddleford's unpredictable rulings had Skip briefly musing about the paradox. But the logic of the illogic was sufficiently familiar to be quickly resolved. Such was the nature of litigation in front of a far-from-brilliant political hack who had failed to devote the time and effort required to master the many complex rules of evidence. Skip quickly refocused on the task at hand and, particularly, the nine exhibits that had been offered into evidence. Except for the first two, the photographs did little more than sharpen the image of the crime scene. Most important, they did nothing to link Morehead to the crime. Skip sensed Judge Biddleford's impatience. Skip said, "No objection to the photographs, except Number One and Two, which purports to show the body of Mr. Grimes lying on the floor. The graphic detail is highly prejudicial."

"Objection noted, but rejected. The position of the body and the location of blood on that body have potential probative value that may assist the jury in determining exactly how the crime in question occurred. That potential outweighs the minimal risk of prejudice. People's Exhibits One through Nine are received in evidence." Judge Biddleford turned to the District Attorney. "Proceed."

"Your Honor, may I show the photographs to the jury?"

"You may."

The better part of ten minutes elapsed as the jury quietly passed the photographs among themselves. Whatever their reactions, they showed nothing. When they were finally done and the pictures handed back to the District Attorney, he said, "Detective Thomas, did you at anytime check the premises for fingerprints?"

"Yes, I dusted for them in the living room, dining room and kitchen."

"What did you find?"

"A number of prints, but apart from those which were simply unidentifiable smudges, they all matched the victim's prints."

"Thank you," said the District Attorney. He walked back to the prosecution table and examined his notes briefly. "No further questions."

"Mr. Maynard," said Judge Biddleford, "your cross-examination."

Skip got up and circled around in front of the defense table. He preferred to ask his questions from that location, rather than over near the jury box rail. Detective Thomas had proved to be an engaging witness. Having him turned kitty-corner away from the jury would make it harder for him to connect with them on a more personal basis. "Mr. Thomas," said Skip, eschewing the witness's title of detective, "if I recall your testimony, and correct me if I'm wrong, you made an initial look around the apartment and later you checked it more closely?"

"That's right."

"Apart from Squeaky's body and the blood, you found no evidence of a struggle; for example, overturned chairs or lamps, broken glass, or knickknacks strewn on the floor. Isn't that right?"

"Yes."

"Isn't it also true that later that day you made an even more exhaustive search of the entire flat?"

"Yes."

"And that search showed absolutely no evidence of any kind of gambling paraphernalia such as betting slips, gaming devices, gambling records or the like?"

"Well...I did find a deck of cards in a desk drawer."

Out of the corner of his eye Skip saw a tiny shake of the head of the elderly male juror occupying the first seat in the second row. "A deck of playing cards in a box?" Skip laced his voice with sarcasm.

"Yes."

"But there was no gambling paraphernalia, was there?"

"No."

Skip moved closer to the witness. "Now, Mr. Thomas, earlier you referred to spots on the floor that appeared to be blood. I'm referring to the spots in People's Exhibits Three, Four, Five and Six. Of your own knowledge you don't know that they were blood, do you?"

"Well...no."

"Now, let's talk about that smear you found located at about five o'clock on the door handle. You first observed that subsequent to the time that you had examined Mr. Grimes's body to see if he was alive and subsequent to the time when Mr. Feinstein came in to confirm the body was indeed that of Mr. Grimes. Isn't that right?"

"Yes."

"You told us that one of the first things you did when you arrived on the scene was to check Mr. Grimes's pulse. To do that you had to touch him, didn't you?"

"Yes."

"Where exactly did you check his pulse?" Skip avoided a leading question because he already knew the answer from Detective Thomas's testimony at the suppression hearing. Perhaps the Detective would slip up. If so, Skip would impeach his answer with the earlier transcript.

"I checked his wrist and then his neck, the carotid artery."

"So, perhaps you got his blood on your hand?"

"I doubt it."

If the detective thought he could dismiss the possibility so easily, he was mistaken. "Earlier you told us there was blood all over Squeaky. Right?"

"Yes."

"Your first concern was for him...whether he was alive. True?"

"Yes."

"Under the circumstances you could have gotten some blood on your hand when checking his pulse?"

"Well...I suppose."

Thomas had given a crumb, tiny perhaps, but enough to satisfy Skip's appetite. "So, the trace of blood on the door handle may have come from your own hand. True?"

"Highly improbable."

"But you can't preclude it?"

Detective Thomas failed to respond.

Pressing the issue would gain little, likely less than the witness's silence. "Mr. Thomas, you told us that there was a pool of blood all around the body. It's also possible that you got blood on your shoes and tracked it through the apartment, isn't it?"

"I was very careful."

"But when you first arrived on the scene, as you already told us, your primary concern was for the man on the floor. You were hoping he was still alive, weren't you?"

"Yes, but as an experienced detective, I was careful with a potential crime scene."

Skip walked forward, much closer to the witness. "Officer Watson was not so experienced. He was a rookie, wasn't he?"

"Yes."

"And he had already announced his departure from the force, hadn't he?"

"Yes."

"On direct examination you indicated one of the first things you did was to check the entire flat for other persons. You also indicated that later you made a more thorough examination, including the kitchen. True?"

"Yes."

"During that time Officer Watson was out of your presence, wasn't he?"

"I guess so."

"So, it's possible Officer Watson tracked the spots of blood with his shoes?"

Detective Thomas heaved a sigh.

"Excuse me," said Skip. "I didn't hear your answer."

"I suppose it's possible."

"And the smear of blood on the door handle may have come from his hand. Isn't that true?"

The witness broke eye contact.

Skip merely waited.

Finally Detective Thomas said, "It may have."

"May have?" muttered Skip softly. His voice quickly grew loud. "The truth be known, you have absolutely no evidence who created that smear of blood, do you?"

"Well...no." A lowered gaze underscored Detective Thomas's concession.

Skip eased back a couple of steps and folded his arms. "Let's talk about fingerprints. You told us you dusted for them, but only found Squeaky's. Correct?"

"Yes"

"Isn't it a fact that you failed to dust for fingerprints until after you had examined both the body and the flat and had Mr. Feinstein confirm that the victim was Squeaky Grimes?"

"Well...yes, but I was concerned about—"

"You've answered the question. It merely called for a *yes* or *no*, not why." Skip took note as Detective Thomas shifted his position in the witness chair. He appeared far less comfortable than when he had first taken the stand. "Mr. Thomas," said Skip, in order to let Mr. Feinstein in and out of the flat, you and he had to use the door handle. Right?"

"Yes, I guess."

"And I assume that you dusted for fingerprints on the interior handle of the front door, the one where you found the smear of blood?"

"Yes."

"And you found no fingerprints there?"

"Nothing other than what appeared to be a print of Mr. Grimes's index finger. Everything else was too blurred to be identifiable."

"I assume you've dusted for fingerprints many times before?"

"Yes."

"And would it be fair to say that if one person touches where a fingerprint has been left, that can blur an existing fingerprint making it unidentifiable?"

"Yes."

"So—it's possible that the killer left his or her fingerprints on the door handle, but you or Officer Watson or Mr. Feinstein deprived us of that knowledge by blurring the killer's fingerprints before you dusted?"

"I doubt it. I was careful."

"But Officer Watson or Mr. Feinstein may not have been so careful?"

Thomas swallowed hard. "I guess so."

Skip walked backed to his chair. Still standing, he gazed at the witness for several seconds. "No further questions."

The District Attorney had no re-direct and called his next witness, Dr. Walter Milliman. The District Attorney took him through the preliminaries establishing his qualifications as a physician with nearly twenty years of experience as County Coroner. He testified that he arrived at the crime scene shortly before noon on the 10th of April, at which time, after examining the body, along with the crime scene, he pronounced Ralph Grimes dead. He estimated that the victim had already been dead for ten to twenty hours before he examined the body. He ruled the death a homicide and fixed the cause as multiple stab wounds, three to the abdomen and two to the back, resulting in a huge loss of blood. Three of the stab wounds were between six and seven inches deep, while one each to the abdomen and back were in the four-inch range. Based upon the depth and width of the wounds, he estimated they had been made with a knife or similar instrument with a blade at least eight inches long and roughly an inch and one-half at its widest point. He further testified based upon his expertise that the wounds were indicative of a blade with a sharply pointed tip and a serrated edge.

Once the prosecutor completed his direct examination, he returned to his seat. Skip stared blankly at his notes. Excusing the Coroner with no cross-examination was hard to imagine, and yet it made sense. There was no doubt Squeaky had been stabbed to death. Nothing in the Coroner's testimony pointed in Morehead's direction.

"Mr. Maynard, we're waiting," said Judge Biddleford.

"Um..." Skip found it too hard to simply say, *No questions*. He got up and walked forward. The outside chance to create another avenue of reasonable doubt inveigled him.

"Dr. Milliman, you indicated that you ruled this a homicide. Correct?"

"Yes."

"Isn't it possible, however, that it may have been a suicide?"

"I doubt it. People don't ordinarily stab themselves, particularly in the back."

Skip had anticipated the response and was ready to deal with it. "But it is possible?"

For an instant the witness's eyes widened. "Given the smear of blood on the door handle and the spots on the floor, I think not."

The less than emphatic denial was exactly what Skip was looking for. "Doctor, you can't say in what sequence these stab wounds were made, can you?"

"No."

"Isn't it possible that Mr. Grimes, standing next to the front door, stabbed himself in the abdomen—perhaps one of the shallower wounds—put his hand there, then touched the door handle and walked across the room, during which time blood dripped causing the spots on the floor. Thereafter upon reaching the spot where the body was found he could have inflicted the remainder of the wounds?"

"Well..." The Doctor peered off into space.

The hesitation buoyed Skip. He gave the jury a glance as he waited patiently.

"People who commit suicide do it with pills or jump out of a building. They don't stab themselves with a knife."

"Doctor, that's what they usually do. But there are exceptions. Indeed Mr. Grimes may be that exception?"

The witness sat up tall. "Mr. Grimes did not die of self-inflicted stab wounds. Besides the three to the abdomen, there were two to the back. They were not self-inflicted."

Skip was only looking to leave the door of suicide open a crack, enough that reasonable doubt about the possibility would remain in the minds of the jury. "But Doctor, a person is capable of stabbing himself in the back, isn't he?"

"Yes." Dr. Milliman turned to the jury. "However, a self-inflicted stab wound to the back, especially a deep one, would be at an angle, not perpendicular to the back. The seven-inch stab wound to Mr. Grimes's back was directly perpendicular to his back. I am absolutely certain he did not do it himself."

Skip felt a lump in his throat. He had fallen prey to one of the most basic miscalculations known to trial lawyers, the reluctance to simply say, *No questions.* Excusing an adversary's witness without any challenge was inherently difficult. The desire to counter an adversary's points, however minor, was inescapable. Temptation could seduce even the most judicious lawyer to turn a blind eye to the potential peril. And Dr. Milliman, an experienced witness, constituted just such a peril. His seeming defensiveness at the beginning of cross-examination may have been a ploy. There was even the possibility the prosecutor had put him up to it. Regardless, Dr. Milliman had turned the tables and waltzed Skip down the primrose lane. The competitor in Skip yearned to fight back. He wanted to explore the wounds and the knife that had caused them. Judgment halted the lunacy. He was playing with fire. Careless questioning could open the door to testimony regarding the suppressed knife. Having it linked to Morehead would be a disaster. Dr. Milliman had fed Skip a piece of humble pie, but at least it was small. Additional questions could turn it into a glut. Skip strolled back to his seat and pretended to examine his notes. He looked up at the bench and said, "No further questions."

"No re-direct," said the District Attorney.

Judge Biddleford glanced at his watch. "The noon hour is already upon us. This is a perfect time to break." He looked over at the jury. "During lunch please refrain from any conversation whatsoever concerning the case. We will reconvene at two o'clock. In the meantime I hope you all enjoy a good repast." His eyes shifted to Skip, as he added, "One that will leave you fit for the afternoon."

Much as Skip resented the innuendo, he found it hard to argue with its propriety. His recollection, foggy though it was, how several months earlier, with *Jack* in sway, he had stumbled in for an afternoon session was hard to erase. Skip had hoped the shameful memory might get buried in the past. Apparently His Holiness had other intentions.

Chapter XIV

Skip plopped himself onto his usual stool, left end of the bar at the *Eagle*. If he returned to the office, he would be drawn to the mail and telephone messages. Enduring such distractions at the end of the day was tolerable, but not over the noon hour in the midst of a trial. Years earlier his trial-practice professor had described the courtroom as all-consuming. As far as Skip was concerned, the characterization was an understatement.

"I'll be with you in a minute," said Loomis, as he drew a couple of drafts for some other patrons.

"No problem," said Skip instinctively, his brain focused on how he might impeach a witness he anticipated the prosecution would call during the afternoon session.

A minute later Loomis placed a large *Diet Pepsi* in front of Skip. Apparently he was determined to obviate the possibility that Skip opt for *Jack's* company. In fact, Skip had already decided on the non-alcoholic beverage.

"What can I get you to eat?" said Loomis.

"The usual, but skip the onions." Skip glanced around to make sure no one was listening and then whispered. "If I were smart, I'd go double on the onions, raw and extra strong. I could blow in His Holiness's face."

"He's giving you the usual hard time?"

The comment set Skip to thinking. Candor forced him to admit that the normally abrasive and arbitrary jurist had shown far less impatience than usual and, more important, discounting legal ineptitude, remarkable fairness. "As a matter of fact, he's behaved like..." Skip found it hard to voice the concession aloud. "...like a member of the human race. A human being."

"You know," said Loomis, "maybe...just maybe, you've been too rough on him in the past. Perhaps he's not the ogre you thought."

Skip bristled. The ever-objective bartender had gone too far. Biddleford was a creep, and a single morning of semi-civil behavior didn't erase years of abomination. Skip let his face do the talking.

Whether Loomis got the message, he didn't press the point. He said, "How's the trial going?"

"Okay, I guess. Of course, there's a long way to go."

Loomis gestured toward the other end of the bar. "The fellow in the green shirt down there said he watched part of the morning proceedings. According to him you had Carter reeling more than once."

Skip chuckled to himself. He had one-upped an adversary before, only to find that when the jury rendered its verdict, he and his client were on the short end. Landing jabs was great sport, but juries were remarkably adept at looking past lawyers' showmanship and sifting through the evidence to reach a just verdict. He said, "We'll see what's what after the dust finally settles."

Loomis's enigmatic expression was at best noncommittal. "Gotta go," he said, and he hurried down the bar where a man in a business suit was waving an empty highball glass high in the air.

Skip eyed his *Diet Pepsi*. He took a gulp. Unlike his pal *Jack*, that perfect mash which blended a pure Lynchburg spring with fine corn, barley and rye, it was nothing more than carbonated water flavored with syrup. Tolerating it was tough, but more important concerns demanded he do so. Harley Morehead's life, whether he would spend the rest of it in prison, was on the line. Great friend that *Jack* was, duplicity, unintended or not, accompanied his friendship. Sure, *Jack* meant well. And he even made Skip feel good. Inhibitions vanished amidst a surge of bravado. But arming oneself with *Jack* meant slurred speech, impaired reasoning and slowed reactions. For all his pluses, in the courtroom *Jack* was a recipe for disaster. The time had come for Skip to go it alone.

Skip eyed his watch—2:13—as Judge Biddleford finally took the bench. Late, as usual.

"Before we bring the jury in, may I see both counsel at the bench."

Skip met the District Attorney there.

Judge Biddleford peered down over his narrow-rimmed glasses at Skip. "Looked like you walked a straight line."

The purpose of the powwow became apparent, and it irked Skip, especially because the Judge had made the remark loud enough that the stenographer and court attendants and perhaps even the spectators in the last row heard it.

"I figured a field sobriety test was in order given the post-lunch show you staged at the suppression hearing. No way would I allow you to reprise that performance now that we have a jury."

Looking up at the elevated bench was always tough, but at that moment Skip felt two-feet tall. He whispered, "All I had to drink was a *Diet Pepsi*."

"Good. So, let's get on with it." Judge Biddleford looked to his left. "Mr. Witmeir, bring the jury in."

Skip headed back to the defense table. As he did, he felt the District Attorney's hand pat his back. Donald Carter was an adversary striving within the rules to win a case, but personal humiliation was not his objective. Having spent many a day in Judge Biddleford's courtroom, doubtless he had taken his share of shots. Empathy was understandable.

Once the jury was seated, Judge Biddleford said, "Mr. Carter, please call your next witness."

"The People call Terrance Winter."

An elderly gentleman, neatly attired, stepped forward and took the oath. He gave his age as seventy-four and was qualified as an expert in the field of hematology with over forty years of medical practice.

"Mr. Winter, on the 10th day of April of this year, did you have occasion to examine blood at the flat of Ralph Grimes at 14 Rock Street?"

"Yes, at about three o'clock that afternoon."

"Was Ralph Grimes's body still there when you conducted your examination?"

"No, but there was an outline on the floor where it had been found."

"And what exactly did you examine?"

"Blood from a pool in the outline, along with some spots on the floor and a smear on the door handle. I had already gotten a sample of Ralph Grimes's blood at the morgue."

Using the pictures already in evidence, the prosecutor had the witness specifically identify the pool, spots and smear. He said, "And what did your examination show?"

"That all of the blood, the pool next to Mr. Grimes's body, the spots on the floor and the smear on the door handle was Type AB, Mr. Grimes's blood type."

"How common is AB?"

"Actually it's the least common. Only about six-tenths of one percent of the population has it."

"Do you have an opinion that you can state with reasonable medical certainty as to whether the blood you found on the premises was that of Ralph Grimes?"

"Yes. Based upon the Coroner's report describing Mr. Grimes's wounds, and given that the fresh pool of blood next to his body, as well as the spots and smears, matched his blood type, and further given the rarity of his blood type, I can state with reasonable medical certainty that all of that blood did indeed come from Mr. Grimes."

"And do you also have an opinion whether all of that blood was a result of his wounds?"

"Objection," said Skip. "As an expert, the witness may express his opinion, but only if he can state it with reasonable medical certainty."

"Dr. Winter," said Judge Biddleford, "can you state with reasonable medical certainty whether all of the blood you found was, in fact, a consequence of the stab wounds sustained by Ralph Grimes?"

"Well...I'd be surprised if it wasn't."

"Doctor, that's not what I asked you." Judge Biddleford's tone was sharp. "Do you have an opinion, one that you can state under oath with reasonable medical certainty, that all of the blood, the pool, the spots and the smear, came from Mr. Grimes's wounds?"

"Uh...yes, as to the pool of blood next to his body."

"What about the spots and smear?"

"Well..." Dr. Winter drew in a deep breath. "Given the extent to which they had dried, I guess its possible they could have been there prior to the stabbing."

Judge Biddleford said, "Objection sustained as to the spots on the floor and the smear on the door handle." He turned to the jury. "Insofar as the witness indicated that the spots on the floor and the smear on the door handle were a result of the stabbing, you are directed to disregard his testimony."

Morehead whispered in Skip's ear. "You're racking up points."

Rather than points, Skip focused on His Holiness. The jurist, though self-indulgent, for a change was actively administering the elements of Due Process.

Before continuing, the District Attorney, perhaps in an effort to regain his footing, reviewed his notes. "Dr. Winter, do you have an opinion, one that you can state with reasonable medical certainty, as to the sequence of events that produced all of the blood stains you found?"

Skip was tempted to object, but decided to hold off. Dr. Winter's inability to establish that all of the bloodstains came from Squeaky's wounds had tied the prosecutor's hands.

"I have theories."

The response brought Skip to his feet. "Speculations from the doctor are not competent evidence."

"Mr. Carter," said Judge Biddleford, "not to be redundant, but the opinions of your expert witness are welcome if, and only if, he can express them with reasonable medical certainty."

The District Attorney nodded and then refocused on the witness. "Dr. Winter, do you have an opinion that you can state with reasonable medical..." The District Attorney's voice trailed off. He gazed silently into space. "I'll withdraw the question." He walked back to the prosecution table taking a moment to again review his notes. "Nothing further."

"No questions," said Skip, a lesson as recent as the morning session still fresh in his mind.

Morehead whispered, "You're doing good. So far, they've got nothing more than an unexplained murder."

Morehead's point was valid, but Skip took little solace. Thus far, the prosecution was merely laying a foundation. Based upon its witness list, the links to Morehead were yet to come.

Dr. Winter was excused from the stand, and the District Attorney called his next witness. A slight fellow with round shoulders, about 5'6", no more than one hundred thirty pounds, stepped tentatively forward and was sworn.

"Please state your full name for the record," said the District Attorney.

"Warren Holt."

"And Mr. Holt, where do you reside?"

"At...uh..." The witness was shaking.

The reaction might have surprised Skip were he uninitiated. But years earlier, well before he was admitted to practice, he watched a woman in Surrogate's Court pass out seconds after taking the stand. Numerous times thereafter he had seen witnesses consumed by nerves.

"Mr. Holt," said the District Attorney. "You're not on trial. Please...try to relax."

"Uh...okay." The man took a deep breath. "I live at 237 Walker Way...uh...that's in Oneonta."

"Good. And how old are you?"

"Uh..." The witness thought for a moment. "Thirty-seven."

Skip eyed the soft-spoken man with balding top. He was a double-edged sword. A tough cross-examination would likely rattle him, but unlike someone glib and cocky he would enjoy the jury's sympathy. A nervous witness with no ax to grind was a dangerous witness.

"Are you married?"

"Uh...nope."

"And what do you do for a living?"

"I work in the grocery department of the A&P...in Oneonta." His fingers were strangling the arms of the witness chair.

"Did you know the victim, Ralph Grimes?"

"Yes, we wuz buddies. But I...uh...like most folks, called him Squeaky."

"And how did you come to know him?"

"I met him at the *OTB* parlor in Oneonta. We...uh...both liked the horses. Him and I would sit together for a couple hours most every Tuesday evening. We done it for nearly four years till he wuz killed. Sometimes he'd give me tips and visey-versey."

"At some time did the role he played with regard to your betting change?"

"Uh...do you mean...did he start taking bets from me?"

"Yes. And, if so, can you tell us how that happened?"

"Well...uh...one day he asks me if I'd like better odds. And I sez sure. And he sez he can get 'em for me. I had my doubts, so at first I bet real small. I won, and he brought the money. Pretty soon, except when he gave me a tip, I was playin' the horses with him stead of *OTB*. His odds wuz a whole lot better. I also bet the numbers with him."

"Do you know if he worked for himself?"

"I knew it wuz someone else, but until last year I didn't know just who."

"How did you come to find out?"

"Squeaky told me."

"And for whom did Squeaky tell you he worked?"

"Objection," barked Skip, desperate to avoid the mention of Morehead's name. "The question calls for hearsay."

"Sustained."

The District Attorney walked back to his table and removed a paper from his file. He took it to the court stenographer who marked it for identification. The District Attorney handed the document to the witness. "I show you People's Exhibit Ten, marked for identification and ask if you recognize it?"

"Yes. It's a note that Squeaky wrote about a month before he wuz killed."

"Where did he write it?"

"Over at the *OTB*."

"Did you see him write it?"

"Yup, in his own hand. And then he gave it to me to keep."

"I offer it in evidence," said the District Attorney.

He took the paper from the witness and brought it to Skip, who read it, not that he needed to. He had read the copy in his file so many times he could recite it word for word. From the first time he had seen it many weeks before, Skip had tried unsuccessfully to find a technicality that would keep the damning note from the jury. Regardless, consenting to its admission into evidence was out of the question. He said, "Your Honor, the defense objects on the grounds of hearsay. The paper represents an out-of-court statement of a third party, not available for cross-examination."

"May I see the exhibit?" said Judge Biddleford.

Skip delivered it, knowing an unfavorable ruling was a forgone conclusion.

Judge Biddleford examined the note. He said, "Defense's objection is overruled. People's Exhibit Ten is received in evidence."

"Your Honor," said the District Attorney, "permission to read it to the jury requested."

"You may."

As the prosecutor stepped forward to get the note, Skip felt a knot in his stomach. The People were about to land their first big blow.

The District Attorney went over to the jury box and said, "Ladies and gentleman, People's Exhibit Ten reads as follows:

> *I, Ralph Squeaky Grimes, work as a runner for Harley Morehead. He is a bookmaker. We had an argument, and he threatened to kill me. If any thing happens to me, you can bet Harley Morehead is behind it.*

"The document," said the District Attorney, "is dated March 12, 1968 and signed by Ralph Squeaky Grimes." The District Attorney walked back to his table. He said, "Mr. Holt, what brought you here today?"

A puzzled look came over the witness's face. "Uh...I came in my car."

"Sorry. That's not what I meant," said the District Attorney. "Did you come of your own accord or for some other reason?"

"Oh...I got a paper, a subpoena, from your office telling me I had to come. Is that what you're asking?"

"Exactly. And that's all the questions I have." He looked over at Skip. "Your witness, Mr. Maynard."

Skip got up slowly. His mind was racing. Temptation, the chance to disclose inconsistencies, was luring him. Judgment dictated caution. Beating up the little fellow was likely to backfire, and it would do nothing to change the note. Skip said, "Mr. Holt, you don't know the defendant Harley Morehead personally, do you?"

"No. But I...uh...heard of him. Stuff about politics."

"You never placed a bet directly with the defendant, did you?"

"Uh...No."

"So, you can't say of your own knowledge that he took any bets, can you?"

"No."

"And you have no personal knowledge—" With the mistake he had made when examining the Coroner still fresh in his mind, Skip cut himself off. The inquiry was too risky. Holt was apt to blurt out that he believed that Morehead had killed Squeaky. If he did, Skip assumed he could get the answer stricken from the record, but having the jury put it out of their minds would be another matter. He said, "No further questions."

Judge Biddleford eyed his watch and then gazed pensively into space for a few moments. "It's nearly four o'clock. We've had a lot to digest today. Perhaps it would be well to adjourn and begin anew tomorrow." He turned to the jury. "Ladies and gentlemen, once again I admonish you to discuss the case with no one. Also, please steer clear of any news media—television, radio or newspapers—where you might be exposed to information about the case. We will reconvene tomorrow at 9:30 A.M."

As the courtroom cleared, Skip began packing up his papers.

"What do you think?" said Morehead.

"Hard to say," whispered Skip. He heaved a sigh. "Unfortunately I suspect things will get tougher tomorrow."

Morehead shrugged.

"Anything you want to discuss?"

Morehead shook his head.

"Then I'll meet you back here at 9:15 tomorrow."

Skip watched as his client left the courtroom. There were moments when he felt Morehead might be innocent. Other times he was far more skeptical. This was one of the latter moments. Regardless, he had to give Morehead his due. Skip had spent hundreds of hours on the case, and he had billed Morehead for all of them, and not at the discounted rates he gave many clients. A guy who could post one hundred thousand dollars cash bail didn't rate that kind of consideration, not that Morehead had asked for any such favors. On the contrary he had promptly paid Skip's bills in full. Whatever else Morehead may have been, whatever he may have done, he was honoring his financial obligations to Skip. Even if it were otherwise, irrespective of personal feelings, Skip would have given his client the best defense possible. But admittedly Skip much preferred being well compensated for putting the People to their burden of proof. And when it came to that burden, Skip had a strategy to make it heavy. Very heavy.

———

"You got a couple minutes?" said Mickey, as Skip came out of the Courthouse.

"For you...always." Skip did a double take. "What the hell are you smoking?"

Mickey held out a candy cigarette. "It's my newest cigarette of choice. I made the mistake of going to the doctor for a change. First time in seven years. He told me to give up smoking, practically ordered me. It's been four days, and I'm goin' nuts. He recommended some kind of gum to help my cravings, but I couldn't stand the stuff." Mickey stared at the candy cigarette. "It ain't a *Camel*, but it's better than nothin'. I gotta have somethin' between my fingers." He studied Skip for a moment. "You still on the wagon?"

"Yeah. I'm trying."

"Is it gettin' any easier?"

The question set Skip to thinking. It was still tough, but arguably less so than a few weeks before. He said, "Sometimes, yes. Other times, no."

"I've got some new information."

"The good kind?"

Mickey hesitated. "A little of both, I guess."

Skip had no desire to go back to the office. He had checked in by telephone with Lucy before leaving the Courthouse, and she had everything under control. He needed to unwind, but at that moment the *Eagle* felt too risky. Regardless, he wanted to stay out in the fresh air. "How about we take a walk to *Doubleday*. We can sit in the bleachers."

"Is there a game there?"

"I doubt it unless the kids from the *Babe Ruth League* have got something going."

As they headed up Main Street toward the ballpark, Mickey said, "The more I learn about Detective Ramsey, the more I'm convinced he's a straight shooter."

"What about his links to Kileen and his insurance agency? Ramsey investigated a few too many accidents with the typical neck and back injuries where Kileen was the agent. And if I recall correctly, there was even one where Squeaky was a passenger."

"I know but..." Mickey took a lick of his candy cigarette and then shook his head. "It's possible Kileen may be scammin' the insurance companies, but I doubt Ramsey is involved. Small town, limited staff may account for his name comin' up so often. Occasionally he gets stuck doin' accident investigations."

"What about that case where the Appellate Division threw out a confession he had obtained? Were you able to learn the details?"

"Yeah. It happened several years ago. The police force was short-staffed due to a flu epidemic, and Ramsey was doin' thirteen things at once. Some guy was caught in the five-and-dime in the wee hours. The guy admitted breakin' in, but Ramsey forgot to give him his *Miranda* warnings before he took a confession. Of course, at the time he wasn't the only one. The Supreme Court had just recently decided *Miranda*, and cops were screwing up all over the country."

Skip shrugged. When he had first taken Morehead's case, the need to attack Ramsey's credibility had appeared important. He had even hoped to link Ramsey to Squeaky. But since Judge Biddleford had suppressed the confession, Ramsey's significance had greatly diminished.

Mickey and Skip turned down Doubleday Court. Skip bought them each a hot dog and a soda at the Bullpen Snack Bar. They headed into *Doubleday*, which was always open to the public, and seated themselves in the stands behind home plate. There was no game, but that didn't matter either to them or the dozen or so other people scattered about the ballpark.

"You mind if we eat first and leave business for later?" said Mickey.

"Suits me fine." After a long day of trial, Skip was famished. Sitting in the site that symbolized baseball's birth was nothing new for him. Ever since he was a child, he had done it. Skip bit into his hot dog. True to form, it had that fantastic, only-in-the-ballpark taste. He closed his eyes. He could see and feel the ghosts of Ty Cobb, Babe Ruth, Lou Gehrig, Cy Young and so many more. As a youngster *Doubleday* was Skip's favorite Cooperstown arena, even more special than the Courthouse. But he loved them both. Many a day when there was no game, he would watch a trial at the Courthouse and then walk to *Doubleday*, sit in the stands and contemplate the courtroom tactics he had witnessed earlier. Skip found striking similarities between litigation and baseball. Both competitions were governed by countless rules, enforced by umpires in dark colored outfits. Lawyers confronting witnesses, like pitchers facing batters, tried to outfox the recipients of their offerings. Just when a fast ball was expected, a curve or even a change-up was delivered. But much as the two sports had similarities, their contrasts were even more striking. At *Doubleday* the players were bigger than life. In the

Courthouse they often battled for their lives. At *Doubleday* a blind ump evoked nasty epithets from the fans, while at the Courthouse spectators expected nothing less than blind justice. At *Doubleday* fans were encouraged to cheer and clap. In the Courthouse spectators who voiced reactions were admonished or even expelled. At *Doubleday* errors were simply statistics from which there was no recourse. In the Courthouse they were grounds for appeal. At *Doubleday* hot dogs and beer and peanuts, whose shells could be tossed onto the ground, were standard fare. In the Courthouse the only ration was water, and the spectators got none. At *Doubleday* a four hundred batting average was Hall of Fame material. In the Courthouse a judicial percentage twice that number merited the wrath of the appellate courts. At *Doubleday* everyone knew the score from start to finish. In the Courthouse there was no score, only a tension-filled moment when the jury rendered its verdict. At *Doubleday* the teams played on inning after inning until there was a winner and a loser. In the Courthouse a deal could halt proceedings at any moment. At *Doubleday* each side wore a uniform. In the Courtroom only a losing defendant got one. At *Doubleday* it was all about physical skills. In the Courthouse they didn't matter. At *Doubleday* the—

"Have you served all your subpoenas?" said Mickey.

The question drew Skip from his reverie. He realized he had mindlessly devoured all but the last bite of his hot dog. He said, "Yup, I served them a few days before the trial started. Morelli, LaDieux, Kileen, Raines, Feinstein, and even Ramsey, though I doubt I'll actually call them all. Did you come up with anything new on any of them?"

"Yeah. Feinstein, like Kileen, has an alibi. A while back I mentioned that Kileen was at a conference for insurance agents in Hawaii from April 6th through the 10th. It turns out Feinstein was in New York City for a couple of days including the 9th. No way could either of them have killed Squeaky."

"They could have hired someone to do it." Skip found the point less than compelling. Based upon his expression, Mickey didn't buy it either. Skip took a pen from his pocket. On the cardboard holder that had housed his hot dog he jotted a couple of notes. "What else have you got?"

"Raines is in bad financial shape. Even though *Artway* has done well—at least if you believe the big shot's boasting—his life in the fast lane has him in a bind. The bank is threatening to foreclose on his house, and he's got credit card debt up the wazoo. Rumor has it he screwed Squeaky out of his share of the business. The little squawker wasn't the type to take it lyin' down. Not impossible that Raines took out Squeaky."

Wheels turned in Skip's head. As with some of the others, he had served Raines with a subpoena *duces tecum,* a subpoena requiring production of records, not merely a personal subpoena. Chances were Raines had a lot to hide. Business dealings with Squeaky, as well as information that would interest the Internal Revenue Service, topped the list. Once on the stand, maybe Raines would resort to the Fifth Amendment. That would be perfect. The jury would wonder if Raines murdered Squeaky. Maybe he did. And maybe he didn't. Regardless, doubt in the minds of the jurors could be enough.

Mickey took an imaginary drag on another candy cigarette. He drew it away from his mouth and shook his head. He bit off a piece. "Who am I kidding? These ain't gonna work." He turned to Skip. "Did you ever smoke?"

"I tried it when I was thirteen, but I hated that tobacco taste. All it did was make me choke."

"You're lucky. Once that nicotine hooks you, you ain't gotta chance. Kickin' a buck-naked Brigette Bardot outta your bed would be a whole lot easier."

A vivid image of the coquette sexpot danced in Skip's brain. "As a single, uninvolved and horny male, why would I?" The thought crossed his mind that if he could have his beloved Megan back, the voluptuous French movie star wouldn't stand a chance. He kept the thought to himself. He said, "With you it's tobacco. With me it's alcohol. And according to an article I read recently, there's a good chance it's in our genes."

"Yeah, just like Bardot." Mickey chuckled and then pointed toward the ball field. "Damn. Here I am sittin' in the grandstand dreamin' about a home run when most times I can't even get to first base." He stuffed the remainder of his candy cigarette back into his mouth. "Not to change the subject," he mumbled, "but a guy I know who was tight with Squeaky told me Squeaky was blackmailin' some folks."

Skip perked up. "What folks?"

"Don't know. The guy didn't know either. According to him Squeaky kept mum on the details. He merely said that too many people had been using him far too long and the time had come to put the shoe on the other foot."

"You think he was referring to Morelli or LaDieux or Raines?"

"All three crossed my mind, along with Harley Morehead."

"What's the name of the fellow who gave you the information?"

Mickey shook his head. "Sorry, I can't say. I gave him my word. And I know what you're probably thinkin', but you gotta understand. I get my information from guys who live on the edge. They trust me. I've got a reputation for doin' what I say. A couple broken promises, and I'll be known as a creep. My sources 'll dry up, and I'll be out of business." Mickey hesitated, seemingly confirming that Skip got the point. "Regardless, my source doesn't know who Squeaky was blackmailin'. Like I told you, Squeaky wouldn't say."

Lenny Gardner. The name popped into Skip's head. "Give me one guess. Just one."

Mickey shook his head.

Skip ignored the response. "Did Lenny Gardner give you the information?"

"I'm not gonna give you a *yes*, and I'm not gonna give you a *no*." Apart from a rare peevishness in Mickey's tone, his demeanor gave no hints. "As I said, the subject is off limits."

Skip wanted to press the issue, but he got the point. Trust was the very reason he used Mickey. Skip's soda can went to his lips. His mind focused on Lenny Gardner. Squeaky's next door neighbor, the man who had hired Skip, had been subpoenaed as a witness for the prosecution. What did Gardner know? What would he say? How did he fit in? Skip could only wonder.

Chapter XV

"For the record, Sir, your name?" said the District Attorney.

"Guy Lewis Devine." Attired in a brown sport jacket and paisley tie, he appeared comfortable, at least as comfortable as one could be on the witness stand.

It was nearly ten o'clock by the time Devine, the first witness of the day, had begun his testimony. Everyone had reached their places before nine-thirty; that is, everyone except Judge Biddleford. Skip had exchanged pleasantries with the prosecutor as both had waited for the jurist to arrive. When he finally appeared, he admonished everyone that there was much to be done and he anticipated all would make judicious use of time.

"Where do you live?" said the prosecutor.

"1023 Lancy Street, outside of Oneonta."

"What do you do for a living?"

"I own an office building where I rent out space. I also operate a self-service car wash."

"And do you know the defendant?"

"Yes."

Only a few questions on direct, and already Skip sensed a challenging cross-examination. With no stake in the outcome, Devine's crisp answers made him credible.

"How do you know the defendant?"

"Through the Chamber of Commerce and the Leatherstocking Club. We've been friends for over twenty years."

"Have you ever done any business with him?"

"He printed business cards and stationery for me."

"Have you done any other kind of business with him?"

"Well...yes."

"And what was that?"

"I placed bets with him." With a seemingly apologetic expression Devine glanced at the defendant.

For Skip the irony was inescapable. How often he had seen it. Individuals, reluctant to hurt a friend, compounded the damage by communicating their reluctance. Damning testimony grew more credible. Skip had another reaction. He was seething. All along Morehead had insisted he was not a bookie. Despite skepticism, Skip had given his client the benefit of the doubt. Skepticism had just become flat out distrust. And if Morehead had lied about being a bookie, there was a good chance he had lied about other things as well.

"What did you bet on?"

"Football, baseball, basketball...you name it."

"Did you also bet the numbers?"

"Yup."

"Approximately how many bets did you place with the defendant?"

"A lot...I couldn't say for sure."

"Well, can you give us some idea...ten, fifty, a hundred or whatever?"

The witness thought for a moment. "A couple hundred or something like that."

"How did you place those bets?"

"Sometimes by phone. Often in person when I saw him."

"Did you place all of your bets directly with the defendant?"

"Well...not all. Sometimes when he wasn't available, I booked them with Squeaky Grimes. He worked for the defendant."

"Do you know if the defendant took most of his bets himself?"

"Objection," said Skip.

"Overruled. I'll allow it." Judge Biddleford turned to the witness. "Please tell us, if you know."

"I was one of a very few regulars from whom he took bets directly."

"How do you know that?"

"He told me a bunch of times. He said I was one of only about a half-dozen big time regulars that he knew he could trust. He said ninety-eight percent of his customers dealt only with Squeaky. Harley was the bank, the money behind the operation. Some folks mighta suspected that Squeaky was just a runner, but they didn't know who was behind the scenes."

"Your Honor, I move to strike what folks suspected. The witness is speculating."

"Sustained."

"Excuse me," said the District Attorney, "but I believe the witness is testifying as to what he was told by the defendant."

Judge Biddleford directed his attention to the witness. "When you indicated that folks figured Squeaky was just a runner, was that something the defendant actually told you or simply a surmise on your part?"

"He told me."

"The objection is overruled." Judge Biddleford turned to the jury. "You are free to consider the last answer."

The District Attorney leaned back so he was nearly sitting on the prosecution table. "Mr. Devine, how would you describe your relationship with the defendant?"

"Friends...good friends."

"And what brought you here today?"

"Your office served me with this subpoena." He reached into his pocket and pulled out a folded document.

"If I...strike that." The prosecutor peered into space for a few seconds before refocusing on the witness. "Let me direct your attention back to the end of March of this year. Do you recall having a conversation with the defendant about Squeaky Grimes?"

"Yes."

Skip's ears were directed to the testimony, but his eyes were surveying the jury. All fourteen, including the two alternates, were totally engaged. There were no blank looks or drooping eyelids.

"Mr. Devine, where did that conversation occur?"

"In the Grill Room at the Leatherstocking Club. We were off in the corner, and the place was fairly deserted. It was a typical March day, and we were bemoaning the fact there was still snow on the fairways."

"Please tell the jury what the defendant told you regarding Squeaky that day."

The witness heaved a slight sigh. "He...uh...said he suspected that the cops might be talking to Squeaky. He was worried that Squeaky would fold up and make a deal and throw him in to save his own skin."

"Did the defendant say what he might do about the situation?"

"Well...uh...not specifically."

"What did he say?"

"That he wouldn't let Squeaky screw him like that."

"And what did you take that to mean?"

"Objection."

"Withdrawn. No further questions." The District Attorney turned to Skip. "Your witness."

"Your Honor, I request a ten-minute recess prior to cross-examination."

Judge Biddleford hesitated. "Well...okay, but not one second longer."

Skip hurried Morehead out of the courtroom down the hallway to a small conference room where he shut the door, restraining the urge to slam it. The moment he was alone with his client, he said, "So, you still claim you're not a bookie?"

Morehead broke eye contact.

"I take that as a change of tune."

"C'mon...you have to understand—"

"Damn it," said Skip. "I don't have to understand anything. I want the truth." The moment he spoke the angry words he had second thoughts. Did he really want to know if his client had murdered Squeaky Grimes? Probably not. He believed in the system. All defendants, guilty ones included, were entitled to a defense. Using only admissible evidence, the prosecution had the burden of establishing guilt beyond a reasonable doubt. The theory was great. But defending a client Skip knew to be guilty would hardly be the same as one who claimed innocence. Enabling a murderer to walk was a doubled-edged sword. Ignorance had its advantages.

"Yeah, I'm a bookie, but that doesn't mean I killed Squeaky."

Skip's brain went into overdrive as he silently repeated Morehead's words. The old negative pregnant had again reared its odious head. The seeming denial had the earmarks of an admission. A part of Skip wanted to press his client. But this wasn't a first office visit. They were in trial. Skip had an obligation to defend Morehead to the best of his ability. Knowing that he was guilty might make it harder to fulfill his obligation. Skip stared at Morehead. It was hard to imagine that one as shrewd as Morehead believed the truth about his bookmaking would not come out. But was it really? How many times had Skip seen defendants faced with compelling proof of criminal misconduct insist they were purer than Ivory Soap? And when it came to politicians, the tendency was greater yet. No matter how strong the evidence of their wrongdoing, with righteous indignation they would maintain their innocence. Skip said, "I think it's best that I excuse Devine without any cross-examination. Keeping him up there will only compound the damage. He's far too credible."

"I understand." Morehead pointed at the big clock on the wall. "We've only got five minutes, and I need to pee."

"Good idea," said Skip. They headed to the men's room and adjacent urinals. Skip's eyes remained focused on his own business. His mind, however, was elsewhere. He wondered if the man with whom he was standing side-by-side might be a murderer.

Judge Biddleford surveyed the courtroom. "Mr. Carter, call your next witness."

"The People call Edward Willis."

A hulk of a man, about two hundred fifty pounds and well over six feet strode forward. With bushy eyebrows, a *Fu Man Chu* mustache and a penetrating stare, he looked like a professional wrestler, the villainous type. Dressed in a tight-fitting tee, his huge biceps and blacksmith-like forearms showed as he placed his hand on the Bible and took the oath.

He seated himself on the witness stand, and the District Attorney quickly took him through the preliminaries.

"Mr. Willis, you're also known by a nickname, aren't you?"

"Yeah."

"And what is that nickname?"

"The Enforcer."

"How and when did you acquire that name?"

"About fifteen years ago in my mid-twenties when I worked as a bouncer at the *Bucking Bronc*, a bikers' bar outside El Paso, Texas."

The District Attorney gestured toward the defendant. "Do you know the defendant Harley Morehead?"

"Yup. I worked for him for the past five years, until just after he got arrested."

"Please tell the jury the nature of that employment."

"I collected money guys owed him from losing bets."

The District Attorney drifted over to the jury box rail, so the witness faced generally toward them. "And just how did you collect this money?"

"I'd go to their homes or wherever they hung out. First I'd ask them for it."

"What if that didn't work?"

"I'd threaten 'em."

"Did you ever carry out any of those threats?"

"Occasionally."

"And how did you go about that?"

"I beat up about four or five guys. Once ya do it to a few, ya get a reputation. Folks know ya mean business and usually cough up what they owe. Don't gotta carry out the threats all that often."

The District Attorney gestured at Morehead again. "Was the defendant aware when you beat someone up?"

"Definitely. I never done it without gettin' his okay first. He decided who needed it."

"Did you know Ralph Grimes?"

"Ya mean Squeaky? Sure. Lotsa folks thought he was my boss. He took the bets and made the payoffs. He liked playin' the big shot. Harley, on the other hand, didn't want no attention. He wuz happy just rakin' in the dough."

"Now, if I refer you back to the weeks just before Squeaky was killed—and I'll refer to Mr. Grimes by that name since that's what you're doing—did you have an occasion to meet with both Squeaky and Harley Morehead?"

"Yup."

"And when was that?"

"I can't tell ya the exact date, but it wuz about a week before Squeaky bought the farm, give or take a day or two."

"If I told you that his body was found on the 10th of April, could we agree this meeting took place shortly after the 1st of April?"

"Yeah, that sounds about right."

"Where did this meeting take place?"

"At Squeaky's flat over on Rock Street."

"Was it pre-arranged?"

"Between Harley and me, but Squeaky didn't know we was comin'. We just kinda popped in about seven in the evening."

"How did you and the defendant get to Squeaky's place?"

"Harley picked me up."

"What kind of car did he drive?"

"A baby blue Cadillac with a white convertible top. It's a real beauty. Always loved ridin' in it."

The District Attorney folded his arms and leaned his hip against the jury box rail. Skip, on the other hand, was not so relaxed. The Enforcer may not have been the most articulate witness, but unlike diving or figure skating, style points didn't count. Juries looked for credibility, and the lug was convincing.

"What happened once you arrived?"

"Harley told Squeaky he had heard a rumor that Squeaky had been talkin' to the cops. Naturally, Squeaky denied it. Just what you'd expect from a little runt like Squeaky."

"Move to strike what one would expect." The technicality proved nothing, but Skip hoped to interrupt the prosecutor's rhythm.

"The jury will ignore the witness's editorial comment." Judge Biddleford turned to the District Attorney. "Continue."

"What happened next?"

"Squeaky told Harley he wuz doin' all the work, and he wanted more money. He said the take had tripled over what it wuz a couple years before and he wuz entitled to at least double what he wuz gettin'. Anyway, Harley, already pissed, blew his top. He said, *You want somethin' more. I'll give it to you.* Then he held up a fist and told me to let Squeaky have it."

"What did you do?"

"I laid a haymaker in Squeaky's gut. He doubled over, and I launched an uppercut to his jaw. Just before he went down, I fired another in his gut."

"What if anything did Squeaky say?"

"Nothin'. Course I doubt he could talk too well just then."

"Did the defendant say anything?"

"Yup. He told Squeaky that wuz just a taste of what he'd get. He said if Squeaky didn't wise up quick, he'd be sleepin' six feet underground. Then he motioned me to go, and we headed out the door."

"Where wuz Squeaky when you left?"

"Lyin' on his living room floor."

"Where did you and the defendant go once you left Squeaky's flat?"

"He dropped me off at my place."

"From the time you left Squeaky's until the defendant dropped you off, did the two of you have any more conversation about Squeaky?"

"Yeah. Once we got in the car, the defendant said Squeaky was dangerous. Said he might have to take the little rat out for good. I told him I didn't want no part of no killin'. Harley gave me a nasty look. He said if he gotta, he'd do it himself."

The District Attorney turned slowly and gazed at the defendant. The eyes of the jury followed him there. "No further questions," said the District Attorney. He walked back to his seat.

Out of the corner of his eye Skip looked at Morehead. Having the Populist Party County Chairman for a client was a distinct liability. Quintessential politician that he was, even when caught with his hand in the cookie jar, he continued to protest his innocence. By playing it cute and denying he was a bookie, he had made Skip's job tougher. Skip got up from his seat. He headed across the courtroom angling back to the bar that separated the combatants from the spectators. He took a place about thirty feet from the witness stand where both the jury on one side and the District Attorney on the other would be watching a tennis match between Willis and himself.

"Mr. Willis, isn't it true that you have a criminal record?" Knowing that Willis would be testifying, Skip had checked him out. He had also tried to speak with Willis, but on the advice of counsel the strong arm had refused.

"Yeah. Ten years ago I served six months in the Herkimer County Jail for assault."

Ordinarily a criminal record was a great device to impeach a witness's testimony. In this case it did little. Willis had already acknowledged on the stand that he was a paid enforcer. The fact that he had once been convicted for assault was no surprise and did little to impair his credibility. Skip had checked court records to see if Willis had recently entered any form of guilty plea. There was none. But Willis had an attorney, and he was testifying for the prosecution. Two and two generally added up to four. If that weren't enough, an article in the *Oneonta Star* had reported that Willis had agreed to testify against Morehead in exchange for a short stint in the county jail. Skip said, "After Squeaky was killed, no doubt you spoke to the police."

"Yeah."

"They came to see you, didn't they?" Whichever way Willis answered, Skip had a strategy.

"Yeah."

"You immediately told them what you knew. Right?" Once again, Skip was ready for either answer.

"Nope. I asked if I wuz under arrest. They said no. And I said I wanted to talk to my lawyer. They said 'cause I wuzn't under arrest, I wuzn't entitled to one. But I knew the game. When they tried to question me, I clammed up. Told 'em I was takin' the Fifth."

"They told you they suspected you of killing Squeaky, didn't they?"

"Not in so many words."

As much damage as Willis had done, Skip saw the opportunity to cast shadows over his testimony. Represented by counsel, the only way Willis would have admitted that he had assaulted Squeaky, rather than maintain reliance on the Fifth Amendment, was if he had a deal. Skip said, "But you knew you were on the police's list of possibilities?"

"Objection. Calls for a conclusion."

"Overruled. This is cross-examination. The witness will answer the question."

"Yeah...I knew they were investigatin' me."

"The police knew you worked as a strong arm, didn't they?"

"I guess so."

"They also knew your nickname and reputation as the Enforcer?"

"Yeah."

"Earlier you told us you've been involved with the criminal system before. You knew to get a lawyer when the police wanted to talk to you. Right?"

"Yeah."

"How long did the police interrogate you?"

"For a while...till I took the Fifth, demanded to leave and see my lawyer. Anyway I didn't tell 'em nothin', least not then."

"What did you do once they finished?"

"I went straight to my lawyer."

"And he made sure you didn't talk to the police until he worked out a deal. True?"

"Yeah."

Skip walked forward a couple of steps. "Tell this jury the terms of the deal you made."

"I'm pleadin' to assault third for beatin' up Squeaky. I'm gonna get five months in the county jail, plus three years probation."

"No doubt your lawyer told you what you were facing for beating up Squeaky if you didn't make a deal."

"Yeah...a few years."

"And he told you that you could face more charges for others you've beaten up, didn't he?"

"Yeah. That's what he told me."

"And you were also worried the police might charge you with Squeaky's murder, weren't you?"

"I didn't kill him."

"Move to strike as non-responsive," said Skip.

"Sustained. The witness will tell the jury whether he was worried the police would charge him with Squeaky's murder."

"Yeah, I wuz."

"So, before you made your deal, you realized you could get decades or even life in prison. Right?"

"Yeah, but I didn't—"

"You answered the question." Skip inched forward. He didn't need rocket science to know the District Attorney had conditioned Willis's deal upon his cooperation. Skip said, "As part of your deal you agreed to testify against the defendant, didn't you?"

"Yeah."

Skip stared pensively upward. "So, let's see if I have this right...by agreeing to testify against Harley Morehead, you got five months in the county jail rather than facing decades or even life in the big house?"

"I'm also gettin' three years probation."

"That's right—you're also getting three years probation." Skip smiled, his gaze moving from the witness to the jury. He was satisfied they got the point. He looked back at Willis. The big fellow was hardly a boy scout who had come forward to do his civic duty. "No further questions."

Willis started to get up.

"Excuse me," said the District Attorney, "I have a question or two on re-direct."

Willis settled back into the witness chair.

"Mr. Willis, did you kill Squeaky Grimes?"

"No, Sir."

"That's all I have." The prosecutor sat down.

Skip was on his feet immediately. "You beat people up for a living, don't you?"

"Well...not exactly."

"Not exactly?" Skip meandered around from behind the defense table and walked forward within a few feet of the

276

witness. "You told us earlier that you beat up a number of people who didn't pay their gambling debts. Isn't that what you told us?"

"Yeah."

"And you got paid for doing that. Right?"

"Objection," said the prosecutor. "This is beyond the scope of re-direct."

"I'm going to overrule the objection. It goes to the heart of the witness's credibility."

The ruling gave Skip pause. In his years of practice never had Judge Biddleford given him such latitude. Where ordinarily he mined Skip's path with stumbling blocks, the jurist was opening doors.

Judge Biddleford turned to the witness. "Do you need to hear the question again?"

Willis shook his head. He turned to Skip. "Yeah, I got paid for bein' an enforcer, and sometimes that meant beatin' people up."

"You knew that was a crime, just like lying under oath. True?"

"Yeah."

"But you did it anyway?"

"Well...yeah."

Skip gestured to the jury. "Give these folks one good reason why they shouldn't conclude that you're not lying today in order to save yourself years in prison?"

Willis sat motionless for several seconds. He glanced at the jury but still said nothing.

Skip waited a bit longer. Finally he said, "I believe we have your answer." He walked back to the defense table. "I have nothing further."

"Nor do I," said the District Attorney.

"The witness is excused." Judge Biddleford glanced at his watch. "Eleven-thirty. This seems like a good point to break for the morning. Before we do, I was wondering, Mr. Carter, how many more witnesses do you have?"

"Just one, Your Honor. Leonard Gardner."

Skip thought he saw traces of a wry smile on Judge Biddleford's face. It may have been Skip's imagination or a reflection of the Judge's reaction to the gay man or, perhaps, Judge Biddleford had a clue about Lenny Gardner's upcoming testimony. An uneasy feeling came over Skip. As the Judge dismissed everyone until one-thirty, ruminations stirred in Skip's head.

Morehead patted Skip on the back. "I told you we're gonna win this thing."

Skip eyed his client. "The prosecution still has another witness. It's far from over."

"C'mon, you sound like Yogi." Morehead pointed in the general direction that would lead up the street to the *Baseball Hall of Fame*. "In a few years when they enshrine him with the other greats, it'll be for his bat and glove, not his smooth tongue." Morehead patted Skip again, this time more demonstratively. "I've been in enough political races to know which way the wind is blowing."

Skip shrugged. A familiar refrain echoed. Never had he seen a criminal defendant so cavalier, especially one charged with murder. It boggled his mind. He told himself that politicians were known to have amazingly thick skin, but how could anyone take the possibility of life in prison so lightly? Skip said, "I'll see you back here shortly after one." He watched Morehead saunter out of the courtroom. Admittedly, the case was going well, but juries were unpredictable, and the District Attorney had one more witness. Donald Carter was not the kind of prosecutor to come to court with an unloaded gun. All along Skip had harbored concerns about Lenny Gardner. As Skip packed his papers into his file, those concerns attained new heights.

Chapter XVI

Skip turned toward the rear of the courtroom as the District Attorney announced the name Leonard Gardner. He wondered if his former client would make eye contact as he stepped to the stand.

Shoulders erect, like a private in the army, Gardner marched forward. If his peripheral vision allowed even a glimpse of Skip, he gave no hint. He placed his right hand on the *Bible*, swore that his testimony would be entirely truthful and then seated himself on the witness stand.

"Please state your full name for the record."

"Leonard Paul Gardner."

"How old are you?"

"Thirty-seven."

"And where do you reside?"

"At 10 Rock Street here in Cooperstown. I rent the upper flat."

"Where is that in relation to 14 Rock Street, the address where Ralph Squeaky Grimes lived?"

"I live in the building next door. If you were facing the front of the houses, my place would be to the left of his."

Gardner was looking directly at the District Attorney. His answers were crisp, and from all that Skip could tell, he was not unduly nervous.

"Please describe the front of the house in which you live."

"It has two porches, one for each flat."

"Is the porch for your flat enclosed?"

"No. Above waist level it's open in front and on both sides, except for a few supporting posts."

As the prosecutor flipped a page on his yellow pad, Skip looked at the bench. It was not uncommon during testimony for

279

Judge Biddleford to appear preoccupied or even disinterested. He was giving Gardner his undivided attention. It crossed Skip's mind that the jurist's dislike for the gay witness might play to the defense's advantage. The right circumstances could give rise to hostility that could influence the jury's evaluation of Gardner's credibility. Skip realized he was getting ahead of himself. He was yet to learn what Gardner would say.

"If I direct your attention back to the 9th of April, the day before Mr. Grimes was found dead, can you recall where you were that evening at about eight o'clock?"

"I was at home in my flat."

"And what were you doing that evening?"

"I was reading a book, *Of Mice and Men,* to be precise."

"Do you recall what the weather was like?"

"Yes, it was exceptionally warm. More like an evening in early June."

"And where in your flat were you reading your book?"

"In my big easy chair in the living room. That's in the front of the house, adjacent to the porch."

"Your big easy chair—where specifically is it located in your living room?"

"Along the wall on the side of the house closest to the building where Mr. Grimes lived."

"Are there any windows in your living room?"

"Yes, three. One on each side and a third in the front."

"You mentioned it was a very warm night. Were those windows open or closed?"

"The two on the sides were open about eighteen inches for cross-ventilation."

A sense of where Gardner's testimony was headed had begun to take shape. A way to keep the jury from hearing it eluded Skip.

"Did there come a time while you were reading that evening that something drew your attention away from your book?"

"Yes."

The District Attorney gestured at the jury. "Please tell these ladies and gentlemen what transpired."

Gardner turned to the jury. "I heard shouting."

"What did you do?"

"I got up and went to the window."

"And what did you see and hear?"

"There were loud voices coming from the house next door, the downstairs flat to be specific."

"And when you say the house next door, are you referring to the building where Ralph Grimes lived or the building on the other side of your house?"

"The one where Mr. Grimes lived."

"And what did you see as you looked out the window?"

"Some light coming from the window of the front room on the side of Mr. Grimes's house adjacent to mine. His window, like mine, was open."

"And were you able to see the people who were shouting at that time?"

"No, the shade on Mr. Grimes's window was drawn well over half-way down."

Skip breathed a momentary sigh of relief. Disaster escaped, at least for the moment.

"Were you able to recognize the voices of the people who were shouting?"

"Well, yes, as to one—Mr. Grimes's."

"How well, if at all, did you know Mr. Grimes before April 9th?"

"We were neighbors…what I'd refer to as acquaintances, not friends, not that we didn't get along. We always said hello, and we had spoken to one another at some length about a half-dozen times over the preceding year since I had moved into my place."

"You indicated you recognized Mr. Grimes's voice. Was there anything distinctive about it?"

Gardner, who up to that moment had appeared poised, displayed an abashed look. For an instant his gaze lowered. "Well…uh…I don't mean to belittle the poor fellow, but he had this really distinctive, high pitched and scratchy voice. It was the kind you just couldn't miss. I…uh…guess that's why folks called him Squeaky."

Skip swallowed hard. Gardner was believable.

"Were you able to recognize the other voice?"

"Objection," barked Skip, fearing Morehead was about to be identified. "The witness already testified that he only recognized one voice."

"Overruled." Judge Biddleford turned to the witness stand. "Did you recognize the other voice?"

"No, Your Honor."

Lips taut, Skip remained frozen, lest his sense of relief slip through the veil of a self-assured mask.

The District Attorney gestured at the jury again. "Please tell these folks what, if anything specific, you could make out from the shouting next door?"

"Objection—hearsay." Skip was grasping at straws.

"Overruled. The witness may answer."

"As I indicated, I heard shouting, and I went to the window. I heard Squeaky say, *I want more money, or I'll go to the cops.* The other fella said, *Don't you threaten me you slimy weasel.* Then I heard Squeaky say, *Stay the hell outta my kitchen.* After that I didn't hear anything for about thirty seconds."

"What happened next?"

"I heard Squeaky yell, *What are you doing with that knife?* Then I heard him scream a couple times, and there was silence. I continued to look down from the window, but I couldn't see anything. I stood there for at least a minute before I went to the front porch. I leaned over the side trying to see into the open window of Squeaky's flat, but from my second floor, looking down at an angle, I couldn't see anything. A minute later someone came out the front door of Squeaky's flat."

"Were you able to tell who it was?"

"Not at that moment."

A bullet dodged, but with more certain to follow, Skip's stomach knotted.

"What did you do next?"

"I went to the front edge of my porch, crouched down and peeked over the side. An instant later a man stepped off the porch of Squeaky's building. He had a rolled-up newspaper in his hand, and he hesitated as he seemed to fold the ends around something."

"Could you tell what that something was?"

"No. But the newspaper once it was rolled and the ends folded was well over a foot long."

"What did the man do?"

"Well...he looked around both left and right and back at Squeaky's place. I stayed low and watched him over the edge of my porch. Then he hurried to a vehicle that was parked along the curb on our side of the street, about on a line between the buildings where Squeaky and I lived."

"In what direction was the car facing?"

"The front was nearer my house and the rear nearer to Squeaky's."

"What did the man do next?"

"He opened the trunk of his car and tossed the newspaper into it."

"Can you identify the car?"

"It was a Cadillac. A blue convertible with a white top."

The knot in Skip's stomach tightened. He stole a peak at Morehead. The defendant appeared as cool as ever.

"What's the next thing you recall?"

"The man hurried around the side of his car and got in on the driver's side."

"How far from you was the man as he got into the car?"

Gardner gazed upward into empty space and mumbled aloud. "Let's see...I was about twenty feet up, and it's about fifteen feet out from the porch to the curb, plus another five to the far side of the car, makes roughly twenty out. So, twenty feet down and about the same out." His hands moved briefly in the air as if making a mental model before he refocused on the District Attorney. "I'd say about twenty-five or, at most, thirty feet from the man to me. It was like the hypotenuse of one of those—what do you call it (he snapped his fingers)—isosceles right triangles." He heaved a sigh. "For a moment there, I was afraid I had forgotten. Hard to believe since geometry was my best subject." He shook his head. "Anyway, getting back to your question, I could probably work it out better using the formula. You know, $c^2 = a^2 + b^2$."

The District Attorney chuckled. "It rings a bell, but it's been a long time, and math was never my forte. If I understand, your best estimate is that the man was about twenty-five or thirty feet from you as he got into his car?"

"Objection…leading," said Skip, desperate to halt the inexorable line of questioning. "And there's no evidence whose car it was."

"I'll withdraw the question and rephrase. Give us your best estimate of the distance between you and the man as he got into *the* car?"

"Between twenty-five and thirty feet."

"What was the lighting like on the street?"

"It was after sunset, but the streetlights were on."

"Can you tell us where the nearest streetlight was located?"

"Yes. Directly in front of the center of the house in which I live. I know because every Thursday—that's garbage day—I lean my trash bag against it for pickup."

Well-spoken and calm, with no apparent axe to grind, Gardner was a devastating witness. The more he testified, the more helpless Skip felt.

"In what direction was the man facing as he opened the car door?"

"Toward me, if that's what you mean."

"Yes." The District Attorney nodded slowly. "Were you able to see him well enough to identify him?"

Skip's grip on his pen tightened to a stranglehold.

"Yes. It was Harley Morehead, the defendant."

A buzz emanated from the rear of the courtroom.

Judge Biddleford rapped his gavel. "Those of you behind the bar will observe decorum. If not, I'll clear the courtroom."

Skip stole a peak at the jury. He could see beyond their stone faces. Harley Morehead was in deep trouble.

The District Attorney took his time. Finally he said, "How did you know it was Harley Morehead?"

"I recognized him. I've seen his picture in the newspaper and on television. All that political stuff he's involved in as Chairman of the Populist Party."

The explanation was no surprise. In the jury selection process when Skip had examined the potential jurors, most were familiar with Harley Morehead.

"Here in the courtroom, do you see the person that you observed that night getting into the Cadillac convertible?"

"Yes."

"Would you point him out for the record?"

Laser-like index finger at the tip of a fully extended arm, Gardner pointed at the defense table. "It's the man seated over there next to Mr. Maynard."

Judge Biddleford said, "Let the record show that the witness identified the defendant."

"Mr. Gardner," said the District Attorney, "as you sit here today, is there any doubt in your mind whom you saw that evening?"

"No...none whatsoever."

"Once the defendant got into his car—excuse me, the Cadillac—what did he do?"

"He drove off."

"And what did you do?"

"I went back inside my flat and looked out the window toward Squeaky's place, but I couldn't see anything."

"And what did you do next?"

"Nothing really." Gardner, who had been largely relaxed throughout his testimony, fidgeted with his tie. "I...uh...thought about calling the police, but I wasn't a hundred percent sure that anything bad had happened." Gardner's gaze lowered. "And I...I didn't want to get involved."

The District Attorney walked back to his table. He studied his yellow pad for a minute or so. "No further questions."

"Mr. Maynard," said Judge Biddleford, "your cross-examination."

"If I may take a moment, Your Honor." He turned to Morehead and whispered, "If there's anything you wish to discuss before I go ahead, I can request a short recess."

Morehead shook his head. His face showed nothing.

From time to time Skip played poker. He prided himself on an ability to read people. Years in the courtroom had given him lots of practice. He had no clue what Morehead was thinking. Skip got up from his seat and walked slowly forward. Gardner was certain to be a tough nut, and the fact that Skip had represented him compounded the difficulty. Skip said,

"Mr. Gardner, you indicated that when you looked out the window of your apartment, you were unable to see inside Squeaky's flat. True?"

"Yes."

"And the reason you couldn't see was because the shade was well over halfway down. Correct?"

"Yes...and I distinctly remember the shade because it struck me how much nicer the window would have looked with curtains."

Skip welcomed the gratuitous comment, as well as a laugh from the rear of the courtroom, one that drew a rebuking glance from Judge Biddleford. Based upon *voir dire* when the jury was selected, Skip suspected juror number five might be homophobic. If so, he was apt to view Lenny Gardner's testimony with a jaundiced eye. Skip said, "So, with your angle and your view obstructed by the shade, you couldn't tell if there were more than two people in Squeaky's flat, could you?"

"No."

"There could have been three or four...or even more people there?"

"Yes, I guess."

Skip drifted across the room toward the jury. As bad as things were, at least Gardner was not giving him a hard time. Skip shifted to a position along the jury box rail, but far from the witness stand. From there he could discreetly survey the jury's reactions. He said, "Once the Cadillac drove off, you told us you went back into your apartment. Right?"

"Yes."

"You indicated that you looked out your side window again but saw nothing?"

"That's correct."

"So, you have no idea whether anyone else left Squeaky's flat after you went inside, do you?"

"No, I don't."

"You also don't know if anyone else went in?"

"That's true."

"As a matter of fact, you never saw Squeaky that evening, did you?"

Gardner thought for a moment. "I guess that's right."

"For all you know, what you heard could have been a tape recording of his voice?"

"Objection," said the District Attorney. "Mr. Maynard is asking the witness to speculate."

"On the contrary, I'm trying to make certain what he knows."

"Objection overruled. The witness will answer."

"Yes, I guess it could have been a tape."

Skip checked the jury. They didn't seem all that impressed. No surprise. If Skip were in the box, he would not have been either. "Mr. Gardner, you told us you didn't recognize the other voice you heard. Correct?"

"Absolutely."

"So, it could have been someone other than the defendant?"

"Yes."

"And that person could have killed Squeaky?"

"It's possible."

"And you would not have seen him leave Squeaky's flat because you were back inside your apartment. Right?"

"Yes."

"Or if someone arrived later and killed Squeaky, you wouldn't have known either, would you?"

"Probably not."

"Earlier you told the prosecutor that the defendant came out of Squeaky's flat carrying a folded newspaper."

"A rolled-up newspaper. The ends were folded."

"Excuse me—a rolled-up newspaper with folded ends." Skip made certain the tone with which he acknowledged the correction was deferential. The minor *faux pas* provided a wonderful opportunity to demonstrate he was doing nothing to browbeat the witness. "Regardless, you have no knowledge what, if anything, was inside that newspaper, do you?"

"No."

"As a matter of fact, it may have been nothing but a newspaper?"

"Absolutely."

Before he had begun his cross-examination, Skip thought an aggressive approach might be required, but with Gardner cooperating, it was possible to remain low key. And that was fortunate. Attacking a former client would be problematic. Skip glanced at the bench. Judge Biddleford knew that Skip had represented Gardner. At any moment the jurist could yank the rug from under Skip's feet. Regardless, Harley Morehead's freedom was on the line, and Skip had to do his best. He said, "You told the jury that after going back into your apartment you didn't call the police. True?"

"Yes."

Back in law school Skip's evidence professor had told them never to ask a material question on cross-examination for which they didn't know the answer. The rule made sense, but like most, it had exceptions. Lawyers, good and bad, took an occasional gamble. Some paid off, while most proved the rule. Skip hesitated but went ahead anyway. "Mr. Gardner, you didn't know for sure if anything untoward had happened next door, did you?"

"No, I didn't."

"And as you sit here today, under oath, apart from voices, you don't know what transpired in Squeaky's flat from the time you heard shouting until the Cadillac drove away. Isn't that true?"

Gardner shrugged. "It is. I really don't know what...if anything...happened there."

Skip breathed a mental sigh of relief. The knot in his stomach that had developed early in Gardner's direct examination had ameliorated. Reasonable doubt might be coming back into the equation, and with some good fortune those doubts could be expanded once the defense began its case. Skip eyed the notes he had made during the District Attorney's direct examination of Gardner. Skip had questions when and under what circumstances Gardner had provided information to the legal authorities. But asking them was dangerous. It would refocus on Gardner's reluctance to get involved, and, worse yet, undo what Skip had just accomplished. He said, "No further questions," and he returned to his seat.

The District Attorney got up. "Mr. Gardner, did you come to court today of your own choice?"

"Not really. I'm here because you served me with a subpoena."

"Apart from your involvement in this case, do you personally know any of the parties or the lawyers?"

"Objection." Skip was on his feet, though hardly on solid ground.

"The basis of your objection," said Judge Biddleford.

"New matter. Beyond the scope of cross-examination."

"Your Honor," said the District Attorney, "this is re-direct. I'm entitled to repair the witness's credibility. And the jury is entitled to know if the witness comes to court with any predilections or biases."

"Your Honor," said Skip, "the prosecution, having called Mr. Gardner to the stand, vouches for his credibility. There is nothing in his testimony as would suggest that he falls into the category of a hostile witness." Skip saw Judge Biddleford's eyes narrow ever so slightly. The reaction would have escaped Skip had he not seen it so many times before, especially in chambers where exchanges were more blunt. Indeed, if the lawyers had been alone with Judge Biddleford in the back room, the jurist probably would have blasted Skip.

"Objection overruled," said Judge Biddleford. He turned to the witness stand. "Mr. Gardner, tell us whether you personally know any of the parties or attorneys apart from your involvement in this case."

Gardner gestured at Skip. "Mr. Maynard represented me in a support matter."

Skip tried to show no reaction. He wondered how the jury was taking it, but he dared not look their way.

"Mr. Gardner," the District Attorney said, "you like Mr. Maynard, don't you?"

"Objection...leading."

"Sustained."

"Do you like Mr. Maynard?"

"Yes."

"Did he do a good job for you in Court?"

"Very good."

"And you wouldn't want to do anything to hurt his case here, would you?"

"No."

"May I see both counsel at the bench," said Judge Biddleford.

As Skip met the District Attorney for the side bar, he was concerned, but also puzzled.

"Mr. Carter, you've made your point." Judge Biddleford's voice was stern but soft enough that the jury couldn't hear. "It's time you move on."

Skip found it hard to believe that the Judge was hard-timing the District Attorney. A moment later when the jurist pointed a finger at Skip, he realized his adversary was not the only one under the gun.

"Mr. Maynard, at the very latest when you received the People's witness list, you had to realize there was a potential conflict of interest. Why you chose to take no steps to address the situation is known only to you. However, rest assured, you and I shall explore it after this case is over." A scowl on his face, Judge Biddleford shook his head. "Let's get back to business."

As Skip headed back to the defense table, he had no doubt that down the road Judge Biddleford would put him through the ringer. Still the tradeoff could have been worse. The Judge could have allowed the District Attorney to continue hammering his point.

Leaning over the back of his chair, the District Attorney stood and peered down at his notes. "No further questions," he said.

Skip quickly evaluated the situation. Admittedly Gardner had done significant damage, but keeping him on the stand would likely compound, not mitigate, that damage. "No re-cross," said Skip.

"The witness is excused."

Gardner stepped down from the stand. As he passed between the prosecution and defense table, he stole a glance at Skip. His expressionless face was inscrutable.

"Mr. Carter, any more witnesses?" said Judge Biddleford.

"The People rest."

Judge Biddleford looked at his watch. "Let's take a twenty minute recess, and then we'll start the defense."

"If Your Honor please, I wish to make a motion to dismiss," said Skip.

"Fine. But since we want to avoid the risk of legal arguments tainting the jury, I'll excuse them first." Before doing so, Judge Biddleford again admonished the panel to keep open minds and not discuss the case.

While the jury was leaving, Skip whispered to Morehead. "This is the motion I told you I would make at the end of the People's case. As I mentioned, we defense lawyers do it as a matter of course. I have no illusions it will be granted."

Once the jury was gone, Judge Biddleford said, "Mr. Maynard, your motion."

Skip got up from his seat and circled around in front of the defense table. He waited a moment making sure he had Judge Biddleford's full attention.

The defense moves to dismiss the indictment on the grounds that the People have failed to make out a prima facie case. Even accepting the entirety of the People's evidence, as a matter of law, there is no basis on which a jury could properly conclude beyond a reasonable doubt that the defendant Harley Morehead killed Ralph Squeaky Grimes. The People have failed to produce even one scintilla of forensic evidence that links the defendant to the crime. Terrance Winter, the People's hematologist testified about various bloodstains he found at the scene. We know Squeaky was stabbed to death, but the bloodstains, all of which came from Squeaky, tell us nothing about who murdered him. More important, they in no way link Harley Morehead to the crime.

Now, let's talk about Leonard Gardner, the only witness who placed the defendant at the scene of the crime within the expansive time frame during which the homicide could have been committed. Mr. Gardner acknowledged he couldn't say whether any violence had transpired next door in Squeaky's flat. Mr. Gardner said he saw the defendant carrying a rolled-up newspaper but admitted he had no knowledge what, if anything else, the defendant might be carrying. This is hardly the kind of proof under the constitutional dictates governing our system of jurisprudence that would permit a guilty verdict. Accordingly, the indictment against the defendant must be dismissed forthwith.

Once Skip returned to his seat, the District Attorney stepped forward. He glanced at the defense table before proceeding.

Your Honor, the defendant's motion to dismiss must be viewed from a perspective allowing the People's evidence every favorable inference so long as reasonable. Mr. Maynard, skillful advocate that he is, instead inveigles us to examine the evidence under a defense-biased microscope. Eddie the Enforcer Willis, who worked for the defendant, testified that he beat up Squeaky Grimes at the behest of and with the defendant present. He further testified that at said time the defendant threatened to kill Squeaky. The defendant clearly had motive. As Mr. Willis testified, Squeaky had threatened to inform the police that the defendant was engaged in illegal bookmaking. Two other witnesses, Walter Holt and Guy Devine, as well as Eddie Willis, established that Morehead was indeed a bookmaker.

Next, let's examine Mr. Gardner's testimony. The subpoenaed witness testified that within the ten-hour time frame that the coroner fixed as to when Squeaky was stabbed to death, he heard Squeaky arguing with someone. Gardner heard Squeaky threaten to go to the cops if he didn't get more money. Then he heard Squeaky say, 'What are you doing with that knife?' There was a scream. A minute later Gardner saw the defendant come out of Squeaky's flat carrying a rolled-up newspaper that he stuffed into the trunk of a Cadillac. Not only did Mr. Gardner positively identify the defendant Harley Morehead, but his description of the vehicle driven by the defendant, a blue Cadillac

with a white convertible top, matched the description
given by defendant's strong arm, Eddie the Enforcer
Willis.
In summary, the defendant had motive and opportunity.
He had threatened to kill the victim. Eyewitness
testimony placed him at the scene of the crime. While
there, Squeaky screamed. There was silence, and
moments later the defendant came out of Squeaky's
flat. What transpired is obvious. Harley Morehead
murdered Squeaky Grimes. For Mr. Maynard to
request a dismissal of the indictment—in other words,
contend that there is no way a reasonable jury could
find the defendant guilty—is absolutely ludicrous.
Accordingly, the motion must be denied.

Judge Biddleford jotted some notes. He gazed pensively into space for the better part of a minute. "At this juncture I'm going to reserve decision on the motion."

If Skip were a rookie, he might have been buoyed by the news. But the handwriting was on the wall. Very often, even when the denial of a motion to dismiss seemed a foregone conclusion, a judge would reserve decision, only to deny it after the defense presented its case. No doubt Judge Biddleford had chosen that route.

Judge Biddleford picked up his gavel and rapped it twice. "We'll reconvene in fifteen minutes."

———————

"You got a moment?"

Even before Skip looked back down the hallway that led from the courtroom, he recognized Kelly's voice. As he waited for her to catch up, he took note of her chic, chestnut suit. That the understated lines of her impeccable professional attire enhanced her feminine charms seemed anomalous. On prior occasions the apparent contradiction had crossed Skip's mind, but never with sound explanation. Regardless, titillating intrusions, nature's enigmatic device for transmuting thoughts and emotions, made Kelly look even lovelier than usual.

"Interesting afternoon," she said.

"You watched it?" Although Skip hadn't noticed her among the spectators, her presence was no surprise. With the wrongful death action she had brought against Morehead on behalf of Squeaky's estate, she had good reason.

"I was in the back row." She motioned to a quiet corner of the hallway. Skip followed her there. "Biddleford is treating you pretty well. If I didn't know him better, I might think him civilized."

Skip jerked back histrionically.

"React all you want. But from where I sit, I'd say he's given you a few breaks."

"Sure, you see it that way because you represent Squeaky's estate." Despite his comment, Skip silently conceded that His Holiness had been remarkably fair. Indeed he had given Morehead more than an even break, most notably suppressing his confession.

"I won't debate the point because I know you don't have a lot of free time during the brief recess. The reason I wanted to talk involves Bernie Feinstein. I understand you subpoenaed him. Unless I miss my guess, you're hoping the jury will have a hard time excluding him as a suspect. And you needn't comment. I'm not fishing for your strategy."

Kelly's assumption was right. Skip's primary defense tactic was to clog the jurors' heads with a laundry list of possible suspects, just enough to leave doubts as to Morehead's guilt.

"Anyway, I thought you'd like to know that Feinstein found Squeaky's big diamond ring hidden away in the apartment and turned it over to me."

"Interesting, but maybe he did it because he was more concerned about being charged with murder than keeping the spoils." The tenuous argument rang hollow in Skip's ears.

"Whatever...but once again I won't debate the matter. What I want you to know is that Feinstein has an airtight alibi. He was in New York City when Squeaky was killed. The prosecution has a rebuttal witness who can verify that. They want you to call Feinstein so they can show the jury that you're grasping at straws in an effort to mislead them away from Morehead."

Most times Skip would have greeted the information with skepticism, but not coming from Kelly. He knew her far too well. No way would she deceive him. Regardless, Mickey had already verified the tidbit. "Why are you telling me?"

"I thought you'd want to know."

"Yeah...but you've got a lawsuit against Morehead. His conviction would put you on easy street."

"In some respects." She thought for a moment. "But the way I see it, at this point money doesn't mean a whole lot to Squeaky. The best thing I can do for him is to bring his killer to justice. And as far as his estate, sure, we want to recover damages, but from the person who murdered him, not someone else."

"Does that mean you think Harley Morehead is innocent?" The possibility buoyed Skip. Kelly had been watching the trial. Perhaps he was swaying her, and, if so, maybe the jury as well.

She shook her head. "To put it in the parlance of my late client, betting man that he was, Morehead is chalk."

"You might be surprised."

Kelly shrugged.

The gesture brought Skip no solace. Once again, she had politely declined to argue.

"Anyway...I think you're doing a great job. It reminds me of the brilliant young lawyer I watched more than a decade ago when I was still in law school." She hesitated. "Don't take this the wrong way, but back then I had a crush on that lawyer. Unfortunately he was married." She patted him on the back. "I'm really happy to see that you've pushed the alcohol aside." Her voice grew soft. "I'm proud of you." She started on her way. With a glance back over her shoulder, she added, "Good luck with the trial."

Skip watched her disappear down the hallway and around the corner. Damn, she was sexy and beautiful and always a class act. Skip heaved a prolonged sigh lamenting the choice he had made five years after Megan had been killed. Admittedly *Jack* had always been there for him, but picking the pal in a bottle over Kelly had been a mistake. Of course, back then, *Jack*, not Skip, was the boss. Skip lowered his gaze, taking in the cold, hard granite floor. At that moment he would have loved to ask Kelly out for Saturday night. It wasn't possible. The canons of ethics prohibited the attorney for Harley Morehead from dating the attorney for Squeaky's estate. Regardless, other business demanded his full attention. He was due back in the courtroom.

"Mr. Maynard, call your first witness."

Skip got up from his seat. "The defense calls James Raines to the stand."

Nattily attired in a blue blazer and gray slacks, and sporting a heavy gold chain that hung where a pair of buttons on his aquamarine sport shirt remained open, Raines stepped forward and took the oath. He looked more ready for a three-martini lunch at the *Leatherstocking Club* than a stint on the witness stand.

The phase of the trial Skip had long been awaiting had finally arrived. Listening to prosecution witnesses build a mound of evidence against his client had been painful. He welcomed the opportunity to fire his shotgun of reasonable doubts. His strategy, however, had an inherent complication. He planned to attack his own witnesses. The rules of evidence precluded the tactic, except for witnesses ruled adverse or hostile by the court. With Judge Biddleford on the bench that was always a challenge.

Skip got up from his seat and slowly walked around to the front of the defense table. "Kindly state your full name for the record, please."

"James Walker Raines."

"And Mr. Raines, where do you live?"

"2613 Willow Street, Cooperstown."

"How old are you?"

"Forty-four."

A momentary frown from Judge Biddleford caught the corner of Skip's eye. Unconsciously Skip had seated himself on the edge of the defense table with legs dangling freely. In his early years of practice Skip had often assumed the casual bearing, sometimes without thinking, but others when trying to lull a witness into a false sense of security. Judgment urged he climb down from his comfortable perch. Instead he closed his eyes for a moment. He felt a dozen years younger. He was remarkably relaxed and eager to litigate.

"Mr. Raines, you're engaged in a business known as *Artway,* aren't you?"

"Yeah."

"And what is the nature of that business?"

"We sell works of art. Mostly paintings, although we're now dealing in sculptures as well. Much of what we sell comes from lesser-known artists. It's unfortunate how many talented individuals never get the recognition they deserve. But we're changing that, all the while getting our customers high quality works with huge appreciation potential at rock-bottom prices."

Skip could have cut Raines off halfway through the longwinded response, but he preferred to let him go on. The advertisement, likely a well-rehearsed spiel, enabled the jury to see that the man on the stand matched his outfit. Like the proverbial used-car salesman, Raines was glib. Trustworthy was another matter. "Do you have a partner?"

"Not now. But Ralph Grimes, or Squeaky, as everyone knew him, was...until he was murdered."

"Was it a fifty-fifty arrangement?"

"Yeah, we were equal partners."

"Please briefly explain to the jury the structure of your business."

Raines turned toward the jury. "An individual who has sold five thousand dollars worth of our art work becomes a franchisor, a certified *Artway* dealer. A dealer gets a percentage of the sales of new dealers that he or she brings in, plus a lesser percentage of their new enlistees."

Skip pressed the tips of his fingers together with his arms forming an inverted V. "If I understand, your business structure is like a pyramid with you—previously you and Squeaky—at the top?"

Raines shifted his gaze to Skip. His tone took on an edge. "The visual image you create may be helpful, but I resent your terminology. It stirs notions of unseemly pyramid schemes."

"Isn't that the nature of your business?"

"Objection!" The District Attorney was on his feet. "Mr. Maynard is impeaching his own witness."

"On the contrary, I'm endeavoring to clarify the type of business in which the witness and the victim were partnered."

"Mr. Maynard, I know what you're doing. Objection sustained."

Skip climbed down from his comfortable perch and took a couple of steps forward. "Mr. Raines, how did you and Squeaky get along?"

"Okay, I guess."

"Okay...you say. Are you suggesting there were some problems?" Skip needed to lay a foundation that would enable him to attack Raines, but he also needed to tread carefully.

"Partnerships have their rough spots."

"What were the rough spots between you and Squeaky?"

Raines shrugged. "This and that. Nothing specific."

Skip moved forward within a few feet of the witness. "Isn't it true that in the Grill Room of the *Leatherstocking Club*, with several others present, Squeaky accused you of stealing monies that had accrued to your partnership?"

"Objection!" The District Attorney was on his feet once more. "The question is not only leading, but counsel is again impeaching his own witness."

"Your Honor," said Skip, jumping in before Judge Biddleford could rule. "I merely asked the witness a question. I have not impeached anything he has said. However, owing to the contentious relationship between the witness and the murder victim, extracting testimony from the witness will no doubt be challenging. I, therefore, request that you declare Mr. Raines to be a hostile witness and allow me to ask leading questions."

The District Attorney gestured at the stand. "The witness has not been hostile."

"Your Honor, my client is on trial for murder. He should be afforded every opportunity to demonstrate his innocence.

We believe we can show that Mr. Raines had motive and opportunity to kill Squeaky Grimes. Since naturally the People did not call Mr. Raines, the defense must, not because we vouch for his credibility, but because we—"

"Mr. Maynard is making speeches, polluting the jury with inadmissible trumpery. The People—"

Judge Biddleford's gavel struck. "Both of you stop." He glared first at the District Attorney and then at Skip. "At this juncture there is insufficient basis to declare the witness hostile. Having said that, Due Process requires that the defendant be afforded the opportunity to support counsel's claim. Accordingly, I will, for the moment, allow you, Mr. Maynard, to ask leading questions. How long that will continue remains to be seen. Proceed."

"Thank you, Your Honor." The phrase, one Skip had begrudgingly uttered to His Holiness many times before, for once was sincere. Judge Biddleford had not only referenced Due Process; he had actually given the fundamental principle more than lip service. Skip refocused on the witness. "Mr. Raines, is it not true that earlier this year in the *Leatherstocking Club* Grill Room, with several others present, Squeaky accused you of stealing monies earned by your partnership?"

"He might have. People say lotsa stuff, and nobody can remember it all."

"You say, *he might have.*" Skip walked back to the defense table and picked up his yellow pad. "Would it help refresh your recollection if I mentioned the names George Landmore, Peter White and Gerard Staunton and if told you that I have subpoenaed all of them?"

Raines sat motionless.

Skip glanced at the jurors. They were intently scrutinizing the witness.

"Mr. Raines," barked Judge Biddleford, "answer the question!"

"Yeah, Squeaky accused me of stealing, but that doesn't mean I was."

"Move to..." Skip had second thoughts. The gratuitous remark, food for the jury, did more good than harm. He drifted over to the jury box rail and said, "It was late March, about two weeks before Squeaky was killed, when he accused you of stealing, wasn't it?"

"Something like that," growled Raines.

"And where were you on the 9th of April?"

"Working, golfing, shopping...home watching TV." Raines glared at Skip. "You pick some random day from way back when. How should I know?"

"If you don't mind, I'll ask the questions." Skip stared Raines down. "Anyone who can vouch for your whereabouts?"

"My wife."

"But she wasn't with you the entire day, was she?"

"She might have been."

"But chances are, she wasn't...I'll withdraw that," said Skip, his comment overlapping with the District Attorney's cry of *objection*. Skip folded his arms. "What was your wife doing on April 9th?"

"How should I know?"

Skip nodded slowly. "So, the truth of the matter is...you don't have an alibi for the day Squeaky was killed, do you?"

"No, but I didn't kill the weasel."

"Weasel...To you Ralph Grimes was nothing more than a rodent?"

"I didn't say that."

"Not exactly...but that's what you thought of Squeaky. Right?"

A simmering Raines remained silent.

Skip eyed the jury. The point was made. He said, "On the day that Squeaky accused you of stealing, didn't you threaten to put him six feet under ground if he ever repeated the accusation?"

"Are you insinuating—"

"I'm asking you whether you threatened Squeaky with words to that effect." Skip marched forward as he spoke.

"Maybe I did, but—"

Skip held up his hand. "Thank you. You've answered the question." Skip walked back to the defense table. He pulled out his chair but before seating himself said, "That wasn't the last time Squeaky accused you of stealing, was it?"

Raines failed to respond.

Skip sat down. Several seconds later, he said, "Nothing further of this witness."

Morehead leaned over and whispered in his ear. "Good job."

Skip scribbled *thanks* on his yellow pad and slid the note in front of Morehead.

The District Attorney got up. "Mr. Raines, did you kill Ralph Squeaky Grimes?"

"No."

"That's all I have," said the District Attorney.

"Mr. Maynard, do you have any re-direct?"

"No, Your Honor." Skip didn't need to prove that Raines was the murderer. Reasonable doubt as to Morehead's guilt was sufficient.

Judge Biddleford surveyed the courtroom. "The four o'clock hour fast approaches. Perhaps this would be a good point to break for the week."

Skip chuckled to himself. Consistent with his familiar *modus operandi*, Judge Biddleford, anxious to get his weekend started, would never work late on a Friday afternoon. The fact that he began late every morning and took long lunches was no reason not to conclude early. Look out for number one, and make sure he doesn't work too hard. In spite of the familiar cynicism, Skip reluctantly conceded that when it came to Due Process, the self-important jurist was treating the principle as more than a dispensable nuisance.

From the lawyers lounge in the Courthouse Skip dialed his office. Paperwork sat on his desk, but nothing so important it couldn't wait until the following week. In the midst of a murder trial he needed to direct all his energies to the task at hand.

"How's it going?" said Lucy.

"Hard to say." Skip prided himself on the ability to read juries, though admittedly the skill was little more than an intuitive guessing game. Regardless, he could not even begin to hazard a guess. "Anything there I need to address?"

"Everything's under control."

The words played dulcet notes in Skip's brain. At such moments, even more than usual, he valued Lucy. He said, "You know, your boss is a mighty lucky guy. How a ding-a-ling like him rates a peach like you is beyond me."

With her typically inimitable cool, Lucy absorbed the praise. "How far along are you in the case?"

"I put my first witness, Jimmie Raines, on the stand this afternoon. He—" Skip cut himself off as another member of the Bar entered the lawyers' lounge. "The weatherman predicts sunshine for tomorrow."

"Company?...Can't talk?"

"Right. I'll let you go."

"Before you do, I've got a message here from Lenny Gardner."

Gardner. Skip silently mouthed the name, trying to imagine what the former client would want. "Did he say why he was calling?"

"No. He said he'd be out of town for a few days, and he'd call you when he gets back."

"Did he leave a number where he could be reached?"

"Nothing."

"Okay. Talk to you later." As Skip hung up the receiver, he pondered why Gardner, the prosecution's most devastating witness, had tried to reach him. Skip needed an answer, and getting one several days down the road when Gardner got back into town could be too late. Mickey would have to try to locate Gardner. Skip left the attorneys' lounge in favor of the pay telephone in the hallway where he dialed Mickey and put him on Gardner's trail.

Skip left the Courthouse, and, after depositing his attaché case in the trunk of his car, started down the street in the direction of the *Eagle.* The old Federal style tavern was not yet visible, but the image of its façade, with green-shuttered windows and heavy oak door, was sharp in Skip's mind. Like *Bali High* from his Rodgers and Hammerstein favorite, the enticing haunt was calling him. And the similarity didn't end there. Besides the chance to unwind, there were other allures, not the least of which was the bottle of *Jack Daniel's* always near the far left of the upper shelf behind the bar.

As he stepped through the door of the storied pub, Skip paused just long enough to eye the bronze plaque bearing the bust of James Fenimore Cooper that hung adjacent to the entrance. The idea that the famous man may have passed that same way many decades before was one small element of Cooperstown's history that had prompted Skip to return to his childhood hometown after law school. He had passed up an opportunity with a large firm amidst the skyscrapers of New York City. Admittedly when it came to architecture, the *Big Apple* had more to offer than tiny Cooperstown. The same could be said for lucrative legal positions. And the renowned metropolis had no shortage of history or excitement. But at heart Skip was a small-town guy. The serenity of Otsego Lake was preferable to the hustle and bustle of Time Square, Fifth Avenue and Broadway. The faint echoes of *Drums Along the Mohawk* played better in his ears than the relentless honks of cabbies blowing their horns. No doubt a ballgame at *Yankee Stadium* was exciting, but the *House that Ruth Built* was only a nice place to visit. In the stands of little *Doubleday*, Skip felt at home. So it was at the *Eagle.*

As he eased forward to his usual spot at the left end of the bar, he loosened his tie and unhooked the top button of his starched white shirt.

A moment later Loomis came his way. The lanky bartender leaned forward and whispered. "Word is you knocked 'em dead in court today."

Skip shrugged. "You mean I put the jury to sleep?"

"C'mon, you know what I mean. Folks are saying it's fifty-fifty whether Morehead killed Squeaky. With odds like that, he's looking more and more like a free pass."

Skip shrugged again. "I'll believe it...if and when the jury gives the word."

"What would you like?"

"A not guilty verdict."

Loomis frowned. "Sorry, that's not on my drink menu."

Skip pointed at the bottle of *Jack Daniel's*. He ignored the unreceptive look on Loomis's face. "On the rocks in a big highball glass."

"You think that's a good idea?"

"No."

"But you're ordering it anyway?"

Skip hesitated. "No…Just answering your question. You asked what I wanted. Doesn't mean that's what I'm gonna have."

Loomis rolled his eyes. "How 'bout a *Diet Pepsi*?"

Skip shook his head. "I need something stronger. Make it half-diet and half-regular. And I'll have an *Eagle Burger*, heavy on the onions, along with a *double* order of crisp fries."

Just before he headed off, Loomis smiled.

A hand on Skip's shoulder caused him to turn. He didn't recognize the face.

"I was in the back of the courtroom today. Just want to say that you did a bang-up job. Don't see how any fair-minded jury could convict Morehead. If you ask me, they may have charged the wrong guy." The fellow immediately moved on.

Though Skip knew better than to prematurely count his chickens, the confidence boost was gratifying. And if everything went as planned when court resumed on Monday, his odds could get even better.

His *Pepsi* arrived. For a few moments he focused on the beverage, but his thoughts quickly re-directed to his upcoming witnesses. For Skip trial work was all-consuming. Years earlier as a rookie litigator, he had fretted over obsessive tendencies until conversations with some of the finest attorneys in the region convinced him such behavior was commonplace among the best.

Loomis delivered his burger and a huge platter of fries. "Someone was in here yesterday asking about you."

"What did he want?"

"It wasn't a he."

The person doing the asking suddenly became more interesting than the nature of the inquiry. "Who?"

"Kelly Lane."

Loomis bore that certain look. Perhaps it was the hint of an enigmatic smile beneath widened eyes that made it hard to describe, let alone fathom. Regardless, Skip knew it well. Loomis had something on his mind, which, for the moment, he was keeping to himself. "What did she want?"

"Just some small talk." His cryptic mask vanished behind a toothy grin.

"You gonna jerk me around?"

Loomis pulled back with arms spread wide.

"Save the melodramatics for your next audition with the local thespians."

"You accusing me of having a boyfriend? Your buddy Biddleford perhaps?" An outrageous scowl confirmed that Loomis was still playacting.

"No, but if you don't stop the nonsense, I'll accuse you of a lot worse. So, tell me, what did Kelly want?"

"Not much. Mainly she was interested whether you and *Jack* were still traveling separate roads."

"If that's all, why'd you make a big deal of it?"

"'Cause her real interest was obvious."

Skip struggled to make sense of the comment.

"Hope you don't wear that blank face in the courtroom."

The desire for an explanation kept Skip from continuing the futile banter. "Do me a favor. Humor me, and explain what you're babbling about."

"Kelly Lane has the hots for you."

"C'mon, you're just saying that to..." Skip's voice trailed off as he recalled her recent flirtation at the Courthouse. "You really think so?"

"I know so." Loomis looked toward the middle of the bar where a burly fellow was calling for a refill. "Gotta go."

Skip reached for a fry. He nibbled, intrigued by the idea that Kelly was taken with him. His skeptical side posed doubts, but when it came to reading people, Loomis the bartender, not to mention amateur psychiatrist, was better than anyone, perhaps even Mickey.

Chapter XVII

Half asleep, Skip reached for the telephone. "Hello," he garbled, as he glanced at the clock. 6:23.

"Hi, it's Mickey. Hope I didn't wake you."

Still struggling for his bearings, Skip let the comment pass.

"Did you read the morning paper?"

"No, as matter of fact, I was sleeping."

"Sorry, but I think it's important. Front page...there's a story about the Justice Department's corruption investigation."

The information roused Skip from what still bordered on a stupor. "What's it say?"

"Morelli has been indicted. He's charged with paying kickbacks to public officials."

"Perhaps our lovely City Manager was indicted also?"

"LaDieux...not as yet."

Skip ran the information through his head. "Wait a second. Why would they indict one without the other?"

"Perhaps Morelli paid off someone other than LaDieux. But anyway, the article doesn't give her a clean bill of health. When asked if she was in the clear, the U.S. Attorney declined comment."

"Interesting...very interesting," said Skip, already beginning to weigh how the disclosures might affect his courtroom strategy. "Does the article include any other details about the kickbacks?"

"Not specifically, but...there was something. Just a sec, and I'll find it." A few moments later Mickey continued. "Here...it says: *A source close to the investigation predicts Morelli may try to negotiate a plea deal in exchange for his testimony against a public official or officials who extorted kickbacks.* There's another interesting tidbit in the story." Mickey paused again. "It says: *The U.S. Attorney declined comment when asked if the indictment of Gino Morelli had any connection to the murder of his former employee Squeaky Grimes.*"

"He declined comment," mumbled Skip. "What do you know about that?"

"You think it might be significant?"

"For the moment I'm not sure." Through the earpiece of the receiver, Skip heard a breathy sound. "Was that a sigh or, don't tell me...you're smoking again?"

There was a brief silence.

"Yeah...those damn candy cigarettes were a stupid idea, especially for someone like myself who's hooked on the nicotine they pack in good, old-fashioned *Camels.*"

"Old-fashioned maybe, but as for good, that's another matter."

"C'mon, don't be judgmental. You—of all people."

The message silenced Skip. His battle with the bottle was far from over. Indeed his thirst for *Jack* was arguably as powerful as Mickey's craving for the tar and nicotine hidden behind the picture of the benign dromedary...maybe more powerful, if there was truth to the notion that the battle with alcohol was a lifelong struggle.

"By the way, I wasn't able to locate Gardner. I checked with his ex-wife and a few others, but no one knew where he went."

"Well..." Skip tried to imagine why Gardner had called the office. Having traveled that route before, he immediately conceded its futility.

"What do you plan to do now that Morelli has been indicted?"

The new charges raised interesting possibilities, but also more than one strategy. "At the moment, I'm not entirely sure."

"You got a minute?"

Halfway up the walkway that led to the Courthouse, Skip turned and stopped as he spotted City Manager Traci LaDieux hurrying to catch up.

She gestured at the semi-circular, stone bench at the nearby monument to the soldiers and sailors of Otsego County.

He shook his head. "Right here will have to do."

"You plan to make me testify today?"

Though not one hundred percent certain, he said, "I subpoenaed you, didn't I?"

Momentary frustration appeared on her face. "So you did. But it's not like there's anything I could say that would help your case. Chances are I'd do more harm than good."

Skip consciously displayed a furrowed brow, a polite reminder that she was a politician, and politicians were renown for words more indicative of expediency than substance.

"C'mon...we've known each other since grammar school." She moved closer, brushing against his arm.

Far from the point of contact, neurons flashed. Her red v-neck sweater had already drawn his eyes to the ample cleavage that pointed to her tight-waisted skirt. As usual, her alluringly attired body had him struggling to keep his gaze north of her neckline.

"Don't misunderstand...I'm not asking you to jeopardize your case in any way."

"What are you asking me to do?"

She looked at him provocatively as she pressed closer. The bell in the steeple of the First Methodist Church chimed nine o'clock. She gazed in the direction of the melodic sound. "Just because we missed the opportunity to make sweet music back in high school doesn't mean we need to repeat that mistake."

Skip felt the pounding of his heart—hard and fast. It was as if Traci had transported him back to his hormone-raging teenage days. A tightened grip on the handle of his attaché case evidenced that thoughts were dictating physical reactions, but it also sparked a reminder, refocusing his attentions. This was not high school. In his hands he carried the fate of his client. He had a legal responsibility. And too, there was Kelly. To quote

Loomis, she had the *hots* for him. Spectacular though a fling with Traci might have been, Kelly was more than just a great body. The image of his beloved Megan flashed into Skip's head. The conglomeration of thoughts troubled, addled and enticed him, all at the same time. He eyed his watch, despite being well aware of the hour. He said, "You'll have to excuse me. I have a case to try." He headed into the Courthouse.

As he began his examination of Gino Morelli with a typical line of innocuous inquiries, Skip eyed the bronze-skinned contractor. With broad shoulders, blacksmith forearms and a face whose every facet was inscribed with determination, he was indeed a formidable foe. Skip was no pushover, but if they were in the alley near *Doubleday Field*, it would have been a mismatch. In the courtroom, however, the rules were different. Highly technical, they were anything but no holds barred, and the weapon of choice, rather than clenched fists, a facile tongue. And one more thing, Skip got to choose all the questions.

Skip drifted over to the jury box rail, about twenty feet back from the witness stand. He wanted the jurors to enjoy an unobstructed view of Morelli's face as he testified. "Mr. Morelli, in the course of your contracting business, was Ralph Squeaky Grimes ever in your employ?"

"Until I fired him."

"And when was that?"

"Back in March. The middle of the month."

"A few weeks before Squeaky was killed? Would that be about right?"

"Something like that."

"How long had he worked for you?"

"Four...or five years, off and on. Usually just a few days per month. He always had more than one job, none of them full time."

"What type of work did he do for you?"

"Framing, some paneling...stuff like that. I used him when I needed an extra hand. He was okay, but he was no master. That's for sure."

"Why'd you fire him?"

"Well..." Morelli shifted his position, pushing back taller in his chair. "He...he wasn't reliable."

"Did he show up for work on days when he was supposed to?"

"Yeah."

"On time?"

"Yeah."

Skip motioned to the jury. "Help these good people understand what you meant by *unreliable*."

"I don't know." Morelli displayed an indignant expression. "You...you just couldn't count on him."

Skip donned a puzzled mask, strictly for effect. "For what?"

"For you know...whatever." Annoyance infected Morelli's tone.

Skip shrugged. "I don't know. That's why I'm asking."

"The guy was trouble. I didn't want him around any more. Okay?"

"You say trouble. What kind of trouble?"

Morelli's jaw clenched. "Personal. Between him and me."

"We'll decide that," said Skip. From the corner of his eye he saw the District Attorney rising from his seat. "Withdraw the comment." He stared at the witness. "What kind of trouble?"

"Personal," barked Morelli.

"Mr. Morelli," said Judge Biddleford, "you will answer the question." Several seconds elapsed. "Tell us the nature of the trouble you had with Squeaky Grimes."

Never turning to the Judge, Morelli looked straight forward. He said nothing.

"Sir!" Judge Biddleford's voice resounded. "Answer the question!"

"The creep was blackmailing me." The decibels of Morelli's response approached that of Judge Biddleford's directive.

Skip inched forward along the jury box rail. "How exactly was he blackmailing you?"

"He threatened to make false accusations against me if I didn't pay him fifteen thousand dollars."

"What was the nature of the accusations he threatened to make?"

"Objection," said the District Attorney. "The witness has indicated the accusations were false. He shouldn't be required to publicize them here in open court."

Skip might have reacted to the spurious argument had he not caught the unreceptive look on Judge Biddleford's face.

"Mr. Carter, we have on the stand a man who indicates he was being blackmailed by the victim. I believe the jury, not the witness, should weigh the credibility of the accusations the victim allegedly made." Judge Biddleford turned to Morelli. "Tell us the accusations."

Several protracted seconds of silence ensued. Morelli, perhaps sensing that an exasperated Judge Biddleford was about to lash out, finally responded. "He threatened to tell the authorities that I had bribed public officials in order to get public contracts. But it wasn't true."

"What did you do?" said Skip.

"I told you. I fired him!" Morelli gritted his teeth.

Skip sensed that with each question Morelli was growing angrier. Just to Skip's right, the jurors, like fans at *Doubleday* caught up in a duel between a fireballing hurler and a prodigious slugger, were absorbed in the back-and-forth exchange. Skip eased into a casual lean against the rail. His smooth sliders had been subtly slipping past Morelli's fuming blasts. A couple of change-ups, and then, at the right moment, Skip would unleash the hard one, high and inside—chin music. He said, "Did he threaten you after you fired him?"

"Maybe...I don't know."

"You don't know or, perhaps, you prefer not to tell us?"

"Argumentative," said the District Attorney.

"Sustained."

"Mr. Morelli, when was the last time you saw Ralph Squeaky Grimes alive?"

"I don't know. About a week before he got killed, I guess."

"And where was that?"

"He came by a house that I was building for speculation just north of Oneonta."

Skip sensed that Morelli's blood pressure had lowered a notch.

"Did you have a conversation with Squeaky at that time?"

"Yeah."

"Was anyone else present?"

"Nope."

"Did he try to blackmail you then?"

"You bet he did."

Skip nodded again, his thoughtful countenance intended for both the witness and the jury. "So, let me make sure I have your testimony straight. Squeaky threatened you the last time you saw him, which was a few weeks after you fired him. Right?"

Morelli's eyes widened with seeming recognition of his misstep.

"Objection—leading." The District Attorney voiced the belated challenge with little conviction.

"Overruled. The witness has displayed sufficient hostility to justify leading questions on direct examination. If need be, I'll make him the Court's witness." Judge Biddleford turned to Morelli. "Did Squeaky Grimes threaten you several weeks after you fired him?"

"Yeah."

Judge Biddleford gestured for Skip to continue.

"So...Mr. Morelli...earlier when you told the jury that you didn't know whether Squeaky threatened you after you fired him, that wasn't true, was it?"

Morelli said nothing.

Skip eyed the witness. The fastball had thumped the catcher's mitt. All along the goal had simply been to cast reasonable doubt on whether Morehead had killed Squeaky. For the first time Skip was seriously contemplating the possibility that Morelli might be the murderer. Skip glanced at the jury. Among the normally opaque faces, he saw the elderly woman at the right end of the first row appear to nod. Perhaps it was his imagination, but maybe she too was thinking that Morelli was Squeaky's killer. Regardless, Skip had plenty of fodder. He looked back at the witness stand. "Mr. Morelli, did you know a fellow, late of this county, by the name of Woody Wilson?"

A puzzled look appeared on Morelli's face. "Yeah."

"Did he work for you?"

"He wasn't my employee."

"But he did work for you in your contracting business. Right?"

"A little...but like I said, he *wasn't* my employee. He was an *independent contractor*."

"While working for you, Wilson suffered a fall that caused a disabling leg and hip injury. Isn't that right?"

"That's what he claimed. But I never believed it."

"How did it happen?"

"How should I know?"

Skip let the sarcastic interrogatory response go unchallenged. The more the jury observed Morelli's caustic tongue, the better. "Wilson filed a Workmen's Compensation claim against you, didn't he?"

"Yeah, but the Board tossed it out because he wasn't an employee."

"Was that because you were paying him under the table, and he couldn't prove an employment relationship?"

"Objection—calls for a legal conclusion."

"Sustained."

"Do you know how Woody Wilson died?"

"I heard it was a suicide. He sat in his car while it was running in the garage."

"When was the last time you saw Wilson alive?"

Morelli's eyes again showed fire. "What's that supposed to mean?"

"Excuse me," said Skip. "Please answer my question."

Morelli glared. "Around the first of May. A month or two before his suicide."

"Did Wilson ever work alongside Squeaky?"

"He might have."

Skip was fishing, but for what, he wasn't altogether sure. If Wilson's death had some link to Squeaky's murder, he didn't know how, and Morelli would never tell him. Skip needed to be careful. If he fished too long, he would undermine what he had accomplished earlier. He said, "When Squeaky began blackmailing you, you became enraged, didn't you?"

"Yeah...Wouldn't you?" Morelli's jaw clenched.

Skip stared directly into the witness's eyes. "Move to strike as immaterial and beyond the witness's knowledge what I would or wouldn't do."

"Stricken. The jury will disregard the witness's comment."

Skip walked forward to the corner of the jury box closest to the witness. "When Squeaky blackmailed you, you threatened him, didn't you?"

"I warned him."

Morelli's growl was music to Skip's ears. "Just how did you warn him?"

A simmering Morelli remained mute.

"We're waiting for your answer," said Skip.

"I let him know he better not mess with me."

Skip folded his arms. "Where were you on the 9th of April?"

"Working."

"What about in the evening?"

"Home watching TV...I assume." A disgusted look showed on Morelli's face. "You expect me to remember some night you pick from out of the sky."

Skip disregarded the gratuitous comment. "Perhaps you paid Squeaky a visit at his flat that night?"

"I didn't go to his flat, and I resent your insinuation."

Arms still folded, Skip stared at Morelli for the better part of fifteen seconds. Finally he said, "No further questions; however, I may wish to recall this witness later."

"If and when the request to recall occurs," said Judge Biddleford, "we'll cross that bridge. No need to do so now."

Skip returned to the defense table. As he took his seat, Morehead whispered, "You think Morelli killed Squeaky?"

Skip turned to his client but merely put his finger to his lips.

The District Attorney got up. He walked slowly forward. "Mr. Morelli, did you kill Ralph Squeaky Grimes?"

"No."

"Do you have personal knowledge who did?"

"No."

"Thank you. That's all I have." The District Attorney sat down.

During the District Attorney's brief cross-examination, Skip had focused on the jury, rather than the witness. Their stern glares hinted that Morelli's self-serving denials were less than compelling. Skip said, "No re-direct."

Judge Biddleford excused the witness. He took a drink of water and then checked his watch. He mumbled aloud. "Ten forty-seven. A bit early for lunch." He turned to Skip. "Mr. Maynard, call your next witness."

"If I may take a moment, Your Honor."

Judge Biddleford nodded.

Skip flipped the pages of his yellow legal pad to his witness list. He still had LaDieux and Kileen and Ramsey, along with evidence documenting that Squeaky had served time for extortion. The fact would demonstrate that blackmail was Squeaky's style. Appropriate questions of the upcoming witnesses would reveal circumstances suggesting that Squeaky may well have been blackmailing any or all of them. Admittedly Kileen had an alibi, but that did not prevent him from hiring a hit man or conspiring with Ramsey to get rid of Squeaky. Skip had already elicited an admission from Raines that Squeaky had accused him of stealing and that Raines had threatened to put Squeaky six feet underground. The list of individuals with motive to kill Squeaky was far from short. For a jury to confidently exclude them all, particularly after a summation that referenced each in detail, would be extremely difficult, especially when the list included Gino Morelli. With motive and opportunity, he came across as the type capable of murder. More and more Skip was beginning to believe that someone other than Morehead had plunged the blade into

Squeaky. Skip again flipped the pages of his pad. He said, "The defense calls Traci LaDieux to the stand."

From her seat in the rear of the courtroom LaDieux paraded forward. All eyes were glued to her. Reading people's minds was no great feat. In her short skirt and low-cut red sweater, the siren reverberated throughout the courtroom. She put her hand on the Bible and took the oath. The dictates of the Holy Book were being tested. Men were doubtless lusting. Their seductress, though seemingly oblivious, encouraged them. Her provocative attire and mien provided ample evidence. The question, however, was whether the evidence she provided from the stand would violate that other biblical law, the one proscribing false witness.

She sat up tall on the stand, a commodious, mahogany captain's chair, situated on a podium roughly eighteen inches above the courtroom floor. Unlike the desk that Lucy had selected for the reception area of Skip's office, the witness stand had no modesty panel. LaDieux crossed her legs, left over right. From his location off to her right, Skip could only imagine the view the prosecutor enjoyed. At that moment rather than begrudge his adversary's prime seat, with more significant concerns on his mind, Skip happily forsook the titillating distraction.

He rose from his seat and circled around to the front of the defense table. "Please state your full name for the record."

"Traci B. LaDieux."

"Where do you reside?"

"At 41 Mohegan Street, here in Cooperstown." Her left foot swung rhythmically back and forth.

Skip eyed the jury. Number five, an athletic-looking machinist, bore an intent, but lowered gaze, seemingly hypnotized by her beguiling red-heeled metronome.

"How old are you?" said Skip, his eyes still directed at the jury, rather than the witness.

Her hesitation confirmed the question had not been well received. Finally, in a voice that was barely audible to Skip and presumably inaudible to the spectators in the rear, she said, "Thirty-eight."

"What do you do for a living?"

"I'm the City Manager of Cooperstown."

"How long have you held that position?"

"Ever since I was elected nearly four years ago."

Skip watched his former schoolmate as she responded. Physically she was every bit as sexy as she was back then, but her manner had changed. It even differed from what he had seen just an hour earlier outside the Courthouse. Traci was all business. She was Cooperstown's answer to Delilah. Skip had never thought of her that way before, but there on the stand her multi-faceted attributes were evident. Whatever the situation, she knew how to play the role. The demure sex kitten—she could wangle and cajole. The tough negotiator—she could drive a hard bargain. And Miss Congeniality—she could turn on the charm, and a whole lot more. She was an actress. She was a chameleon. She was also a politician. But whatever the role, she was always a woman. About that, there was no doubt.

"Were you here in the courtroom when Gino Morelli testified?"

"I was."

"Do you know Mr. Morelli?"

"Yes."

"How do you know him?"

"He's a businessman, a contractor here in the area. As City Manager I know most all the local business people."

"During your tenure as City Manager, did he ever do any work for Cooperstown?"

"Yes."

"More specifically, did he do any work on the Main Street beautification project near the *Baseball Hall of Fame*?"

"I believe he did."

"Was that work done with competitive bidding?"

"Offhand, I don't recall. The public works department handles those contracts."

"But they're under your control, aren't they?"

"Technically, but naturally I look to my professionals, the City Engineer and his people, when it comes to such matters."

Skip had more questions about the project, but for the moment he decided to jump ahead. Fencing too long with the slick City Manager, he could lose the jury's attention, though in the case of the five males, the risk was greatly reduced.

"Did Mr. Morelli ever do any work for you personally?"

"You mean like repairs in my office?"

"No, for you personally, outside your capacity as City Manager. For example, at your home?"

LaDieux gazed into space, her deliberative expression revealing nothing.

"Ms. LaDieux, did you hear the question?" said Judge Biddleford.

She turned to the Judge. "On the advice of my attorney, I decline to answer."

Judge Biddleford's eyes widened. "Do you mean you're taking the Fifth Amendment?"

"That's exactly what I'm doing."

Skip had anticipated the possibility, though hardly so soon. He said, "Did Mr. Morelli finish the basement of your home?"

LaDieux turned to the Judge. "Your Honor, I've already indicated that on the advice of counsel I'm taking the Fifth Amendment."

"That is your right," said Judge Biddleford. "But you are a witness, not a defendant, in this proceeding, and Mr. Maynard is entitled to ask his questions. Once he does, you may assert your Fifth Amendment privilege as to any or all, but only one question at a time."

Skip welcomed the turn of events. It was playing right into his hands. He had already filled the jury's heads with the possibility that Morelli had killed Squeaky because Squeaky was blackmailing him. If LaDieux testified fully, at best she might confirm the blackmail. But by taking the Fifth Amendment, she had given Skip the chance to play his own constitutional card. "Your Honor," he said, "the witness's refusal to answer my questions is depriving my client of a fair trial. Facts surrounding a blackmail scheme in which the victim was engaged are being kept from the jury. Gino Morelli, a man with no legitimate alibi, had motive to kill Squeaky Grimes. Unless the jury hears the details of that motive, my—"

"Your Honor," shouted the District Attorney, leaping from his seat. "Mr. Maynard is again poisoning the minds of the jury with his speeches."

Poisoning may have been too strong a word, but Skip was knowingly blowing smoke in the jurors' faces. On summation he planned to resort to the old adage, trite though it was, that there was fire behind the cloudy veil. Indeed he was beginning to believe that Morelli, not Morehead, had killed Ralph Squeaky Grimes. Regardless, he only needed to create a reasonable doubt. "Excuse me," he said, "but my client is on trial facing life in prison, and Mr. Carter pretends a full disclosure of the facts is superfluous. To him perhaps, but not the Constitution of the United States. Due Process demands a complete and fair airing of all the details. The—"

"Mr. Maynard," said Judge Biddleford.

"Confrontation of witnesses is guaranteed by—"

"Mr. Maynard!" bellowed Judge Biddleford. He pounded his gavel. "I appreciate your concerns, but this is not a sales convention. Save your speeches for summation."

"But Your Honor, with all due respect, the prejudice to—"

Judge Biddleford hammered his gavel repeatedly. "Mr. Maynard, I'll not have your histrionics in my courtroom. I understand your point. I will take it under advisement and rule on it at the appropriate time. For the moment, I am reserving decision. Therefore, let us continue with proper decorum. Understood?"

Skip heaved a sigh. "Yes, Your Honor," he said, still hoping to reap additional mileage from the situation.

Judge Biddleford turned to the jury. "Ladies and Gentlemen...counsel, along with me, have just engaged in some considerable dialogue. The exchanges present certain legal issues beyond the scope of your considerations and, therefore, I am admonishing you to ignore them as if they never transpired."

"Your Honor," said Skip, halfway between the defense table and the bench.

"What now?" growled Judge Biddleford.

"The jury needs to consider the prejudice to the defendant owing to a witness taking the Fifth Amendment."

"Mr. Maynard, you are trying my patience. That discussion is closed."

"But—"

"One more *but*, and I will hold you in contempt. If you believe the jury needs a particular instruction, present it to me in chambers. If, and only if, it is appropriate, will I include it in my charge to them before they retire for deliberations." Judge Biddleford glared at Skip. "Once and for all, do we understand one another?"

"Yes, Your Honor."

Judge Biddleford turned to the jury. "Once again we have had an unfortunate exchange. Once again I admonish you—"

From behind, Skip heard a thud. The spectators in the back breathed a collective gasp. Skip turned and saw Harley Morehead crumpled on the floor next to his chair. Like a bovine struck down with mad cow disease, he writhed and moaned.

"Mr. Maynard," shouted Judge Biddleford, "if this is another of your familiar theatrical antics, you're in contempt and on your way to jail." Judge Biddleford pounded his gavel.

"It...it's no stunt. I assure you," said Skip, already half way to his client.

"Is there a doctor in the courtroom?" Judge Biddleford waited a second. "Bailiff, get an ambulance!"

Down on his knees, Skip put a hand on Morehead's arm. "Harley... Harley, are you okay?"

Morehead moaned inaudibly.

"Can you hear me?"

Morehead continued to moan.

Chapter XVIII

"Are you Skip Maynard?"

Still in shock, Skip looked up from his seat in the small waiting room at the Mary Imogene Bassett Hospital and nodded.

"I'm Doctor Hersot." He shook the hand that Skip extended as he stood up. "The nurse tells me you're Mr. Morehead's attorney and he has no family."

"That's correct," said Skip. "How's he doing?"

Dr. Hersot's expression turned somber. "It's not good. He's had a massive heart attack. He's conscious, but it's only a matter of time."

"You...you don't mean that he...he's not going to make it?"

Dr. Hersot nodded. "I'm sorry...but that's how it is. It would take a minor miracle for him to pull through." Dr. Hersot hesitated. "Make that a major miracle."

"How...how long does he have?"

Dr. Hersot shrugged. "A few hours...a day. I don't know for sure."

"Can I see him?"

"Yes. As a matter of fact, he wants to see you."

Having to tell his client there was no hope was like delivering a guilty verdict on a charge carrying a mandatory life sentence. On second thought, even worse. "Does he...uh...know the situation?"

"Just before I left his room, he asked me. When I hesitated, he said, *five hundred-to-one the grim reaper will have me before midnight*. I told him it might not be that quick, but he knows the score."

"Okay to go in now?"

321

Dr. Hersot nodded.

As Skip started across the hall, he paused and looked back. "Any suggestions about what I should say?"

"I've been doing this for twenty-five years, and I've never found any great phrases for times like this. Anyway, being a lawyer, you're probably better than I with words."

Skip shook his head. "Situations like this weren't part of the law school curriculum."

A wry smile appeared on Dr. Hersot's face. "In med school they told us to be compassionate. Unfortunately there's no easy way." He shook his head. "It never is, especially if you've got a heart."

Skip inched toward Morehead's room. Before entering, he hesitated hoping to conjure some appropriate phrases. Unlike a courtroom argument, planning was futile. He took a deep breath. Inhaling the antiseptic odor of the hospital did nothing to cleanse his mental wounds. He pushed the door ajar and poked his head inside. "Okay to come in?"

A nurse, who was standing alongside the bed, looked his way.

"Are you Mr. Maynard?"

"Yes."

"Come right in." The nurse turned to Morehead, putting a hand on his shoulder. "Mr. Maynard is here. I'll prop you up a little higher, if you'd like."

"That would be good," said Morehead in a voice that was barely audible.

The nurse pushed a button on the side of the bed frame raising Morehead so his back was elevated at about a thirty-degree angle. She motioned Skip, who was still standing by the door, to draw closer. As he did, she said, "I'll leave you two alone." She stepped out closing the door behind her.

"How you doing?" Skip shriveled amidst the vapid echo of his ridiculous question.

"It's okay," said Morehead, seemingly conscious of Skip's discomfort. "The pain's not all that bad, most of the time." His normally burly voice was shaky.

"Anything I can do?" Once again the absurdity of Skip's question had him cringing.

"You have a magic wand?" Morehead displayed a slight smile.

Skip forced a smile of his own. He found it hard to believe that Morehead was providing the humor.

"Turns out I got more than bad indigestion. All those *Tums* I've been popping the past few years weren't doing the job. I might better have gotten myself checked out." Morehead groaned, perhaps from pain or maybe, regrets; most likely both. "No matter now. It's water over the dam." He looked Skip in the eye. "The Doc told you I'm not gonna make it...didn't he?"

Skip found it difficult to respond.

"You know I'm dying. This is no time for sugarcoating."

Skip laid a hand on Morehead's shoulder and rubbed it. "I'm sorry. I just wasn't prepared for this."

"Me neither."

A lump formed in Skip's throat. Tears were welling up in his eyes. For months he had been battling for Morehead's life. Suddenly when his client needed him most, Skip was helpless. "I...I don't..." *Jesus.* He chastised himself. *Can't you do better.* He managed, "Dr. Hersot said you wanted to see me."

"Yes...it's important."

"I'm listening."

"The nurse is gone, isn't she?"

"Yes."

"And the door closed?"

"Absolutely."

"I...I've got some bad news."

Could matters actually get worse?

"I killed Squeaky Grimes."

The thunderous blow sent Skip reeling. Just when he had finally begun to believe his client was innocent, a confession.

"Did you hear what I said?"

"I...I heard you."

"There's more." A plaintive wail nearly muddled the words.

Whether physical or mental anguish was behind the dirge, Skip couldn't say. Perhaps both.

"Don't you want to know?"

At that moment, not really. Voicing what he felt was unacceptable. "Tell me," said Skip.

"I killed Woody Wilson too."

"Wilson?...You didn't?"

"I did."

Skip stared at Morehead in disbelief. Perhaps his condition was causing his imagination to spiral out of control. Skip suspected the wishful thought was nothing more than that—a wishful thought. "But why would you kill Wilson?"

"It's complicated." Morehead groaned. This time his physical pain was evident.

"Here, I'll get some help."

"No...please. Just stay and listen."

Skip nodded.

Morehead gestured at the side of the bed. "Can you raise me up a little higher?"

Skip held the button down increasing the bed's tilt as far as it would go, roughly forty-five degrees."

"Thanks. That's better." Morehead took a deep breath. He exhaled slowly. He gazed at the ceiling and mumbled to himself. "Where should I start? Squeaky is as good a place as any." He looked at Skip. "Squeaky was blackmailing me. As those fellas testified at the trial, Squeaky was the runner for my bookmaking operation. I was the money, but I stayed in the background. Only a handful of my customers ever knew I was involved. Most everyone dealt with Squeaky. One day, out of the blue, he demanded a third of the profits or he'd go to the cops. I tried to reason with him. Then I had Eddie work him over. Squeaky refused to accept the message. Even when I went to his place, I hadn't planned on killing him, but the creep was impossible, and once it became apparent he was gonna squeal, one thing led to another. It happened pretty much the way Gardner told it in court."

Skip shook his head.

"I don't blame you. It's gotta be disappointing to find out your client is a murderer."

"That's not why I was shaking my head. I was struck by the irony. Early on—in fact, most of the time while I was representing you—I thought you were guilty. That isn't to say I didn't think we had a good shot of getting you off based upon reasonable doubt. But as the trial went on, especially after Morelli testified, I really began to believe you were innocent."

"Sorry to burst your bubble." Morehead studied Skip's face. "You got a funny expression. Whatcha thinking?"

"About Wilson. Why did you kill him?" Skip no sooner asked the question than he anticipated the answer. "Let me guess. Did Wilson somehow discover that you killed Squeaky. Is that why you killed him?"

"No. It's far more complicated." A look of chagrin came over Morehead. "It has to do with your late wife, Megan."

"Megan?" The mention of her name sparked an explosion in Skip's brain. Emotions, long repressed, gushed forth. "What does she have to do with it?"

"Wilson knew whose car struck and killed her."

Skip's jaw clenched. "Don't tell me you slammed into Megan and then left her in the road to die!"

"God...no."

"Then who did?"

"Judge Harold Biddleford."

"Biddleford...That no good son of a bitch!" Rage prevented Skip from logically analyzing the bizarre disclosure, not that logic would have explained it. Skip's fingers clenched into fists. He pictured the pompous jurist seated in his robe on the bench. If His Holiness were actually there, Skip would have pounded the bastard into oblivion.

"Do you want to know the details?"

Much as Skip did, for the moment they were secondary to his fury. Still he quelled his anger enough to respond, "Let's hear them."

Morehead took another deep breath and once again exhaled slowly. He looked away from Skip. "The evening your wife was killed, Biddleford and I had played golf together earlier at the *Leatherstocking Club*. After golf we hung out in the bar for about three hours drinking. Both of us were drunk as skunks. Back then I had a place off Route 20, up near the north end of Otsego Lake. Biddleford was driving me home when he struck your wife while she was jogging. At the time she was on the shoulder four or five feet to the right of the pavement, but

Biddleford was so plastered he hit her anyway. He was going about sixty, way over the limit, and all over the road." Morehead paused, still not making eye contact with Skip.

"Did he at least stop?"

"Yeah...and then we walked back. She was clearly dead. I told him we should call the police. With no one else around, Biddleford insisted we take off. That's what we did."

You son of a bitch. If his client weren't dying, Skip would have voiced the sentiment.

For an instant Morehead made eye contact. "I'm sorry."

Skip merely gritted his teeth. At that moment he couldn't bring himself to extend the smallest indulgence, regardless how contrite the dying man might be. Skip simmered silently for the better part of a minute before he finally said, "I still don't understand why you killed Wilson."

Morehead's chin sank into his chest. "As I told you earlier, it's a long story."

"Let's hear it!"

"Well...as you probably know, Wilson was a body man. A damn good one. I knew that and arranged for the repair of Biddleford's car. Wilson's place was out of the way. That also helped. Anyway, when Wilson finished fixing Biddleford's *Mercedes,* it looked as good as new. No one, except for the three of us, Biddleford, Wilson and me, had a clue it had been involved in an accident."

Thoughts of Megan stirred renewed anger. Skip suppressed it knowing that this was a time for information.

Morehead struggled to clear his throat. "Biddleford knew I had saved his bacon. He also knew I could bury him. He promised me over and over again that if ever I needed a favor, I could count on him." Morehead chuckled. "As Populist Party Chairman, a politician, I made it a practice of accumulating obligations. And sure enough, when I killed Squeaky, the day finally came when I needed that favor. To put it bluntly, I was desperate. The moment I got home from Squeaky's, I dialed Biddleford. I asked for his help. But I didn't call hat in hand. Instead I dropped a hint that if he didn't cooperate, his cat would slip out of the bag. I was in deep trouble, but I had him over a barrel. He told me to sit tight. He said that once he thought it through, he'd be over to my place. I wasn't sure what to expect, but in the meantime I covered my bases. I may not be the quickest press in the print shop, but I've spent enough hours in the back room to run a shrewd operation."

What Morehead meant about covering his bases was unclear, but with more important disclosures seemingly at hand, for the moment Skip avoided the temptation to interrupt.

"Sure enough, about an hour later—Biddleford seemed as desperate as me—he showed up at my door with a cockamamie scheme." Morehead thought for a moment. "Hard to believe, but the harebrained idea actually worked."

"So, what were the details of this scheme?"

"To call Detective Ramsey and confess."

"To what!"

"Call Detective Ramsey and confess." Morehead's face bore what appeared to be a self-satisfied look. "Biddleford chose Ramsey because another confession he had obtained had been suppressed by the courts. The plan was that once the body was found and the murder made news I would call Ramsey and tell him I had some information about the crime. But I had to insist that he come to my house alone if he wanted the information. When he arrived I gave him my handwritten statement saying that I had killed Squeaky. Naturally, he arrested me. Once I got down to the station, in accordance with Biddleford's instructions, I clammed up and demanded an attorney."

The more Skip heard, the more questions he had, but he put them aside and continued to listen.

"After I was bailed out, I took the position that Ramsey had put a gun to my head to force the confession. Biddleford scripted my whole story. Supposedly Ramsey told me he planned to shoot me if I didn't sign, and after he killed me, he planned to put my fingerprints on a lead pipe he had in his cruiser and claim he had shot me in self-defense when I had come at him with the pipe. Of course, the entire story was a fabrication. Ramsey never threatened me at all. But that didn't matter. It gave Biddleford an excuse to throw out my confession. He promised to do it. He also told me to hide the murder weapon, the carving knife, where the police were sure to find it once they had my confession. I hid it in my shed, but not too well. Biddleford said he wouldn't let the knife in evidence either. Something about a poison tree. I remember you told me about that too."

"Fruit of the poison tree," said Skip, intrigued by what he was hearing. "When an illegally obtained confession leads to other evidence which would not have been otherwise discovered—in this case the knife—the other evidence, like the confession, must be suppressed." While he explained the legal technicality, Skip's brain was working overtime. Certain things began to make sense. For the first time he understood why His Holiness had been indulgent, rather than his usual surly self; why he had granted Skip an adjournment until the next day when Skip had returned to court under the influence of *Jack*; and why, shock of shocks, he had granted the motion to suppress. Skip also understood why all along Morehead had seemed so confident about the outcome. But other aspects of the case remained as inexplicable as ever. Skip said, "Why of all people did you hire me to represent you?"

Morehead smiled.

The deviousness of the look elevated Skip's already aroused curiosity.

"Needless to say, I wasn't thrilled with Biddleford's plan. The damned thing seemed crazy. And too, I didn't trust him. That's why I chose you."

"Huh...come again?"

"It sent a signal to him that he better not cross me. All I had to do was tell you that he killed your wife, and you would have gone to the ends of the earth to get him."

Skip now had that information, and already in the back of his mind he was trying to figure out how he would get even with the bastard. The goddamn statute of limitations for manslaughter had already run on the hit-and-run accident. The possibility that His Holiness might get off had Skip's thermometer shooting up again. But for time being he needed to refocus on the bizarre puzzle. He said, "I still don't understand why—and for that matter, how—you killed Wilson."

"Well, it was—" Morehead grimaced in obvious pain.

"You okay?"

"Not really."

"Maybe I should get the nurse."

Morehead shook his head. "I've got a lot to say and not a lot of time. So, let's keep going." A thoughtful look appeared on his face. "Where was I?"

"You were about to explain Wilson's murder."

"Oh, yeah." He adjusted his position a trifle. "Wilson was never a problem until he got hurt working for Morelli. After that he was almost a cripple. He could hardly do anything. Because he was getting paid under the table, he couldn't prove he was Morelli's employee. The Workmen's Compensation Board turned down his claim for benefits. He was disabled with virtually no income. He went to Biddleford demanding the Judge do something about it. Biddleford said he couldn't. Claimed he lacked jurisdiction. Whether that was legit or just an excuse, I've got no idea."

"It was legit," said Skip. "The Workmen's Compensation Board is an administrative agency. By statute the exclusive remedy is what's known as an Article 78 Proceeding brought in Supreme Court. Biddleford is only a County Court Judge. He had no subject matter jurisdiction over the case." Skip observed the confused look on Morehead's face. "To make it simple, Biddleford had no authority to hear a challenge to a decision of the Workmen's Compensation Board."

Morehead shrugged. "I guess that's what Biddleford was saying. Anyway, Wilson didn't buy it. He got pissed. Having fixed Biddleford's car following the hit and run and keeping quiet all these years, he wanted Biddleford to take care of him. When it didn't happen, he demanded forty grand. Otherwise he said he would go to the police. Biddleford said he'd pay, but he needed a couple weeks to get that kind of money." Morehead gestured at a pitcher on the nightstand. "Can you get me some water?"

Skip obliged. Once Morehead had finished drinking, Skip said, "So, how did Biddleford react to Wilson's demand?"

"He treated it as a death wish." Morehead chuckled. "He said we needed to get rid of Wilson. No way would he pay the creep forty thousand, and even if he did, chances were once the money was gone, Wilson would be back demanding more. Initially I refused to kill Wilson, but Biddleford convinced me we were in the mess together. I realized that if he went down, I would too." Morehead laughed, though his facial expression reflected no humor. "Funny," he said, "what you'll do when you're facing life in prison."

Skip waited a moment for Morehead to continue. When he didn't, Skip said, "So, how did you kill Wilson?"

Morehead took a deep breath. "Biddleford had me pay Wilson a visit. I pretended to be sympathetic. Even gave him five hundred dollars, which I took back afterwards. While he was getting me a beer, I came up behind him and stuck a chloroform mask over his face. It was easy, big as I am, and him, short, skinny and a near cripple. He was out like a light. I carried him out to his car and put him in the driver's seat. I gave him another dose of chloroform for good measure. Next I turned on the engine and stuffed a couple rags in the exhaust, not that it was necessary. Then I stepped outside, shut the door and watched from the side window of the garage, just to make sure he didn't wake up." Morehead gave Skip a look as if anticipating a reaction.

Vexatious thoughts and emotions boggling his brain, Skip remained tight-lipped. Two murders, and at long last he knew who was responsible for Megan's death, and he was in no position to do anything about it. Morehead was his client. Everything he had communicated to Skip enjoyed the protection of attorney-client privilege.

"With all I've told you, all you gonna do is stare into space?"

Skip heaved a sigh. A part of him, the legally trained portion, discouraged him from giving his dying client a hard time. Megan would have encouraged him to simply move on with his life. But Megan deserved better. He said, "I'm sorry, but I'm having a hard time dealing with what you've told me."

"Hard time?…Why?"

Why! The question infuriated Skip. "My wife was killed by a hit-and-run driver. For years I've had to live with that horror, never knowing the truth. At long last you tell me, and I'm supposed to play the deaf mute."

Morehead shook his head. "You missed the point."

Despite the fact Morehead was dying, Skip could no longer restrain himself. He jabbed a splenetic finger into his own chest. "*I* missed the point!"

"You heard me right. And before..." Morehead grimaced. Obvious pain had halted his words. For several seconds he writhed. Finally he said, "The things I told you—I'm not asking you to keep them a secret."

"You're not?"

"No...I'm not."

Skip hesitated, his cynical proclivities working overtime. "Why?"

"What the hell. I'm dying. That, plus you deserve better. You did a tremendous job in court. If I were making book on the case—and let me tell you when it comes to that business, I'm damn good—I'd lay one-to-nine I was on the road to an acquittal. Almost a sure thing." Morehead heaved a sigh. "Too bad the case won't ever go to the jury. I'll get a mistrial. Right?"

The question spawned an unwelcome thought. The last thing Skip wanted was for Morehead to revoke his waiver of attorney-client privilege, but ethics demanded a full understanding of the waiver. Skip said, "If you die at any time prior to conviction, the charges against you would have to be dismissed. The District Attorney, as the representative of the People, cannot pursue them after your death. In other words, apart from your misdemeanor bookmaking conviction you had years ago, you would die with a clean slate."

"A clean slate. Whad'ya know about that?" Morehead managed a grin.

Skip kicked himself. Following the canons of ethics, putting his client's interests ahead of his own, sucked.

Morehead pulled his arm out from under the sheet that covered him. He put his hand on Skip's arm. "You know," he said, "you're one helluva guy."

Welcome though the compliment may have been, it did nothing to assuage Skip's frustration.

"C'mon, don't look so disappointed. I'm not gonna screw you. Sure that clean slate sounds sweet, but, what the hell, will it really matter once I'm looking up at dandelions?" He looked Skip in the eye. "You're free to use everything and anything I've told you, however you wish."

Morehead's selflessness caught Skip by surprise. Morehead was a louse, but at that moment, a sympathetic louse. Skip eyed his dying client. He put a hand on Morehead's shoulder.

"You going soft on me?"

"You're...uh..." Skip's tongue tangled in the face of conflicting emotions.

Morehead grimaced once again. The painful episode persisted for the better part of a minute. Finally he said, "You're giving me too much credit. I got ulterior motives. The way I figure, with two murders on my resumé, I need to score all the points I can before the grim reaper ships me north or south. And too, my relationship with Biddleford was purely business. I never cared for the prick. The thought of him dancing on my grave is too hard to take." Morehead's voice turned weak. He squeezed Skip's arm. "You make sure you do a job on him."

"I'll...uh...try." The sight of his client slipping away made it hard for Skip to speak the words.

His face red with discomfort, Morehead coughed several times. "Look, I got an excuse for this voice. You, on the other hand, are a different story." Morehead's head went back against the pillow, and he closed his eyes.

During his years as an attorney there had been many tough moments, but never had Skip watched a client die. He bowed his head as he wiped a moistened eye.

"Damn—can't a guy get a moment's rest without you bawling." Morehead's entire body tightened, and he let out a yelp. "Sorry, that one hurt." His voice was little more than a whisper.

"I know." Skip thought to tell Morehead to let go, but the words wouldn't come to his lips.

"Promise me you'll get Biddleford."

"I...I'll try."

"Try? That the best you can do?"

"Without you and Wilson, I...I won't have any evidence."

Morehead tapped himself lightly on the forehead. "Damnation. I almost forgot." He took a couple of deep breaths. Trying breaths.

"Don't try to talk anymore."

"Jesus!" His eyes directed at the ceiling. "I'm half over the cliff, still with important stuff to do, and you want me to pack it in." He coughed some more. "In my jacket you'll find my key ring. The smallest key opens a strong box that's buried two feet behind the back left-hand corner of my shed." Morehead gasped for a breath. His eyes started to nod but reopened. "In the box you'll find pictures showing the damage to Biddleford's Mercedes."

Skip didn't have the heart to tell the dying client that old photographs of a damaged car wouldn't prove that Biddleford had killed Megan. Regardless, the statute of limitations had expired on the hit and run.

"There's a..." Morehead gasped for breath. He couldn't find the air. His eyes closed. This time they did not reopen.

Skip looked at the monitor on the pole alongside the head of the bed. Its intermittent beeps had ceased. The line was flat.

———

Arms folded, shoulders higher than usual, Judge Biddleford surveyed the courtroom before turning to the jury. "Ladies and Gentlemen, it seems we have had a rather unfortunate turn of events. The defendant's episode here in court yesterday was far more serious than we imagined." Judge Biddleford's deep voice was uncharacteristically somber. "It is my very sad duty to inform you that he passed away last evening. Under the circumstances this trial can proceed no further."

Seated alone at the defense table, no client at his side, his jaw like a drawn bow, Skip wrestled with the urge to strangle the pontificating bastard who had killed his wife. Having to listen to the bogus expression of dolor only compounded Skip's ire. No doubt Biddleford was celebrating Morehead's demise.

"All of us came to this forum determined to do justice not only for our community, but also Ralph Squeaky Grimes. Justice, however, sometimes comes in ways we do not fully comprehend. Whether that has occurred in this case, we can only speculate. Much as I wish that you good folks would have had the opportunity to deliberate the outcome of this case, the law dictates that it must be taken from your hands." Judge Biddleford turned to the District Attorney. "Mr. Carter, I understand you have a motion."

"Your Honor, given the defendant's death, the People, obliged as they are, move that the murder indictment against the defendant Harley Morehead be dismissed."

Judge Biddleford turned to Skip. "Mr. Maynard, I presume you have no objection to the request."

Skip glared at His Holiness. How dare he speak of sad duties? How dare he preside over such a mockery? And how dare he invoke the word *justice*? By itself the hypocrisy fueled rage. Knowing the arrogant jurist had gotten away with Megan's death rendered the fury ineffable. With clenched fists shaking beneath the defense table, Skip, his ability to respond constrained, remained mute.

"Mr. Maynard, the Court is entertaining a motion to dismiss the charges against your client."

Skip drew in a slow breath. The part of his brain armed with formidable tools of Socratic legal training clashed with irrepressible wrath. He took another breath. This was not a time to seethe over things he could not control. Morehead, his deceased client, was still entitled to Skip's best representation. Never rising from his chair, his voice a torpid monotone, Skip said, "On behalf of my late client, I concur in the request to dismiss the charges."

Judge Biddleford, his squinting eyes dominating an inscrutable mask, appeared to study Skip. "The motion is granted. The indictment against the defendant Harley Morehead is hereby dismissed."

Teeth grinding, Skip grappled with grotesque irony. Morehead, though guilty, had just been cleared, and who but the man with whom he had conspired was making the pronouncement. Skip gazed at the mural of the scales of justice. What a joke. What a goddamn joke. Still he found it hard to deny that in a way, albeit perverse, in Morehead's case justice had been served. Would it have been any better had

Morehead survived? Highly unlikely. In all probability His Holiness would have granted the motion to dismiss made several days earlier at the conclusion of the prosecution's evidence. The jury would never have gotten the opportunity to deliberate the case. And even if they had, one could make book that they would have acquitted.

Judge Biddleford turned to the jury. "On behalf of myself, as well as the attorneys and the citizens of Otsego County, my sincere thanks for your attention and indulgence throughout this trial. Without you our system of jurisprudence would not have worked."

Liar...Charlatan...Murderer. Skip longed to leap from his seat and scream the epithets. Helpless, he bowed his head.

Judge Biddleford reached for his gavel. He rapped the bench. "This Court is adjourned."

As the courtroom emptied, Skip sat motionless. He stared blankly into space. "Damn it," he muttered. "Damn it!" Several minutes passed. He looked around. He was alone. The acoustically perfect hall was eerily silent. But the quiet was paradoxical. A deafening roar was echoing in his head. A conglomeration of emotions surged forth. Rage. Impotence. And loneliness. Terrible loneliness. It reminded him of the days, weeks and months following Megan's death. He closed his eyes conjuring her image. He needed her. He desperately needed to hold her in his arms. But that hadn't happened in the days following her death, and once again it wouldn't. He tightened the seal of his eyes, hopelessly trying to escape himself. The futile gesture prompted an image of the one friend who had been there in the dark days following the accident. Come whatever, Skip could always count on *Jack*. Admittedly *Jack* had his drawbacks, but when push came to shove, when all else failed, and when loneliness became unbearable, *Jack* was there.

Eyes still closed, almost in a stupor, Skip sat for several more minutes. Conflicting ruminations kept him frozen in place. *Jack's* knack for lifting Skip from the depths was undeniable. But *Jack* was a dissolute companion. The relief he provided, an escape from reality, was never more than temporal. Inevitably his helmsmanship guided Skip through an endless maze, one that drove Skip deeper into the depths.

Chapter XIX

Before leaving the Courthouse, Skip dialed his office. As always Lucy had everything under control. He drove home and spent most of the day in bed. He checked the bar in the basement and the bottom shelf of the credenza in the den on the outside chance that *Jack* might be hiding there. He knew the search was useless because many weeks earlier he had been careful to eliminate all traces. What he would have done had he actually found *Jack* stowed away was an open question.

The following morning he dragged himself out of bed and drove to the office. He stopped on the way at the *Grand Union* and picked up a dozen roses. When he arrived at the office, Lucy was already at her desk. He handed her the flowers along with an envelope.

"What's this?"

"Just a tiny gesture communicating that an overindulgent, eccentric boss appreciates having the world's best secretary, receptionist and office manager."

She opened the envelope. Her eyes widened at the sight of the enclosed check.

"It's a very well-deserved bonus."

"I...I'm..."

"Don't tell me. You would have rather I brought you a pizza from the *Pantheon*."

She shook her head. "This will buy all the pizzas even *I* could want." She smelled the roses. "They're beautiful. Thank you...for both the flowers and the check."

"Thank *you*."

She studied him for a moment. "You've got that funny look. What's on your mind?"

Thank goodness he didn't play poker with her. And thank goodness she didn't sit on his juries. She read him like a billboard. He said, "How have you managed to put up with me all these years?" Her dismissive expression caused him to add, "No...I'm serious."

"Why? What's wrong with you?"

"C'mon, days like yesterday when I didn't come back. And what about the countless afternoons when I showed up around three after drinking my lunch?"

She shrugged. "So?"

"How do you tolerate it?...Even more so, me?"

She shook her head. "Tolerate...You've got it all wrong. Because as far as I'm concerned, I've got a great job and a terrific boss. And just to get that confused look off your face, I'll explain. You pay me well. More important, you treat me with respect; you allow me to exercise my judgment; and even when I make a mistake, you never, ever put me down. Very simply, you appreciate me. And I appreciate that."

Skip consciously displayed a broad, even amorous smile.

"What's that about?"

"What do you mean?" he said, though he fully understood her question.

"C'mon...you know you can't fool me. Out with it."

"Well..." He hemmed and hawed. "I was just thinking—if you weren't already happily married, I'd snatch you up."

"Skip Maynard...you mean to tell me after all these years you didn't realize that you and I *are* married." She sat up tall. "Not many girls who can brag that they've got two wonderful husbands, a Platonic one by day and an intimate one at night."

"Does your husband know you have two husbands?" Even as the droll revelation was rolling off his tongue, Skip was conscious of its inherent absurdity.

"Not only does he know...he approves. For some strange reason—I can't imagine why—he likes you."

"Well...he probably has bad taste." Skip ignored Lucy's feigned indignation. He was still digesting her unique, but very welcome take on the situation. He said, "You know what—you, my dear, are a bigamist."

She leaned back. "And a very happy one at that."

337

Seated at his desk, Skip perused a stack of about a dozen telephone messages. Corbin Dudley, a childhood friend, had been rear-ended by a pickup truck and wanted Skip to handle his case. Ezmerelda Waldemeir, the eighty-something spinster wanted to change her will for the umpteenth time. Freddy Parker wanted to sue his next-door neighbor for allowing his dog to do its business next to Freddy's mailbox. On down through the pile Skip went until he came to the last. Leonard Gardner had telephoned and requested a call back. Skip stared at the message. For several days since Gardner had left his first message, Skip had wondered what his former client wanted, but with Gardner out of town and no way to reach him, Skip could do nothing except wait, albeit impatiently. Once again Skip tried to imagine what Gardner wanted. Conjecture was futile. Skip picked up the telephone receiver and dialed Gardner's number.

"*Sublime Coiffures.* Lenny speaking."

"Skip Maynard returning your call."

There was a momentary silence. "I...I want to apologize."

"Apologize...for what?"

"Court...what happened. I...uh...shoulda been more up front with you."

That would have been nice. Though Skip contained the sarcasm, he couldn't bring himself to offer words of absolution.

"I didn't want to get involved. I thought that if I kept quiet the whole thing might go away. It didn't work. The District Attorney subpoenaed me. I didn't have a choice. And once I was on the stand, I had to tell them what I knew about Squeaky's murder."

Skip wished that Gardner had told him before the trial so he could have prepared better, but, nevertheless, it was hard to blame Gardner, especially knowing it would not have changed the outcome. "I understand."

"I appreciate that."

"One thing I don't understand is why you hired me for your support hearing." Gardner had previously given him an explanation, but Skip still harbored doubts.

"I didn't have a lawyer when my ex and I got divorced. We agreed on terms, and I signed a paper that her lawyer drew up. When she took me back to court for more money, I realized I'd better get an attorney, especially after my first appearance in front of Judge Biddleford. Right off the bat, it was obvious he had it in for me. It was hard to say whether he disliked me more because I was gay or because I had let my wife down. Anyway, I was certain he would put the screws to me."

"But that still doesn't explain why you hired me."

"Well...after your client was arrested for Squeaky's murder—with him being my neighbor and the things I had seen and heard—I went to court to see what was happening. I was impressed with the way you handled yourself at the suppression hearing."

Skip had heard the same explanation before. Reluctantly he bought into it the first time. Upon reiteration it was gaining credibility, but... He thought back to the first day when he had returned to court inebriated after lunch. "Did you see the entire hearing?"

"No, just the second afternoon when you were mainly cross-examining the prosecution's witnesses. You did a helluva job. Though I have to say—and please don't take offense—I was surprised to later read in the newspaper that Judge Biddleford had tossed out Morehead's confession."

Skip had a pair of reactions. First: Had Gardner been there for the first day of the suppression hearing, he would have hired a different attorney. Second: Gardner's assessment whether the confession should have been suppressed was on the money. What Gardner didn't know was that His Holiness was fixing the case.

"Again, I'm sorry if I made your job harder, and I'm sorry too about Harley Morehead dying."

"I appreciate your sentiments." Skip was about to terminate the conversation.

"There's one more reason I called. Do you remember when I bumped into my friend Darrell outside the Courthouse?"

The reference failed to click.

339

"It was right after you requested that Judge Biddleford excuse himself from my case. That's not the word you used, but anyway you wanted a different judge, one who'd give me a fair shake."

"Recuse...I remember the motion, but I can't recall what transpired outside the Courthouse."

"Darrell and I talked about a bet whether the *Yankees* would win the World Series this year."

The mention of the bet partially jogged Skip's memory. "Well—I remember you discussing some kind of bet. So, who won?"

"I did. Darrell is an avid *Yankees'* fan, and needless to say, for a change, it wasn't their year. But all of that is neither here nor there. What's important are the terms of the bet. If he won, I had to clean the apartment for two months. But if I won, he had to announce to the press that he had an affair with Judge Biddleford."

The information fully jogged Skip's memory. "Now I recall who Darrell is. How could I forget the scene outside the Courthouse when he told Riley Ripley of *TV Seven News* that he had been intimate with Judge Biddleford?" Skip thought for a second. "But if I understand what you're saying, the story was a fabrication?"

"Complete and total."

"Why'd you do it?"

"How would you feel if you were gay and you had to appear in court before a judge, a man supposedly free of bias, who was openly homophobic. The son of a bitch, despite an oath of impartiality, was determined to screw me, and no doubt he would have if you hadn't negotiated a settlement. When I made the bet with Darrell, I was anticipating the worst, and I decided that two could play the same game. I wanted to shaft him the same as he was screwing me."

Skip greeted the disclosure with mixed emotions. Delight that His Holiness was getting comeuppance was inescapable, but conscience questioned whether he could let the deception pass. He said, "Why are you telling me?"

"I'm not sure. Second thoughts, I guess. You were my lawyer, and as I've said in the past, you did a great job. I might have told you about the bet sooner, but the last thing I wanted was to throw a monkey wrench into your case while you were defending someone for murder. In fact, if your client weren't gone, chances are I never would have told you the details of the bet."

A side of Skip preferred ignorance, but another delighted in the ironic perversity. Skip leaned back and closed his eyes. The familiar mural of the blindfolded woman holding the scales of justice came to mind. His Holiness was getting away with the murder of Woody Wilson, just as he had gotten away with killing Megan. Morehead, the only one who could tie the arrogant jurist to the crimes, was, as Lenny had said, gone. If nothing else, the story of the gay affair would ensure the jurist's defeat in the upcoming election. Liberals despised his homophobia. Conservatives were outraged. And those in the middle condemned his hypocrisy. Seeing him driven from the bench would be far from justice. At best, a miniscule consolation. But that was better than nothing. Skip said, "You're no longer my client. So, I really shouldn't advise you."

"That's fine. I didn't expect you to. But I wanted to let you know what I had done, in case you wanted to voice an objection. You treated me well, and fair is fair."

Skip had all he could do to keep his sardonic laugh to himself. Gardner had no clue about the horrendous inequities His Holiness had perpetrated. "If I understand what you're saying, you intend to let Darrell's rumor persist.

"Exactly. Unless you demand otherwise."

Skip allowed several silent seconds to pass before ending the call.

———

Skip pressed his intercom. "Yes?"

"Mickey Shore is here to see you."

"Send him right in."

The moment Mickey stepped through the doorway, Skip gestured at the cigarette tucked over the detective's ear. "Is that the real thing or just candy?"

Mickey pulled it out and held it close for Skip to see. "It's the genuine article. Fine *Camel* tobacco." Mickey raised it to his nose and inhaled slowly. "No way I'm gonna give these up. Chances are they'll be the death of me, but..." His voice trailed off with a shrug. "You still off the sauce?"

Skip nodded. He took no delight in rubbing it in. Nevertheless, he was pleased with his success. Seeing Mickey underscored more than ever that renewing his friendship with *Jack* would be a mistake.

"You're a better man than I," said Mickey.

"Hardly." Though the response was instinctive, a moment's afterthought confirmed the conclusion. They each had their dependency; similar, yet distinct vices. Mickey was hooked on tar and nicotine. The need was physical. Skip, on the other hand, drank to escape. Several months earlier he had wondered if his need was physical too. Time had seemingly proved the contrary. Sweats, shakes, and the like—he had endured none of the withdrawal symptoms. Admittedly there were times he had longed for a drink, mainly when stress mounted. *Jack* was his ticket to leave reality behind. Sobriety, however, had educated him, mostly about himself. The bottle did more harm than good. Sooner or later the effects wore off. The reality he tried to avoid was still there, and, compounding matters, it grew more daunting, especially with a hangover.

"Yesterday another lawyer I work for, name to remain unmentioned, was talking about you."

"I can only imagine his comment."

"Apparently you can't. He said Cooperstown's most-talented trial lawyer has returned following a decade in absentia."

The accolade caught Skip off guard. Such praise, commonplace at one time, had become a distant memory. To the extent it still crossed his mind, the recollection described someone he no longer knew.

"Too bad about Morehead. Last night, what with the case over, I talked with one of your jurors. He said the prosecution proved diddly-squat. He was sure the jury would have acquitted. Regardless, he said a conviction was off the table.

No matter how the other jurors voted, he planned to hold out even if the sun ceased to rise. "

Skip debated whether to tell Mickey that Morehead was guilty. Morehead had authorized the disclosure, but why sully the dead man's reputation with such information. It would be one thing if it would foster some positive consequence, but disclosure merely for the sake of gossip was best left unspoken. Skip said, "Were you able to dig up the strongbox from behind Morehead's shed, the one for which I gave you the key?"

"Yup. It was right where Morehead told you. And damn if it didn't contain some mighty interesting stuff."

"Such as?"

"Photos of the damaged *Mercedes* that killed your wife." Mickey handed Skip two eight-by-ten black and whites.

His blood boiling at the mere sight of the pictures, an incongruous thought burst into Skip's head. *How did Mickey know this was the vehicle that had struck Megan?* Skip examined the photographs, one showing a 1956 *Mercedes* with a damaged front right corner and the other, a close-up of the damage. He checked the backs for labeling that might explain the anomaly. There was nothing. He said, "Morehead told me about the pictures just before he died." He pointed at the one that displayed the entire vehicle. "How did you know this was the car that killed Megan?"

"There was something else in the strongbox." A sly smile punctuated Mickey's reply.

"What?"

Mickey held up an audiocassette.

"What's on it?"

"A recording of a conversation between Morehead and Judge Biddleford."

Skip assumed it had been made about the time the photographs had been taken, before Wilson had repaired the damage to the vehicle. The possibility that the tape might provide proof that Biddleford was responsible for Megan's death was provocative. Though it wouldn't revive the manslaughter statute of limitations to prosecute the bastard, the world would know what he had done. If Gardner's bet hadn't killed His Holiness's chance for re-election, this would. Instead of a judge, he would be a pariah. Another confusing thought popped into Skip's head. He said, "Wait a second. The cassette couldn't have been made at the time of the accident. Cassettes hadn't been invented yet."

"No fooling." Mickey leaned back. "Aren't you interested in knowing what's on this thing?"

"You bet. So don't leave me in the dark."

"I've got a cassette player in the trunk of my car. I can get it if you want. The conversation goes on for the better part of half an hour." Mickey started to get up.

"That's okay," said Skip, his curiosity begging immediate satisfaction. "Tell me the highlights. We can listen to it later."

"Well—" Mickey tugged at the *Camel* that was back behind his ear. "My trip to the car was supposed to provide a cigarette break." His face bore a plaintive expression.

Skip spun his chair so it faced the credenza behind him and pulled out a pack of matches. "Go ahead." He struck a match and helped light Mickey's cigarette. "By the way, you're the first to smoke in my office."

Mickey shrugged. "Look at it this way. If your sacred space has to lose its maidenhood, you couldn't have a nicer fellow do the honors."

"Sure," said Skip. "But now that you've got your fix, tell me what's on that tape."

Mickey took a long drag. He hesitated and then exhaled the smoke through his nose. "As I said, it's a conversation between Morehead and Biddleford. It took place soon after Morehead killed Squeaky."

"Hold the phone. You know that Morehead killed Squeaky?"

"Sure."

"But earlier you talked about him being acquitted?"

"And he would have if the jury ever got the chance to render a verdict." Mickey took another drag. This time he blew the smoke from his mouth. "But that doesn't mean he was innocent. In fact, he details the whole crime on the tape."

Thunderbolts crashed in Skip's head. "Are there any discussions how he might get away with it?"

"Are there ever. Once he reminds Biddleford how he helped him cover up the hit and run, Biddleford guides him chapter and verse through a plan that will enable Morehead to beat the rap. He tells Morehead to confess, how he'll suppress the confession and ultimately dismiss the indictment before the case ever reaches the jury."

As Mickey continued, Skip reveled amidst a surge of adrenaline. He now had evidence, Biddleford's own words that would prove Biddleford had helped a felon avoid prosecution, obstructed justice and breached his duties as a judge. Forget about merely defeating His Holiness on Election Day; the creep would have a new home, the state prison at Dannemora. Another thought popped into Skip's head—Morehead's curious deathbed comment about covering his bases the night of Squeaky's murder. Skip now understood what the shrewd politician meant. He had set up a tape recorder.

Mickey eyed his cigarette, which had shrunk to a half-inch. "Mind if I have another?"

"Be my guest."

Mickey used the remains to light another *Camel*. "By the way," he said, "the other side of the cassette is rather interesting too."

"Oh really," said Skip, though he was still preoccupied with the joy of the earlier disclosures. "What's it about?"

"It's another conversation between Morehead and Biddleford."

Skip's attention immediately perked.

Mickey took a puff. "It was apparently recorded a couple of months after the first conversation. In it Biddleford sweet talks Morehead into killing Woody Wilson. Your dear client chloroformed Wilson and then left him in his car with the motor running, where he died from carbon monoxide." Mickey blew a smoke ring. Self-satisfied, he watched the nearly perfect loop hover gently in space. "See that. I told you all along that Wilson was murdered."

Skip focused on the smoke ring. He nodded slowly. "Damn, if you weren't right." Skip passed up the opportunity to tell Mickey that Morehead had already told him how Wilson had died. Skip had bigger matters on his mind. The flip side of the cassette was an even bigger hit than the first. There was now proof, once again His Holiness's own words, that he was a co-conspirator to murder. Charges for obstruction of justice and the like had just become small potatoes. His Holiness would be on the short end of a murder indictment. Chances were his ticket to Dannemora would be one way. Skip gazed up at the ceiling. He envisioned the mural on the Courthouse wall. Occasionally camouflaged truths tilted the scales at wayward angles. The system was far from perfect. The wheels often ground slowly. But sometimes...sometimes there was justice.

Several weeks had passed since Morehead had died. Election day had come and gone. The very day Skip had gotten the tapes, he had given them to the District Attorney. An indictment charging Judge Biddleford with a litany of felonies, not the least of which was murder, had guaranteed the jurist's defeat at the polls. Still he had refused to resign from office. The voters, however, in what was a staggering landslide, had given him the boot.

From the time Morehead had been arrested right through his trial, the case was center stage in the local media. Interest, as well as coverage, magnified dramatically with the revelation that Judge Biddleford had masterminded a plot to obstruct justice and commit murder. Television and newspaper reporters were constantly at Skip's doorstep. Interviews with the jurors who never got the chance to deliberate Morehead's fate indicated that Skip's exemplary defense would have certainly produced an acquittal. New clients, not just criminal, were banging down his door. Business was booming. He had begun interviewing for an associate and a secretary to assist Lucy.

Most mornings Skip was arriving at the office even earlier than Lucy, and many evenings he was staying late. But he didn't mind. Not since the early years of his career, when Megan was alive, had he brought such enthusiasm to his practice. Diet and regular *Pepsi*, a fifty-fifty mix, had become his beverage of choice. He had grown to like it, even preferring it to *Jack*, so long as the comparison included the drawbacks of

346

the smooth guy from the Lynchburg cave. The need to escape, even the opportunity, had lost its lure. He enjoyed what he was doing, along with the sense of being in control. One factor, far more than anything else, had brought about the change. There was finally closure to Megan's death. No longer was it an unsolved mystery. His Holiness had been identified as the hit-and-run driver. The fact that the statute of limitations would prevent his prosecution for the accident made no difference. People knew he was responsible; he was off the bench; proceedings to disbar him had commenced; and his prosecution for Wilson's murder, among numerous other charges, was well underway. Stripped of his black robe, it was only a matter of time before the unscrupulous Judge, who for years had haughtily reigned and deigned, would don a prison jump suit.

It was a week before Thanksgiving, an invigorating autumn morning. Skip had just filed some motion papers at the Courthouse. Rather than heading directly back to his office, he ventured further up Main Street to the *Baseball Hall of Fame*. Many weeks had passed since he had last visited the shrine, and the time to renew his annual pass was at hand. After paying the fee, he went directly to the large hall with the inductees' busts. Cobb, Ruth, Gerhig, the legends of bygone eras were all there; and Williams, DiMaggio and Foxx, the heroes of Skip's own childhood, had their places as well. Skip toured the room taking a moment to touch each statue. The world of baseball had so much in common with *Jack's* world. Grown men, like the boys of *Never, Never Land*, escaped reality playing a child's game. Bearing bats and gloves and balls, they were bigger than life to the hoards of fans who joined in their fantasy. Men, some old enough to be ballplayers' grandfathers, linked their very identities to the exploits of their favorite players and teams. Like *Jack*, the fantasy played a pre-eminent role in their lives. But unlike *Jack*, baseball rarely crippled their ability to address the reality that remained once a game's final out had been recorded. Baseball and *Jack* were similar, yet disparate aphrodisiacs. At various times in Skip's life, each had played that seductive role.

By the time Skip had met Megan, for all intents and purposes he had already outgrown baseball and moved on to the law. He was yet to discover *Jack*, not that he needed him then. Together with Megan, the law, not that it could hold a candle to her incomparable glow, became his aphrodisiac. Skip still had his memories of Megan. He would cherish them always. But the time to move forward had arrived. All but oblivious to others who were in the hall, with knees bent and hands cocked as if holding a bat, Skip planted his feet about ten feet from the bust of the famed fireballer Lefty Grove. "Bring it on," said Skip, bracing for life's next pitch.

He headed out the Main Street entrance of the Hall of Fame. He gazed left in the direction of his office but turned right toward the adjacent park. Another quick right and a left just a minute later brought him into the old cemetery. He paused several seconds at the grave of James Fenimore Cooper and then continued to the rear where Megan was buried. Ever since her death, Skip had regularly visited Megan's grave. In the days following Morehead's death, his visits had grown more frequent. Alone in the rear of the quaint and storied burial ground, Skip would close his eyes and lay a hand on Megan's gravestone. He could feel her touch as he softly told her the newest details of His Holiness's downfall.

Back when she was still alive, he and Megan often strolled Cooperstown's tree-lined streets. Her hand in his, Skip held the world, a peaceful one, replete with love. Fall was Megan's favorite season. Skip was more of a spring person, but he cherished their autumn walks. As he stood beside her grave, a huge pin-oak leaf floated gently to earth, its angular border coming to rest against the edge of his shoe. Skip inched his cordovan wing tip until the leather sole hovered just above the leaf. He closed his eyes. He slowly lowered his foot. The crisp foliage crackled. So many times Megan had paused to eye a fallen oak leaf, perhaps from the same tree. Carefully she would press her shoe to the symbol of changing seasons, savoring the rustling symphony of what she called nature's percussion. Skip rubbed the sole of his wing tip on the leaf's crushed remains. The faint sound seemed distant, but he knew it to be near. Megan was too.

Skip opened his eyes. They met those of a squirrel, an acorn in its mouth, only a few feet away. Motionless, the squirrel cautiously watched for several seconds. Then it scampered off. A long winter, the season of rest, lay ahead. Skip pressed his hand against Megan's gravestone. "Rest well, my love." A tear slid down his cheek. "Rest well."

Skip ran his hand over the marker caressing the top corner. A thought he had entertained a thousand times before revisited. If only it had been he, not Megan, on the road that fateful night. The notion was followed by a familiar sequel. If he had been the one struck by the drunk driver, more than anything he would have wanted Megan to go on. Doubtless she would have wished the same for him. He had done a poor job of it. But finally he was making headway. And at long last there was no reason to turn back. The promise he had made at her grave all those years earlier, the unkept vow that had denied him closure, had finally been fulfilled. Biddleford, the hit-and-run driver, had been identified, and he was being brought to justice.

Skip turned and started to walk slowly from the cemetery. Standing by the entrance gate about fifty yards away, he spotted Kelly. He paused just long enough to wipe the remains of a few tears from his eyes. He then continued in Kelly's direction. "What brings you here?"

"Just happened to be passing." An abashed look accompanied a momentary drop of her gaze. "That's...uh...not quite accurate. The truth is: I called your office. Lucy guessed I might find you here."

"Must be really important for you to rush over rather than leave a message." Beneath Skip's facetious tone curiosity bubbled.

"Uh...not really, but..." Her customary poise was lacking. "I hope I'm not intruding." She gestured in the direction of Megan's grave.

"Not at all. I was just leaving." He waited several seconds. "You still haven't told me what brings you here."

"I...I want to ask you for dinner this Saturday."

Skip's eyes widened amidst a conglomeration of thoughts. "Do you think that's a good idea, what with you handling Squeaky's estate?"

"Assuming that would be a problem—and I'm not so sure, now that Harley Morehead is gone—it's academic. I'm no longer involved with the estate."

"You're not?"

She shook her head. "I turned it over to Pete Cameron."

"Why?"

"Uh...Can't you guess?" Her awkwardness was more telling than her words.

Skip glanced in the direction of Megan's grave. "I'd love to come to dinner."

Kelly smiled.

Skip felt a glow, the kind that had been absent far too long. He said, "Given our past, you sure you want to put up with me, even just for dinner?"

Kelly nodded. "I've had my eye on you for a long time. I hated when we broke up, but competing with *Jack* was more than I could handle."

"How can you be certain he won't get in the way again?" Skip's instinctive habit of playing devil's advocate had him kicking himself. Was he so stupid, the proverbial fool who represented himself, that he needed to hire a lawyer just to arrange a dinner engagement?

"I can't be one hundred percent sure...but nothing in life is. Anyway, I've watched you the past few months. I'm convinced the old Skip is back." She hesitated. "That, plus I've gotten some inside information."

"Inside information?"

"I've been talking to Lucy."

"Lucy!"

"According to her you're not just a great boss but also the terrific lawyer who hired her back when he first hung out his shingle." Kelly appeared to study Skip for a moment. "I hope you're not going to give her a hard time. Frankly I was reluctant to tell you that I had talked to her, but I felt it only fair."

Despite a poker face, Skip had no intention of giving Lucy grief. True, he might have a bit of fun with her, but real grief—no way. With what she had put up with over the years, not to mention all her great work, he had no right.

"So…is she in Dutch?"

Skip shook his head. He said, "Can I walk you back to your office?"

"You could, except I've already got a date."

Pangs of jealousy instantly percolated.

Kelly gestured across the street. "Dr. Harvey, my dentist, has his drill ready and waiting to grind one of my molars. I'll bet you're envious."

"Very."

"Sure." She glanced at her watch. "I'm due there in five minutes. I'd better go." She started to walk away but turned back. "How does six o'clock sound for Saturday?"

"Perfect…and about that appointment, I hope your dentist knows that his next patient is the loveliest woman in all of Cooperstown."

"I'll be sure to tell him." Kelly blushed and then headed across the street.

Skip watched her until she disappeared into the office. Recollections of their relationship, the intimacies they had shared when they had previously dated, ignited warm feelings. The characters had been right; unfortunately the timing was not. Skip wasn't ready. But that was then. He turned and gazed in the direction of the cemetery and Megan's grave. Her reassuring voice was blithely encouraging him to move forward. Another tear fell from his eye. Not from sadness. Strictly joy.

CPSIA information can be obtained at www.ICGtesting.com
Printed in the USA
BVOW070105121212

307881BV00001B/1/P

9 781621 371625